Kvithavet

Nakraim Sai

DAUVRÁK

Ringmark

KISTESTIKK

MURGATA

TUNGESKARET

Lunga

Tysna

Nákla-zing

ÆRUNAS VEI

Florian's
Parlors

PROF DOLIG'S VEI

HAERGATA

Brenn-
Torget

Corpse Bay

Nakla
College

NÁKLA-WALL

Kloft

Vinter-
hagen

BODSRABBEN

MYNTSLAGET

Herad

RINGKOLLEN

Shodda

n
Eskran

GUDEBRO BRIDGE

Mattagap

Náklaborg

SKJEPNASNARET

LYKTELØKKA

hill

The
Jannseyr
home

Jólshov

STEINNLEIA

Vazghelling

Kvalbukt

VETA

Blægge

Rogness

tan

Náklav

IRON WOLF

VARDARI — PART 1   SIRI PETTERSEN

IRON WOLF

Translated by Tara Chace

Arctis

This is a work of fiction. Names, characters, places, and incidents are from the author's imagination or are used fictitiously.

This translation has been published with the financial support of NORLA, Norwegian Literature Abroad.

To the wolves I run with.

And to you. You who are afraid. You who are held captive by inconceivable worries, by a merciless dread that can overtake you all of a sudden, when you least expect it. You who are fighting a war against your own body, fearing the sound of your own heartbeat. This is your book.

PROLOGUE

Nafraím opened the jar and sniffed the fish roe. The eggs were fresh, but there weren't very many of them. He emptied them onto the linen tablecloth, which soaked up the remainder of the salt water.

He rolled one of the reddish pearls between his fingers and squeezed it slightly. The consistency was perfect, that gelatinous membrane you only got from *harving* roe, but it was hardly bigger than a barleycorn. This would require concentration and a steady hand.

He cracked his knuckles and pulled the lamp closer. The flame flickered, an irritation he would have to live with until he got the gaslights working. Three explosions in one month were reason enough to cast doubt on the entire experiment. Luckily, he had unlimited time to figure it out.

He rotated the magnifying glass, pulling it over the desk. The copper mountings squeaked. He adjusted the screws and tightened the frame around the lens. A makeshift instrument, he would be the first to admit, but this project had tremendous potential. And would also have to wait. First things first.

His fingers became a pale, grooved landscape under the magnifying lens. He picked up one fish egg and punctured the membrane. Then he squeezed gently. A drop of oil grew around the hole. It trembled, came free, and dripped onto the tablecloth below. The trick was not to squeeze too hard, because then the egg would tear.

There was a delicate balance. He pressed until the membrane was flat between his fingers, then took a deep breath before the hard part.

He pulled the stopper out of the flask of blood and stuck the tip of the hypodermic needle down into it. It looked like an instrument of torture. An oblong glass ampoule, secured in a macabre silver casing. He had never felt comfortable with syringes, even though he had been handling them for as long as he could fill them with one hand.

Steady now.

Carefully, he brought the tip of the needle to the surface of the fish egg. They fused together. The needle sank in, and he pushed until the blood trickled out. It was always a captivating sight. To begin with, the membrane seemed closed, reluctant. But then it sucked in the needle before swelling up like a bellows to become a hungry, bloodshot berry.

His hand started trembling, triggered by ancient pain, and he twisted his arm slightly, enough to regain control. He set the blood egg back in the jar and picked up a fresh fish egg. There was a knock at the door.

"I'm busy, Ofre," Nafraím answered without taking his eyes off his work.

"Sir, he insists." Ofre's voice came through the oak door, muted.

"Everyone insists. Unless it's the Queen, I don't want to see anyone."

It was quiet for a bit, but he knew Ofre was still standing there.

"Sir, he says you will *want* to talk to him."

Nafraím poked a hole in the fish egg and said, "Then ask him to come back tomorrow."

"Sir, he says . . ."

The pause made Nafraím look up, inadvertently curious to hear what would come next.

"He says he's a monk, from Surtfjell Temple, and that he has a sign from . . . the devil?"

Nafraím pushed the magnifying lens aside and sat up in his chair. He realized how dark the workroom was. The light from the lamp didn't reach the top of the heavy bookshelves, and the shadows made the room strangely unfamiliar, filled with alarming silhouettes. The models and instruments, maps and drawings. The workbench with its copper piping and flasks, like some mechanical monster. There was a time when this light would have been insufficient to work by. His vision would have failed him, but that was a long time ago. Far too long ago.

Ofre cleared his throat outside the door.

"I'll ask him to come back tomorrow, sir."

"No, no . . . Come in, Ofre."

Ofre opened the door and took a modest step in. Nafraím wrapped up the linen cloth with the fish roe and put it in the desk drawer. He wiped his fingers on his handkerchief and put on his gloves.

"Sir?"

"Yes, send him down, Ofre."

The old estate master's eyes surveyed the shelves with their anatomical specimens in alcohol.

"Are you sure you wouldn't prefer to come up, sir?"

"Ofre, I'm too old to concern myself with other people's sensitivities. Send him down."

Ofre nodded and, bracing his knees, made his way back up the spiral staircase. A few minutes later, he came down again, no longer alone.

"Brother Laurus from Surtfjell Temple, sir," he announced, showing the man in. Then he closed the door, changed his mind, and popped back in. "Tea, sir?"

Nafraím shook his head, and Ofre disappeared again.

The monk remained, standing in front of the door. Nafraím hadn't seen him before, an attractive man, somewhere around thirty, with a gullible appearance. His rain-soaked cloak was rimmed with mud, and his shoes showed uneven wear. He clutched a bundle to his chest and directed his eyes downward.

Nafraím realized that the monk had never seen a warow before. He felt a twinge of guilt. He should have visited the temple more often, strengthened the ties to those who had followed him for generations. But the years passed so quickly. He waved the monk closer.

"Laurus? We haven't met before," he said, unsure whether that was an apology. "But I might have met your predecessor?"

"No . . ." The man looked up and met Nafraím's gaze. This seemed to make Laurus nervous, so he hurried to add, "But you met my predecessor's predecessor."

"Ah . . ."

The monk took a couple of steps toward the desk, but his feet seemed to grow heavier as he walked. His eyes roamed over the instruments and stopped on a heart stored in yellowed alcohol.

"Wolf," Nafraím explained, unsure whether that helped the matter. The monk nodded energetically, as if he had never thought otherwise, while he gaped at the instruments in front of him. He reached out toward the shiny switches on the gas burner.

"Don't touch!" Nafraím leapt out of his chair.

The man pulled in his hand, backing away.

Nafraím calmed himself and repeated the words: "Don't touch. Don't touch . . . anything. Let's see what you've got."

Laurus set the bundle on the desk and untied the straps. He unfolded the cloth, revealing another cloth underneath. He opened the second cloth and revealed a glass bowl, half-filled with dirt. A tiny, green shoot stuck up from the dirt.

"From where?" Nafraím asked, even though he knew the answer.

"Svartna, sir. In the middle of Vargrák."

Nafraím peeked at his pocket watch. "It's late, Brother Laurus. You must be hungry and tired. I suggest that you stay until tomorrow. Go upstairs and ask Ofre to make up a room for you, as well as some supper."

"That's very generous of you, sir," Laurus said, looking down. "Bless you." Then he disappeared up the stairs with poorly concealed relief.

Nafraím lowered himself into his chair. He stared at the green shoot and knew for certain that he was looking at his own death.

He had always imagined that the end of everything would come like a beast of prey, an enormous rage, ancient, with teeth and claws. It seemed unreasonable for it to announce its arrival through this delicate, new life.

Two leaves splayed out like a thin book; a book that would tell tales of the monstrous things he had done, sins he would have to answer for—and sins he had many, over six hundred years' worth. But few were worse than the ones he would be forced to commit now.

THE NEWBIE

The newbie was the worst kind, a city schlub who thought he was a wolf hunter after his first night in Svartna. He had an awkward, forced chumminess about him, and he talked nonstop. Juva was on the verge of stuffing snow in her ears just to block him out.

Instead, Juva stood and started rolling up the sleeping furs. Let the rest of them sit there nodding indulgently while the newbie clowned around, wasting valuable daylight. She had woken up at the crack of dawn for this? She'd lit the campfire so the rest of them could wake up to food and warmth. They had eventually crawled out of their snow caves, a group of seven this time.

It was usually six. Six was better.

The newbie had been the last one up. Even so, he had planted his butt by the fire without pitching in, and he was still sitting there yammering away, his mouth full of food. He should be packing up his stuff, getting ready—as ready as he could get, anyway, with that equipment.

Juva hauled the pelts over and put them in the sleigh, sneaking peeks at him. His leather boots were new and wide open around the calf, more suitable for shuffling around in the streets of Náklav. He had gotten soaked yesterday and would again today, too. His crossbow sat planted bow-down in the snow, as if he couldn't tell the front from the back. If he ever got around to shooting it, there would be ice in the arrow groove. The arrows stuck up out of a quiver on his hip, and they clinked against each other as he moved. The only wolf they would get close to would be a deaf one.

Juva glanced at the others and discovered that Broddmar was studying her as he scraped up the last spoonful of fermented groats in his bowl. She turned her back to him and buckled on her straps. The pack had belonged to Father, so it had always been a little too big for her, but the leather was worn soft and had stopped chafing ages ago. She had also made some good improvements: a strap across her chest, which lessened the weight of the crossbow on her back; a large bag on her hip belt; and a sheath for her skinning knife. She tightened the buckle that held the arrows firmly to her thigh. They sat in a row, with their poisoned brown steel tips safely hidden. They had to be easy to draw but sit securely enough to tolerate a fall. For the newbie's sake, she hoped he wasn't using poisoned arrows; he would probably kill himself the minute he stumbled.

She heard Broddmar's footsteps behind her in the snow.

"Hey, Juva . . ."

"No, I'm not taking him."

Broddmar didn't respond right away. Unlike the newbie, he usually thought before he spoke, but then, he was old enough to be her grandfather, so presumably being strong and silent came with age. That was why Broddmar made the decisions. And now he had decided that they would bring along this runt who, at best, would waste their hunt and, at worst, risk their lives.

"Fine," Broddmar said eventually. "When we split up, he'll come with me."

Juva tightened the strap around one of the sleeping hides until it looked strangled, like a furry hourglass.

Broddmar cleared his throat behind her back. "I don't think those hides are planning to run off anywhere."

She turned around and tilted her head discreetly toward the newbie, who was bragging to the others about his crossbow.

13

"*You're* the one who always said the team is no stronger than its weakest link!" Juva objected. "Look at him! He's never hunted before. He's a kid!"

Broddmar's cheeks became a little more sunken, evidence that he was hiding a smile.

"You're nineteen," Broddmar pointed out. "He's at least ten years older than you."

She narrowed her eyes, and he hurried to add, "Listen . . . He's seeing a good friend of Muggen's sister, so Muggen couldn't tell him no. It's just this one time, Juva."

That last admission soothed her irritation. He knew he'd made a mistake. He smiled encouragingly, with a broad gap where Father had once knocked out his front teeth. He only had his molars left in his upper jaw, which made her name sound like *Jufa* whenever he was stressed. It was charming, and he used it for all it was worth.

"He's going to screw up," she muttered.

Broddmar's shaggy wool mitten patted her on the shoulder before he turned around to go. She grabbed his sleeve.

"You owe me, Broddmar. The next time you dress in red, I want to go with you."

Broddmar glanced over at the others, but no one could hear them over the newbie's nonstop talking.

"No, Juva, you won't be coming. Let it die now. Lagalune would have my hide if I let you come, and I'm not idiot enough to run afoul of your mother."

As if she cared.

Juva let him go. There was a limit to how much teasing Broddmar would permit. She trusted him, in spite of the newbie. If Broddmar felt safe with him, so should she. But worry wriggled like worms in her belly. It wasn't because the fool was inexperienced. She had been that way herself a few years ago. It was more than that. He was nervous, restless. He was careless where he stuck the crossbow, as if it wasn't actually important, as if he wasn't actually out here to get leather or wolf teeth at all.

She wished she had never learned to read people. It wasn't something anyone could forget. Whether she wanted to or not, she picked things up just from how people moved, the words they used. It made her feel like a thief, robbing them of the chance to show her who they were on their own. She already knew more about the newbie than he knew about himself. She just hoped she was wrong.

The others had begun to stir. Hanuk kicked snow over the fire, which sizzled until it died. Lok squatted, lacing on his snowshoes. His rust-red hair reached down to the ground in that position. He nodded to the boots that belonged to the newbie, who still hadn't stood up yet.

"You're not afraid of going home with frostbite, eh?"

Juva was relieved that someone had finally said something. Lok sometimes had a big mouth, but he meant well, brimming with emotions as he was. He cried for no reason and missed his kids after half a day. And even with four mouths to feed, his shoes were still better than the newbie's.

"What, these?" the newbie asked, pulling in his feet and looking down. "These cost a premium price, I can assure you. They're from Kastor in Sakseveita, the best shoemaker in Náklav! He has a waiting list, but I—"

"I don't doubt it," Lok cut him short. "But we have extra shoes and mittens for anyone who needs them."

"Yes, that won't be me, you know. I've got the best that money can buy." The newbie nudged Lok's shoulder with his fist, as if they shared a secret. "Plus, I've got fate on my side. I went to the blood reader not three days ago. She has a waitlist as well."

Juva held her breath.

That's all we need.

"And she said you couldn't freeze to death?" Lok asked.

"Basically. She said I had barely started my life."

Juva rolled her eyes. How gullible could you be? The wording was a dodge, and she had heard it a thousand times. All the blood reader had said was that he was young. His having a long time left to live was his own conclusion.

Hanuk burst out into a magpie-like laugh. "Doesn't sound like a guarantee that you'll get old," he pointed out.

The newbie leapt to his feet, clearly shaken that anyone would knock the fortune he'd put stock in. He started bumbling his way through the fable about how the blood readers had gotten their powers from the devil himself in wolf's clothing. As if everybody in Slokna hadn't taken in the fairy tale about "The Sisters and the Wolf" with their mother's milk.

"That's bullshit," Muggen said. "Right, Juva?"

Juva clenched her teeth. Broddmar jabbed Muggen in the side with his elbow and he jumped. Muggen glanced up at Juva, ashamed at his slip of the tongue. Typical. He was as dim as a rock but as imposing as a mountain.

The newbie caught that and came over to her, eagerly. "Why is he asking you? You know blood readers?"

"You could at least tie something around those," Juva said, pointing to his boots. "So you don't get snow down inside them. We're not going to turn back because your toes get cold."

"Do you? Are you related to blood readers?" Apparently he wouldn't let himself be distracted from the question.

"If I say yes, will you tie some leather around your shoes?"

She turned her back to him, but he slipped around in front of her and leaned against the sleigh. "You're too pretty to be so touchy."

"If a blood reader told you to dive off the side of Ulebru, would you do it?" She gave the sleigh a jerk, and his elbow slipped off the edge. He didn't say anything, and it dawned on her that he was actually thinking about it.

16

Juva had had more than enough. She strode rapidly toward the woods, and the others hurried after her.

"Who is she?"

She could still hear the newbie behind her.

"Juva," Broddmar replied.

"But who *is* she? What's her family name?"

"Hunter. She's Juva Hunter."

"That's not a blood reader name, is it?" His question ended in a grunt. He was stumped.

Juva continued into the charred trees that gave Svartna its name. They looked like rivers of ink against the white snow; it was easy to get lost here. There were no colors or life, and nothing new could grow. Enormous spruce trees spread their branches above her. Even their needles were black, some hard like rocks, others delicate like dust.

A punishment from the gods, they said in the village in general about everything that took place in Náklav—sinful city people, sinful money—and in a way, they were right. Coins had long since overtaken the gods' place in the capitol.

Juva studied the snow for tracks as she walked. The winter's darkness had just begun to ease, but light was still scant. The upside was that almost every footprint belonged to wolves. Few animals strayed into the dead, nutrient-poor woods in Slokna. Wolves were the exception. They could put enormous distances behind them, and easily crossed the narrowest swath of the deadwoods in one day.

She stopped, listening, certain that she had sensed something, but the only sound she heard was the creaking of snowshoes and the runners of the sleigh Broddmar pulled behind him.

There it was again, the disturbance in her chest, as if someone was breathing on her heart.

"What is she doing?" the newbie asked.

He was hushed into silence.

17

Juva kept walking, slower and more carefully. The tracks appeared right in front of her—those of a young wolf, alone. She raised her hand and made the signal to those behind her.

"What is it? What does that mean?"

"She says there's a stray wolf."

"How can she know—"

"She can sense them. Now shut up."

If he says one more word, I'll smother him in the snow.

Juva unlaced her snowshoes and tossed them in the sleigh. The others followed suit and prepared. She lifted the crossbow off her back, put her foot in its stirrup, and pulled toward her until the string clicked into place. Then she followed the tracks to the edge of a steep slope and signaled that they should split up.

There was a hollow between the trees ahead of her. The snow billowed down the slope in big drifts, like waves in a white sea. She slowly crept to the south, confident that Lok and Nolan were behind her. Broddmar had taken the others to the north.

She got down on all fours and crawled along the slope. The wolf had stopped by a snow-laden boulder down in the hollow, as if knowing it would be harder to spot against the gray stone. It pricked up its ears and its yellow eyes wandered along the tree line along Broddmar's side of the hollow. Juva wriggled her way forward. If they didn't manage to surround it, they wouldn't stand a chance.

A little click broke the silence, a crossbow being spanned.

Damn it, the newbie!

The wolf broke into a run—in the wrong direction.

"Muggen!" Juva screamed as she slid down the slope on her back.

Muggen with his longbow was the only one who could hit the wolf at that distance. She didn't even see the arrow coming before it sank into the wolf, throwing it onto its side. Its paws continued running even as it lay there, in sheer denial.

The newbie cheered and came running down the slope. He tripped, sailed some distance on the snow, then scrambled back onto his feet and approached the quarry.

"Wait!" Juva reached out her arm reflexively, even though she was much too far away to stop him.

The newbie didn't see or hear her, blinded by his eagerness for the kill. He knelt in front of the dying animal.

Anguish welled up in Juva. "You're going to get bitten!"

But the newbie didn't listen. If she shot another arrow at the wolf, she risked hitting that imbecile instead.

Juva tossed her crossbow aside and took off running toward him. She had to wrestle her feet up out of the snow with every step. The newbie grabbed hold of the arrow sticking out of the wolf's fur.

Juva yelled as she ran: "Move!"

The wolf's upper body jumped. It snapped its jaws and sank its teeth into the newbie's calf. She heard a crunch. He fell over backward in the snow, screaming and kicking. Then Juva was there. She grabbed hold of his hood to pull him away. He waved one arm and clung to her lower leg with the other. She lost her footing and fell onto her back in the blowing snow. She stared up into the wolf's frothing mouth. Steamy breath and canines. Sharp, white knives.

Juva stared at those teeth. Remembered them. She had spent a lifetime forgetting.

The wolf snarled, a primal sound that paralyzed her body. She knew she needed to act, but she couldn't move. This was her fault. She had made this happen. Her own words about the newbie raced through her head.

He's going to screw it up.

You're going to get bitten.

The wolf's mouth came at her. She heard several shouts, and suddenly, her arms woke up. She pulled a bolt from her thigh belt and drove it up into the wolf's abdomen with both fists. For an instant, everything stood still. The wolf trembled. Her gray mittens soaked up the blood. They became saturated with red.

It's going to drip!

She tossed her head. The drops rained onto her cheek, and she rubbed her face feverishly against her arm so as not to get blood in her mouth. The motion weakened her arms, and the wolf collapsed on her, hot and heavy. Its nose was wet against her neck, its breath coming in short jerks. The animal's heart beat with hers, a race for life. Slower and slower. Until it was only hers left.

She heard the sleigh, its runners cutting through the snow with tremendous speed. Muggen's face appeared, powerful and wide-eyed. He heaved the wolf off her and pulled her to her feet with his club-sized fists. Juva felt her tears coming. Then the fear hit her, way too late now that it was over. She gasped for breath and thought she was sobbing until she realized the sound was coming from someone else. The newbie.

Broddmar tried to pull up the bloody leg of the newbie's pants, but the young man wailed and dragged himself further from Broddmar, leaving an ankle-wide trail of blood in the snow.

"We need to turn back," Broddmar said.

Juva stared at the newbie. She had heard the crunch of bone when he was bitten. Why didn't he want anyone to look at the wound? Suddenly, she realized why he didn't have proper shoes.

That damned idiot! May he rot!

She lunged forward and sat down astride his thigh, ignoring his protests while she held him down and yanked up his pants leg. His hose were torn, gaping around a curved gash that was bleeding heavily. Something gleamed in the wound, glass shards from a little flask he had strapped above his ankle, hidden within the wide boots.

A storm of rage awoke in Juva. She ripped off the strap and held the flask up in front of the newbie's face, grabbing hold of his jaw and forcing him to look. He raised his arms to protect himself.

"It's to spike my coffee!" he squealed. "Rye whiskey! Get off me, you crazy bitch!"

Juva threw the strap aside and stomped her foot down on his chest.

"What in Gaula were you thinking?!" she yelled. "You think you're going to live forever, don't you, if you drink enough of it? Or are you just in it for the high? Just where are you on the idiocy scale?"

"You were right, Juva," Broddmar said, pulling her away. "Now let it go."

"No!" she screamed, fear and rage shaking her body. "Leave him here! He could have gotten us killed! He's a damned blood dealer!"

For a second, she feared that the others wouldn't believe her, wouldn't see him the way she did. Maybe they didn't catch his fretfulness and fake friendliness, how he had pulled in his feet when they asked about his boots, as if he had instinctively wanted to hide them. Regular people were lucky. They grew up in families where you didn't learn to look for things like that.

But the flask left no doubt. The others gathered around the newbie. Polite, diplomatic Nolan had a rare stitch of scorn at the corner of his mouth. Hanuk, that ray of sunshine from the icy wastes of Aure, didn't have a single laugh line at the moment. Redhaired Lok was in tears, of course. But the one who was taking it hardest was Muggen—huge, naïve Muggen. He hung his head and his underbite looked worse than usual beneath the hood of the moth-eaten cape that had given him his nickname. He stared at the newbie with disappointment—not only disappointment, but guilt for being the one who had brought him along.

Broddmar squatted down beside the newbie, who had begun to sweat despite lying in the snow.

"You could have cost us our license with this depravity. That is not what we do here. The blood is for the stones, and only for the stones.

Do you hear? Be glad that flask was empty, otherwise I would have let the Ring Guard handle you."

The newbie gulped.

Juva could not calm down. Fear fluttered in her chest, and she felt shaky.

Hoggthorn. I need hoggthorn.

Her hand found her belt bag, but she hesitated. Didn't want the others to see her fighting her panic. Hanuk came over to her and pulled off his hood. His black hair lay plastered on either side of his face, like the wings of a dead crow. He was carrying her crossbow.

"This wound up under the runners," he said, hooking it into place on her back carrier. Hanuk was always the one to pull the team back up when they were down, and it helped to see that his dimples had returned. "That was close, Juva! But everyone's alive and, thanks to your quick thinking, we have a wolf to field dress. Go change your mittens."

That simple command made her feel steady on her feet, which was no doubt his intent. She pulled off the bloody mittens and tossed them aside. They would never again be wearable. She cleaned off her hands in the snow, digging her fingers in deep in case she had gotten any blood under her nails. They were chewed down, but still . . . She found an extra pair of mittens in the sleigh and pulled them on, grateful for the warmth. She grabbed some rope as well and started tethering the wolf's hind legs together while the others debated how they would get the newbie up onto the sleigh.

Her body calmed down as she worked. Broddmar came and helped her pull the carcass up the slope to the nearest tree. She rapped on one of the charred branches. It seemed sturdy enough, not the porous type that was used as fuel. You could never be sure about corpsewood.

Juva threw the rope over a branch, and then Broddmar pulled the wolf up by its feet until it dangled above the ground. None of them said anything. They had done this so many times before that words were unnecessary.

Broddmar pulled a bloodskin out of his backpack and gave it to Juva, a safe weight in her hands. It was heavier than a normal waterskin, since it was bigger, with a double bag to prevent leakage and a stopper secured with steel rings and locking clips. The black skin was even embossed with the Náklav city seal on one side and the Ring Guard seal on the other. No one would ever have gone to so much trouble for water.

Juva opened the stopper and steeled herself against the smell of rotten red clover. It was a disgusting mixture, but without it the blood would coagulate. She held the skin steady against the wolf's neck, found the most promising artery, and pounded in the knife-sharp spout with her fist.

The bloodskin slowly swelled between her hands. They filled three skins before the animal bled out, and in the meantime, the others got the newbie up the slope. Broddmar carried the bloodskins over and placed them in the drawer in the side of the sleigh. The newbie didn't even notice what was being loaded on beneath him. He had more than enough to pay attention to with Muggen picking pieces of broken glass out of his leg. Juva hoped it hurt like crazy, enough that he gave up hunting for the rest of his life.

She lowered the wolf's carcass and drew her skinning knife from her belt. Then the gloominess set in, the grief at watching a life ebb away, and at the same time knowing that this was what it took to feel safe.

She stuffed her hand into a chainmail glove. She had to be careful not to cut herself because the hide was delicate and time was short. She clutched the little knife shaft in her fist and let the metal slice its way under the skin. When she was done, she broke the teeth out of the wolf's jaw. The sound didn't bother her anymore, not like it had the first time. She wiped the teeth off, wrapped them in a cloth, and put them in her bag. Broddmar came back and doused the pink cadaver in oil. Then he set it on fire.

Flames in Svartna weren't like flames in the city. Out here, flames always seemed so strong, the only thing with any color as far as you could see, deep orange and alive against the black, dead forest. The flames ate their way around the carcass, carrying the smell and the life up into the trees. Juva's pulse finally stopped pounding in her ears.

She had burned it, burned the wolf.

Broddmar had once said that she was the most reluctant hunter he had ever met, and he thought that had to do with her father's death. But it had to do with a thousand things. Father. Mother. Blood reading. Nightmares. Heartbeats.

She didn't kill wolves for the money, and certainly not for the joy of hunting. She killed because she had to. Because the world would rip apart at the seams if she stopped.

TASTE OF BLOOD

A sharp pain in his jaw tore Rugen from his dreams. Had he been beaten up, robbed while he was sleeping it off? He felt for his coin pouch. It was still there, if nearly empty.

He grudgingly opened his eyes. People were sleeping on the bench in front of him, men and women. Intertwined like a litter of puppies. Strangers he had a vague sense of having been best friends with a short while ago. Now the thought made him ill.

He tried to raise his hand, but it wouldn't move. What the hell, was he paralyzed now? He peered down at the hairy arm resting on his stomach and realized that it wasn't his. It belonged to the man snoring beside him. Rugen groaned and tried to focus. How out of it had he been?

He wriggled. The stranger flopped onto his back without waking up, revealing a coin pouch on his belt. That could hold a nice sum of money . . . No, he felt too lousy. Besides, he remembered having liked the guy. A failed beer brewer from Grimse, who spoke Norran poorly, and had come straight here from the ship. No one who came to Náklav by sea was rich.

A new jolt of pain. It radiated from his jaws all the way up into his skull. What the wolf slit was this? This was the last time he would drink liquor at the same time. He needed to get up and walk it off.

Rugen forced himself up, rubbing his lower back. The bench cushions were so meager they might as well have skipped them. The candles on the table had melted together into a shapeless sludge, the wicks drowned. A simple tavern, fair enough, but was it too much to ask that they swap out the candles?

The air was stifling. He glanced over at the window before he realized it was fake. The tavern was in a basement, so the wall was decorated with mullions and painted to look like glass. If he wanted air, he needed to go outside.

He grabbed his jacket from under the sleeping Grimselander, threw it on, and listened at the door. The noise level suggested that the evening had reached its peak. He heard bellowing, toasting, and the unmistakable scraping of chairs and tables that suddenly found themselves in the way of drunk people.

Rugen pulled his hood over his head, opened the door, and snuck out, his back hunched in case he owed anything. He was met by an acrid fog of tobacco smoke and men swaying as if they were on a ship's deck. He sensed that he was doing the same thing. What was he doing here? He, who worked for the richest, drank with the noblest, and screwed the wives of the most powerful—one of them from behind with her shoes on, who, afterward, had given him her pearl-trimmed pillowcase to remember her by. He'd sold it that same day.

He grinned at the memory and the jab came again, an intense pain that made him touch his jaw. A couple of guys looked at him. This was not the time to throw up. He had to go up to the stone ring, to the civilized part of the city.

Rugen made his way up the stairs into the dark alley, which was narrow even for Náklav. He knew merchants so rotund they would've gotten stuck. The alley opened out into the Sailway, a street that had a unique ability to channel the cold in from the sea. Ice sparkled between the cobblestones. It was extremely cold, always cold. And dark. He hid his fingers inside his jacket sleeves and cursed the stone gates. If it hadn't been for them, people wouldn't fucking live here. But the gods must have a rotten sense of humor, because as it was, hundreds of thousands lived in Náklav. The world's busiest city, even though it was so far north that a man could freeze his dick off before he had shaken off the drops.

He yawned to stretch the stiffness in his jaw. He spat and tasted blood.

The cold crept into his chest. This was no normal hangover. It wasn't like any he had ever experienced before, anyway. He needed to see what was going on, find a mirror. The tavern he had come from would never have something like that. He needed to make his way into the city, to the parlors. He rubbed his jaw with his thumb. It felt tender, but the pain wasn't constant. The worst of it was the fear of another jolt.

He crossed Ulebru Bridge without being swept away by the gusts off the sea, and turned left into Nattlyslokket, a street that ran under a vaulted ceiling with lamps lit with corpsewood. He had never liked the effect. Corpsewood burned without flames, with a nasty glow that made him feel like he was seeing ghosts.

He stopped in front of a leaded shop window that jutted out from the wall. He leaned forward, toward the wobbly reflection of his own face. A skeleton stared back at him. He gave a start—but it was just a drawing on a card. There were several of them hanging in the window, he saw. The sort of fate cards that blood readers used.

He'd had his way with one of them last year. Or was it the previous year? A blood reader, not a skeleton. A delightfully spirited girl who used to ride his chest like a mare in the night. He had borrowed money from her drawer and steered clear since. Truth was, it still bothered him a little. Was that why he was having pains? Had she put a curse on him or something? Rugen swallowed and stared at the death card. Was this an omen?

Cursed nonsense!

The shop sign squeaked in its wrought iron fastener above him, swaying in a gust of wind. He hurried along, up to Kaupatorget, where the frost-covered statue of a dead city councilman guarded the surrounding buildings. Candles burned behind colored glass windows in several jettied projections that jutted out over the street as far as the law allowed and a bit beyond.

He heard amateurish harp music coming from Florian's Parlors and followed the sound through a colonnade until he spotted the parlor. The sort of place that always had a man posted just outside. High society believed he was there to open the doors for them. Everyone else knew he was there to screen who was allowed to enter in the first place.

Rugen hesitated. He had worked there a few years earlier, but he would be the first to admit that he was not at his best right now. And he didn't have anyone inside who could vouch for him anymore. But his jaw throbbed with pain. He had to see what the hell was going on.

He pulled his hand through his hair, tried to make himself look as if he belonged, and then walked right up without giving the guard a glance. The mistake most losers made was to smile and be pleasant. They might as well wear a sign on their chests saying they had never been there before. The real admission ticket was an aura of arrogance.

The door was opened for him, and he proceeded into the lobby. The contrast with the tavern he had woken up in left a bitter taste in his mouth. These walls were divided into golden panels, decorated with paintings of fish that existed only in the imagination. Lavish glass doors opened into the parlor. He could make out the vaulted ceiling inside, covered with sea green glass in wrought iron frames that made it look like the whole building had sunk into the sea. He couldn't even imagine the cost.

The people sitting inside were the type who never needed to wonder whether they belonged. They acted important in their embroidered vests, stiff winter dresses, pins, and hair ornaments he could swear were made of dead beetles. Glasses clinked, and their jewelry glittered in the glow of thousands of burning candles.

This was where he ought to be. He knew better than any of them how life was meant to be lived. Prosperity was completely wasted on such shitty, boring people.

The guy he had woken up with had putrefied for weeks aboard a ship from Grimse. No one in here would survive two days on a ship—but, then, they didn't need to. They paid the fee for the stone gates in Nákla Henge without blinking; they never needed to waste their hours or days traveling from one end of the world to the other. Rich people's time was sacred. Maybe that's why they came here, too, secretly hoping for more time?

Rugen tasted blood. He slipped into the bathroom.

They had upgraded it since he had last been there. Copper pipes ran along the ceiling, down the shimmering blue walls, and right into a silver sink. No pump, but taps for hot and cold. Damn, if only he had a fraction of this money.

A mirror was mounted on the wall over the washbasin. Rugen saw himself framed in silver and had to concede that it was sheer luck that he had made it in. He looked like he hadn't slept in several days. His brown curls, which he was pretty sure were his key to the ladies, clung to his sweaty scalp. It must have been the transition from the frozen street to the warm parlor.

Rugen leaned toward the mirror and opened his mouth, not knowing what he was looking for. He ran his tongue over his teeth. What a moron he was. Nothing was wrong, he was just hungover.

This verdict was shattered by a new jolt of pain. It came as a pulse and would not relent.

Fucking Gaula, to the depths of Drukna!

He punched the wall with his fist, but the pain did not abate. He spat blood into the sink. Red rain in a silver bowl. A realization took shape and left him shaky, nauseated. He cocked his head to the side and opened his mouth again. Wiggled a tooth with his fingers. Was it a little loose? By holy Jól's slit, it was loose! Panic flooded through his body and stole his breath away. His throat tightened so he couldn't make a sound.

Why, why was this happening? Had he taken too much? No, he had never overdone it. At any rate, not enough to . . .

His train of thought was interrupted by a deep booming in the distance. *The Dead Man's Horn.* The sound spread like freezing cold through his chest, relentless, devastating, a grim warning of just how real his problem could become.

Rugen rested his forehead against the mirror, staring down at his knuckles, which whitened on the rim of the sink. He was dreaming. This was a nightmare. He hadn't left the basement tavern yet. This wasn't happening. He smashed his fist into the mirror and heard it break.

The harp music from the parlor seemed distorted, an auditory mirage. Sitting beside the sink was an open egg made of mother of pearl, with three little perfume bottles inside. Perfume! How completely absurd! The most useless trinket he could imagine right now.

The room began to sway. He braced his hands on the broken mirror to keep his balance. He pulled a shard out, long and sharp like a knife. He pressed the shard to his wrist, hesitated, trembling.

Cut! Do it!

But he knew he didn't have a chance of succeeding. The world might look different tomorrow. Maybe he had gotten some bad stuff and started imagining things. A bad trip, that was all. He let go of the shard. It tinkled as it hit the basin and dragged red spit toward the bottom.

He needed help.

But this wasn't something he could go to his new friends with, and he didn't have many old friends left. The list was far too short.

He heard himself laugh. His breath fogged up the mirror, and he was relieved to no longer see himself in the shards.

The only useful name he had on his list was possibly more frightening than his problem, so what the fuck should he do?

Pull it together! Everyone has a toothache at some point.

He took a deep breath. He would wait and hope it was something else, that's what he would do. A toothache was nothing to go berserk over. There were far more substantial things to fear.

And from out at Knokle, the Dead Man's Horn resounded in affirmation.

NÁKLAV

By the time they finally reached the coast, where Náklav reared up from the sea, Juva could have collapsed and slept right there in the snow. Even at this time of the day, the lights glittered in the blue darkness. Hundreds of thousands of them, crammed together on the large island. Two islands, actually, but the smaller one nestled in against the larger, as if the two had once been a single entity. No matter what, they were overpopulated, both of them. Náklav was so bursting at its seams that you could hardly see where the buildings ended and the cliffs began. Locals joked with visitors that the outermost buildings sometimes toppled right off.

The hunting group had been pushing themselves to the bone for half the night to get the newbie back before his wound caused trouble. He'd consumed a quarter barrel of rye and was snoring in the sleigh, which Broddmar and Muggen pulled between them. The wolf hide was rolled up on the back of Juva's pack because the newbie had complained about its stench.

Juva knew how he felt. Every time the wind grabbed hold of the hide, it smelled like bloody game, and she felt like she was still lying trapped under the wolf's hairy body. It made her heart flutter in her chest. She had managed without hoggthorn for a few weeks now, but this hunt had asked too much of her, awakening the fear that always slumbered within her.

She stifled it by thinking of the flames as they walked through

Naar. The village ended at the foot of the bridge that crossed to Náklav. They prepared to say their farewells before they reached the bridge gate, since Lok lived there. Hanuk, too, but he was going to handle the sleigh, so he had to come across with them and unload the newbie.

Naarport was more of a fortified tower than a gate, massive and black, with snow on the windward side. Broddmar showed the hunting card to the gate guard, who disappeared inside and came out again with his boss, a completely humorless representative of the Ring Guard, who rubbed his eyes like he had been roused from sleep. He was pulling the handcart, as he usually did.

Broddmar opened the drawer in the side of the sleigh and loaded the three black bloodskins onto the cart. The grumpy man signed a piece of paper as he inspected the hunting party with a self-important expression. Juva was overtired and mostly wanted to tell him to knock off pretending like he had any control. Sure, he would lock the blood in a chest, and then it would be transported right to Nákla Henge without any stops along the way. But all the same, some of it would go astray, and that would cost lives.

But she kept her mouth shut. Not only because she'd be an idiot to provoke the men dressed in black with the ring seal on their chests, but also because the piece of paper he held in his hand was what they needed in order to get paid.

Broddmar took it and stuck it in his pocket.

"We have a new guy here who had an accident." Broddmar nodded at the sleigh. "Bitten in the leg."

"Who bit him?!" The watch commander stared at Broddmar.

"No, no, not a person. Bitten by a wolf. A hunting accident, that's all."

"All right." The watch commander rolled his eyes. "Unload him here and we'll send him to the infirmary in Kviskre by carriage."

He barked an order to the other guards and threatened Broddmar that he would pull them for the carriage trip next time before disappearing into the tower with the handcart. Juva retrieved her crossbow from the sleigh and roused the newbie. The gate guard came over to lift him out, and the newbie stared dopily up at them. Juva resisted the temptation to tell him they had informed on him for attempting to steal blood.

The idiot had ruined their season, as if the period between the far-too-black dark time and the spring equinox wasn't short enough already. Broddmar needed to serve in the Ring Guard, and Lok was expecting his fifth child. Would they even manage to squeeze in any more trips?

She might get by on what little money she had, but there wasn't going to be a new crossbow.

Hanuk took over the sleigh, nodded goodnight, and headed back into his village.

"So it's just the four of you going across?" one guard asked. "Then we need to see your mouths."

It's happened again . . .

Muggen opened his mouth without asking any questions. This wasn't the first time they'd had to show their teeth. Juva opened wide while the guard stared into her mouth. He seemed embarrassed, so he didn't do an especially thorough job. Presumably because they were there so often they were considered familiar. She glanced over at Broddmar, who muttered something quietly to the other guard. She pricked up her ears but didn't catch any of it.

Nolan blinded the guard with a smile, which was checked post-haste. He always got off easy, proper as he was. He was well-groomed and spoke in a polished way, but he knew the most obscene jokes and he usually asked the most obnoxious questions.

Once they were finally permitted to make their way across the bridge, having to move felt cruel. Juva's feet shook from being forced to walk again. The sea thundered against the massive bridge pilings. If they'd managed to remain standing, she could, too. The bridge was called Sixth, and the dumbest thing visitors could do was to ask the guards what had happened to the first five. That joke was so tired that anyone asking risked being refused entrance.

The icy wind off the fjord bit into Juva's cheeks but eased up as soon as they made it through the city gate and into the endless fortress of buildings that was Náklav. Juva asked a gate guard if he had a runner available, and he confessed that he had taken pity on two who were waiting inside the tower. He pounded on the door and a young lad she recognized came out, looking sleepy.

"Runner, miss?"

"Could you go to Ester Spinne at Myntslaget 7? You've been there before. Tell her that Juva is back, two days too soon. We ran into problems and only got one animal."

"Yes, miss! Ester at Myntslaget 7. Juva had problems two days too soon, is back with just one animal."

Juva was too tired to correct him. "Ester will pay you," she said.

The boy was just about to run when it occurred to Juva to ask him to wait until the morning bell rang.

Muggen said goodbye and turned right onto Rautan, while Nolan headed up toward Muunsvei. Juva and Broddmar walked along Villfarsveien together. Neither of them said anything. Juva could tell he was thinking from the way he clicked his tongue against the roof of his mouth, but he wouldn't answer her if she asked. Either about the tooth check or what had happened.

They walked in silence past the soft lights through Taakedraget, until they reached Hidehall. She was used to being greeted by the frivolity of the ale house as she approached, but it was quiet now. When she was little, the whole hall had been just for hunters. A massive stone building, on the very edge of the cliffs, where they prepared and sold their goods. There weren't very many hunters now, but there were more people. So half the hall had been converted into a tavern. There was more money in beer now than in hides. But the name had stuck and the tavern was still called Hidehall.

Broddmar wished her a brief goodnight and disappeared into the building next door. Juva let herself into Hidehall the back way. The common room was empty but not cold, thanks to the fireplace wall in between the room and the kitchens. There were glowing embers behind the fire screen, a dim light that barely reached the antlered skulls decorating the log railing that ran along the gallery above.

All she wanted to do was sleep, but she needed to salt the hide so it wouldn't sour. She walked into the salt room, her feet heavy. She scraped some overlooked remnants off the wolf hide, salted it, and folded it in half twice in one of the salt casks, which she shoved onto one of the available shelves on the wall. She ought to put the teeth she had in her bag in alcohol, but that would have to wait for tomorrow.

Juva dragged herself up the stairs to the gallery and let herself into her bedroom, which was more like a tunnel. A passage over the alley to the building next door, but that exit had been blocked off eons ago. She had just enough space for her bed bench at the far end, and on the coldest nights she had to leave the door to the common room ajar. But it was cheap, and anything was better than home.

She took off her backpack and crossbow. Dropped her jacket right onto the floor. Pulled off her shoes. They were stuck as if by suction to her swollen feet. She wasn't up to anything more than that. Even brewing hoggthorn tea felt like an insurmountable task. Juva flopped onto her bed and fell immediately into a deep sleep.

PORTENT

Juva spread her things across the scarred wooden table in front of the fireplace in the common room. She placed everything in neat rows so she could see what needed to be done. The sleigh runners had done a number on her crossbow, and it needed attention. Her chain mail glove had a hint of rust at the thumb. The leather around Father's hip flask needed conditioning. His embossed name was almost unreadable under the grime and grease spots.

Little things. Hardly enough to keep her mind busy for an hour.

She emptied out everything that was in the backpack so she could clean it as well. What else? She had swapped out the candles in the chandelier, which was a term slightly too generous for the clump of antlers under the roof beams. She had preserved the candle wax so the tavern could repour them. The wolf teeth had been placed in alcohol. She had scrubbed her bloody clothes until her fingers were numb. Everything was rinsed and hung up to dry. The only thing left to wash was herself, but that would have to wait until afterward.

Her body was stiff, the hunt sabotaged. The newbie had kept going on and on about blood readers, and Juva had ended up on her back underneath a snarling wild animal. But even so, she had made it through the morning without any hoggthorn. That should feel like a victory, but all she felt was anxious, as if all the things she didn't have answers for were making her heart more fragile.

Juva sat down at the table, took a sip of tea, and tried to find some peace in the things that remained unchanged. She was sitting in the same hall—surely even the same chair!—that Father had once used. He had looked at the same vaulted wooden ceiling and the same stone walls. The same antlers along the railing up on the second floor, which cast trembling shadows in the glow from the fireplace. He had surely also thought that the shadows looked like claws. He had salted hides in the same dented casks and made soup in the same copper pots. Even his coworkers were the same, Broddmar and Muggen, anyway.

The silence was broken by a creaking door.

"Juva? Where's my girl?" Ester's voice squealed from the porch.

For a second Juva feared bad news, but then she realized that Ester was there because of the runner she herself had sent. Still, when Ester called her *my girl*, that meant trouble.

The old woman came waltzing in as if she owned the place, which was fine since she actually did. She stopped in front of the opening to the kitchen. Shook her head at what she saw inside, presumably water bloody from washing the clothes and hunting boots drying over the hearth.

"Men!" she said brusquely. "They live like the animals they hunt."

Juva didn't bother to clarify that most of the mess was hers, lest Ester decide to give her accommodations to someone else. The rent she demanded was laughably low for Náklav, and Juva had nowhere else to go.

"So," Ester leaned on her cane and sank heavily onto the chair beside Juva. "What kind of problems? Are you all right?"

"Oh . . . yeah, we just had to turn back. Nothing serious."

Ester looked at her with sharp, gray eyes and raised her eyebrows. "Mmm. I see that. You have blood in your hair."

Juva brought her hand to her long, blond tangles that, sure enough, were caked with blood.

"I haven't had time to bathe."

She hadn't had time to dress properly, either. Only the long stockings and a stretched-out sweater, since she still needed to get into the tub. She pulled her feet up under her and tugged down the sweater sleeves to protect her hands as she held the hot mug.

Ester leaned back in her chair. She was a notch older than Broddmar, surely nearing seventy, although Juva had never asked. But she dressed and acted as if she had her whole life ahead of her. Or maybe more as if nothing could hurt her. Juva would have given anything to feel that way.

Ester had wrapped a white scarf around her head, the way women from Ruv often did. It was secured over her forehead with a gold pin. Her sealskin coat shone in the light from the fireplace, and she drummed her wrinkled, ringed fingers against the knob atop her yellowed bone cane. The top was carved like a fist. Rumor had it that it had belonged to her husband, and that she had killed him with it when she was young. Juva hadn't asked about that either.

Ester pursed her brown-painted lips as if she was tickled by something. "So, no serious problems, but enough to have to turn back?"

"Yes, we had a newbie along. He got bitten. He won't be coming next time, let's just put it that way."

"Bitten?! How the Gaula did he manage to get bitten? Was he trying to ride the animal?"

Juva chuckled and her tea went down the wrong way. She searched for words that wouldn't reveal that they had set out with a blood slave and risked their hunting license. She would leave it to Broddmar to share that.

"No idea," she replied. "He didn't make it that far. He just muscled his way in there before the wolf was dead. Would you like a cup of tea?"

Ester's gaze drilled into hers. She was by no means gullible, but she didn't ask any more about the matter. That was another sure sign that something was weighing on her, just as sure as *my girl*.

"Tea? Jól deliver me from evil, that sounds disgustingly healthy. Don't you people have any wine?"

"No, we usually get it from them when we have something to celebrate." Juva nodded to the door that separated the hunting hall from the tavern.

"Oh," Ester mumbled, disappointed. "Then I suppose I'll get you something you can have on hand. It wouldn't look good if I let the hunters go thirsty!"

Juva set down her cup and lifted the crossbow from the table. She supported the stock between her knees as she waxed the string.

"They checked our teeth at Naarport," she said. "Did the Dead Man's Horn sound?"

Ester tapped her cane against the floor and her eyes widened. She looked a little like a stout bird. "Yes, by golly, they found a man at Bløgge with half his face gnawed off! Gnawed! How's that? That's the worst I've heard in my whole life!"

"Not worse than that guy last year with the missing throat."

"No, but—"

"Or the woman whose stomach had been—"

"Yes, yes, but it gets worse and worse!"

Ester leaned on her cane and got up from the deep chair. It looked like her bad hip was hurting her, but she never complained. Aside from when she would occasionally ask men to fetch her some wine. In those moments, suddenly, she could barely walk. She liked young men racing around for her. She had said that she enjoyed pretending it was because she was still beautiful and not because she was rich.

Ester opened a voluminous coin purse with a clever kiss clasp and took out a few coins, which she set on the table. They seemed out of place between the skinning knife and the chainmail glove. It was almost thirty runes for a single hide. Something was definitely wrong.

Juva studied her. "You haven't even seen the hide yet," she objected.

"Oh shush," Ester snorted. "Let me pay decently if I want. Be smart, my girl."

She served up a harsh smile that faded into concern. Juva steeled herself for what was coming, but that was hard since she had no idea what to expect.

"How do the other hunters treat you, Juva?"

"They couldn't be nicer." Juva resisted the temptation to urge her to get to the point.

"You know you can tell me if anything comes up, right?"

"Yes, thank you."

"Can you handle some bad news?"

"That depends on the news."

Ester looked a little shocked that Juva hadn't been surprised, but she didn't have a chance to respond before the door to the tavern opened. A bloodred silhouette appeared in the doorway. Red dress, red cape, and red veil over the face, but Juva didn't need to see it to know that this was the bad news.

She shot up from her chair, only barely catching the crossbow before it fell to the floor.

"Solde?!" She stared reproachfully at Ester. "You brought my sister?!"

"Of course not," Ester responded, touching her earring. "But I may have mentioned that you were here," she added, a little more guiltily. Then she waved her gloves at Juva to make light of the whole thing. "Don't look at me like that, child. Was I supposed to say no to a blood reader?"

Ester nodded in greeting to Solde and disappeared out the back door without waiting for a response. No response was needed. She was right. No one said no to a blood reader.

Solde tossed her veil back behind her head and revealed her face in a carefully studied motion she had surely spent the morning perfecting. Juva stared at her in astonishment. It felt like half a lifetime since she had last seen her, even though in reality it had been closer to six months.

The heavy winter dress and cape were sewn from a dizzying red so bright that she could have replaced the lighthouse at Kleft. The skirt was stiff and wide enough to be squashed by the doorway. The waist was tied with a red ribbon, so tight that it made Solde's hips stick out unnaturally.

Solde was three years younger than Juva, but dressed like that, people would think it was the other way around.

Juva took a deep breath. Her sister had always embraced her role as blood reader, but this was completely over the top. This was a protest. A warning. The jewelry was the finishing touch, primitive in contrast to the dress. Long leather straps decorated with silver Muune's moons and bones featuring runic cutouts. Solde was steeped in the mystique that blood readers made a living claiming to understand.

Solde sailed into the hide hall and wrinkled her little button nose. "What *is* that smell?"

"Blood and entrails, mostly." Juva had hoped to shock her, but Solde maintained her icy mask. When you were well trained in how to read people, you knew what to hide about yourself. Juva realized that she probably did the same thing, more often than she liked to think about.

Solde's hair was blonder than Juva's own. Almost white and pulled tightly back. It made her look bald from a distance, a skull. Her neck disappeared into the stiff red collar, as if her clothes were devouring her. She was a dead girl in a dress that would consume her, slowly but surely.

"You live here? Really?" Her sister pulled off her red gloves, finger by finger, as she peered around.

Juva spotted her thumb ring, and for a second, she thought it was a blood reader claw, even though Solde hadn't inherited yet or been accepted into the guild. But it was no claw, just a black bird skull that bent over her thumb joint. The beak reached almost to her thumbnail. A visual exercise for the day when the claw would be hers.

Solde's gaze wandered around the room until it stopped on Juva with feigned shock, as if she had only just noticed her. "Oh, but for heaven's sake, you're a mess!" she exclaimed.

"What are you doing here, Solde?" Juva set the crossbow on the table.

"I'm trying to tell you that someone pooped in your hair," Solde said, coming closer.

Juva turned her back to Solde and went into the kitchen. She tried to steady herself by resting her hands on the counter, then realized that they were shaking. Her pulse quickened.

Hoggthorn. I need hoggthorn.

She opened the tea caddy and looked down at the black leaves with orange bits of dried hoggthorn. The sight of them gave her the courage to wait. She refused to give Solde the satisfaction of seeing her off-kilter. She heard Solde's shoes click-clack across the floor on her way to the kitchen. Solde stopped in the doorway. It would take a lot to get her sister into a kitchen, and at the moment, she truly looked as if she had never seen one before.

"What next?" Solde asked with distaste. "Will you move onto the rafts? Find a shack to live in with an old fisherman or something?" Her laughter was sharp with scorn, a specialty Solde had mastered at far too young an age.

She looked Juva in the eye, and a flicker of uncertainty darted over Solde's face. She recovered with a theatrical sigh. "Mama is sick," she announced.

Juva pushed the tea caddy back onto the shelf. "She isn't sick."

"She is, too!" Solde put her hands on her artificially big hips, finally

43

looking like the defiant child she was. "She's been confined to her bed for several days, and I've hardly left her side!"

Juva pushed past Solde in the doorway, quickly, so the red dress wouldn't eat her as well. She sat down in front of the fireplace again and picked up a bolt from among the things she had laid out on the table. She started polishing its steel tip.

"Just so we're clear, Solde, I have no doubt that she *said* she's sick."

"Do you really think I can't tell the difference?"

Solde came over to the table and started touching Juva's things with her long fingers. It was as if two worlds that should never come in contact with each other collided: the one Juva wanted to live in and the one she didn't want to remember.

"Don't touch that." She brushed Solde's hand away from the crossbow.

Solde picked up the jar containing the bolt poison.

"Don't touch that either," Juva snapped, snatching it away from her. "Unless you feel like throwing up your own lungs. Fine, so she's sick. So what?"

Solde looked like she was considering sitting down, but evidently the chair wasn't up to her standards or she concluded that it wasn't possible in that dress. So she remained standing.

"She wants you to come. Not that I understand why, because it isn't going to make any difference, Juva. But since she's sick, you could at least come by and say goodbye. And pick up the rest of your things."

Juva had planned to pick up the rest of her things anyway, and she wanted as little to do with the inheritance as possible, especially the job of blood reader. But the matter-of-factness with which Solde wrote her off made her knuckles whiten around the bolt.

Solde started poking at the leather thongs around Juva's sketchbook. Juva slammed the palm of her hand down on it and pulled it toward herself. No one could see her drawings, least of all her sister.

She felt her throat constrict. Memories crowded into her head and her anxiety threatened to take the upper hand. She needed to get Solde out of here and drink some hoggthorn.

"Have you said what you came to say?"

Solde looked extremely cheerful not to have been contradicted about the inheritance. She turned her back so the skirt swept across the floor.

"You do as you please," she announced. "I did my best."

Juva gave a brief laugh. Her sister had done precisely as she had been asked to, no more, no less.

Solde opened the door to the tavern, and the conversation in there immediately went silent. Juva could see the looks the patrons gave the blood reader, some in fear, others in hope. One elderly man stood up and folded his hands in front of him as if in prayer. Juva couldn't hear what he said, but he probably wanted to know what they all wanted to know. How long he had left to live.

Solde turned to Juva and smiled. The resemblance to a skull was complete. Death in red, surrounded by people who wanted answers so badly. Then she slammed the door shut between them.

Juva got to her feet and stormed into the kitchen. She picked up the pot. Empty. It was empty. She put her strength into the water pump, with forceful thrusts, pumping in time with her heartbeat. Only a few drips emerged from the tap.

"Damn it, what the . . ."

She fought against the panic, leaning on the pump and using her body's weight to coax out the droplets. Then the water started to flow, all at once. Juva put some in the pot and set it over the hearth. She looked around for the cup and realized it was in the living room, a small problem that suddenly felt insurmountable.

Get a grip, Juva!

She took a fresh cup from the shelf. She thought it probably belonged to Broddmar. She dropped two pinches of hoggthorn tea into the bottom, shifting from foot to foot while she stared at the pot. She couldn't wait, and poured the lukewarm water over the tea, then sat down at the kitchen table.

The leaves hadn't even unfolded before she took the first sip. Good? No. Bitter filth that made her throat constrict. But she knew it helped. She had been drinking it since she was a child. An anxious child, they had said, who got palpitations at the least little thing. But that wasn't true. Other people were afraid of the strangest things, things she had never been afraid of: the dark, the northern lights, the highest seaside cliffs plunging into the sea, and idiotic portents like faces in the embers or entrails that lay the wrong way after the animal was slaughtered.

But there were other things that made her dizzy with fear, things people couldn't understand, because they made her remember that gruesome things could happen because of her. Had she conjured up the wolf again? Was that why Solde had come?

Juva took a big gulp and felt her heart calm. She had killed the wolf and burned its remains. That should stave off a day of catastrophes at any rate.

She knew that wasn't logical, not something a person thinking clearly would do. But it didn't feel like she could change that. She hadn't made these rules.

She sat down with her drawing book in her lap. A soft, leather-bound book that had saved her life many times over. She opened it in the middle so she wouldn't have to see her earliest drawings, the ones that were folded and tucked between the first pages. Some of them were ten years old.

She found a blank page and started drawing. The pencil felt safe in her hand. She had made it herself out of a charred branch from Svartna, with string wrapped around the chewed-up end. Her hand moved as if in a trance, and she had no idea where the picture came from. The devil took shape, as he always had. An animal-like body on two legs, sinewy and naked, like a skinned wolf. The head was as much man as animal, with chalky-white eyes and fangs. Alluring. Deadly. The animal in her life.

She tugged the page out of the book and threw it in the fire. The devil yellowed before he caught fire and became engulfed in flames. He curled up into glowing ash and disappeared.

Juva closed the book and leaned back in the chair.

She could breathe again.

BLOOD READER LINEAGE

The ice fog crawled in from the ocean to settle over the city, but Juva didn't need to see to know where she was going. She had grown up there, unlike all the visitors with their eyes wandering between their guidebooks and the copper signs, hunting for Náklav's famous treasures and curiosities.

Juva approached the crossroads, and her feet grew heavier as if reminding her that she was going the wrong way. Straight ahead, the street continued all the way up to Nákla Henge, the stone gates that churned out the endless stream of visitors from the entire world. The narrow Lykteløkka twisted off to the right. There was no difference between locals and visitors there. They were all after the same thing: blood readers.

Juva took a deep, cold breath and turned right. All she had to do was sign for Solde to get the inheritance and leave again. Then it would be over. She would never need to have anything to do with Mother, Solde, or any other blood readers ever again. Just this once, then she could live her own life, invisible, free. Maybe save up enough money to leave Náklav for good and find a place with solid ground under her feet, a place without blood readers and without vardari.

Lykteløkka was undisputedly the blood reader street. People flocked to have their fortunes told all over the city, of course, but this was where the power was. You could see Jólshov out on the tip of Skodda from here. That was the Seida Guild's headquarters, and the blood readers who belonged to the guild were easy to find. You just had to follow the red lanterns.

Red was reserved for the genuine ones, the *real* blood readers, as if anything about them was real. They had tried to obtain an exclusive right to use lanterns, but even the Seida Guild couldn't stop people from hanging lights by their doors. The city court had decided to limit the color, not the lights. The result was that the entire street was full of what the guild called amateurs, with yellow and orange lanterns. Every now and then, one would show up that was so close to red, the owner would be fined and have to swap it out.

Juva pulled her hood well over her head. The icy fog shrank the already narrow street and intensified her sense that she was heading into a trap.

Additions stuck out of every conceivable building surface. New construction permits were rarer than a winter solstice, but people were people. They figured out how to circumvent the rules and build anyway. Passages, bridges, and stairs popped up faster than the city council could register them. And the elegantly drawn maps that were sold to the tourists were rarely updated.

In a number of places, the buildings had actually grown together over the street or been connected with elevated walkways of stone and wood with little windows. Visitors called these "Nákla bridges" without ever suspecting that the walkways were one of the things locals argued over most. People would even join two bay windows into a full elevated closet-like passageway that could be rented out for a tidy sum. That was Náklav in a nutshell.

Juva stopped in front of the Sannseyr residence, the family home she had left at the age of sixteen. It had been a long time since she had set foot there, and the sight bothered her more than she wanted to admit.

The stone building was the last in a row, large enough that the others seemed cramped in comparison, as if the dark blood reader's house was slowly but surely displacing them. Tower-like additions with ashwood timber framing bulged out on the second floor. The windows were tall and slim, with mullions, and wavy glass panes that prevented anyone from seeing in.

Between the two front doors hung a heavy lantern made of red glass, which made the fog bleed.

Last time. It's almost over.

Juva still had the keys in her bag, but it felt wrong to let herself in to a house that was no longer her home. She walked up the front steps and used the knocker on the main door. It was slim and made of solid forged iron. Lagalune had once talked about replacing it with a bigger one, to make visitors feel smaller. Juva had never forgotten that.

The door was opened by a stranger, a girl in a black dress that was buttoned all the way up to her chin. She pulled a book out of her pocket and opened it using the ribbon bookmark.

"First time? You need to use the other door. That's the one for the waiting room for visitors. Do you have an appointment?" Her index finger ran down a list of names and stopped at the one she assumed was Juva's.

"No. I'm . . ."

"I see. In that case, you can come closer to the weekend, on Flodsdag." The girl placed a hand on Juva's arm and looked at her with what an inexperienced viewer would interpret as concern. "Because I know you need this."

Juva bit her lip to keep herself from telling the girl to save it. Her feet itched to leave again, but this wasn't going to be any easier later. She had to get this over with.

"I'm Juva, Juva Sannseyr. Lagalune is my mother."

The girl's chin dropped for a second, but she quickly recovered. "Forgive me, Miss Sannseyr. I didn't know . . ."

"Juva."

"J-Juva. I didn't know you were coming today."

"Neither did I. Is Lagalune in?"

"Yes. Or, well . . . Lagalune has been under the weather for the last few days. She's in her chambers now, meeting with the other two members of the Guild, but they've been talking for a long time, so I'm sure they'll be done soon."

The girl moved aside to let her enter, but Juva remained on the stairs. "And Solde?" she asked.

"Solde is out."

Not exactly chained to Mother's so-called sickbed, then.

"I'll wait," Juva said.

"Um . . . People usually wait inside?" The girl looked at her, clearly at a loss.

Juva forced herself to cross the threshold. The door closed with a clang behind her, heavy and metallic. It was an unpleasantly final sound and triggered the anxiety in her heart that she had known would come.

"Shall I take your jacket, Miss Sannse . . . Juva?"

"No, thank you. I won't be staying long."

That seemed to be a significant weight off the girl's chest. She excused herself. Juva remained standing alone in the front hall, which looked the way it always had, so gloomy that she might as well have been in Drukna. She took in the dark walls with thin gold stripes around the panels, and the ink-black stairs that curved their way up to the gallery. The railing was so intricate that it looked like black lace. Under the highest part of the stairs sat the centerpiece of the house: the fireplace that separated the front hall from the library. An enormous, burning maw. Its flames were the only sign of life. There were more than enough fireplaces in the home since this row of houses was farthest out by the sea, on the edge of the southern cliffs.

There was a long runner carpet on the floor depicting the phases of the moon and a black bench against the wall with a back that looked like a rib cage. It was damned uncomfortable, but that was also the point. Everything in this accursed house had a purpose.

Visitors were supposed to feel inferior, helpless in the face of a dark power. The skeletal bench and the shelves of grotesque curiosities hinted at a world where the rules were different. A carved skull, an hourglass, an antique plague mask—all suggesting that even death wasn't the worst thing that could happen.

Juva hated it, hated the whole house, and she had never been able to shake the feeling that it was mutual. She could feel her own heart here, as if it sat right under her skin, beating in a frightening, shaky rhythm. Inside these walls, she had never had control, never been able to trust anything.

Juva put her hand against her pocket to make sure the hoggthorn berries were there, in case things got too bad.

I am not a child anymore!

This felt like a test. The house was testing her, but she didn't live there anymore. She had won, and she felt an intense need to prove it. The door to the blood reader's room was open. Juva picked up her chin and walked in. There he was. The wolf.

He loomed before her, painted across the whole wall in shades of blue and black. He was a dark outline filled with stars. To stare at the wolf's body was to stare into the night sky. His eyes were two white fissures, almost glowing. He seemed cunning, the devil, as he bent over a woman who was vanishingly small against his body.

The sister in the fairy tale, the one who survived.

Juva held up her hand to the motif, which had scared the wits out of her when she was little, but she couldn't get herself to touch him. Down at the bottom, there was a signature by the one paw, so untamed that it was illegible. *Síla Sannseyr*, her great-grandmother. The woman who had bought the estate from the harbor master at the time. It was a miracle that the painting had survived Mother's penchant for changing things up. But no doubt that was due to the fact that the painting had a clear mission: to remind people of where the blood readers' so-called powers came from.

Three sisters went out to hunt. They caught a wolf, which was no ordinary wolf, but the devil in wolves' clothing. He said that if they let him go, they would always know where he was. Always know where the evil was. Death, disease, ill-will—nothing would be hidden anymore, not from them. The women said yes, and the wolf shared his blood with them. That's how they became blood readers.

The eldest of the sisters, the one in green, realized right away that she herself was evil and threw herself off the cliff. The middle one, dressed in blue, went home and realized that she had married an evil man. She attacked him and he killed her. The youngest of the sisters, the one in red, realized that the devil was everywhere. In every heart. She did nothing and survived. Since that time, the blood readers have always known where the devil is.

Lies.

Layer upon layer of lies and fairy tales, milked by the Seida Guild for generations. There could hardly be a room in the world where more make-believe had been so convincingly dished up. Day in and day out, a temple to the imaginary, born in a bloodthirsty frenzy.

Juva heard someone cough and she jumped. It came from the waiting room, so it was surely a customer waiting to spend all his money.

Not my problem.

She turned her back to the wolf and looked around. The west wall was right up against another building, so there were no windows, but there was a fireplace in each corner. A round wooden table stood in the middle of the floor; it was speckled with little dots that looked like rust. Blood from thousands of customers.

53

A box with iron fittings, as if to protect the world from its contents, sat on the edge of the table. Juva opened the lid and peered down at the bone cards. For blood reader cards, they were exquisite, she would be the first to admit. They were smaller than her hands and almost wafer thin, made of yellowed whale cartilage, supple and strong. Durable enough that the cards had survived many generations of Sannseyrs. They would surely survive Solde as well.

The pictures and patterns were colorless, burned onto the bone. The raven sat at the top with his gaping beak and grim gaze.

Destiny. Primordial Power. Change. A Stranger.

Would she ever forget their meanings? Everything she'd had to rehearse from the time she learned to walk? Next to the cards sat the claw, the articulated silver thumb ring, which poked holes in the skin.

Someone coughed again, and Juva shut the lid. How long did they keep people waiting? She opened the double doors to the waiting room. A woman stood up abruptly, her eyes hopeful. Her hope faded when she realized it wasn't the blood reader, and she sank heavily back into the chair again, staring down at the purse she clutched in her lap.

Juva didn't want to know anything about her, but the impressions wouldn't stop coming. Reading them was elementary. Her name was Vera if the staff woman's little appointment book was right. The way she had sat down showed that she had been waiting for a long time. She held her money, not possessively, but with a conspicuousness that indicated she couldn't actually afford to be there. She was scarcely older than Juva, and the slight bulge of her abdomen spoke for itself. Pregnant and didn't want to be? No, she made no attempt to hide it.

"I had an appointment." The woman smiled apologetically at her. "With Solde Sannseyr. But it was a while ago, I think. Maybe she doesn't want to see me?"

She forgot you or most likely doesn't give a damn about you.

Juva closed her eyes. This wasn't her problem. This was not her business, not at all. She should leave. But she knew she had already lost that battle. She sighed.

"I'm Juva, Solde's sister. Why are you here, Vera?"

Juva hated herself for using the woman's name. It was a cheap trick, but it worked. Vera leapt to her feet again, eager to believe anything at all. The look in her eyes contained a touching trust that no one in this house had earned. She peered down at her coin purse and then up at Juva again.

"I . . . Is there any way that I could get less than . . . just a half appointment?" Her hand slid toward her belly.

"You're afraid for the baby," Juva said, calculating her own tone of voice. If she was right, the girl would interpret that as true-sight. If she was wrong, she could pretend it had been a question.

Vera nodded. "My mother died having me. And the wolf-sickness is spreading! People say there's bad blood in the city. I asked Solde the last time I was here if Jól wanted to hurt me. If the gods are going to take me, too. My husband . . . He won't be able to bear it if . . ."

"And Solde said that she was sure she needed to see you again to know?" Juva tried to smile through her growing anger.

To suck the last of your money out of you.

"She said something was wrong!" The woman gulped. Her eyes welled up. "Something she couldn't see clearly, but that might happen. I had to come back. I don't know what you want me to do!"

Juva grasped the woman's hand and squeezed it between her own. She closed her eyes and adopted a mask of concentration.

Self-loathing ate away at her from the inside, even though she hadn't claimed to be reading the woman's blood. Not in so many words.

After a bit, she released the woman's hand and looked at her again.

"You have to help the gods to help yourself, Vera. Can you do that?"

Vera's hand flew up to cover her mouth and she let out a little sob. "I'll do anything!"

"Good. Go see a doctor. Explain what happened to your mother, and make sure that you're not alone as your time approaches. That's all you need to do, and you never need to come here again. No one here can tell you anything you don't already know."

The woman nodded and opened her coin purse.

Juva stopped her. "Save your money for the baby. You're going to need it. They're not cheap."

Vera clearly interpreted that as a good sign and her eyes overflowed. She wiped away her tears with a clenched fist and mumbled *thank you* before disappearing out the door with a level of relief that Juva would not have thought possible only a few moments before.

Enough! Never again!

Juva returned to the blood reader room and heard the voices of two women out in the front hall. She recognized them. Ogny Volsung, master of the Seida Guild, and Maruska Auste. Sannseyr, Volsung, and Auste. The backbone of the guild, and the family names all of Náklav knew.

They were walking toward the front door as Ogny complained that this was a terrible time to dither and that Lagalune needed to make up her mind or be prepared for reprisals.

From the warow . . .

Juva put her hand to her chest to calm her fluttering heart. Gaula take the blood readers *and* the warow. She waited until the front door closed after them, then marched down the corridor to Lagalune's bedroom.

The door was open, revealing the dark four-poster bed, surrounded by tall candlesticks. Lagalune sat in a chair by the window, which curved out over the open sea. There was ice on all the little windowpanes and one was cracked after years of battling the harsh weather.

She spotted Juva and tapped a thin cigar on the ashtray. She wore her black hair loosely up. Her lips were painted a matching black. She looked deceptively young, despite her almost fifty years.

Juva remained in the doorway, her heart pounding, which she did her utmost to hide. "Solde said you were sick."

Lagalune stood up, set down her cigar, and pulled her dress over her head to change without any shyness whatsoever.

"Of course I'm not sick! Have you ever heard of a sick blood reader?" She tossed her dress on the bed and stood there exposed, in a perilously tightly-laced white corset. She looked around and found a skirt slung over a chair back. "But how else was I supposed to get you here?"

"Ask, like a normal person?" Juva said with a shrug.

Lagalune tied the skirt around her waist. She took another puff of her cigar and blew a cloud of white smoke out of the corner of her mouth as she watched Juva.

"Where are your things?" she queried.

Juva's feeling of horror grew into a nauseating certainty. Her mother had never intended this to be a short visit.

"I have my things where I live."

Lagalune pretended she hadn't heard and started adjusting the pins in her hair. Juva's eyes roamed around the room and stopped on the little glass flask on the dresser, filled with fish roe, little red beads that would never rot or smell. Blood pearls. And Juva knew where they came from.

Vardari. The eternal ones, the warow . . .

The nausea turned bitter in her mouth. Her mother always claimed she needed it, to heighten her senses so that she could read better. She could say whatever she wanted to, but even blood readers weren't above the law. Wolf blood was just as forbidden for them as for that damned newbie who had ruined their hunt. In the worst-case scenarios, they could come down with wolf-sickness.

57

The most disgusting effect of the wolf blood was the confidence it seemed to give people. Juva had seen that even as a child. The memories flowed through her, unwelcome and violent. She used to call it blood certainty. Mama was blood-certain.

Lagalune took the hairpin she had held between her teeth and jabbed it into her bun.

"You are insanely stubborn, Juva. You must get that from your father. Or Broddmar. You spend way too much time with that toothless old man. He has a habit of making things up." Her eyes wandered down Juva's body. "You haven't let him between your thighs, have you?"

Don't take her bait!

Juva tensed her jaws. "Why am I here, Lagalune?"

Her mother took on her mortally insulted face.

"Juva, aren't you a little too old to pout? I understand that it's easier to blame me for everything that is wrong in life, but you simply need to outgrow that. Sometimes things happen that aren't actually about you! Do you think I would have invited you here if it wasn't important? We need to discuss the future, whether you want to or not."

Invited? Pout? Blame?

Juva felt exhausted already. "What are you talking about? Just give me the papers and I'll sign! Let Solde take everything she wants—the house, the job. Anyway, she can't get rid of me fast enough."

Lagalune picked up a knot of black beads from the nightstand and attached them to her ear. They dangled in long strands alongside her neck.

"Solde is too . . ." Mother opened a mirrored cupboard and studied herself as she searched for the words, ". . . irresponsible."

"Irresponsible? *Solde* is too irresponsible?" Juva would have laughed if it wasn't so tragic.

"You know what I mean! She's . . . sadistic."

"Sadistic?"

"Don't play dumb with me, Juva. It doesn't suit you. She takes pleasure in other people's misfortunes. She's immature. Holy Muune, the girl was only eight when she trampled your cat to death! You used to be a bright girl. Don't tell me you don't see that?"

Juva felt drained, trapped, yet again, in a drama somehow mysteriously constructed to relate to her. And yet again, she lost her grasp on reality. Had that really happened, or was her mother just making things up?

"What cat?"

Lagalune took another puff of her cigar and lifted her breasts into place in her corset.

"The cat! That striped stray cat you took in? Don't you remember?"

"Paws?! You said he was killed by snow falling off the roof!"

"I never said that!" Lagalune waved her hand dismissively. "But it doesn't matter. I've prepared your room. You'll stay for a few days in any case. We have a lot to plan."

Juva leaned against the doorframe. Was this a tasteless joke? A test? Some kind of revenge?

How had she survived her entire childhood in this house?

And she couldn't even start with this nonsense about her staying. Even the thought was absurd! After almost three years on her own, it was painfully obvious that this was not normal behavior. This was Lagalune. This was the blood readers. It didn't matter at all to them whether something was real or not.

"You look pale, Juva. You take hoggthorn, don't you? Remember what Dr. Emelstein said. You need to take care of your nerves."

Juva couldn't find the energy to respond. She clutched a couple of whole hoggthorn berries in her pocket and fought the feeling that the world around her was swaying.

BANISHED

Rugen paused at what he thought was Lutvannsveita. It was hard to tell in this labyrinth of a city. And now, on top of everything else, it had started to snow. He'd made his way under bridges and overhangs to avoid getting drenched, but damp flakes stuck to his hood.

He shielded his eyes with his hand and squinted into the alley. It continued underneath a narrow building that hung pinched between two larger buildings. A sad hovel, but yes, he was in the right place.

The second-floor window was just barely an opening, but a candle flickered inside, so unless she had moved, she was home. He definitely wouldn't find a sink here, but he had run out of alternatives.

Besides, they hadn't had a fight, had they? It had just sort of fallen apart on its own, the way such things usually do. It had started with the letter she had written back then, which he had never answered. But for all she knew, it could've gotten lost. Letters went missing all the time in Náklav, especially when they were intended for someone like him, someone who moved from place to place. She couldn't possibly be mad about that. Either way, it was completely crazy to expect someone to answer a four-page letter full of questions, right?

A new jolt shot through his jaw. His hand moved reflexively toward his face, but there was nothing he could do. It was like a needle was drilling from his lip to the bridge of his nose. He had to get to safety. Find shelter, with someone who could take care of him when everything was going to Drukna.

Rugen entered the archway under the house and found the door. He pushed his hood off, pulled his hand through his hair, and knocked. A fat woman in a nightcap opened the door a crack. She was hiding something behind her back, presumably a knife. This wasn't the best neighborhood in the city. Gods knew he deserved better.

He tried to look as if he were expected. "Hi, I'm going upstairs. I'm a good friend of Aletta's."

"Alette?"

"Alette. That's what I said."

The woman opened the door a little more but remained where she was, so he had to squeeze past. Either she hoped to stick a knife in him or she was hankering for a man's touch. It was hard to tell with women. He felt like they often wanted both.

Rugen climbed the stairs and stopped outside Alette's door. He could hear some sort of noise inside but wasn't sure what it was. He practiced smiling and then rapped his knuckles against the door. It grew quiet. Then he heard quiet fiddling with the lock and realized that she was trying to see who it was. Rugen bent down, turned his face away from the light on the wall, and grinned at the keyhole. The door opened a crack.

"What in Gaula . . ." Alette stuck her head out and looked around, as if she expected him to have brought more people with him.

Her dark curls were heavy and unwashed. She was sweaty and generally looked a little sick.

"Hi . . . Can I come in?"

"Come in? You can get lost, Rugen. You're the last thing I need right now." She tried to close the door, but he managed to push his foot into the opening.

"Did I do something wrong? Are you mad at me for something?" In cases of doubt, it was always best to play dumb.

"Rugen, I can't deal with you right now. Just go."

Rugen searched for some memory that could explain her resentment, but he was certain their parting hadn't been so bad that she'd refuse to let him in. Still, no two women were alike, so he could never be sure. He needed to play his best hand here.

He leaned his forehead against the door. "I'm sorry?"

"It's fine, Rugen. Now go!" She squeezed the door against his foot so hard that he swore.

Fucking bitch. Didn't she realize what it had cost him to come here? There was no way he would take this shit if he had any other choice!

"Alette, I mean it. I need help."

"Not as much as I do." She disappeared and he heard her let go of the door.

Rugen darted into the room. It seemed smaller than he remembered. The bench under the window opening took up the whole width of the place. The black cast-iron oven was the only place to make food, and a ladder led up to the loft where the bed was. The bed barely had room for the both of them; he had experienced that firsthand. It was so close to the ceiling that she could brace her feet up there, and he remembered that as a definite advantage.

He smiled, but she wasn't looking at him. The closet door was open and she was packing her clothes into a worn suitcase that looked as if something had been chewing on its corners. This was apparently about something other than him. He felt both relieved and slightly disappointed.

"So, what's going on?"

"It's none of your business anymore. Say what you need to say and get out of here." She walked over to the window and peered down at the street. She drew the apron that was serving as a curtain across the window.

"Alette . . ." Rugen grabbed her arm, but she pulled free.

"I don't have anything to help you, Rugen. No money, no blood pearls, nothing. You're in the wrong place, do you understand?"

He was on the verge of saying that she had a warm bed to lend if she was going somewhere, but that wasn't going to be enough now. He had to take it easy if he was going to clinch this. Besides, she was lying. Her bag was hanging open from the coat peg, and the little coin purse inside did not look empty.

"Where are you going?"

"Wherever." She stuffed a wool sweater into the suitcase as if she hated it.

"Could you relax for a minute?"

She stopped and looked at him. She wasn't wearing any make-up—and she usually wore a lot. The bodice of her dress wasn't laced up. She looked tired and unkempt. Her swollen eyes welled up.

"No, Rugen, I cannot relax! I'm done! I'm dead!"

He walked over and pulled her to him. She softened in his arms and began to cry.

"You're not going to die, Alette. Just stop." He ran his hand over her hair, burrowed his fingers into it, and felt himself growing hard.

She tensed and pushed him away. "You don't know shit, Rugen!" She bared her teeth at him like an animal.

For a second, he thought she had lost her mind, but then he noticed the canine tooth. It was sharp, a little shorter and paler than her other teeth, new, not grown in all the way.

"What the wolf-snatch?!" Rugen backed away.

Alette tried to close her suitcase, but it was too full. She pressed both hands down on the top, several times, as she sobbed. He felt sick to his stomach. He had been prepared for a lot, but not for this.

"How? You never used that much, did you?"

"That much?! I never used any before I met you!"

Rugen suppressed a pang of guilt. He wasn't up to being anyone's scapegoat, not now. He started pacing back and forth, the few steps there was room for. This shouldn't be happening. The odds were practically zero! Wolf-sickness was an empty threat, something you said to troublemaking teens to keep them off blood. People rarely came down with it, and only the ones who couldn't control themselves as far as he knew. And now there were two of them in the same room? What the fuck was going on?

He pulled his tongue over his own teeth, relieved that he still had his canines. He had more time than Alette. Unless he'd already started to go crazy and none of this was really happening . . .

The thought made him shudder.

"Fuck, Alette." He pulled her close again, as if to make sure that she was real. "I don't know what to do."

"No, you never did know that, Rugen." She sounded defiant, but she didn't pull away from him.

"Have you been taking more than before?" he asked, knowing that he was searching for answers more for himself than for her.

"No. And no, I haven't bought from strangers. Neither have any of the others I've heard about."

"What others?"

She looked up at him. "Others with wolf-sickness. Rugen, they're checking people at the gates again. How out of it are you?!"

He'd heard about that, but people always talked. And it never had anything to do with him.

"I thought wolf-sickness was, I don't know, something made up, an excuse for hunting rabble-rousers or outlaws, poor people, people traveling illegally. I thought . . ."

"Does this look political?!" She retracted her upper lip to reveal the canine tooth, which was bleeding from the root.

"What are you going to do?" he asked, looking away in disgust.

"What do you think? I'm getting out of here before the red hunter comes breathing down my neck and I get my arteries cut and bleed out!"

Her fear was as raw and naked as his own, a frightening mirror image. He considered telling her that he was in the same situation. Surely that would comfort her. But the risk was too high. What if she couldn't keep her mouth shut? Or would they have to stay together? Would he be forced to hang out with her while she turned into a raving predator? Hell, no. Alette had never had the same strong will he had. She was a lost cause. He couldn't go down with her.

All he needed was a place to sleep so he could figure things out tomorrow.

"It'll work out, Alette." He took her hand and pulled her toward him again. "Don't be scared. I'll stay here tonight, and I can take care of things here until you come back. It'll be all right."

Alette pulled away and steered him toward the door. He resisted, enough to sneak his hand into her bag on the wall. He stuck her coin purse in his pocket. Then he relented and let her push him out. She did it more forcefully than he expected. He nearly fell down the stairs.

"Go to Drukna, Rugen!"

The door slammed shut. He stood there staring at it. It seemed so final and solid, all the more so for being the last of a long string of closed doors he had encountered in his life. Had the world always been this way? Had people always only thought about themselves?

Rugen ambled down the stairs and reluctantly made his way back out into the snowy weather. He checked Alette's coin purse and found three measly runes. A good party, nothing more. The bitter part was knowing that this city was full of money—it just wasn't in his pockets. Where could he pick up a little of the excess?

At Nafraím's . . .

If there was such a thing as vardari, Nafraím was one of them. Rugen shuddered. He had never liked the thought of them. Gaula only knows what was true and what was made up, but one thing was certain: It wasn't just trade that brought people from every corner of the world to Náklav. It was also the rumors of something unpleasant living in the shadows, of people who never aged. But how many of those who came here actually believed that the warow existed?

And of those who believed, how many came hoping to become one of them?

Why would anyone want to live a day longer than they had to in this vale of tears?

Who was it who'd told him that? Someone he'd been drinking with? Yes, that watchman who had been fired. Everyone knew it, he had said, that the worst outlaws worked together. You could take a pig who sold wolf blood in a bar and you could take his boss or his boss's boss, but sooner or later someone would say *stop*. Somewhere at the top were people you never saw, heard, or touched. People you never got close to without paying for it. The watchman had been happy that he'd only been fired, that he hadn't ended up in Drukna. Later, he had thrown up all over himself.

Rugen's thoughts had tormented him that night. More than a year earlier, Nafraím had given him a job to do, and he had screwed it up. Was he lucky that he hadn't been executed, or was it only a matter of time? Had he signed his own death warrant by running away without admitting that he had screwed up? Nafraím was a powerful man, and if he was one of *them* . . .

Rugen looked around, suddenly aware of how alone he was. The snow had really started dumping down. He sought shelter by a staircase under a narrow arch. The cold crept into his bones. His feet had gotten wet, and his toothache was unbearable.

Was this how it was going to end? Would he freeze to death and be fed to the stones? Would his blood mix with blood from wolves and from base outlaws and flow in the gutters under Nákla Henge so that others could travel and enjoy life?

Rugen leaned his forehead against the wall. He slammed his hand into the stone and moaned. This wasn't him! He wasn't a poor fool from the boats, nor a scoundrel. He liked a party, but he didn't throw up on himself. He wasn't afraid of powerful men. He should *be* one. He didn't belong on the streets. He belonged at home among those who had it all.

Nor was he some blood slave. He used very little. And rarely. He used the blood pearls for his own enjoyment because it was wonderful, but never enough to risk wolf-sickness. He wasn't one of those idiots who believed wolf blood would give him eternal life. That had never been his goal.

But, then, he had never been dying before.

THE WITNESS

"Do you know what people from Fimle call Náklaborg?"

The queen reached for the teapot, and a servant over by the door sped toward her. She stopped him with a discreet wave and filled both of the cups on the table herself. Nafraím took that as a worrying sign that she desired a confidential conversation, which he was very much not in the mood for.

"They call it the ugliest castle in the world!" She pointed around the room with her hand, as if to emphasize how absurd that was.

Nafraím didn't have the heart to tell her that *everyone* called it the ugliest castle in the world, even here in Náklav.

"They've only seen the outside, Your Highness."

She looked around with a dissatisfaction the room by no means deserved. True, it was intimate, for Náklaborg, but magnificently finished in blues. A sea blue ceiling rested on pale blue beams that met in the middle. It was like being caught under a bluebell.

Nafraím squirmed uncomfortably. The crackling from the fireplace gave him the troubling sense that the room was on fire behind his back. "Who told you that, Your Highness?"

"King Margen. I came from Skaug the other day."

"Skaugians say exactly the same, but perhaps King Margen neglected to mention that?"

She smiled. "So, you think we've reached the point where architecture is being used for political games?"

"Your Highness, Thervia gained its independence three hundred years ago because of a throw pillow."

The queen broke out into a contagious laugh. She was a warm woman. Soft in a way that made her unbreakable. Nafraím had seen regents come and go for centuries, and he found himself fervently hoping that Queen Drøfn's reign would last a long time. But, naturally, that required him keeping his distance, and she made that more difficult than he liked to admit.

"The worst thing is that he's putting me in a bind," she said despondently. "If I renovate, he'll think it was because of him, that he insulted me, right? So now I can't do anything with this black colossus!"

"You could invite him for a tour, Your Highness. Show him this 'black colossus.' Explain to him that people are little more than their history, which can be read here in each stone."

"I think I'll need to take the tour myself first," Drøfn said, her lip curling into an embarrassed smile.

Nafraím surprised himself by laughing. "Humility suits you, Your Highness, but this multitude of blocks has been everything from a lighthouse to a fortress for thousands of years. No one can know its whole history."

"No one other than you, you mean?"

The queen sipped her tea and studied him over the rim of the cup. Nafraím cursed himself for having led her so easily down the wrong track. The question of his true age was surely just around the corner and, once it came, it usually wasn't long before changes needed to be made. New role, new history, new bribes. In the worst cases, it also cost lives. The world wasn't the same as before. Nowadays, there was hardly anything that didn't get recorded. Inheriting from himself used to be a simple matter. Now it was an exhausting and risky process. He needed to lead Drøfn where she really wanted to go.

"I've inherited many books, Your Highness. But I know more

about the disease than I do about Náklav's history. I presume that's why I'm here?"

The queen set down her cup and looked at him. "Klemens doesn't trust you. You know that?"

"He's a wise man."

"Are you saying that he's right?"

"I'm saying it would be unwise for the Ring Guard commander-in-chief to go around trusting people."

"That's exactly what he said." Drøfn chuckled. "But he also says you're a brilliant scientist, and that we can thank you for the fact that the gates still work."

"He's far too generous, Your Highness."

"He *also* says that you folks have the disease under control. Do you have it under control, Nafraím?"

"It would be a miracle if we did, Your Highness. Wolf-sickness has many names in many countries, and has plagued mankind since time immemorial. All we can do is live with it."

"We can live with three cases a year, but three cases a month? Think of the ripple effect! There are those with the disease, and then the poor victims of the bestial attacks, the people left behind . . . What am I supposed to say when the sovereign council convenes? That all we can do is live with it?" The queen smoothed her heavy skirt, which was just as blue as the room. "I had hoped you would give me a better answer than Klemens."

Nafraím took a sip of tea as he weighed his words. "Klemens is right," he said finally. "The Ring Guard is in control to the greatest extent possible. This is not a plague. It has never been contagious from person to person, even though that is easy for people to forget when we see this type of . . . concentration. Klemens is a practical man. He says it like it is, not like a politician would say it. If you ask me what you should tell the sovereign council, then that's a completely different matter."

"Well?"

"Your Highness, I'd say that the last several cases clearly originated from the same supply source, which has gone astray. It is possible that poachers caught a wolf on their own, or that an unfaithful servant stole a bloodskin from the load. It could even have been smuggled here from another country despite the watch. There are a lot of possibilities. The blood was probably sold and used a long time ago, so we've already seen the worst of the damage. If the esteemed men and women of the sovereign council are still worried, then you could suggest eradicating the wolves."

"Eradicate the wolves? Are you crazy? Am I supposed to propose a measure that would destroy the stone gates? That would mean financial and political ruin for all of Slokna!"

"Precisely, Your Highness." Nafraím smiled.

"Ahh." Her eyes brightened with understanding. "The sovereign council would react exactly as I just did. And be forced to admit that the side effects of the wolf blood are . . ."

"Something we must live with. That's right, Your Highness. But, of course, that doesn't mean we won't do our utmost to close any holes. The Ring Guard does not take it lightly that blood is going astray, and they have just begun discussing the penalties for . . . Your Highness?"

The queen's attention was stolen away by a little boy who came running in. He was wide-eyed and dressed in full winter gear, like a furry baby seal.

"Mama, you've got to come see this! The thing in the henge is moving!" The queen's son pulled the queen to her feet.

"What are you talking about, Eljas?"

"Nákla Henge! The iron cross in the middle of the stones came to life just now!" The prince's eyes darted between them as he struggled to put what he'd seen into words.

The queen's brother and his wife also hurried in with half of the court on their heels, all equally excited.

Nafraím cautiously got to his feet so that no one would see how unsteady he suddenly felt.

A lady's maid helped the queen into a white winter coat and explained: "He means the Witness, Your Highness. The old verdigris tower in the middle of the stone circle. They say it's come to life! The sleighs will be right here, Your Highness."

"Oh goodness." The queen smiled at Nafraím. "This must be the biggest misunderstanding of the year, don't you think? Come, Nafraím, let's go see!"

Nafraím attempted to smile.

She's right. It's a misunderstanding. It must be.

He followed them out onto the palace square, which was teeming with life. The members of the court, servants, children, horses, and dogs were all in a jumble, ready to rush out onto the Gudebro Bridge. Náklaborg *was* an ugly castle, but Gudebro was one of the wonders of the world. A wide canal built atop the old walls that encircled the top of Kingshill, it was full of water and frozen almost year-round. From the castle square, it arched eastward toward Tunga, sparkling like the northern lights, elevated high above the city on enormous pillars that vanished down in between the buildings.

The servants helped the royals up into the sleighs. The horses stamped on the ice with their studded horseshoes, their puffs of breath visible in the cold. Nafraím felt like more of a foreigner than he had in a long time. This was nothing to them other than some exciting news. For him, it was the end of the word.

"Come with us, Nafraím! We're going all the way out to the point, where we'll have a view of the henge."

"Much obliged, Your Highness, but—"

"Ah, of course," the queen said with a wave of her hand. "You'll want to go down there and see properly. Yes, of course. Tell Klemens that I'm excited to hear your report. See you later!"

Her sleigh departed, ploughing ahead through a cloud of fresh snow.

No, Your Highness. We've seen too much of each other already.

Nafraím hurried through the gate to the nearest of the main staircases leading down from the old wall. He nearly slipped multiple times, but sheer fright drove him along; he knew that if it turned out to be true, there was nothing he could do.

Of course, it's true. Haven't I known for a long time?

For several years, deep down, he had felt it. He'd tamped down the restlessness with work, moving one game piece or another, just in case.

He maneuvered his way between people who hadn't heard the news yet. They walked as if they had all the time in the world. Bells tinkled in shop doors as visitors hunted for unique objects to show off back home, completely unaware that nothing would ever be the same again.

The wall around Nákla Henge towered at the end of the street, and the news had spread there. People were thronging outside the gates, but the guards stood their ground. They had closed the gates while they did their research. Presumably their leading experts were already inside—historians, scholars, mechanics, every type of academic. A man who had run so hard he had lost his hat and mittens pointed in frustration toward the college as he argued with the gate guards, who eventually let him in. The crowd let out a collective groan of displeasure.

Nafraím had to take a different way. He followed the street around the enormous ring wall. He had to look up to see the wall itself, since the city's most expensive businesses were packed around it. It hadn't always been like that, and he had been slowing the changes for a long time, but little by little some positive aspects had become apparent. No one noticed a door in a city full of doors.

73

Nafraím stopped in front of the entrance, a simple oak door between two shops that sold antique maps, shells, fossilized eggs, and shocking objects in glass jars. The oak door seemed like it could belong to either one of them, but it belonged to neither.

He fumbled with the keys and let himself in. The space inside was nothing but a narrow corridor that led straight to an iron door in the ring wall that surrounded the henge. The hinges creaked, complaining about how long it had been since anyone had been here. It was cooler inside the wall and as dark as it could get. It never got completely pitch dark anymore. There were always shades of gray.

He found the staircase and started climbing. He heard the muffled sounds of agitated people through the thick wall. His concern grew with every step. He didn't stop until he was all the way up and could let himself out onto the narrow balcony along the inside of the wall, just underneath the wooden cupola.

He walked over to the railing and looked down at Nákla Henge.

It's true.

The round courtyard below him was hectic. This had once been a place of peace, as close to sacred as anything could be in Slokna, but now it was a place of commerce. On the ground floor, the gallery had been converted into shops the whole way around even though this was the most expensive place there could be to run a business. The people working there had come out of their shops and teahouses to see. They crowded around the stone circle in the middle. Sixteen tall, rough-hewn monoliths of massive, black stone. They stood in pairs. Eight pairs. Eight gateways. Náklav's pulsing heart.

No other city had more stone gateways or greater prosperity. They were the source of power, money, knowledge, and diplomacy. Nafraím had seen close to seven hundred years of progress, and he knew how essential they were.

It never ceased to amaze him how much people took them for granted, even though no one actually understood them. The scientific and religious explanations were both far-fetched and tenuous, but the gates were no longer treated like a miracle. Fossilized bird eggs and wineglasses made of shimmering beetle shells, *that's* what they gasped about. Boxes you could put money into and have a mechanical doll give you your fate seemed to be a bigger mystery than traveling between the world's cities in the blink of an eye.

But they were marveling now.

They were jockeying for space to see, while the Ring Guard held them back. Nafraím could watch the whole miracle from above. In the middle of the stone circle stood what people had taken to be a decorative antiquity, a pillar, old as Gaul. Formally it was called the Witness, but it went by many names: the Pathfinder, the wolf walls, Votna Tower, the devil's cross . . .

Despite all the names, no one down there was sure of its purpose. The only thing they had been certain of was that it would stand there for another eternity, as unchanging as the stones around it.

Until today.

Nafraím supported himself on the railing, painfully aware that he was the only one who could see the end of everything in each motion.

From up there, the pillar looked like the blade of a three-edged sword, planted in the ground. Three large walls that met in the middle. The iron cross, as the young prince had called it. Though it wasn't iron, it was copper. Oxidized over centuries so that it appeared to glow in that ghostly, blueish-green hue that was so common in Náklav.

Three animals sat atop it, at the outermost tip of each of the walls: a raven, a wolf, and a stag. They stood with their necks bowed, as though they were looking down at the people thronging around them.

The walls were taller than the height of three men and resembled the inner workings of a clock, an enormous, mechanical wonder with dials, rings, and cogs. And on the one wall, they had begun to turn in different directions and speeds, seemingly under their own power. The raw edges squealed as centuries of patina was rubbed away.

And as the most attentive of those down below had noticed: the raven was missing the orb from its beak. It was as large as a head, but a head would have been less alarming. The orb had fallen down into the track on the inside of the wall, triggering the mechanism, which in time the scholars would discover.

Nafraím felt a certain relief that the orb had come from the raven's beak. The wolf and stag still had their verdigris copper orbs wedged in their mouths.

There's still hope.

Experts were running around measuring, sketching, and arguing about what they saw. Some were studying the characters engraved on the dials. Phases of the moon, seasons of the year, constellations, days and gods, everything in núr. It was an extinct runic language, but they would surely agree on that soon. After all, they had books to help them. They were well-dressed, prepared to keep going for as long as the city council was willing to accept the lost income from travelers. From where Nafraím stood, they looked like hares, mere prey scurrying around below the far larger animals on top of the Witness.

The business owners on site were growing restless. They were talking to the gate guards, presumably about how long the closure would last. It could hardly be long. There were few things Náklavites disliked more than losing money, so Nafraím guessed they would reopen the stone gates within a few hours.

They hadn't always been so easy to open. At one time it involved primitive rituals where wolves were slaughtered, their blood used to color the stones red. At that time, people believed that only bleeding stone would let people through. Now there were pipes underground that brought the blood to the base of the stones, hidden from sensitive visitors, under decorative gratings like any old sewer. The gates were opened every morning and closed every evening, simply by turning a faucet in the Ring Guard's office.

The world was different than before. But luckily not completely ready to end.

Nafraím knew he'd have a lot to do going forward. He needed to approach Lagalune again. The blood readers could no longer remain in control; it wasn't safe. He took a deep breath, reminded himself that it could have been worse, and headed for the door. He heard a thud and then another thud, resistance from the awakening cogwheels mixed with shouting. He walked back over to the railing and stared down.

All three of the walls in the Witness were in motion.

Three orbs were missing. The raven, the wolf, and the stag stood with empty mouths wide open. The sight ate its way into his heart and set it sprinting. The animals gaped. They gaped as if in shock at everything he had done. They were censuring him. Nature was censuring him, hauling out memories of ancient sin, as clear as if it were yesterday.

Nafraím looked up at the wooden dome. It had an eye in the middle, a hole to the sky. Snowflakes strayed in and danced down to the Witness. His arm began to ache, like an old man's joints. Chaos prevailed down in the courtyard below. None of them had ever seen the walls move, only him. He had been there when they stopped more than six hundred years ago. He had seen the dials rotate before, slower and slower until they had finally stopped altogether. Winters had come and gone, and finally people had forgotten that it had ever moved.

The Might was back.

He had suspected it, felt it, seen the green, sprouting evidence long ago. And now it was clear for anyone to see. Anyone who knew

or who had even heard of it. None of the mortals down in the courtyard, that was for sure. But the warow . . . they knew. Speculation
and panic would follow, accusations, conflicts.

War.

Nafraím couldn't stand war. It was an intolerable solution among
humans and even worse between vardari. Not to mention the
wolf-sickness. Who knew what that would mean for the blood users.
The queen's words ran through him like a whisper.

Do you have it under control, Nafraím?

He had lied to her.

Nafraím walked back into the wall. He locked the iron door behind him and leaned against it. It was cold against his back, biting
through his coat, through his skin. He stood there with his eyes
closed in the darkness. It smelled stuffy, dead.

He had run out of time.

Many of the warow didn't value time, but he had always tracked
it, had always understood what a gift it was to have an unlimited
amount of it. Precisely because he hated being busy. Hated having
to act quickly. Quickly often meant unwisely. But soon the vardari
would gather, and the questions would come. Disagreements would
divide them. He needed to find out where he stood. What was he
willing to sacrifice? *Who* was he willing to sacrifice?

A cold, tingly feeling arose in his chest as if he were coming down
with something. It took him a while to recognize the feeling as fear.
Raw and nauseating. All-consuming. Just as he remembered it.

THE WAROW

The chair did not get any more comfortable no matter how much Juva shifted her position. The other visitors didn't seem to have the same problem, but then they were also the type of people who hung out at teahouses, well-dressed and leaning forward, engaged in their conversations and quick to laugh. They radiated a carefree ease she couldn't remember ever having experienced.

They were also the class of people who could afford expensive blood readers, and the thought of being recognized made her queasy. Juva turned her back to them, to the extent possible, and reminded herself why she was there. Not just because Ester was paying, but because it was Nákla Henge. This was where the wolf blood was used, and maybe also where it had been stolen from.

The hunters were never sloppy in their routines. They handed over the blood at the bridge each time. And yet, an irritating sense of responsibility irked her. She was part of the problem.

It cost fifty skár just to get in to see the stones, even if you weren't going to travel. So this was a welcome opportunity to snoop around a little.

If they ever finished eating.

The round table in front of her was loaded with golden brown tea breads, frostberry cream, and sweet, brown butter oat crisps, a transparent attempt to apologize for Solde's visit to Hidehall.

Every time Juva set her cup down, she was afraid something

would fall off the edge. But Ester kept ordering, clearly determined to make the host's life into an ordeal. He stood over their table, scanning for an empty plate to swap out for a full one.

Was that how the blood was ending up on the black market? A host or hostess? Or someone else who ran a business here? These were expensive spaces to rent. Maybe someone was desperate enough to pad their earnings.

Desperate enough to spread wolf-sickness?

"It's marvelously mysterious, isn't it?" Ester said, craning her neck toward the window, which looked like an arrangement of bottle bottoms.

Juva's thoughts were elsewhere, so it took her a second to understand that Ester was referring to the Witness, the calendar, or clockworks, or whatever it was, in the middle of the stone circle, which had started to turn. The whole city was talking about it. Juva certainly would have been talking about it herself if her head weren't full of Mother, Solde, inheritances, and blood pearls.

Her glass of sour beer was replaced with a fresh one, even though there was still a little beer left in the glass. She expressed her thanks and made an honest attempt at a smile before she took a big swig to drown her frustration.

"What do you think it means?" Ester asked, leaning over the table toward her, putting a teapot in imminent danger.

Juva looked out at the stone henge in the middle of the courtyard. The Witness rose in the center of the circle. People often said that the three walls looked like a three-edged sword, but she thought they looked like open books. Three mechanical books of patina-green copper, fused together into a tower with their spines together.

Each wall had an animal statue on top, gaping at nothing. The orbs they always held in their mouths were inside the walls now, she had heard. A part of the machinery of rotating dials, which had never moved before.

No one had any idea why the orbs had fallen out, or what drove the inner clockworks inside the walls, but, of course, a succession of blood readers claimed to have foreseen the occurrence.

There were many travelers out there as well. They were slower than they would have been otherwise, because they were transfixed, staring at the spinning dials and ticking gear wheels. Complete strangers were exchanging words, discussing the phenomenon before handing their travel passes to a member of the Ring Guard, walking between the stones, and disappearing. Others, in turn, appeared between the stones, stopped to look, and needed to be nudged along so they wouldn't be in the way.

"It must come from the blood," Ester said, answering her own question.

"No." Juva understood what she was thinking, but that didn't make any sense. "It must be something new. The wolf blood has always been used to open the gates, but the walls have never moved before. Maybe it's something in between?"

"In between what?"

"In between the stones."

"There's absolutely nothing in between the stones. Don't tell me that you've never used them? Holy Jól, then we'll have to go at the first opportunity!" exclaimed Ester, slapping her linen napkin on the table.

Juva glanced around them, but no one was paying any attention to them. "Yes, I've used them. I went to Haeyna and Kreknabork with my mother, but it's been a long time. She prefers to travel alone or with the other two."

"What other two?"

Juva lowered her voice.

"Ogny and Maruska, the Seida Guild. You know, the blood readers? They travel to Kreknabork every year, just the three of them."

Juva didn't remember the trips as anything other than a moment of black void that had made her vaguely queasy. She also hadn't been allowed to bring her backpack when she was little.

"There *is* something between the stones," she continued. "Otherwise, they wouldn't have the rules about what you can bring. Never more than you can carry on your own, and not too heavy, because it can get lost in the undertow. So, the things people lose and don't manage to hang on to . . . where do they end up? I mean, it happens all the time that merchants lose things, and they must end up somewhere. So, there's something between the stones."

Ester put her hand on her cane and stared at her with that pursed smile of hers.

"You don't like mysteries, do you?" she said.

Juva took another swig. The sour beer made her feel more secure, less afraid that her heart would start pounding, like at home. Although that was mostly about who you were with. Ester was fine. Old people made her feel calm, like things would last, even her heart.

"I like mysteries," she replied. "But I don't like the lies that can be told about them before they get solved."

"You're not very favorably disposed toward them, my girl." Ester fondled the handle of her cane with ring-laden fingers.

"Toward who?" Juva asked, even though she had no doubt who Ester meant.

"Your mother. Or the rest of the Seida Guild. But even something you despise can bring good with it."

"Good?" Juva stifled a snicker. "I only needed to say the word *lie* and your thoughts went straight to the Seida Guild, so what good can come from them?"

Ester raised her hand and signaled for the check.

"Do you know, I see a lot of myself in you, Juva. You're a young woman and a wolf hunter. I'm an old woman and a peddler. We've followed our hearts, and no one has stopped us."

"Why would they stop us?"

The host came over and set a slate on the table on which he had neatly written down everything they had eaten and drunk. Juva saw the total and choked on her beer. It had been three years since she'd lived as a Sannseyr, and she'd forgotten what extravagance was.

Ester set a stack of coins on the slate, watching her with that bird-like gaze.

"They would have stopped you if they dared," Ester said. "Me, too. Holy Jól knows, they've done their best. But fear of blood readers means fear of women. The Seida Guild's power has given us freedom. Without them we would have a king, not a queen."

Juva wanted to ask what freedom was worth if it came from fear, but then she remembered the rumor that Ester had murdered her husband and didn't say anything.

Ester got up, almost without help from her cane. Juva slung her backpack on, and they walked out into the courtyard together. There was something captivating about the whole thing. The sound of the mechanical dials and the wonder of the travelers. Juva got chills. Some called it a sign of the end times, but in Náklav, a sign of the end times was just an attraction.

You needed a travel pass to go near the stones, so they had to make do with following the gallery around, observing from a distance. Juva used the opportunity to search for weaknesses in their security. There weren't many.

Nákla Henge was an impenetrable fortress. A dark ring wall with three gates, each facing a different direction. The metal doors in the gates could boast of being the largest in the world. Useless in practical terms, so there were smaller doors set into them, which were ordinarily used. They were well guarded.

The wall had three stories of galleries. The arched openings were newer, that was easy to tell from the small, precise brickwork. Only the top story was in its original condition, intact, with narrow embrasures. They faced inward, toward the stone circle, which had always seemed odd. As if a traveler had ever been a threat.

The roof was only two or three hundred years old. A staggeringly large wooden cupola, which far exceeded the construction abilities people would have had when the ring wall was built. The wood in the roof was laid out in thousands of ridges, like the gills beneath a golden poisonous mushroom. The hole in the middle reinforced this impression. It looked like someone had snapped out the stem, so the scant daylight could filter in. It meant that people couldn't climb over the wall, either.

And even if they could, the Ring Guard had guards on both the inside and outside. There were guards stationed by each pair of stones, too. So, eight men on duty, just there.

The blood ran through pipes, hidden underground, all the way to the stones. Maybe someone could get to it if they pried up one of the gratings on the ground, but when would they have a chance to do that in such a busy place? It seemed impossible. But there had to be a weakness somewhere. Most likely someone corrupt in the Ring Guard. Someone was obtaining wolf blood for the vardari and then selling it to people like Mother without thinking about how it could lead to wolf-sickness.

Wolves, wolves everywhere.

Juva's eyes were drawn to the wolf statue atop the Witness. It looked lifelike in the column of light from the roof. The animal was arching his back with his hackles up as it scowled down at the people who came and went between the stones.

Why have you come to life? Why now?

She remembered the wolf in the woods, its foaming jaws over her, and she tore her eyes away. This was not a place to have palpitations.

Ester returned their visitors' passes at the gate, then they each went their own way. Juva would have preferred to go straight to

84

Hidehall, but she walked toward Lykteløkka anyhow. Three sour beers had made her optimistic. She had everything she needed in her backpack and could stomach just this one night so her mother could say what she needed to say.

Her mood wilted as soon as she let herself in. The home she had grown up in wasn't like other houses. It felt alive. The memories sat in its walls and breathed, felt, waited. The black front hall was like the entrance to Drukna, her private realm of the dead, where everything she wanted was quashed, and everything she despised was nurtured. Lies, insecurity, shame. And fear.

Nightmares, sweaty palms, and palpitations, ever since she was seven years old. She had drunk more hoggthorn tea in the last few days than she normally did in a month because she knew she had to come back here. Hoggthorn calmed the heart, but it couldn't change the past.

Juva peeked through the little conversation window into the waiting room. There were two people in there, a man and a woman. The door to the blood reader room was closed. Good—at least Solde was busy.

There was a fire in the hearth under the black stairs, and on either side of the chimney were open archways leading into the library. Juva had always felt safer in there than anywhere else in this house. Books were filled with fates, both better and worse than her own, and that had always been a refuge from Mother's hysterical fits and impulses.

Juva strolled into the room, which was lined with books from floor to ceiling on both of the long walls. The dark shelves jutted out in places, creating little nooks where she used to hide. The only windows were on the short wall all the way at the far end. They curved out at the sea, like the stern of a ship.

Corpsewood glowed on an open hearth in the middle of the room, surrounded by a deep leather sofa, a couple of chairs, and a lacquered bar cabinet. An unfamiliar wadmal coat hung neatly over a chair back. Otherwise, everything was the way it had always been.

Even the idiotic fate machine. It sat by the chimney, between the doorways. Built like a cupboard, a fair bit taller than her. The lower portion was decorated in runes, platitudes of the sort you found at any old "mystical" market. The top portion was a glass cage protecting a very poorly taxidermied raven. Big, black, and moth-eaten. Its eyes stuck out a little and the household servants had decided that it followed them with its gaze, a rumor that, of course, Lagalune made no effort to dispel.

There was a coin slot in the front and ten skár would make the poultry move and tip out a cup of runic dice. A cheap, generic fortune, in the home of the city's best paid blood readers. The irony of fate, literally. Lagalune loved it because she imagined there was a difference between what she and the bird provided. Juva disliked it because she knew that both were equally wasted. But at least the bird didn't demand more than the price of a loaf of bread. She didn't even want to know what Lagalune was charging these days.

Juva heard a door open and voices from the corridor that ran alongside the library. It was her mother and a man. Juva realized that she recognized his voice.

It's him!

That certainty sent a chill of fear through her body. Her anxious heart beat irregularly and loudly in her chest. The control she'd imagined she had vanished without a trace.

Nafraim! The warow!

Vardari were in the house. Those pigs who gave Mother blood pearls and who surely made a good living off of disseminating them throughout the entire city without worrying about wolf-sickness.

Juva hid next to the raven cabinet, reflexively, as if she were a child again. Her backpack squeezed up against the chimney.

"... the amount of time is immaterial. It doesn't change the indisputable fact that we've reached the end, Lagalune." His voice was strained, dangerously controlled.

"It's not up to me. There are actually several of us." Mother. Her words were more confident than her voice. "What do you think they're going to say, Nafraím? This is in our blood. We've been doing this our whole lives!"

"By my grace and favor. The wolf is ours, was always ours."

The voices grew nearer as they followed the corridor toward the front hall.

"We have no guarantee of that. Should we allow ourselves to be influenced into breaking a tradition, a pact, on your word alone? You need to look at this from our point of view. For all we know, this could be a coup on your part. Do the other warow know you're here?"

Juva's eyes widened. That question was beyond bold, it was a dangerous accusation. The silence was so fraught that she didn't dare breathe. Oh, depths of Drukna, they were going to hear her heartbeats. They could probably be heard all the way to Naar!

"Vulgarities are uncalled for, and they don't make an answer any less necessary. Yes or no, Lagalune?"

Another silence. An audible breath, Lagalune taking a puff of her cigar.

"No."

Juva's hand flew up to her mouth, an unexpected delight mixed with the fear. Who dared to say no to a warow, right in front of his face?

Lagalune Sannseyr, that's who.

Suddenly it hit Juva that it was his coat hanging over the back of the chair.

Shit!

"All I can do is say that I'm sorry," Nafraím said.

These words were more frightening than anything else he had said, and she could swear he wasn't lying.

Juva retreated into the front hall. She nearly stumbled on the stairs, but managed to take a couple of steps up before her mother and Nafraím came in and spotted her. Juva stopped, with her hand on the railing, as if she had just walked in the front door.

Breathe calmly. Count the steps.

But right now she couldn't have counted to ten if her life depended on it. The artery in her wrist quivered, quickly and unevenly. She stared at the warow. If she hadn't known better, she would have said he was around fifty. The few wrinkles he had were exactly the same as when she was a child. And maybe even when her mother was a child?

Pull it together, Juva! Everyone dies!

The myths said they had fangs, the warow. But it wasn't true. Nafraím was treacherously ordinary. Slim and well-dressed with short, dark hair. His eyes were intense and curious, youthful. Had he been a stranger on the street, she would have thought he looked good, that he was a well-read man. A teacher, maybe.

But Nafraím was no teacher. He was her mother's source for her blood use. He was the shadow that had always rested over this house. He had been there before her father died, and that was what the vardari meant: Death. Misfortune. Blood.

Juva felt sick to her stomach. She stood there frozen on the stairs as he glanced at a pocket watch, which few people were privileged enough to own. His hand seemed stiff, as if it wouldn't bend properly, and he was wearing gloves. The gray wadmal coat she had seen in the library was draped over his arm.

"Can I get your coat?" she heard herself offering without knowing for sure why. At best it was a desperate attempt to pretend she hadn't been in the library. At worst it was a misplaced sense of loyalty to her mother, a way of asking him to leave.

Nafraím looked at her in surprise. "I have it here, but thank you for offering, Juva." He said her name slowly, as if he were tasting it.

Lagalune stood behind him, her thin cigar between her fingers. It dropped ash onto the floor, but her mother didn't seem to notice. The corner of her mouth twitched, and she stared at Juva with a world of warning in her eyes.

Nafraím's eyes roamed as he put on his coat, as if he had never seen the black front hall before. His eyes found Juva again. "I sincerely hope you escape . . . all this," he told her. Then he turned the handle, nodded to them both, and walked out. The door closed behind him.

Juva crumpled onto the stairs and took a breath. Seeing him standing there . . . right there. The nightmare forced its way into her mind. A childhood dream she thought she had forgotten. It was dark, and she knew she ought to be asleep. But she had heard something, hadn't she?

She had come downstairs, to right where she was sitting now. And there, on the floor in front of her, where Nafraím had just been, sat a rusty iron cabinet. An enormous metal chest standing on end, and she wanted to see what was inside.

No! That never happened. Mother said it was a dream!

"Juva?" Lagalune came over to the stairs.

Juva clutched the railing with a clammy hand. Father had died that night. And it was her fault, her shame. She had conjured the wolf that had taken him, conjured the devil, the devil Mother had said she should never talk about because it was only a dream, a fairy tale.

Lagalune reached out her hand to her. Juva raised her arm protectively, to defend herself. But against what? Her memories flowed together until she could no longer distinguish what she had imagined from reality. Mother was right, she made things up. Fantasized. Always.

Juva spun around and dragged herself up the stairs, like an animal on all fours, pulling her backpack along behind her. She ran down the long hallway and into the bedroom she hadn't used in many years.

She lit the oil lamp. The flames lapped at the yellowed glass as she groped in her backpack for her book and flipped through it, her hands shaking. Back, back, until the loose pages. The oldest pictures she had.

She found a drawing in which the lines were so naïve, it had to be at least ten years old. A man with sharp teeth like an animal. Juva rolled up the piece of paper and stuck it down into the lamp's reservoir. The flames suddenly grew, spitting out soot. She turned the paper upward and let it burn until the flames reached her fingers and she was forced to let go.

The last corner of the paper wafted down toward the floor, curled up into a delicate, black ball with embers running along it. Then it went out.

Juva pulled a hoggthorn berry out of her pocket and started chewing on it. She felt like she was being chewed to pieces herself. The guilt had eaten away at her since she was a little girl, eaten its way into her body and lodged there. She had done as her mother had asked and pretended as if it had never happened. Father had been injured hunting, they said. He died of a fever.

But he hadn't. Father had been killed down there, in the front hall, because she had conjured the wolves. They were everywhere.

In the woods, in the blood, in the dreams, on the walls—even between the stones in Nákla Henge. And now they were waking up.

WOLF-SICKNESS

Juva took a swig of whiskey and looked at the man who had squeezed his way in to sit at her table in the crowded tavern of Hidehall. He sat with his back to the enormous wine barrel that filled the one wall niche. She didn't want to talk to anyone and was about to get up and escape into the hunting lodge where she could be in peace when he pulled out a book and begun to read, as if he hadn't even noticed her.

So, not the worst sort.

After a brief chat, she had learned that his name was Lodd, that he came from Undst, and that he was reading the holy book, a fanatic. So, the second worst sort. But she stayed seated anyway. He was a welcome distraction from the chaos in her thoughts about her mother and the warow and her shame at the breakdown she'd just had at home.

"I'm not saying that you folks don't have a faith," Lodd said. "I'm saying that you've stolen what you believe in."

"Everyone has stolen what they believe in," Juva protested. "Or do you think your gods were the first?"

"We only have one," he said.

Juva rolled her eyes. "And you think Náklav stole the one god you have?"

He laughed and that made him almost beautiful. He leaned forward and rested his elbows on the table.

"No, you didn't steal God, you stole the devil, and that tells you a lot about Náklavites, doesn't it? You have dozens of gods, but none that you worship. Nary a temple in the whole city, aside from Jólshov, and even that is really more of a collection of banquet halls. No, the only thing you embrace with such passion is the devil. And he came from us."

"You're wrong about that, Lodd. We've always had the devil. We have ancient folktales about him."

"You *think* you do," Lodd said, raising an index finger, "but you had the wolf. People in Slokna have been obsessed with wolves since the dawn of time. But then you sauced the myths up with our devil, and now they're one and the same. The devil and the wolf."

"And in Ruv they have the snake," Juva said with a shrug. "So what? It's not stealing; it's learning. Náklav has more travelers than any city in the world, and we've learned to get by without help from the gods."

"Is that so?" He leaned back again. "Wolf teeth as talismans against disease? Longshoremen who read portents in fish guts? Not to mention Lykteløkka—there's a lot of people there. Aren't Náklav's famed blood readers a type of god, for those who can pay for the answers?"

"You mean pay for the fantasies?"

Her answer seemed to surprise him, but his smile widened, and Juva could swear that he had suddenly become downright attractive. She hadn't touched a man since Rugen. *Damn Rugen.* A couple of months of buttering her up, and now she was forty runes poorer. He had stolen from her and then disappeared. She squeezed her backpack between her feet to make sure it was still there.

Forty runes, she couldn't believe what a fool she had been. The only comfort was that his life would never be any better.

Mine, either.

Lodd pushed the sacred book aside. "You seem smart for someone so young and so cute . . ."

Ah . . . Time to go.

Juva swirled her glass but left the last little bit of whiskey. Best to keep a clear head now that she had to go home again.

She wished she didn't care and could simply leave her mother and Solde to their own fates. They had only themselves to thank for flirting with vardari and using blood pearls. Nothing good ever came from that sort of thing. But self-inflicted misery was probably the worst kind. Besides, she couldn't forget that her mother had contradicted Nafraím. The warow had asked for something, something he felt she owed him. Even Mother wasn't dumb enough to steal or borrow something from the vardari, was she? But she was dumb enough to say no. Mother had said no to a warow.

Juva felt something akin to pride, but it was baseless.

The wolf is ours, he had said. What wolf?

Is Mother in danger? Is that why she asked me to come back home?

Juva got up. Lodd looked as if he wanted to object, but a deep rumble in the distance sent a wave of silence through the tavern.

The Dead Man's Horn! Another killing!

The lingering sound carried well through Dragsuget and had sounded far too often the last few months. Half-drunk men suddenly sobered up and hung their heads. A few of the patrons left without finishing their beers, frightened back to their homes by the knowledge that someone with wolf-sickness was out on the streets. Rut darted around the bar counter and locked the door. The Dead Man's Horn tended to put a damper on the mood.

Juva snatched her jacket and backpack, tossed Lodd a quick farewell, pushed her way through to the door, and then hesitated. It didn't take long before people started craning their necks toward the windows and whispering.

Wolf-sickness. The hunter. The bloodhound.

Juva peered out the tavern window. It was barely snowing, but enough to reveal the wind. Broddmar stood outside in the crowded

93

courtyard leashing up Skarr. The gray wolf stood calmly as Broddmar tightened his harness. The animal turned his head toward the tavern, and people recoiled away from the windows, everyone at once, like a school of fish.

If it hadn't been for Skarr, Broddmar would have been impossible to recognize. Dressed in red from head to foot, like an open wound against the dark stone buildings. The red leather coat sat tight around his waist but fluttered free around his thighs. His face was hidden behind the red mask, which looked uncomfortably like a muzzle.

The red hunter. The bleeder.

He was going hunting—proper, meaningful hunting that actually made a difference, that could save lives. Or would cost him his own, even if the garb would do a good job of protecting him. The leather around his neck was reinforced with steel flaps that no canine teeth could pierce. They gleamed in the light of the lamps, enticing her with a purpose that she never got to be part of, because he always said no.

People feared him and needed him. He got to feel useful but denied her the same. She mostly wanted to yell that he wasn't anything to send shivers down your spine. He was an old man missing half his teeth.

Broddmar and the wolf left the courtyard.

No, wait!

People cautiously restarted their conversations, relieved that the hunter wasn't coming into the tavern. Juva pulled her hunting belt out of her backpack. She cursed, unlocked the door, and darted outside, strapping on the belt as she jogged after Broddmar. It was a challenge since the crossbow bolts and knife dangled off the belt and needed to be strapped around her thighs. She tied the laces as she limped along like an injured hare, afraid she would lose sight of Broddmar. She lost him anyway.

Luckily, Taakedraget was covered in fresh snow, which made it easy to follow the wolf tracks north all the way to Nattlyslokket. The street ran through a long, colonnaded archway, and the only snow was what had blown in.

Ugh, deepest Drukna!

Had they walked this way or not? She ran to the next alleyway but didn't find any footprints there, either. Juva stood still for a moment, perplexed, but then it hit her that she knew how to do this. This was her job, hunting wolves. She'd just never done it in a city.

Wolves belonged in the woods, not in the alleys of Náklav. Still, Broddmar had always said that she had a sense for the wolves. She knew where they were.

Juva took a breath and gathered her thoughts around her own heart. She stifled the fear that always came with the fibrillations and concentrated on that fragile sensation of fellowship, of being close to something dangerous that could smell her heart.

The sensation grew stronger even though she was standing completely still. Suddenly, she understood what that meant. They were heading toward her! Of course, Broddmar had to stop at the nearest guard booth to find out where to go, and that was near Ulebru Bridge. She ducked into an alley off Nattlyslokket and waited until she spotted them again, one on two legs and the other on four, disappearing down a side street. She squeezed past a couple who stood terrified, staring after the red hunter with his wolf.

She rounded the corner onto Smalfaret and stopped. The narrow street was blocked by a crowd of people swarming together in front of a door. The lamps were spaced far apart, and it was hard to see what was going on in the darkness but not hard to guess. Juva climbed up onto a deep window ledge to get a better view.

What she had at first thought was a door turned out to be an opening in the wall with a stone staircase inside of it. People stood, seemingly unable to act, around a figure who lay sprawled at the bottom of the stairs on his back, legs on the stairs, torso in the street, arms splayed out. It was a young man, scarcely older than she was. Lightly dressed. Two fingers bent at an impossible angle, as if he had fallen and tried to catch himself. The snow was bloody around his head, a red halo. Snowflakes drifted down onto his face, onto his wide-open eyes, but they didn't close. They just kept staring uncannily up at the northern lights, which flickered wildly over the rooftops. A gash on the side of his neck gaped open.

Someone had bitten him. Eaten from him.

Where was Broddmar?

A pair of officials from the city watch, dressed in black, were acting as though they couldn't hear the crowd's questions as they kept them away from the body. One of the watchmen said they were waiting for the Ring Guard and the bleeder, but also that there was no confirmation that wolf-sickness was the cause. He didn't look like he believed that himself. People stood by their front doors, ready to flee inside if that should be necessary.

Juva spotted a cat coming down the stone stairs. It stepped over the dead man's hand as if he were just a rock in the cat's way, before slinking away along the wall. At the crossroads farther down the street, the cat abruptly stopped, arched its back, and ran away.

Broddmar . . . He went a roundabout way.

Broddmar came walking along with the wolf on its leash and looked right up at her, as if he had been studying her from the shadows for a long time. The heat rose in her cheeks and she felt angry with shame. She stared back at him. The dead man gave her every right.

You see? People are dying! You can't refuse to let me help!

The look in her eyes hardened. She would show him that she didn't fear death or blood, that she was strong enough to become a bleeder, a red hunter. She doubted he would be impressed, but it was impossible to know.

The minute people spotted him, they pulled back, pressing against the walls of the buildings, some right below Juva. Even the city watch took a few steps to the side. Who did they fear more: the wolf or the red hunter?

Broddmar led Skarr over to the body. The hackles on the back of Skarr's neck were already up before he even began sniffing. He curled his flews and growled. The stir that ran through the crowd suggested that everyone knew what that meant.

Juva heard a woman mutter that the dead man should have gone to see a blood reader and possibly saved his own life. The man next to her responded that the whole city should have their blood read, for free, so people knew where the next attack would happen.

Juva managed not to get mad. The fate people feared was no longer a fantasy; it lay bleeding in the snow in front of them, a random and inexplicable evil they would gladly have paid the blood readers to avoid. If she herself had believed, what would she be willing to give to know that it wouldn't be her lying there next time?

Then the Ring Guard arrived, in force and easily recognizable by the symbol they all wore on their chests: sixteen white dots in a circle representing Nákla Henge. They had brought a horse pulling a black hearse carriage, which only barely fit in the alley. There was no longer a shred of doubt that the death was related to wolf-sickness. The first guard talked to Broddmar, while several others placed a blanket over the dead man and dragged him up into the hearse. His limbs were still limp. He couldn't have been lying there long.

The onlookers seemed paralyzed, but none of them protested or cried. Maybe the dead man had lived alone? Or maybe he was an outlaw, or nameless? Juva hoped not. His fate was tragic enough without his also being sacrificed to the stones, diluted into wolf blood, no more worth than water in soup.

A female Ring Guardian with sunken cheeks and dead eyes walked around and chatted with people. She rattled off lies about there not being any other cases of wolf-sickness in Náklav, and that they shouldn't listen to gossip, just tell her their names and what they had seen.

Juva realized that she needed to get away, or she would be forced to say who she was in front of all these people. She looked around for a way out and spotted a man who was heading away from the crowd. He looked over his shoulder at the hearse. An anxious, pale face. Brown hair stuck out from under an unsuitably thin hat.

Rugen?!

Anger cleared away her shock from the blood and death. Fucking Rugen! She hadn't seen him in a year. Not since he had run off with her money. Juva slipped down from the window ledge and elbowed her way through the crowd to set out after him. The game was up with Broddmar, anyway. He had seen her, and it was hopeless to think she could spy anymore.

"You, girl!" A man from the Ring Guard grabbed her and held on to her. "This is Náklav. You can't carry a weapon here! Who are you?"

"I have a hunting license!" Juva replied, craning her neck, but Rugen was gone.

"*You* have a hunting license?" The guard released her with a mocking snigger.

Juva clenched her teeth to keep from saying anything she would regret. This bonehead had let Rugen get away and ruined her chances of getting her forty runes back. She opened her belt bag and took out the waxed cover with the hunting card inside.

The guard snatched it from her and inspected it. "Did you steal this? Aren't you a little young to have a hunting license?"

"Sure," Juva replied. "I was a little young when I started. Three years ago."

His expression made it clear that sarcasm was not the way to go. Other people were staring at his interrogation and Juva felt uncomfortably suspect.

"I took over from my father," she added. "And I just got here, so I haven't seen anything at all."

The guard didn't seem convinced. He stared at her hunting card as if he were searching for something incriminating. "Juva Sannseyr? Is that you?"

The people behind her started to whisper. She heard her own name wander from mouth to mouth.

"You're a Sannseyr?" A lady took a step closer. "A Sannseyr in the Seida Guild? Shouldn't blood readers protect us against things like this?"

The others nodded and mumbled their support.

Juva had the overwhelming sense of not having any time to waste. She snatched the hunting card out of the guard's hands and looked around for Broddmar, but he was already out of sight. The mood was fraught, but she didn't think anyone would touch her. That was the only blessing of being a Sannseyr. No one would dare hurt a blood reader. But she had to get away.

The hearse blocked one direction and the crowd the other. She was trapped. The man who had said earlier that everyone should be blood-read for free grabbed her hand.

"Lass . . . Check us first! What can we expect? Will we be victims?"

"Why don't you read everyone, so we all know who's going to die?" someone else asked.

Juva would have laughed if it weren't so tragic. For a second, she considered playing along. Blood read them all and say they were safe. But just the thought made her sick to her stomach. She had told someone's fortune only once in her life. That was Father.

Never again.

Juva gulped. She stuck her hunting card in her bag and felt the linen sack with the wolf teeth. She clutched at them like the straws they were and emptied them out onto the ground.

"I have wolf teeth!" she said, and pulled away.

It took only a second before everyone threw themselves down on the ground like animals. They scrabbled at the teeth and some started pushing. The Ring Guard yelled and attacked the aggressors. Juva broke into a run, heading away from the chaos.

Her heart was pounding in her chest and her eyes were freezing cold with tears. She cursed the whole city. Damn the blood readers and everything they had made people believe. Damn Rugen, who was an asshole liar and scoundrel, and damn Broddmar, who refused to let her be useful. And she cursed herself, because she had just given away the teeth Ester had already paid her for.

Her knees buckled, and she stumbled on some steps on the street. She slipped into a recess under a building with a turret and caught her breath. Closed her eyes. All she saw was the dead man's gaze, so clear as if he were still staring up at her. It wasn't the blood or the open throat that turned her stomach. It was the helplessness of just lying there while the snow melted on his eyeballs.

In her imagination, she saw the man's pupils sink down and disappear, until his eyes were chalk-white and more alive than they had ever been.

WHORING

Rugen ran until his chest burned, panting through the narrow streets, up stairs and under footbridges, haunted by what he had seen on Smalfaret. The red hunter, the bleeder, the reaper. The man had a hundred names, but only one job: killing the wolf-sick.

I'm one of them.

His jaw pain, his loose tooth, the tingling in his body as if his bones itched . . . The scaffold of excuses had collapsed. All that was left was an impossible truth. He was wolf-sick, doomed to die.

The northern lights chased after him, unruly flames across the heavens, growing less inky black with every night. He had been so insanely thirsty for the bright spring sunlight, without suspecting that he would need the darkness to hide.

His lungs forced him to slow down, and he realized he was on his way to Skjerpe, Alette's neighborhood, where the hunter was surely going. He wheeled around and headed toward Herad.

Just how good is a wolf's sense of smell?

It couldn't find him before his teeth came in, could it? When would that happen? How long did he have? And what the fuck was he thinking, running around out there on his own?! He needed to find some people! As many people as possible, as many odors as possible, and vanish into a crowd.

He ducked into the first ale house he spotted, and it was reassuringly busy. He caught his breath while he peered out a chink in the door. No hunter to see, but the gods knew there were a lot of places to hide in this city.

Relax. He's after Alette.

Rugen stomped the snow off on the slushy metal grate, set ten skár on the bar, and asked for a beer. The bartender was a thin-haired man with a gullible look, who took out four of the coins and left the rest. The mug came quickly, and Rugen rushed a gulp, which went down the wrong way. He cleared his throat and pounded on his chest with his fist. What in Drukna was this? This dishwater looked like beer and smelled like beer, but he couldn't find words for what it tasted like. No wonder it was cheap.

"It's the boiling wort," the bartender said. "You get used to it."

"Why in Gaula would I want to get used to this?" Rugen asked and stuck the rest of his money back in his wallet.

The bartender leaned closer. "Because you don't get drunk and unruly from it." He lowered his voice before continuing. "You're new here, right? There's a lot of folks who can't tolerate beer, you see. It's too much of a good thing. The ones who come here do it because they need to drink less. Or to work up their courage for Kefla."

"Kefla?"

"The blood reader around the corner. Just a young girl, but they say she's better than anyone in the Seida Guild. Eerie as the spring tides, and she refuses to read drunk folks."

Rugen rolled his eyes. Toothache, wolf-sickness, manhunters, and to top it all off, he had stumbled into an ale house that only served grain juice? Really, which gods had he annoyed? But he took another swig, knowing full well that it could have been worse. He could have been Leife, for example, finished off on Smalfaret and hauled away in a hearse.

She killed him.

Leife was an acquaintance of Alette's, so who else could it have been? Lovely, willing Alette . . . Was she capable of killing someone that way? It was impossible to picture, but wolf-sickness turned people into wild animals. Sooner or later. And she had been relatively nuts when he had last seen her. Had he not been smart enough to get away, he would be dead now. She could have bitten his dick off! The thought made it hard for him to hold his mug steady.

What if she came after him? No, Alette was done for. The hunter never made a mistake. He would find her and yank the canines right out of that soft mouth of hers. She would be bloodied and bled to the stones, just like she'd feared. What a damned tragedy.

Rugen forced down more of the so-called beer and tried to drown his memories of her body. Her butt quivering to his rhythm. He would have warned her if it was possible—of course he would. But most likely it was already over. There was nothing he could do; he had barely gotten away himself.

If their roles had been reversed, he would never expect her to sacrifice herself for him. That would have been a complete waste. Not that there was any risk of that, since there wasn't a soul who would sacrifice themselves for anything at all. People mostly thought about themselves. Even so, they sank to the bottom. They let themselves get sick, let themselves be used and die. They simply lacked the will to lift themselves out of misery. Take a look at the two old men at the end of the bar, who were downing wort by the bucketful as if it could heal. They were no better off than him, and tomorrow they would drink themselves senseless somewhere else.

Pain ripped through his jaw. Rugen let out an involuntary moan. He had almost forgotten how much it hurt. He left the rest of his fake beer behind and went out into the cold. The snow on the side street was piss colored from the golden glow of a light he couldn't see.

What was it he'd said, the bartender? Kefla? *Better than anyone in the Seida Guild . . .*

Rugen went around the corner and looked up a narrow passage

that ran between the buildings. Crooked from time and weather, half-timbering well on its way to disintegrating. Even so, at least one person was living there, with a couple of little window openings and a smoking chimney on one side. A stair tower was nestled against the nearest row of buildings and a blood reader light hung next to the door, homemade from a ball of yellow yarn.

What a joke. This was a far cry from Lykteløkka. How desperate would you have to be to throw your last few coins away on this?

Rugen knocked. The truth was that he couldn't afford not to. He could be dead within the hour, butchered by the murderer in red. He needed to know.

After a while, the door opened a crack and a girl with bristly black hair peeked out. She couldn't be older than twelve. Red freckles sat densely across her nose, like a scrape on her golden-brown face. She must be from Ruv or something.

She looked around as if to check that he was alone.

"Come in," she said with a voice like a boy's. "And if you try anything, I'll stab you."

Rugen was caught off guard and couldn't think of a good retort. Then it dawned on him that this girl herself was the blood reader. He followed her up and into the narrow room inside the catwalk. It was dark, and far too hot, thanks to a cast-iron stove burning at the far end. A couple of window openings in the long wall gave glimpses of the street below. In the middle of the floor was a table with two stools, crooked as driftwood. Uninformative figures made of bone hung from the ceiling.

This ought to be cheap.

"Three runes," she said, as if she had read his mind.

She gestured for him to sit at the table, and he sat, even though the price was steep.

"Three runes? That's just as much as blood readers in the Seida Guild charge . . ."

"It's nowhere near as much," she replied, plunking herself down across from him. "Not that that matters. Seida Guild is Seida Guild. I'm Kefla, and my price is three runes."

Rugen snorted. "You can't compare yourself to them. You're a child! And not even from here. Any idiot can see that."

"*You* were the one who compared me to them, not me. And I was born here in Náklav, which is more than you can boast. Give me your hand."

How the wolf's twat could she know where I was born?!

Rugen gulped. "Nothing to get worked up over, I guess. It's fair to haggle. Or are you going to serve me up some lies now?"

The girl watched him through narrowed, brown eyes. "Worse than that, man. I'm going to tell you the truth. Three runes."

"I have two," Rugen said. He wanted to add that he doubted she was worth it, but blood readers were blood readers. You didn't joke around with them; the look in her eyes confirmed it.

Rugen made a show of emptying his coin purse onto the table. Two runes and six skár. And a pill box that he hurriedly put away again. It contained a blood pearl, which could be sold if he didn't use it himself.

The girl considered the coins for a while before she grabbed his hand and punctured his skin with a sharp ring. He pulled away reflexively, but she had a good hold and held his hand over a little pewter chalice of water. Blood trickled from his palm down into the water. She stared at the dancing blood, for longer than he liked, before letting go of his hand and passing him a rag for his wound.

"You want to know how long you have left, even though you know you're already dead?"

If the girl felt anything at all, she hid it well. Rugen wrapped the rag around his palm and contemplated her. He mostly wanted to tell her to go to Drukna, but she made him feel insecure, and obviously she had delivered the goods.

"I'm still breathing," he responded dryly. "So I hope you have more than that to offer."

Kefla nodded at the pewter chalice. "Drink, but don't swallow."

Rugen felt his gorge rise. Drink his own blood water? What the fuck kind of sick method was this?

"Don't act like you're not used to the taste," she said, just as coolly. *Confounded witch.*

What if she ratted him out? Blood readers had to maintain client confidentiality, at least the ones in the Seida Guild did, but who the fuck could trust a hardnosed twelve-year-old girl? Best to maintain a good tone. Rugen emptied the chalice into his mouth. It was salty and disgusting. Worse than the beer from around the corner, and he had to fight to keep from spewing it out again.

"Sea water," she said. "If you didn't take it when you were a newborn, it'll taste disgusting. Here, spit."

She set a bowl of water in front of him, and he spat. He felt sure she was tormenting him on purpose.

"Fresh water tastes too good to do the job or something?" he asked, as harshly as he dared.

"Fresh water won't do. If you're born in Slokna, then you take sea water three times in your life: when you're born, when you get married, and when you die," she said, as if he were some idiot from Undst. As if he hadn't made his share of jokes about how "taking the water" could mean either marrying or dying. There was no denying it was funny, but he doubted she was old enough to see the humor, so he kept his mouth shut.

"If you want to know what will happen between the first water and the last, then you need to drink it again. The sea carries your fate within it, just as much as the blood."

Kefla placed her hands around the bowl and stared down into it. His blood colored the water pink, and darker stripes swirled like smoke near the bottom. She said nothing. Did nothing.

"So? What do I need to do?" Rugen was running out of patience.

She looked up at him. The light from the fire brought her freckles to life, made it look as though she were disintegrating.

"That depends on what you want to save," she said. "Your life or your soul."

"What the fuck is the difference? What good is my soul if I don't have my life?"

The girl shrugged. "If you don't know, then you need more than my help. But, hey, it's your life, man. To save it, you need to take the way out. You already know what it is, but you've been too much of a coward to take it."

Nafraím...

Rugen wanted to know what he should say, how he should approach the warow this time, but Kefla continued to stare into the red soup.

"Three marks of fate," she said under her breath. "The devil. You have the devil in you. You are wolf spit, bearer of the worst seed, and she can't change that."

"She?"

"The heart. The other mark is the heart you broke. What you ruined can ruin you. The heart is the only thing that can tame the animal."

Juva...

Rugen could have listed many hearts with whom he had warmed himself, but Juva was the job he had messed up for Nafraím, so this couldn't be a coincidence. He needed to clean up. The warow could save him.

"And the third mark?"

"Loss." Kefla folded her arms in front of her chest, as if to say that she was done. "Death. Everything that can end will end, and you will see it."

"Great . . . What happened to telling fortunes about cute girls and long trips? Doesn't that kind of thing still sell?"

"I promised you the truth, man. You've received it. There's nothing more to say."

Rugen stood up. For a second, he considered grabbing back the money. The girl was a little shrimp. She wouldn't be able to do anything other than poke him with her sharp ring. But he couldn't risk her blabbing about his wolf-sickness or sending the Ring Guard after him. And despite everything, she had given him the answer he needed. He had to go to Nafraím if he wanted to save his life. That was exactly what she had said and that meant there was still hope. He wasn't doomed.

Kefla opened the door, and he was relieved to be able to leave her, even though he reluctantly had to concede that he did feel better.

He reached the end of the street and came out onto a road he recognized as Lykksalige Runas Vei, not so far from Nafraím. If Nafraím still lived in the same place, that was. Whenever they had met in the past, it had always been at Florian's Parlors, right around the corner.

Rugen could taste his own fear as he walked. Which was worse: being slaughtered by the red hunter or going to see a vardari? The closer he got, the less clear he was of the answer. He contemplated what the mood would be like and realized that he had done the same thing at Alette's place. People were so damned complicated. Why should he be forced to feel ashamed or beg every time he needed someone?

He had been given a job, and he had done his best to find out what he could about the blood reader girl. Before he had taken her money and run off . . . But Nafraím wasn't the type to pout about that kind of thing. Vardari didn't pout, did they?

They just kill you.

He reached Dauvrák, the eeriest street in all of Náklav. It reeked of prosperity, but that wasn't the issue. It was situated way out on the far edge by the sea, and the buildings people called "hanging houses" gave him the creeps. They seemed like typical Náklav buildings at first glance. Dark, ancient two-to-three-story stone buildings, but they were far bigger because the majority hung over the edge of the cliff, anchored in enormous crevices in the cliff face. The lights in the windows made it look like the houses were melting over the edge and down into the sea.

Rugen stopped outside the last house in the row. It had something so rare: a little courtyard in front with an old pine tree that curved up from the snow. The gate was closed but not locked. A cast iron plaque hung over the handle bearing a coat of arms. A wolf killed by a spear, with the family name *Sai* underneath. It wasn't painted or anything. One might think it wasn't meant to be seen.

Sai . . . Nafraím Sai? Was that right? He couldn't remember having been told a family name.

Rugen crossed the courtyard, walked up the two stone steps, and rapped the knocker ring against the door. It was opened by an elderly, slightly pretentious man who looked like he was dressed for a party even though he gave the impression that he had never been to one.

"Good evening. How may I help you, sir?" he said, and it didn't sound like he was kidding. Rugen snickered. Someday he should get himself one of these, too, a snob to open the door and ask how he could help. But Rugen would never make it to that point if he didn't take this chance.

"Nafraím? Are you his servant? I need to talk to him."

The servant raised a narrow eyebrow.

Should he have used the warow's name? Did the vardari use their own names or did they swap them out when they got . . . old? A landslide of questions came to mind, and none of them made him any calmer. He had to pull himself together.

Don't believe hysterical hearsay.

The servant cleared his throat. "I'm the Master's estate manager, yes. Whom may I say is calling?"

"Calling . . . ? Oh. I work for him."

The estate manager stared at him.

Rugen gulped. "I used to work for him. Or I did a job for him. Once."

"You're welcome to come inside and wait." The estate manager stepped to the side. "I'll have to see if my Master is available to meet with the gentleman."

Rugen stifled a nervous laugh and stepped into the foyer. It conveyed a subtle wealth that was so old and matter-of-fact that it appeared to take no effort. So understated that it was plain. The gallery had a wooden railing and rested atop completely ordinary wooden pillars. Heavy tapestries with faded motifs hung on one wall.

Why choose wood and tapestries when you could afford gold? Gold, mirrors, and precious stones, at least that was something people could understand. This seemed like an affront to everyone who had grown up eating porridge.

Rugen walked over and felt the closest wall hanging. It smelled like old rope, woven in shades of blue and gray. He had to step back again to see what it depicted. A flock of wolves on the run, all in the same direction, as if they were being hunted across the fabric.

The tapestry next to it was red, but the picture was baffling. He took a couple of steps back. Hearts? Was that a pile of hearts? Oh to Drukna, how gross! What was wrong with beautiful women with bulging breasts? Were there not enough tapestries with images like that?

"Few would have dared to come here. I will give you that."

Rugen jumped and turned toward the voice. Nafraím stood in the shadows under the stairs. A well-groomed and surprisingly attractive man, despite being old enough to be Rugen's father.

Or great-grandfather? Great-great-grandfather?

Rugen pulled his hood off, realizing that his scalp was sweating. Nafraím's words contained too much, both that he shouldn't have come here and a reminder that he hadn't finished his job. What should he say in response? Rugen's first thought was to laugh it off, pretend not to understand the implication. That was how he survived when he was on thin ice, with charm. But he instinctively knew that the warow would not be as patient as other people.

"I screwed up. I know that. And I wouldn't be here if I didn't have to be."

Nafraím watched him for a time, giving no indication of what he was thinking. Finally, he came closer and opened a door beneath the gallery.

"I hope you can deal with heights," he said, walking through the door without waiting for an answer.

Rugen followed him down a glossy wooden staircase that twisted in a spiral so narrow that he felt hungover. Little windows recessed in deep niches gave glimpses of the sea, which he became uncomfortably aware was beneath him. He was no longer on solid ground.

They came down to a study, or a sort of workshop that smelled like alcohol. One wall arced out toward the sea, and Rugen avoided looking out the window's many small panes of glass. Copper pipes wound around underneath the ceiling, coming down in a cluster in the middle, where an enormous lamp was attached to them. It was ugly, like an oversized wine bottle glowing white with corpsewood.

Rugen had an intense feeling that he was in the wrong place. The workbench was covered in drawings, glass flasks, and instruments, and he had no idea what they were for. And what was that disgusting thing in the alcohol? Was that a heart? He pretended he hadn't seen it and poked at a model instead. Brass balls of various sizes, moving in circles around each other. New balls branched out from some of them like a kind of tree.

"The universe as we presume it appears," Nafraím said, sitting on an upholstered sofa in front of an unlit fireplace.

He gestured for Rugen to have a seat in the chair across from him, but Rugen felt reluctant. The chair seemed too deep, and if he ended up needing to make a run for it . . .

"It's cold out, but you're sweating," the warow said. "You're tensing your jaws and you smell like blood. And they just found a body on Smalfaret. Was that you?" He spoke slowly and intensely, but seemed unaffected by his own question.

"No! What the fuck?!" Rugen immediately regretted his outburst.

He looked at the calm figure on the sofa and felt like he had been fooled. He needed to show that he was more dignified if he was going to have any hope of obtaining the help he needed. He sat in the deep chair.

"No," he repeated, with what little he had in the way of restraint.

"But it could have been?"

Rugen looked at the man, unsure whether he was claiming Rugen was a murderer or if he already knew that Rugen was wolf-sick.

Nafraím sighed. He started to stand up again.

"No, wait!" Rugen raised his hands in panic. "You're right. I'm sick, and I don't understand why. I've always been careful. I haven't done anything to deserve it!"

Nafraím took a lozenge from a little box in his pocket and settled himself more comfortably. "Unlike the others, you mean?" Nafraím asked.

There it was again, that wry smile, a joke Rugen didn't get. He felt exposed, angry, scared. Honesty seemed like the only method.

"Listen . . . I should have sent word that it didn't work. I did what you asked, as far as that went, but you know how women are, right? You can never know with them, and in the end, it just didn't work out. But there was nothing more to find out, I do know that! The girl isn't interested in becoming a blood reader, and she's not going to change her mind. It's the other one, the younger one, who's going to take over and I told you that. So you got everything you needed to know."

Nafraím rubbed his knuckles as if they were hurting, but nothing in his face suggested that he was in pain. His one hand seemed weirdly motionless.

"She saw through you," he said. "You bored her."

Bored her?!

Rugen clenched his teeth. "It wasn't like that, not at all. I gave it everything I had. And I had her, but then I took money from her. All right? I needed it, and it wasn't going to last much longer, anyway."

Nafraím stood up, watching him with an intense look of appraisal. Rugen had an uncomfortable feeling of being insignificant, a little boy. It wasn't fucking right.

"A blessing in disguise if nothing else," Nafraím said. "If that was how it ended, then it can be put right. Wait here and don't touch anything."

The warow vanished through a door.

"So can you help me or not?" Rugen flew out of his chair.

The silence that followed was humiliating. He worked up his courage and walked closer to the windows, peering out where there was no frost. Far below him, the sea undulated in big swells that made him feel unsteady. Across the fjord, lights gleamed from a throng of ships down at the new wharves in Kviskre. A couple of the lights went out as a ship sailed into the shafts in the cliff wall. The smokehouses. Rugen had put up with the job of longshoreman for less than three weeks. The tedious drudgery, the rotten pay, the same crap work the rest of his family had done. He hadn't moved to Náklav to reek of smoke and whale blood.

Nor to die of wolf-sickness.

"Are they loose?"

Rugen jumped at Nafraím's voice. He was far too jumpy these days. On edge, always on his toes.

"Huh?" He turned to the warow.

"Your teeth? Are they loose?"

Rugen felt around with his tongue, although he did that obsessively, all day long, so he certainly knew how things stood. "One of them is a little loose."

Nafraím lifted Rugen's chin and stared into his mouth, as if he were examining a horse. "Well, you still have some time, and I can give you a little more. But I can't do anything about the red hunter, so stay alert." He set a flacon containing something resembling syrup on the windowsill. "This will slow the progression some. You will still struggle with pain, but it will be less intense and less frequent. It will also thicken your blood, so you won't bleed to death from a scratch."

"A scratch? I can bleed to death from a scratch?!" Rugen hated hearing his voice break.

"Not if you take this," Nafraím replied calmly. "Drink a thimbleful a day, no more. It will give you time, but it won't change the outcome."

The outcome . . .

Rugen stared at Nafraím, but the man's empathy seemed superficial at best. It felt idiotic to ask outright, but he clearly wasn't going to get anything for free.

"So, what will change the outcome?"

"Nothing," Nafraím said with a cautious smile, as if he had been expecting Rugen to ask this. "Which is to say . . . nothing short of this." He pointed to himself. A discreet gesture, but the import was clear.

The only cure is to become like him.

Become a vardari, a warow, someone who no illness could touch, no matter how deadly. Rugen suddenly felt shaken. It was a test. A promise of what could happen if he just did the job correctly this time.

"It's yours if you want it." Nafraím nodded to the flacon. "But if you take it, you also take the job. Do you understand?"

"What do you want me to do?"

"What you didn't manage to do last time. The circumstances are more complicated than you suspect, and you need to learn to see better. Listen. Lagalune Sannseyr is the core of the Seida Guild, and a lot is going to happen in that house in the future. I need to know what. Juva is back. Why? Lagalune is lying and saying that she's sick. Why? I want to know where Lagalune goes, where has she been, and what places she talks about. I want to know who she meets and what they say. The Sannseyr house is a hive of secrets, and you need to shed your notion that you already know everything worth knowing. But most importantly: I want to know which of the girls inherits her mother's job, who is taking over her seat on the Seida Guild. I want to know the instant it's decided, and no one in Náklav should know before me. Do you understand?"

Rugen rubbed his sore jaw, not sure if he was about to take on an impossible task. Juva was going to be furious, and he would have to cook up an insanely good excuse. If he could even manage to explain before she shot him with her crossbow. For a moment, he considered asking if he could try his hand with the little sister instead, but Solde Sannseyr had probably never been with a man, and the day she was, it would surely freeze his dick off.

There was also the question of the forty runes. Rugen pulled his hand through his hair and looked at the floor. "I need to pay back the money I took from her. I won't have a chance if she doesn't—"

"You'll have the money."

Rugen licked his lips. The man didn't even ask how much they were talking about. How did it feel to have so devilishly much, and would he ever get to feel that himself?

Nafraím moved toward the spiral staircase. Rugen grabbed the flacon and followed him up into the foyer while he thought about

Juva and how he was going to attack this situation. She was definitely cute, nice breasts. Blonde and not vain, with narrow, suspicious cat eyes. She was hard to get to open up, and he knew that she would never really let him all the way in. But she fucked like she didn't have long left to live and by all the gods how he loved that sort. But how in Drukna was he going to warm her back up again?

Rugen stood alone in the foyer while Nafraím went to get the money. He didn't come back again. It was the estate manager who brought it. He held out the well-filled leather coin purse between two fingers, as if it were dirty.

Rugen felt like he was shriveling up. He had never had trouble charming his way into coins, clothes, or beds, but that was with women. Women *wanted* to be divested of things, they gave things away on purpose, to feel superior. But this was different. This made him feel like he'd never be able to get hard again. He was a whore for the vardari.

DEVIL'S COCK

Nafraím climbed out of the carriage and gave his neck a sorely needed stretch. He could see several people doing the same thing farther ahead in the caravan, which would continue onward to the east coast. If time had permitted it, he would have found a private coach in Kreknabork and traveled alone.

The journey had been trying, stuck with a young woman and her newborn. It could have been pleasant enough if it weren't for the woman's mother, who had nagged incessantly about everything her daughter was doing wrong. The baby was being held wrong, fed too little, and dressed too warmly, not to mention making all the wrong noises. Ultimately, Nafraím had felt compelled to politely request that she spare everyone's ears and instead speak only when she felt something was being done correctly. The woman had swelled up like a bellows, and he had thought for a second that she would burst, but she didn't respond. Nor did she say anything else for the rest of the journey. Shortly thereafter, both the daughter and the baby had fallen asleep.

Nafraím looked around while the coachman lifted his suitcase out. They were in the middle of the wilderness by a small river. The woods were dense as far as he could see, and the only sign of life was a couple of dilapidated hunting or fishing cabins down on the riverbank.

"Are you sure this is the right place?" he inquired.

The coachman handed him the suitcase and pointed down to the cabins. "I swear by my bones, my Lord. You see Vanakrog right down there. Not a ring-city, exactly, but you'll find food, ale, and shelter."

The caravan crawled away through the mud that the snow left behind. Nafraím pulled the piece of paper from the chest pocket of his coat and read it again, as if it might have changed during the journey.

From Kreknabork, take one of the caravans east toward Hamvær. Stop in the village of Vanakrog, ask for the devil's cock. When you find it, I'll have seen you.

He stuck the slip of paper back in his pocket, picked up his suitcase, and followed the road down toward the cabins, trying to avoid the worst of the mudholes. He regretted his choice of shoes and was well prepared to be teased for the rest of his outfit, too.

If it had been up to him, they would have met in Kreknabork, naturally. But he would be the first to admit that you could learn a lot from traveling this way. Mostly you learned to be grateful for the stone circles.

Plus, he was depending on goodwill, from both Faun and Seire. He didn't think they would withdraw from the pact, but you never knew. People changed, especially those who had lived for centuries. He had painful experience of this.

The cabins seemed a bit sturdier closer up, and he took the chance of entering the one that was reminiscent of an inn. He ignored the looks from the lone patron and walked over the plump woman behind the counter, who allowed her gaze to roam shamelessly over his outfit.

He cleared his throat and was about to ask for "the devil's cock" but then realized that he didn't remember any words for the male organ in Fimlandish. He would have to improvise, not exactly his strength.

"I'm looking for the devil's . . . thing."

"A Devilish Thing? Well, if that's a kind of beer, we don't have it here."

"No, no. It's a place, I think. Or a statue." He gestured helplessly toward his crotch. "The devil's . . . item . . . pole."

"Oh! The devil's cock!" she replied, laughing easily. "Then you need to go across the bridge, into the woods. Follow the path to the left. Not to the right. If you come to the waterfall, you went the wrong way." She checked him out again with her eyes. "You're not exactly dressed for it. It's a good hour's walk."

"I'll take my chances," he replied dryly. He set five Fimlandian kroner on the counter. "And what am I looking for?"

"A tree, an old pine that's growing right out of the rock wall, over a lake. You'll understand when you see it."

He thanked her and left. The door wasn't thick enough to muffle the outburst of laughter from the woman and the one patron inside. Nafraím smiled and proceeded over a rope bridge that crossed the river. The path led uphill, through dense spruce and pine, evergreens set against the rust-colored ground. The sun had already returned here, unlike Náklav, but he couldn't see it, only sense it behind the horizon.

Nafraím felt like an intruder in the wilderness, an undetected stranger. He had traveled far too little in recent years. He had sat around in Náklav with his projects and forgotten how enormous the world was and how big the still uninhabited portions of it were.

In cold hollows, he saw that the snow was receding. Yellow tufts of flattened straw stuck up on the hillsides. His thighs were starting to feel tired, a rare sensation.

He squeezed his way between two rocks and emerged onto a heather-covered hillside with a view over a uniquely green-colored lake. And there, on a protrusion over the water, the devil's cock revealed itself in all its glory.

The pine tree clung to the edge of the cliff with a nest of roots. The trunk was enormously strong and bent down toward the water before swinging up again, sloping up toward the sky with a cluster of needles, its shape unmistakable.

Nafraím set down his suitcase and shielded his eyes. He studied the phenomenon until he began to feel a tingling in places he had not felt any life in for years.

"Magnificent, isn't it?"

The voice behind him was also unmistakable. He turned around and threw his arms around the broad-shouldered Faun as well as he could.

"Faun . . ." Saying his name out loud felt like a caress on the lips.

Faun's hand found the back of his head and pulled him closer. He whispered in a raspy voice that made Nafraím close his eyes against Faun's naked torso.

"You smell like you're standing on the edge of the world, Naf. Sea and smoke, wine and perfume. As if you have no idea where you belong." Faun took a step back, holding him at arm's length and inspecting him. "But, yes, I see where you belong. Come," Faun said, nodding to the path. "I have a better viewpoint, and Seire is waiting."

Nafraím followed Faun, which allowed him to enjoy the sight of him without reservation. The wild man was undeniably beautiful, like the natural setting they walked through. Young, strong, and bestial, with an intense blue-eyed gaze. But there had never been anything hurtful in him, not even during the wolf wars, before he had become a warow. The brown hair seemed to grow like roots down his strong, muscular back, gathered with straps and bone beads.

The cold never seemed to bother him, a gift no other vardari had received. Not for the first time, Nafraím wondered if the blood had changed Faun in some unique way.

The path continued as a grass-clad mountain ledge, before it cut up toward a protrusion above the lake that was crowned by tall spruces. In their shadow stood a pyramid of logs, wrapped with mats of heather. Nafraím started to laugh. He would have called it a bonfire, yet Faun called it a meeting place. Smoke rose from the middle.

Faun stopped outside the structure. "You're quieter than usual," he remarked. "Have you seen nothing but human beings the last ten years?"

"That depends on how you define yourself."

Faun laughed. Calling him an animal was no insult. He belonged in the forest more than any other place. It was for his sake that they were meeting there—and so no one would see them together.

The hide was pulled away from the opening and Seire let them in.

"Faun is neither man nor animal. He's become a myth, I hear." Her smile was wide and dazzling.

Nafraím had steeled himself for seeing them, both of them, but apparently that had been a wasted exercise. Almost seven hundred years had passed since their first meeting, and they still made him feel young and uncomfortably self-conscious.

Seire sat down on a log by the fire pit and poked around in the embers with a stick. She was intentionally avoiding looking at him, he knew that. She enjoyed giving him time to study her first.

The wind snuck in the opening and caught her rust-colored curls. They caressed her brown skin, which was full of pale freckles. And they weren't only on her face. The thought warmed his groin.

He took off his coat and draped it over one of the seating logs. Only then did she turn back around to him and break out in laughter.

"Naf, what in heaven's name are you wearing?" She pointed to the pocket of his embroidered vest. "Is that . . . Is that a handkerchief?"

Nafraím flung up his arms. "This, dear savages, is the latest fashion in the civilized portion of the world, where you two would be put in a cage so people could pay to see you."

Faun chortled. "I hear we still disagree on what can be called *civilized*."

Nafraím let them amuse themselves at his expense. He enjoyed it, knowing it would become serious soon enough. He waited until they had settled down again before he opened his suitcase, located the leather box, and emptied it out. A handful of canine teeth rolled out onto the reindeer hides that covered the floor.

"Wolf-sickness. This is from just the past two months. Also, there are new shoots springing up in Svartna again, in the middle of the dead belt in Vargrák. That's been going on for many years now. And a little over a week ago, the Witness woke up—as you both and every single vardari in the world know. There's no point in denying it. The Might is back."

No one responded to him. This wasn't news to any of them. The campfire crackled and spit out sparks. It smelled like smoke and wilderness. Nafraím had a strong sensation of having traveled back in time, of being at the beginning again, but maybe that was how it should be when everything was about to end.

Seire was the first to break the silence. "Are you two scared?"

Faun shook his head, without hesitating.

Nafraím did not feel as brave. "We made a mistake," he said, "and we have to pay for it. I feel that in every nerve."

"Come on," Seire said, sending him a smile that ate up his fear. "What's the worst that could happen?"

"More wolf-sickness," Faun said, "and maybe blood readers. That does complicate things for anyone who hangs out in the cities. If people can sense you again, I mean. Maybe you need to move out here with me?" He grinned.

"These are only practical challenges," Nafraím said, fidgeting fretfully. "Far from the worst thing that could happen. The others know just as well as we do what this could mean. How likely do you think it is that the vardari will all agree on one solution? Not a chance in the sea. This will mean the end of the peace."

"You expect war?" Seire leaned over and picked a little scrap of something off his vest.

"What do *you* expect?" Nafraím eyed them both.

Their silence was answer enough.

Nafraím had to say what they were all thinking. "The worst thing that could happen is that *they* come back. Yes, I know it's been almost seven hundred years, and I know it's unlikely, but it's a very real possibility. That small possibility will tear the vardari to pieces. And this isn't a prediction for the future. This is going to happen quickly. Some have already called for a gathering."

"You want to act before the meeting." Seire stood up and stared down at him. "That's why we're here."

He could see that she had understood, and that she was struggling herself.

"The race for the source will be bloody, and there's not a single warow who knows where he is. The others will . . . " Nafraím gulped.

"You don't need to ask us, Nafraím." Faun put a hand on his thigh. "We are one, we three. We started this, and if you want to end it, then we'll end it. That was the pact."

Seire ran her fingers through her hair, although she looked like she might want to pull it out. She started walking in a circle around the fire. "What the fuck are you so afraid of?! This isn't the end. We've only just begun! I've gotten a woman onto the throne in Grimse, elected by the people! Hera, the elected! Do you have any idea how long that took?"

"We all have projects, Seire," Nafraím rubbed his forehead with his fingers. "I'm working with a doctor in Náklav and we've built an instrument that shows things you could never have dreamt! Everything you see around you is alive. We can see it, measure it, and fight disease with it. I've found a way to burn corpsewood that emits gas, and if I can figure out how to avoid all the damned explosions, then an eternal flame can burn on every street! But everything comes to an end, Seire."

Nafraím felt empty and exhausted again.

Seire crossed her arms in front of her chest. Strong arms over incredible breasts. All he wanted was to feel her against him, but first he needed to get her in on the pact.

"Seire, every single warow we have created is passionate about something. I'm positive Domnik hasn't slept since he founded the national bank. He believes money will make the whole world as rich as Náklav. Do you think he'll voluntarily give up a project like that? Give up and lie down dead? Not to mention Eydala. No, we can't leave this decision up to the vardari. It's ours to make."

Seire closed her eyes for a second and took a deep breath.

"Well, have you talked to the blood readers?" she asked.

"Yes, I tried." Nafraím nodded. "They do not want to give up the devil."

"Then they have sealed their own fate," Seire said.

Nafraím felt the fear in his body release. He had won. She was in.

"But someone will try to torture the answer out of them," she said. "Someone could gain control of the source. What do you suggest that we do?"

Nafraím hesitated before responding.

"I've searched for him. There isn't a single vardari who hasn't searched, even though we've always hidden that from each other. There are indications that suggest that Kreknabork is the place, but I must admit that I have no idea where. The Seida Guild has done exactly what they were supposed to: kept the secret. The good news is that if I don't know it, then no one else does, either."

"So you want to go after the blood readers?" Faun asked. The discomfort in his blue eyes was easy to read.

"We can't risk a new war over the source," Nafraím said with a sigh. "That would cost far too many lives. Killing the initiated blood readers is the cleanest way out I see, the least risky. Lagalune Sannseyr is sick, and that's a good place to start."

Faun stood up abruptly, cocking his head to the side, as if he smelled something. "He's here!" he announced. "Come on!"

"Who's—" Seire began, but Faun shushed her.

"Don't say a word. Lie down!" Faun went over to the entrance and lay down on his belly.

Seire did the same, so Nafraím joined in with no idea of what to expect.

Faun cautiously pushed the animal hide door aside and they peered out at the devil's cock, the crooked tree, nature's showy erection. An elkr stood out on the rocks, the biggest deer Nafraím had ever seen. Its antlers stretched out to the sides, farther than his own arms could have reached, the points extending up into the sky.

It was spectacular, a ruddy brown and muscular. It walked over to the edge of the cliff and leaned forward to reach the crooked pine. It snorted. Its breath showed white in the cold air, forming frost on its muzzle, and it stamped one hoof against the tree trunk as if to test if it would bear its weight. Nafraím didn't dare breathe. Was the animal really going to step out onto the tree trunk?

"I wanted you to see him," Faun whispered. "The king of the forest. He wants to get hold of the outermost branches with needles, but he'll never reach them. There isn't a tree he hasn't eaten from, apart from the devil's cock."

The elkr took a couple of steps back and took a bite of the heather on the rocks but did not seem satisfied. It stood there, peering at the pine that extended out over the lake, so distressingly beyond reach. The colors of the forest had faded, but somewhere behind the mountains, the sun had set fire to the sky. The elkr roared and tossed its head. Something was wrong. Its antlers began to sag. Seire and

Faun warmed either side of Nafraím's body, and he could sense that neither of them dared to breathe either. The elkr made a tremendous leap and shed its antlers. The massive rack landed in the heather and lay there. The king of the forest shook its now unadorned head, bounded in between the trees, and disappeared.

"Before midsummer he will be back, even bigger and stronger," Faun said, watching him and Seire.

"If he doesn't die first," Seire said dryly. "But we got a glimpse of its greatness if nothing else."

Faun's eyes took on a faraway look. "All the blood we have on our hands . . . If we had known back then, would we do it again?"

"I would," Seire said with a grin. "Damn right I would. I don't regret anything. Do you?"

"I regret Eydala," Nafraím said spontaneously and honestly.

None of them moved. They rested close together as the fire spit sparks behind them.

"We had a good run, didn't we?" Nafraím asked.

"The best," Seire replied. "But we're not dead yet."

Her brown eyes burrowed into him as if she wanted to devour him, and Nafraím felt his heart shaking the rust off itself. She lay down on her back, unlacing her top to reveal her breasts. They both lolled to the side, her nipples each pointing in opposite directions. His hand found them without his brain needing to think. She unlaced the top of his pants, and Faun helped her pull his pants all the way off. He climbed up onto her and entered an indescribably wet heat. Alive, he was infinitely alive. Faun came up behind him and his weight sent Nafraím deeper into Seire.

Several hundred years had come to an end, but right now . . . right now, he was embraced between woman and man, the first three, together again. And they weren't dead yet.

SCOUNDREL

For the umpteenth time, Juva pressed her finger against the spring and squeezed the trigger. The crossbow made a stiff click, and she was forced to acknowledge that the damage exceeded her repair skills. The sleigh runners had messed up the mechanism.

She wouldn't need it for a long time, but that was little consolation. Lok and Embla were expecting a baby and Broddmar was busy hunting people, not wolves, so presumably the team had done their last hunt of the winter. And if they were to fit in a trip before the spring run, she wouldn't be able to afford a new crossbow anyway. Thanks to Rugen.

Stupid bastard.

She had been fully aware that he was bad news, but it had been easy to ignore. He was easy to spend time with. He never demanded to know anything at all, because he never revealed anything himself, liar and blood user that he was.

But is he a murderer?

The cold crept in and numbed her arm, which rested against the window. What had he been doing there, by that body? She hadn't told a soul that she had been in Smalfaret, just heard them talking about it. Solde had eaten up all the grotesque rumors about the killing, which were far from what Juva had seen, while Lagalune had praised the public fear as good for business. What in heaven's name was wrong with these people? Juva swore she'd never have kids.

She tossed her crossbow on the bed and looked around the attic room, which had been hers since she was little enough to fit standing upright on the windowsill. Now she had to sit with her knees pulled up to fit there.

Far below her, the ocean raged against the cliffs. Scary, many people thought. Like Ive, the kitchen girl, for example, who had always refused to wash the windows unless the shutters were closed—but she was generally skittish. Even a flock of wolves couldn't have chased her into the wine cellar, which she believed was haunted.

Juva didn't care about ghosts or cliffs. What she feared was her own heartbeats, and the sound of the ocean helped her forget them.

The tide was low, so she could see the rotten pilings from old wharves. Black and crooked, they stuck up like charred fingers, and she remembered that she used to think it was Gaula, the queen of Drukna, who had died there. Now Gaula floated on her back in the deep, like all the sailors whose lives she had claimed. There was something comforting about it, too, having a dead god outside her window, in a city that was obsessed with how long you could live.

Blood readers, warow, and wolf-sick . . .

Her heart gave a couple of fidgety beats, and Juva leapt to her feet. She had to stay busy, so she wouldn't think about it. There were limits to how much hoggthorn a person could consume.

She took her notebook out of her backpack, which still hadn't been unpacked. It wasn't going to be, either, because that would be like moving back in. She was not there to stay. She was there to finish. A day or two, maybe, because her mother had finally set the inheritance process in motion. A man from the bank had been there, along with a legal expert. With a little luck, she would be able to sign and leave as early as that night. Then at least she would avoid any more arguments with Solde.

Juva sat down on the bed and turned up the oil lamp. She unwound the strap from her notebook and opened it. Flipped back through it, lured toward the earliest sketches, the ones that gave her goosebumps. Wolves. Wolves and teeth, that's what she had drawn. Always. Each time was like a painful birth, an exorcism, to get what was rotten out from within her, that which had suddenly reawoken when she saw Nafraím again and started remembering.

I'm crazy.

She had thought that her whole life, that she lacked what was needed to be normal. She drew wolves and wolfmen and then she burned them, because that would prevent terrible things from happening. Because that reduced her feelings of guilt, shame. What kind of normal person did stuff like that?

She was like the crossbow: seemingly fine, but damaged when you looked closely.

"Maybe you can make a living as a street artist when you move out?"

Juva jumped at the voice and slammed her book shut. Solde stood in the doorway with a smile so fake, it was as if she had just invented the expression. Juva got up to close the door, but Solde squeezed in.

"Do you think I'm an idiot, Juva?" she hissed.

Juva was dying to say yes but knew nothing good could come from that. She left the room instead, but Solde came rushing after her, her bone jewelry rattling.

"We don't want you here! Not me and not Mother! She's dragging her heels with the paperwork because you're pressuring her, that's why it's taking time. You think you can steal this from me!"

Juva stopped and turned to face her. "This?" she snapped. "What do you mean *this*? What in Drukna do you think I want from this godforsaken house?"

Solde's mouth made an expression as if she had eaten something bad, but she didn't have a chance to respond before Ive came out from the storeroom with a stack of linens in her arms. The kitchen girl mumbled an apology in the awkward silence and slipped past them down the hallway.

Solde waited until the girl had disappeared around the corner before launching back into it, more quietly this time. "That is so freaking transparent, that false humility. I'm sure you can trick those farm fools you hunt with, but you can't trick me, Juva. You've never managed to trick me! This house is mine, and the seat on the Seida Guild belongs to me!"

Juva bit her lip. She had sworn she wouldn't let herself be provoked, but Solde made that next to impossible. Solde *wanted* a confrontation and had grown more and more hysterical as time passed without the papers being signed. It was as if she expected some divine intervention that would suddenly make Juva interested in staying there, and the fear turned her into a little monster.

It's not her fault. It's mine.

Solde was ruined. She had been living along with Lagalune since the age of thirteen, because Juva had abandoned her in this rat's nest of secrets and deceit. Alone, with Mother's warped reality.

A door banged open, and Mother came swaggering out of her study with a man on her heels. He was gaunt, with thinning hair, and he was struggling to close a leather folder as he stumbled after Lagalune, who was sweeping down the staircase. She took a puff of her cigar and spotted Juva and Solde.

"Solde, I need you to run an errand for me." She didn't wait for a response, and Solde didn't hesitate to hurry after her.

Juva wished she felt confident that she would soon move out of there for good, but she wasn't able to shake the thought that something was brewing. Transferring the house and the money to Solde should be a simple matter, since Juva was more than willing to give it all up. So what sort of drama was Lagalune up to?

She's planning something, and it's going to affect me.

That feeling gnawed away inside her chest. Blood readers inherited both the house and the business, that's how it had always been. But what if Mother intended to split it up or something? Solde would come totally unhinged, and Juva didn't want anything at all from Lagalune. Or was she planning for them to live there together? Like some sort of protection against the vardari?

Juva snuck into the study in the hopes of getting a glimpse of the paperwork, a hint of what was to come.

The study was one of the few places in the house where she had been happy as a child. It was warm and a woody brown, not black and gloomy. Nor was it made to manipulate people, so it was liberatingly empty of everything having to do with blood reading. Juva had found it the most mystical room in the house, maybe specifically for that reason.

It has always been Lagalune's, but it still reminded her of Father. He had left his mark on it with down-to-earth things. Two deep chairs, one with an upholstered footstool that was faded in the middle where people's heels had worn away the pattern. A collection of skulls from little rodents on the mantle. An antique crossbow, supposedly one of the first ever made in Náklav, hung on the wall. Next to it hung a cluster of paintings of Mother's favorite places. Kreknabork in Fimle, with tall wooden houses by the harbor. Haeyna in Grimse, almost as big as Náklav, with light stone houses and domes. All were henge cities, with their own stone travel rings, but none of them were bigger than Nákla Henge, with its seven destinations.

Eight, if you counted the dead pair of stones. The one that fanatics thought led to Drukna.

Juva had never believed that Drukna was real, and most people said the only thing those dead stones led to was the bottom of the ocean. Fatal, of course, so they had been closed for centuries.

She put her hand on the wooden wall panels, remembering that she used to press on them because they looked like concealed doorways or hatches. Other children searched for secret passageways and treasure. She had mostly been searching for a way out.

131

In the middle of the room sat the desk, made of polished oak, sadly bereft of the revealing paperwork she had been hoping to see. A faded green blotter, an ashtray made of bone, with Lagalune's thin cigar butts, and two cups with tea rings in the bottom. But no will. No property title deeds.

Perhaps this was a good sign. Maybe she had let her imagination run wild. That's how it was with her, that was what Mother had always said. That Juva was afraid of nothing, and believed dreams were reality, imagined things.

But it wasn't imagination. Not all of it. If only she could distinguish what was real from the rest . . .

She heard someone knock on the client door, a sound that had been constant through her childhood. Always someone at the door, always strangers. And they wanted to know things no one had the power to tell them, about illness and love, about how long they had left. Only the most cynical of people would take it upon themselves to rattle off lies to them for payment. And that was her family.

Juva had sworn never to tell another fortune.

She glanced up at the painting of her father. A handsome, blond man with stubble. Broad shoulders. Strong. On the frame it said "Valjar 1428." Painted the year Juva was born.

She had stood there right below the picture, and he had sat down on the footstool in front of her with that playful look she had loved. He had reached his hand out to her, as if she were already a blood reader, even though she was only seven. A game, an innocent game.

So, tell me, how old will I get to be, Juva?

The memory threatened to become clearer, so Juva looked away and walked over to the windows that faced Lykteløkka. She leaned her forehead against the glass to cool her thoughts. The mind was like corpsewood embers, a constant smolder that would maybe never go out.

Outside, the red lights dangled like drops of blood in the twilight. People pushed past each other on the narrow street. A man stopped at the bakery, which had already started selling sun kringles, even though it'd be almost two weeks until the first sun-day. The golden baked goods seemed to tempt him, because he lingered there. Then he turned to face the Sannseyr home and Juva recognized him right away.

Rugen?! What in Gaula?!

Juva pulled back, behind the heavy curtains and peeked out at him. What the fuck was he doing there? He seemed nervous, standing pressed against the wall, as if he was waiting for someone he didn't actually want to see. Then he took a couple of steps toward the house, toward her, but then changed his mind and walked back again.

Was he planning to rob her again? Her anger flared up like a backyard brush burning. Juva rushed out of the study, taking the stairs down in big bounds, jumped into her shoes, and ran out onto the street in just her sweater. She saw his back disappearing up the shortcut to Skjepnasnaret and followed him. Suddenly, he slowed down as if he had forgotten something. Juva stopped instinctively. Then he started running.

He knows I'm after him!

Juva ran until she was so close that she could hear him panting. She threw herself at his back and tackled him. They tumbled to the street, and he flailed his arms around wildly while crying like a baby. Juva sat down astride him and trapped his arm under her knee so he couldn't hit her.

"You cost me a new crossbow, you maggot!"

"Juva?" Rugen stared up at her with terrified eyes.

Then he collapsed and started laughing. She realized he had thought she was someone else, someone he was actually afraid of.

"Who else would it be? Why were you gawking at our house? What do you want, and where's my money?"

Rugen tried to get up, but she had his elbow trapped with her knee.

"What do you want, Rugen?"

Two women walked by, each with a sun kringle. They hesitated for a second but seemed to quickly and correctly conclude that the idiot on the ground deserved the thrashing he was getting and walked on.

Rugen caught his breath and calmed down. He looked at her earnestly. "I need help, Juva."

Help?

Juva searched for any sign of a lie but realized that was the truest thing he had ever said to her. She got up and let him stand back up again, but only so it would be easier to push him up against the wall. Rugen put up no resistance whatsoever. Quite the contrary, he was so amenable that she felt even more irritated.

"I don't give a shit if you need help. You stole from me!"

"Yes." He gulped and stared at the ground. "Yes, but you need to—"

"I don't need to do anything, Rugen, not a thing. I have nothing to say to you. It doesn't matter what happened or why. I just need my money back. Otherwise, I'm going to jam my ruined crossbow down your throat. You got that?"

A man with a dog walked by and Rugen tried to back out of the way, but there was nowhere for him to go.

What is he afraid of? What in Drukna has he gotten mixed up in?

The man didn't even glance at them, just continued around the corner out of sight. Juva saw an opening in the wall nearby and pulled Rugen into it with her. It was a cramped vestibule with a stone staircase leading up, the same type that that body had been found in. She pushed him backward until he was sitting on one of the steps and leaned in over him.

"I don't care what you've done, Rugen. The only thing I'm certain of is that you have only yourself to thank."

"Juva—"

"Don't even think about it! Save your efforts for someone else."

Rugen pulled down his hood and ran his hands over his face. "Juva . . . Juva, I'm sorry about that. You have no idea how sorry I am about it, about everything. I was an asshole who stole from you, although I had no choice. I had to do it!"

Juva stared at him. He was genuinely scared, not that that mattered.

"No one *has* to steal," she said, but regretted it as soon as the words left her mouth because it gave him an opportunity to explain.

His mouth took on a bitter twist.

"No. You wouldn't believe it if I tried to explain it, and I can't do that anyway. I can't say anything other than I'm sorry. I was an idiot who ran off like a rat. I was an asshole who never showed up again. I get why you hate me and that's fine, Juva. But I came to give you your money back. Here."

He took out his coin purse and handed her four gold coins, twenty runes.

"This is only half, but you'll get the rest soon, I promise. If I live that long, and right now, *that's* up to you."

Juva stared at the coins with growing embarrassment. She hadn't thought he had them or would ever give them back. He just didn't seem like the type to go to the trouble. Had she been wrong about him? Had she been imagining monsters again? The gods knew she didn't always have a handle on what was real and what wasn't.

Stop making stuff up.

That's what Lagalune had always said, blind to the fact that Lagalune herself had gotten rich off of making things up.

Juva stuck the coins in her pocket and mumbled, "Help with what? Did you steal from the wrong person again?"

Rugen shook his head. "I promise, I'll explain once this is over, but I need a place to stay. Just for a few days."

"Not with me."

"There's no risk to you," he said, as if that was what she was concerned about. "This is only about me. If they . . . If anyone . . . Listen, I didn't want to run off, Juva. I never intended for it to be like that. It was good between us. Don't you remember?"

He pulled his hand through his brown curls and smiled tentatively with his full lips. She had always thought they made him look pouty.

But she did remember, and they had been lovely months. He had been so simple and straightforward. Not looking to get his fortune told, he just wanted to have sex with her. And it was right on the mark. She had told him that she was never going to become a blood reader and he had just shrugged, never asked for any reason.

But she didn't owe him anything. Quite the contrary.

"Forget it, Rugen. If this is a matter of life and death, then maybe you can use my room in Hidehall, but I need to ask Ester first."

"No!" He grabbed her arm. "Don't ask anyone, Juva. Don't say a word. I can sleep at your family's house, on the floor. You won't even need to see me."

"On the floor?" Juva took a step back. "What in Drukna did you do?"

"Not me. It was someone else who did it, but not me." He stuck his hands in his pocket, clearly freezing. She was starting to feel the cold, too, now that her anger had subsided. She wrapped her arms around herself.

"Blood pearls. You took blood pearls from someone, you addict."

"Oh, who are you to talk, huh?" he said, suddenly defensive. "Don't you take those damned berries?"

Juva was relieved at his attack. That was the only excuse she needed to say no. Even if she knew that he was right. She was as addicted to hoggthorn as he was to blood pearls. She turned to go.

"No! Juva, wait!" He grabbed her. "I'm sorry! I really messed up. Blood pearls. Money. Wrong people, wrong place. But this doesn't have anything to do with blood, I promise. Not with the vardari, either, you don't even need to ask. But I would never have come here if I wasn't desperate. I promise I won't be in the way, not in anyone's way. Juva . . ."

Juva felt her anger begin to fade. She was actually considering helping him, which irritated her to no end. She ought to leave him sitting there on the stairs and hope Gaula took him, but she couldn't bring herself to say that. His last words lingered in the air like his warm breath, still visible in the cold air.

I promise I won't be in the way, not in anyone's way.

Of course he would, and maybe that was an advantage right now? She wouldn't have to feel so alone in the house, and it would confound Solde.

Juva suppressed a smile and pulled Rugen to his feet. "One night, no more. And if you touch anything in the house, then I'm going to force you to eat it. You got that?"

She turned her back to him and left. He hurried after her without saying anything, and she didn't look at him again until she let him inside. The heavy wrought iron door squeaked in protest before banging shut. There was something delightful about bringing him there, something perverse. Rugen was an idiot in trouble, without a doubt a dirty stain on Solde's blood reader paradise. It felt cathartically wonderful to sully the house.

Juva took off her shoes and walked into the front hall just as Lagalune emerged from the blood reader room on unsteady legs. She reached out for the skeleton-like bench to support herself, tilting forward as if she were completely drunk.

"Mother?"

Lagalune looked at her, pale as a corpse, her face drawn. Black hairs had come loose from her updo and were stuck to her neck.

"Juva . . ." she gasped. Then she fell to the floor.

THE INHERITANCE

Juva hesitated, slowed by her suspicion that what she was seeing was an act. Lagalune curled up on the floor, her arms around her belly. She moaned as if she were having convulsions. She would get up again, very soon. For sure.

"Lagalune?" someone asked from the reader room.

A client. Mother had been in the middle of a blood reading.

The seriousness pulled Juva out of her trance. She ran over, knelt down in front of her, and supported her head in her lap. Mother's body was heavy and powerless. Juva struggled to clear her mind. She knew that time was running out, knew there was something she ought to do, but she didn't remember what.

Never let them see a weak blood reader.

Meaningless childlore, but the only clear thought she had. She asked Rugen to shut the door to the reader room so the client wouldn't see her mother helpless.

"Mother?"

Was she breathing? Juva forced her head to the side and dug her fingers into her mother's black-painted mouth. Her tongue felt warm and swollen. Her mother jerked with a spasm and vomited. Bloody vomit poured out onto the carpet, soaking into the phases-of-the-moon pattern like an eclipse.

Mother . . .

She couldn't lie like that, she would suffocate. Juva took hold under her arms and pulled her up higher onto her lap. The blood reader claw on her thumb scraped the floor. Juva pulled it off and threw it aside. The articulated ring rolled across the carpet and lay pointing up at the ceiling. Juva heard something break and turned. Ive stood with her hand over her mouth with a sea of glass shards in front of her. Someone yelled. Doors slammed.

Solde? Where was Solde?

Heimilla came running, her skirts lifted over the broken glass. The mistress of the house took charge without hesitating. She sent Ive out to fetch Dr. Emelstein and sent the new blood reader assistant into the waiting room to chase the people home.

Gomm, the cook, ran in, wiping his hands on his apron. He helped Juva lift Lagalune to her feet.

"Burn him," Mother mumbled as if she were dreaming. They supported her into her chamber and got her into the black, four-poster bed.

Juva untied her mother's jewelry, long cords with bone adornments, which had wrapped around her neck.

"Juva?" Her eyes darted around, as if she were blind. She reached out a hand and felt her way up Juva's arm.

"I'm here, Mother." The words thickened in her throat.

"What did you give her to eat?" asked Rugen, who stood in the doorway staring into the kitchen.

Gomm wilted and stammered an answer. "What *hasn't* she eaten? She . . . she eats like a bear. I haven't . . . ."

Juva stared at Rugen. He was the wrong man in the wrong place at the wrong time. A scoundrel. An asshole. A blood slave. And now he was scaring the wits out of the cook with his speculations.

"Go, Rugen! Leave us!" She pointed for him to leave.

Rugen shrugged and left the room. The cook hesitated but followed him.

"Burn him, Juva. You have to burn him."

Juva found a glass of water on the nightstand and tried to get her mother to drink, but she brushed the glass aside and raised herself up in the bed. This ended in a coughing fit. Blood rained over the pillow, and her mother stared at it. Then she lay down on her back, suddenly calmer, and started to laugh. An unpleasant, out of place laughter.

"He fucking has balls. May he rot," she mumbled with a macabre, bloody smile.

Nafraím. He poisoned her, and she knows it.

Juva felt paralyzed. Numb. Unable to act or feel.

Lagalune tightened her grip around Juva's arm and looked at her, her eyes suddenly clear. Her smile faded. "Juva . . . You have to . . ." Her voice failed. She gulped and tried again.

"You have to burn him, Juva. Burn the devil! You mustn't let them get him. Find my cards and burn him. The devil is the blood, Juva. The devil is the blood. It would break Solde. She's not like you. You wanted to, difficult child . . . You know that, Juva. You saw him. Do you remember? The iron wolf? You called him . . . the iron wolf."

Juva stared at the pale hand clutching her forearm, as if it wanted to pull her with it to Drukna. A chill chased down her spine.

The iron wolf . . .

The words bored into her head, and it felt as if her skull would crack. The memories came like a flood, all at once. She felt helpless, drowning. She was little. She had drawn the wolf for the first time. Mother had been so strange, so furious. Threw her drawing into the fire and hit her. Juva reached for her cheek now, frightened that the pain could feel so fresh.

Then Mother had laughed at her. Had said she was making it up, that she should never speak of him. The iron wolf. The wolf in the cupboard. The devil. All these names, for a monster they had forced her to forget.

And now she was lying there pleading with her to remember? Juva's shock darkened into anger. How dare she? How in Drukna did she have the audacity to ask her to remember?! After a life of enforced forgetting? Laughable and confusing. Why?

Because she's dying.

That certainty stopped the flood of memories. Lagalune pulled her hand across her lips. Blood and black lip wax colored her cheek. A final show. Mother's very last drama, and it wasn't even hers. This was him, Nafraím. The warow brought death with him, always had, ever since Father.

The vardari wanted to kill Mother because she had said no. To what? What was it that they wanted that Mother didn't want to give them?

Mother smiled, her teeth black. She wheezed like someone who had drowned.

"Solde . . . Don't leave Solde alone. She will never be able to endure it, you know that's true. It was always true. The devil is *your* destiny. You are the blood reader. You've felt it your whole life, Juva. The paperwork . . . The desk. Your name. All . . . yours."

Lagalune squeezed her eyes closed in a grimace of pain. "I should ask, Juva. I should explain, but you're as stubborn as Svartna. Don't let them get the devil. Burn him!"

Her pupils shrank to pinpoints and a pungent odor of feces revealed that she had lost control of her body.

"They won't get him, Mother," Juva said, and put a hand on her mother's forehead. It was warm and clammy.

Her mother fixed her eyes on her. "Juva, what have I always said about the devil?"

Juva didn't know if she should laugh or cry. So, so many things had been said about the devil in that house, more than any child should hear, and more than anyone could remember. Mother's eyes took on a faraway look, as if she were focused on something else, far beyond Juva. Then she let go of her life. Her face wilted. Her cheeks went limp.

Juva turned her back on her mother but remained seated on the edge of her bed, staring at a couple of drops of blood on the floor near the door. She felt completely empty. She knew that was wrong. That wasn't what she was meant to feel.

Reverberations from the front door echoed through the house, voices in the front hall, then a wail that could only have come from Solde.

The sensible part of her mother's feverish words blew through her chest like an icy wind.

The paperwork . . . All yours.

If there were inheritance papers, she needed to find them before Solde did, find them and destroy them. Juva yanked open the nightstand drawer and groped for the key she knew would be in there. She pushed away the flask of blood pearls and felt the key under her fingers. Solde's footsteps clicked down the hallway. Juva stuck the key in her pocket and closed the drawer.

Solde came sweeping in and stopped abruptly in front of the bed. She put a hand over her nose and took a step back. Her eyes were wide in disbelief. She looked at Juva and her shock faded. Gave way to something else, something far uglier. Her upper lip pulled up in an animal-like expression.

"You're going to try for it now, huh? Lie your way into the house and the job?"

Juva closed her eyes. Those words embodied everything she hated about blood readers. The irresponsible wordplay that allowed them to speculate, accuse, and decide without considering the consequences. How could such small words contain so much nastiness?

She looked down at her own hands and had the uncanny feeling that they were nailed to her thighs. One nail for each of her mother's words.

Solde. Don't leave her alone.

"What did she say?" Solde asked, slipping around the bedpost to come closer.

Her red wool skirt was wet from the snow along the bottom and a cluster of ice crystals glittered like broken glass at the waist. She still had her shoes on, and she was holding their mother's ring in her hand, the blood reader claw. She must have picked it up from the floor in the front hall as she learned Mother was dying.

It occurred to Juva that, although Solde was the one who was more like Mother, Solde hadn't loved her, either. But Solde was only sixteen, and regardless of how she felt about Mother, she had never had the desire to leave home. This was all she knew, all she had wanted. To become a blood reader, to gain a seat in the Seida Guild. The ring she clutched was more important than her mother's life.

Solde pointed the silver claw at her. "No one will believe you, Juva. No one! You don't even need to try. You know what you are, you hunting whore! You belong on your back underneath old men in Hidehall, not here. *I'm* the one who's the blood reader, and I can tell you exactly who you are!"

Juva imagined that she could taste her words, like a rotten apple, bitter and spoiled. She shook her head.

"No, Solde. All you're telling me now is who *you* are."

Solde's hand twitched, as if she were going to lash out, but she would never dare go that far. She leaned toward Juva and hissed. "What did she say? Answer me!"

Juva felt emptiness mixed with a slight thirst for revenge. She could take everything from Solde now. Everything she had owned, everything she had desired. Her overly nasty mouth could be shut up, once and for all. But what would she do then, a broken sixteen-year-old girl? This was all she had and all she could do. And Juva didn't want it, not for anything in the world.

Juva looked up. They weren't alone in the room anymore. Heimilla walked over to the bed and closed Lagalune's eyes. Gomm and Rugen stood in the doorway as if paralyzed. Friesa, the new assistant blood reader, was behind them. She was crying. She was the only one.

They were looking at Juva, all of them, and she realized that her sister wasn't the only one who wanted to know what Mother had said. The serving staff also wanted to know. The Seida Guild would come to find out. And soon all of Náklav would demand to know. Who was the next blood reader in the Sannseyr house?

Juva stood up. Her feet tingled, as if they were asleep.

"She said it was yours, Solde. It's all yours."

An enormous weight seemed to dissolve within Solde. Her shoulders lowered, her face softened, almost like Mother's had done, and the blood returned to her lips. A perverse relief, by a bed that stank of death. Juva pushed past her, past the others, and left the room, relieved that they had let her go. She had to act fast, before it occurred to Solde to look for the paperwork.

She made sure that none of them were following her before she climbed the stairs in the front hall and entered the study. The fireplace was dead, the room dark and cold. The wind had picked up outside, making one window tinkle faintly, like a child just learning how to whistle. Father peered down at her from the painting on the wall, and her courage threatened to fail. But she was so close now. This was the last thing she needed to do. Then she could go back to the life she had had before Solde had turned up in Hidehall, back to being Juva the Hunter. Although now she would hunt different wolves.

The vardari will pay for this. For everything.

There was a drawer on either side of the desk and both were locked. Juva heard the front door downstairs again. Probably Ive with Dr. Emelstein, as if there was anything he could have done. She had to hurry.

The ashtray was on the left. The only thing Mother did with her left hand was smoke, so it must be the right drawer. Juva stuck the key in the lock and turned it. It made a small click and she pulled out the drawer. The papers she had feared would be there were on top, presumably the last thing Lagalune had done.

There were two sheets of paper and they were identical. Juva picked one up and skimmed through the text, which was far too ornate to have been written by Lagalune. It was the lawyer's work, with a blue seal from Náklabank. All her mother had done was fill in Juva's name on a thin, black line in the middle of the text and signed at the bottom.

Lagalune Sannseyr, it said. With a hurried signature she had left the house, the wealth, and the seat on the Seida Guild to Juva.

Why? Mother must have known that Juva would refuse, so what was the point of such drama?

She thought she would have time to explain.

A smaller sum was set aside for what the document coolly termed the "non-heir," a poor consolation that would never be enough for Solde.

Juva lit the oil lamp and screwed the wick up until the flame started to darken the glass with soot. She rolled up the two pages and said a silent prayer that one of them was meant for the bank and that they didn't already have a copy.

Then she did what she always did: set fire to the pages.

Usually, she never had a clear sense of why she did this. All she knew was that she needed to, otherwise terrible things would happen. The wolf could awaken. Someone could die. But this was no wolf she was burning, and she knew exactly what catastrophe she was averting as the flame devoured the paper. This was no hysterical act fueled by anxiety. This was the beginning of freedom for both her and Solde.

She tossed the burning pages into the fireplace. They curled up into a black ball, which she crushed into dust.

She glanced up at Father again. He was the same as always. Valjar. Immortalized on a canvas. There was a painting hanging next to his, a smaller one of her and Solde, which had been painted just before Father died. Juva was only seven, but she thought she looked older. Solde was four and hanging onto Juva's back with her arms around her neck. Juva had never liked the picture. It looked like her little sister was trying to strangle her.

She put out the oil lamp and left the room. At some point, she would need to put the key back in her mother's bedroom. Juva started down the stairs but stopped on the step she had stood on when Nafraím was there.

Her memories had been in absolute chaos that day. They seemed tidier now, thanks to her mother's words.

Iron wolf.

This was where she had dreamt she had seen him. Made it up. Imagined it because it had never happened. That was what Mother had said. Juva was difficult and anxious, a disobedient child, who was never to speak of the wolf again. Not to draw him, either, because he was the devil, her mother had said as she'd thrown the drawing in the fireplace. Burned him.

Do you want him to become real? He will if you talk about him, and he will do gruesome things!

The fire in the front hall was going out and she heard muffled voices from her mother's bedroom. Dr. Emelstein and Solde, and Freisa who was still crying. Someone had opened the door to the blood reader room again. There was still time to find the card if she wanted . . .

She felt like an idiot for even having that thought. Was she supposed to fall for her mother's drama, even after she was dead? Burn a card without any idea why?

Because Nafraím wants it?

Juva had been burning devils her whole life, so why not one

146

more? It couldn't do any harm, and it was what her mother had wanted.

She slipped into the reader room. Mother had been in the middle of a reading, so the box was open and the wall lamps were lit. Her chair lay overturned on the floor. Juva felt a sinking feeling in her chest, a sudden grief that she forced back. If she was going to grieve, it would have to be later.

She picked up the cards. Pale, leaf-thin whale cartilage with black images. It would take corpsewood to burn them, and even then, they'd probably only melt. It had been just a week since she had stood there, thinking that the cards had survived many generations of Sannseyrs and would surely survive Solde as well.

She looked up at the wolf spread across the entire wall, painted by her great-grandmother Síla.

We drew wolves, both of us.

Juva hesitated with the cards in her hand. She was about to destroy something that was older than she was, older than her mother and her grandmother. It felt wrong, a completely unexpected feeling, seeing value in something that had to do with blood reading.

A silent laugh died away before it reached her lips. She had spent a lifetime fighting her way out of this house and now that her mother was dead, she was finally free. What kind of crazy time was this to become sentimental? It was too late to think about her roots now.

The cards were small, smaller than the paper cards many of the other blood readers used. The illustrations were captivating, bordered with symbols and runes, but with simple lines. The moon, the raven, the knife, the secret . . .

The devil.

The card with the devil did not stick out in any way Juva could detect. The picture depicted a strong man with a wolf head, not unlike what she usually drew herself.

"Juva? Has anyone seen Juva?" Solde's voice cut through the entry hall.

Juva put the cards where they belonged and closed the box. If she was going to burn anything, she'd have to do it later. There would always be time. That was the only thing she knew for sure about the devil. He never went away.

THE CARD

Juva had woken up before dawn after sleeping as heavily as the dead, which must have been a first in that house. Heimilla had already notified the Seida Guild, who sent the body washers right away. Three women, so old that they seemed only weeks from Drukna themselves, but they worked as if they had never done anything else. They were plainly dressed, in wool and linen, with sleeves that could be gathered up and secured above the elbow, as if they were going to help with a calving.

They prepared Mother for the mortuary chamber in Jólshov. Washed her and dressed her in a black lace dress. Her lip wax was removed. Her hair was braided and artfully put up in a way she herself had never been in the custom of wearing it. The blood reader makeup and the sallow skin on her cigar fingers was all that revealed it was Lagalune and not some complete stranger lying in the four-poster bed. Juva had the uncomfortable realization that this was her mother's actual appearance. Everything else had been a mask.

The next to arrive were Ogny and Maruska, Mother's closest friends, who would need to lead the Seida Guild on their own now. No, they would lead with Solde. That thought seemed absurd.

Ogny Volsung was over seventy, with skin like shriveled leather. Her cheeks drooped, her eyes were sunken, and her ears were weighed down with iron rings that looked like shields. Little amulets jingled on her forehead from a chain she had secured in her gray hair. She ordered Gomm to make blood cookies and pound cake, as if she owned the house, and when she yelled with her hoarse voice, a tendon in her neck tensed so that it looked like she had swallowed a stick.

Maruska was younger, around fifty, with eyes that made Juva feel like she was being stabbed. Her red hair sat stiff as a lacquer bowl, and the corners of her mouth turned down in a perpetual sneer. Together they were everything people associated with the blood reader guild: smug and inflexible with a phony aura of mysticism that Juva had spent many years learning to see through. Solde, with her paltry sixteen summers, would be eaten alive.

It would break Solde. She's not like you.

Mother's words tormented her thoughts, but Juva had done all she could do, given Solde what she wanted. The inheritance letters were burned. The key to the desk was back in the nightstand drawer. It was over. All that remained was to survive the wake.

If she managed that, it would be thanks to Ester, who had come by with a welcome bottle of whiskey. In addition, Juva had already greedily downed three mugs of hoggthorn tea and was so little aware of her own heart that she could have been dead.

Her anxiety lay dormant. She was numb.

She hadn't seen Rugen since yesterday. Maybe not so strange since she had asked him to leave, but she hadn't expected him to listen, just like that, without any further ado.

Slowly but surely, the Sannseyr home filled with people from all over Náklav, who, to varying degrees, had mastered the balancing act that a blood reader wake required. Grief for the deceased and joy for the heir, a split state that even Solde appeared to be struggling with. Although the most difficult aspect for her appeared to be the tight skirt that forced her to take small, mincing steps, rendering her useless for any practical purpose. Not that she had anything else to do besides receive the stream of congratulations and condolences.

Ogny, Maruska, and their daughters, who were getting up there in years themselves, claimed much of Solde's time and her ghostly smile grew ever stiffer. Almost as if she had no idea how to relate to the sisterhood she had dreamt of becoming part of. The Sannseyr portion of the governing threesome—Sannseyr, Volsung, and Auste—was in place.

Juva did her best to be invisible, and that wasn't difficult. People avoided exchanging more words than absolutely necessary with her. They offered their condolences with shifty eyes that revealed they were speaking of the death but also of the loss of the estate and the land. Juva had gone from being a Sannseyr to being a hair in the soup.

She slunk around the house and overheard the most incredible things. Lorn Selver, a loud jarl and estate owner, was appraising the house along with another stick-in-the-mud from the commerce guild. They were excessively impressed with the black foyer and its magnificent staircase. Two boys were pushing and poking at the glass cabinet with the stuffed raven, hoping to obtain a free fortune. The raven didn't budge.

Two members of the Seida Guild, Ilja and Flo, stood in the foyer admiring Mother's gloomy decorative objects as they talked about how Gyta was such a dull month to die in. Lagalune was probably clawing at the shroud covering her for not having managed to die on the spring equinox. Then the spring run might even have been canceled.

Juva recognized her mother's banker. He was sitting on the skeleton-like wrought iron bench with a plate of blood cookies in his lap, and she imagined that he was eyeing her distrustfully. Did he know that something was wrong with the inheritance? Had Lagalune told him her actual plans?

As if she ever told people what her plans were.

Some people said that the death had been sudden. Others said she had been ill and had known she was going to die. After all, she was a blood reader. There were rumblings about food poisoning, which was Dr. Emelstein's conclusion. Juva had to bite her tongue not to divulge the answer.

She wasn't sick. She was murdered by the vardari.

She'd already had that conversation with the family doctor yesterday. Food poisoning? When in the entire history of Slokna had anyone ever thrown up their lungs due to bad fish?

Emelstein knew it, and he knew who was responsible, that much was clearly written on the cheerless look in his eyes. He had set down his bag, folded his hands in his lap, and acknowledged that by definition "unnatural poisoning" required an agent to perform the act.

It had taken Juva a second to understand what he was trying to tell her. A murder required a murderer, and no one would go after the vardari. At best, it would remain unsolved; at worst the law would take the easy way out and come after her or the cook. Dr. Emelstein's generous description—using the term "food poisoning"—was meant to protect them.

That thought was heavy as a stone, and it pulled her down until all she said and heard was dark and ugly. Afterward, Dr. Emelstein had given her more hoggthorn and asked how her heart and her panic attacks were.

"Jufa . . ."

She jumped. Broddmar, with his toothless pronunciation of her name, caused something inside her to break. He pulled her to him with just one arm and patted her casually on the back. He didn't say a word about her mother or how sorry he was.

"Rough weather is rough weather," he mumbled. "Nothing more to say about it."

Juva took a step back and found her equilibrium again. "Next time you dress in red," she said, "I'm coming. You can't use my mother as an excuse anymore."

Broddmar subtly scanned the room and then pulled her into the shadows under the stairs. "I can use the fact that I don't want to have to come here again for *your* wake."

"Are you saying I'm not as good a hunter as you?"

"Juva . . ."

"No! No, Broddmar, no more excuses. If you don't want me along, then just tell me the truth. Am I too bad a hunter to hunt with you?"

Juva knew she was good enough, and she knew he would never say otherwise, but he chewed on his gums as if he were going to try.

"So that's all you want?" he asked. "Permission to hunt sick, innocent people, and sacrifice them? A red hunter, a bleeder, a bloodhound—was that what you dreamt of becoming when you were a little girl?"

"They aren't innocent," Juva said, looking away. "They're blood slaves. They know they can get sick, and they know that, when they do, they will turn into killers!"

Broddmar grasped her chin and forced her to look at him. "Juva Sannseyr, wolf-sickness did not kill Lagalune and it did not kill your dad, either. You despise everything with canine teeth—wolves, people with wolf-sickness, the vardari. You blend them all together into one enemy that only exists in your head. That is not healthy. You get that, right?"

Juva pulled free. "Don't you dare," she hissed. "Not you, Broddmar. She said the same thing my whole life, that it was all in my head. I grew up in a cursed house with a mother who made me believe I was crazy, and no one can do that to me again. I know what I'm talking about. *Never* say it's crazy, do you hear me? I hunt wolves for the same reason you do, because it's a job, because the city needs the blood for the stone gates. But what we live on, others die from. I go on the wolf hunts and wolf-sickness is an effect that I'm responsible for. You think it's crazy, that I'm hunting a nightmare, but the truth is that it's our damned duty to clean up!"

Juva struggled to keep her cool. She had to shut up and let her argument sink in with Broddmar. He didn't need to know what really drove her. No door was closed to a red hunter. She could use the whole city, armed, free to collect canine teeth. She could get closer to those who were actually responsible, the ones selling the blood and creating addicts.

Broddmar pulled his hand over his sunken cheeks. The inconsolable look in his eyes told her she had won. "We can discuss it," he said.

Juva didn't have a chance to enjoy her victory because the guests had suddenly started flocking into the foyer, just inside the front door. So many people had come and gone that she hadn't noticed that someone was knocking again. Juva craned her neck to see what the commotion was about. A messenger from the court, with a letter of condolences from Queen Drøfn. Solde received it and put on the performance of her lifetime—grief-laden, humble, and grateful, without seeming overwhelmed.

While the guests swarmed around Solde, Juva sensed movement out of the corner of her eye. The door to the blood reader room had closed, as if someone had gone in there. It must be Ive or one of the other staff members. No one else would have gone into the home's most sacred space in the middle of a wake. Would they?

The devil. Don't let them get him.

Juva left Broddmar and made her way through the crowd of people to the other side of the foyer. She opened the door a crack. Ogny stood at the table with her fingers on the card box, as if she had just opened it. She spotted Juva and her hand twitched reflexively. That was revealing, but she covered it by letting out a relieved sigh and putting her hand to her chest.

"Oh, Juva! Muune preserve me, you startled me!"

Juva didn't respond. Her heart fluttered as if it were shaking off the hoggthorn. Mother's final words hadn't been a fever dream. The evidence was right in front of her.

The silence around them thickened. A rare touch of doubt crossed Ogny's face, and she appeared to recognize that some explanation was required. She stroked her wrinkled hand over the rust-colored stains on the table.

"Dearest Lagalune . . . It's unfathomable that she's gone. I still feel close to her, in here."

"You're missing the queen's condolences," Juva said, walking into the room and pointing to the door.

Ogny took the hint. "An old person like me is always the last to know," Ogny said with a fake laugh as if she knew that her claim fell down under its own unreasonableness.

Juva waited until she had left the room, then she flipped through the cards until she found the devil.

Find my cards. Don't let them get him.

Juva had assumed that her mother meant Nafraím and the rest of the vardari. What if she'd meant the Seida Guild? Ogny and Maruska? And what in Drukna did that seventy-year-old guild master want with a blood reader card that could be bought anywhere in Náklav?

The devil is the blood. It would break Solde.

Juva glanced up at the wolf, Síla Sannseyr's mural. A contract with the devil, that's how the blood readers had gotten their powers, which had never been anything other than an extremely ordinary insight into human nature, made keener by blood pearls. Was the devil in her hand an access card to the wolf blood? A code to buy from Nafraím?

But why was Ogny looking for it, in that case? Didn't she have her own? And why did Mother want her to burn it? Was it dangerous in the wrong hands? Maybe it could be a way to prevent Solde from becoming a blood user . . .

Consideration? From Lagalune? Hardly.

Juva pulled up her shirt and wedged the card under the corset stays, pushing it up toward her bra. The devil felt cool against her skin, like a warning.

Did Mother die for this? Why?

Juva was fumbling around in the dark and she hated that, had done far too much of it. Her whole life was a patchwork quilt of distorted fragments that refused to fit together. But now at least she had something she never had before: the certainty that the fragments were real. And that she had been subjected to that grotesque confusion deliberately and on purpose.

The iron wolf.

The beast she had been drawing since she was a child had been real, not imaginary. Father had been killed by someone with wolf-sickness, a bloodthirsty beast. What still didn't make any sense was why they had kept that a secret. Why lie about it?

Juva feared that Broddmar was right. She was crazy. She was mixing up her mother's words with memories and fairy tales. All she knew for sure was that the card pressed against her skin was real, both to the Seida Guild and to the warow, and that was reason enough to destroy it.

She opened the door and slipped back into the busy foyer. The queen's messenger had left, and Juva couldn't see Solde or Ogny anywhere. But she heard a familiar voice beside her.

"Who the wolf crotch *are* all these people?"

Juva turned to Rugen, who sat on the armrest of the skeleton bench. Where had he been? And why was he back again? Wasn't his crisis over? She didn't have a chance to ask before he pulled her to him and pretended he was hiding from everyone else.

"Save me, Juva," he said, unexpectedly playfully.

His hands were warm around her waist. Warm hand against the cold devil. Juva pulled away, mostly because she actually was happy to see him, a realization she would have preferred to do without.

PROMISES

Rugen was struggling to keep his eyes open. It was early, and Gaula knew he hadn't exactly been sleeping well the last few weeks. Death had begun circling dangerously close. Leife was taken by Alette, Alette was taken by the hunter, and Lagalune . . . Well, everything indicated that she had been killed by the man he was supposed to meet now. When you added a toothache and his general impecuniousness, that was more than enough to be called a curse.

The blood cravings had gotten stronger. Plus, he was running low on the sketchy brew. He would have given a lot to sink into a bed made with silk sheets with fistfuls of blood pearls and stay there until Drukna took him, but he had a job to do. The only job that could keep him alive. If only he could steer clear of that menace dressed in red with the wolf . . .

The streets lay silent and veiled in fog. He could hardly see his own feet but could hear his footsteps on the cobblestones and the distant rhythm of the ocean. The buildings leaned over him and it felt like the beginning of a nightmare. He reached the end of Skjepnasnaret and almost walked right into a ladder. Fear blew through his chest, but it was only a repairman who kept the lamps lit and running.

"Slow down, man!" he heard from the top of the ladder.

Rugen didn't bother to answer and kept walking, unable to shake his jitters. He was constantly on pins and needles because it wasn't just the bleeder who was hunting now. People were terrified of wolf-sickness, and someone had been murdered down by the rafts. It was discovered too late that the victim didn't have wolf-sickness. He was just a confused weirdo with crooked teeth. Not that anyone cared about people from the rafts—drinkers, drudges, and whores that the city didn't have room for, literally. They built wooden shacks on floating pallets, which the storms smashed to splinters almost every single year.

In one sense, the riffraff had done that nitwit a favor by saving him from a death by drowning. But talk about being in the wrong place at the wrong time.

With the wrong teeth.

Rugen rounded the northern tip of Kingshill and was nearly mowed down by a horse and cart. He was so used to traveling in narrow alleyways that he forgot to look. He needed to pay attention, stop thinking so much.

He spotted Nafraím at the foot of the stairs, right where he had promised to be. Rugen was still thinking about the raving laborer from the rafts, and the contrast couldn't have been greater. Nafraím was so impeccably dressed and refined that it seemed old-fashioned. He stood with his hands behind his back, wearing a double-breasted coat with a high collar. His leather cap was lined with fur and had ear flaps. It looked like the sort of thing the warriors wore in old paintings from the 1200s.

The very idea that the gate guards would stop someone like him or ask him to bare his teeth was downright laughable. Nafraím had an unassailable charm: powerful, rich, and a warow.

And a murderer.

Rugen pictured Lagalune Sannseyr sprawled in Juva's arms vomiting blood. Food poisoning, the doctor had said. Pure lies, everyone who had been in the house when it happened knew that. But it was probably the safest cause of death to list, because who besides the vardari would dare to kill a blood reader?

Rugen stuck his hands in his pockets as he approached so they wouldn't reveal how nervous he was. The question was no longer whether this man was a killer, but whether that changed anything.

Rugen set that thought aside. The time to come to terms with that was in the future. Because right now, Nafraím and the yellow filth in the little bottle were all that stood between him and the wolf-sickness.

Nafraím turned his back to him and started up the long staircase along the walls around Kingshill. "So . . . food poisoning, huh," he said as Rugen struggled to keep up.

Fuck.

He had hoped Nafraím wouldn't have heard the doctor's conclusion yet. Then he could have shared it as a bit of news, gained some ground, and used that to obtain more of that medicine.

Nafraím waited for him to catch up again before he continued. "But still no date for Solde's investiture? Are they unsure?"

"No, they talked about waiting until Lagalune's sepulture, that's all. It's coming. Guaranteed. Solde is totally into it already. Rather hysterical, if you ask me. I did say she would inherit. It could never have been Juva. She doesn't give a damn about these things. Seriously, I don't think she would have taken the position even if she was an only child."

"Well, it's unlikely that she would have had any choice then," Nafraím replied, giving no indication of being winded.

Rugen was struggling to keep up. His thighs burned with each step, and there was a seemingly infinite number of steps, built right into the wall that surrounded Náklaborg, the highest point in the city.

They reached the top of the lowermost section of the wall, and Nafraím was gracious enough to let him rest. The man looked like he could be anywhere between forty and sixty, but even so, he wasn't sweating. Was that a vardari thing? Great, that's just what they need-ed, for them not to even notice normal people's toil.

"Where are we going?" Rugen asked, regaining control of his breathing.

"Gudebro."

Rugen didn't bother to point out the obvious, that no one was allowed to cross Gudebro Bridge without a passport, and he wasn't particularly interested in defying the gate guards right now.

"Who was at the wake?" Nafraím asked, starting up the next flight of stairs.

"Who? Half the city must have been there!" Rugen regretted his statement right away. It was sadly obvious. He hurried to continue. "The Seida Guild, obviously. Ogny Volsung, that old prune, and the redheaded one. Their daughters, too. I think everyone from Juva's hunting team stopped by. The servants, of course. The cook makes the best pound cake I've ever tasted. The lady of the house, Heimilla, and a kitchen girl."

"I know who works in the house," Nafraím replied dryly.

"Oh, well, everyone who means anything was there. People in the commerce guild, banking people, a jarl . . . Lorn something or other, and a messenger from the queen came."

"Of course. Did you see or hear anything useful? Did the Seida Guild discuss any excursions or trips?"

"Yes, Lagalune and the two old blood reader ladies usually go to Kreknabork every year and have been to Skippalun several times. That must be significant, because there are paintings of both of those cities on the wall of the study. Then there's Hidehall, where Juva really lives. The hunting team uses a cabin sometimes in the woods, but that doesn't have anything to do with the Sannseyrs."

Rugen knew that none of this was of any use to Nafraím, and the silence that followed made him feel weak. He wished there was something to hold on to, but there was no railing, even though no one would survive a fall from up here. Couldn't they have made the steps a little wider at least? Rugen wasn't sure how much more of this he could take.

He looked up. In front of Nafraím, a round tower hung on the outside of the wall. It had an open passage that the stairs ran through. A gate guard sat inside the tower and stood up as soon as he spotted them. Nafraím showed him his hand, and the gate guard glanced at one of his silver rings. They were allowed to proceed without so much as one word being exchanged.

Rugen felt a touch of dissatisfaction over how simple that appeared to be. He had to remind himself that he had always known that's how it worked, that some people had it easier than others. Every single fight in his life was waged on the battlefield, but it was a war he aimed to win. Wasn't that why he was there?

They reached the top of the wall, and the city lay at their feet. Rugen rested against the stone wall and stared down at the shingled roofs with their ash-wood shingles laid in a fish-scale pattern that could be discerned through the rime frost. Many of the roofs were topped with strong wooden pegs meant to prevent the snow from slipping off and crashing down onto the streets below, where the mist crept like smoke. He had the impression that he was looking at the old ruins left after an enormous fire. A Náklav from a bleaker era.

He could see all of Ringmark and Skodda. The tip of Tunga in the north and the ships on their way into Dragsuget, to Nyhavn. So many people, determined to squeeze in on top of each other on an island with steep cliffs. Why?

The wooden dome over Nákla Henge stuck out among the other roofs and gave him his answer. The stones. It all had to do with them.

Rugen felt dizzy. He pulled back from the edge and turned toward the fortress that towered up from the middle of the hill. Náklaborg. Not exactly gorgeous, it required some goodwill to call it a palace.

A greenish-black colossus in a shell of walls that had half disintegrated. It looked like someone had started peeling the fortress and given up. But it was sumptuous on the inside, he had heard that from multiple girls who had worked in the kitchens there. It made them lustful, toiling away over pots and pans.

Rugen sighed.

"So, what are we doing here?" he asked.

"Be patient," Nafraím replied and kept walking.

Gudebro glittered before them, a snake of shiny ice that ran all the way around Kingshill. It wouldn't have been possible to stay on one's feet if it hadn't been for the narrow cobblestone footpaths on the other side.

Rugen followed Nafraím out onto the scariest part, an area that jutted out from the wall and hung poised over the rooftops. A snake's tongue on stone stilts, because some megalomaniac regent had wanted to go for a walk without encountering ordinary people. Rugen couldn't blame him. He would surely have done exactly the same thing.

Gudebro didn't lead anywhere. It just ended abruptly, a perilous promontory into mid-air. Buildings clung to the bridge supports below him, as if they had become greedy and started to devour the bridge. Rugen felt unwell, but Nafraím continued out to the end, seemingly unaffected.

"How are your teeth?" he asked.

"It's just the one that's a little loose," Rugen said, feeling with his tongue. "But I need more of that glop."

Nafraím stopped and let out a brief laugh. "That glop, as you call it, is an incredibly sophisticated mixture of exceedingly rare ingredients. It's not something you can simply pick up anywhere."

This is a negotiation.

Rugen swallowed. It felt as if his mouth had dried out.

"So, what else do you need?"

"I need you to stay where you are for a while longer. A lot is going to happen in the Sannseyr home going forward, and it is of utmost importance that we remain apprised. Do you think that can be arranged?"

There was no other answer but yes. Rugen had nothing to bargain with, other than his own time and a chance of finding out the answers that Nafraím needed.

"Sure." Rugen snorted. "I've been with the girl before and I can promise she hasn't forgotten it. Those were the best months of that wildcat's life. Give me a couple of days."

Nafraím regarded him with a hint of distaste.

Rugen felt his smile fade and groped for slightly more refined words. "I'll find out what you want to know, that's what I'm trying to say. But it would help if you could explain what you're looking for, then I won't have to fumble around blindly."

"I can't be any clearer than I was the last time."

"So, what then? Where they go, who comes and goes, what they talk about? You obviously haven't met Solde; she couldn't keep her mouth shut if her life depended on it, but that's fine. If you need a dissertation on fashion, furniture, or who's sleeping with who in this city, then I'll get it. Could I have more of that gl . . . sophisticated mixture now? Or should I just throw myself off this bridge since I'm going to die soon anyway?"

"Maybe so. If you care about anyone around you, then that would no doubt be the best solution. For them."

Rugen clenched his teeth and felt the nagging pain in his jaw. Nafraím's words were ruthless and delivered so quickly. He hadn't been prepared. Was that all he had to look forward to? An emerging madness, which was doomed to end with him chewing on people's necks?

Nafraím opened his coat, untied a pouch from his belt, and handed it to Rugen.

"It's enough to cover the debts you ran out on. And make sure you give Juva Sannseyr the rest of the money you owe her. She won't trust you until you've settled your account."

Rugen took the pouch without asking how he knew she had only received half the amount. The money felt delightfully heavy.

Nafraím smiled without looking away from the horizon.

"You're taking too dark a view of it, Rugen. Wolf-sickness doesn't need to be a death sentence. If you're strong enough, you can emerge from it unscathed. You may live for a long time yet, with a little help. A year, twenty years, or several hundred."

The words grabbed Rugen like hooks and held him firmly. He thirsted for answers but had no inkling of where to begin.

"Several hundred years? Are you serious? Why didn't the bleeder catch you a long time ago? And aren't the ones like you supposed to have the canine teeth? I've heard that warow are people with wolf-sickness who don't go crazy, but what the fuck . . . I've seen people with wolf-sickness, man, and they're not like you."

The warow regarded him with fire in his eyes.

"No," Nafraím said. "They're people like you."

Rugen felt like he'd been punched. Longing and rage fought within him. He didn't know what he wanted most, to bludgeon Nafraím or throw himself at his feet. But what would he bludgeon him for? Telling the truth? People with wolf-sickness didn't live in the hanging houses. They weren't swimming in money, and they didn't have rings that granted them free passage to the best life had to offer. The people who had wolf-sickness were the people in the rafts, blood slaves, addicts.

Nafraím took off his gloves and pulled out one of his teeth to reveal a perfect animal's canine that had been hiding underneath. Rugen stared at it, nauseated and wobbly. Nafraím pushed his hollow tooth cover back into place with his thumb and put his gloves back on as if nothing in particular had just happened.

"We all have different methods. Some use false teeth, some file them down, and a few keep them just the way they are. The shock you're feeling right now isn't about teeth, Rugen. You're grasping around, looking for a reason. You don't trust yourself, so you wonder why *I* do. But it's not you that I need to trust, it's your self-preservation instinct. The only thing I can be absolutely sure of is that you will always be the most important person in your own life."

Rugen knew he didn't have the upper hand here. He was talking to a warow, and he had no idea whether his words were insults or compliments. He was helpless, and he opened his mouth to say so, but Nafraím stopped him.

"Shh. Follow me, it only lasts for a second," he said and pointed.

A golden glow grew between the mountains on the horizon and set the ocean on fire.

The sun . . .

"It won't be visible from the city for a few more days," Nafraím said quietly, as if he were afraid of scaring it away. "You have to be up high to be first."

Rugen gaped. The first sliver of the spring sun, and it was as if it was conjured up by a vardari. For all the merciful gods, a real warow. The longing grew in his chest, a sudden desire he had never felt the like of. *Life.* He needed to live, to become one of them, raised up over darkness and winter, not having to go without anything. This was what he was born for.

To Drukna with red hunters, debts, illness, and whores. He deserved so infinitely much more. Rugen felt tears coming, as if he were a little kid, but he didn't have the strength to control himself. His heart was naked and laid bare. His body wild and hot. He had a pouch full of money in his hand, the sun was burning in the ocean, just for him, and he was on Gudebro with the man who could make him mean something.

Rugen couldn't tear his eyes off Nafraím. If the man had asked it, he would have split his ass for him. Gotten down on all fours on the cobblestones and taken him, without hesitating. Rugen feared that his thoughts would show outwardly, but the warow just eyed him and smiled cautiously.

"So . . . Shall we go down and buy sun kringles?" Nafraím turned and started back. He nodded toward Náklaborg. "I would have introduced you, by the way, but I'm afraid her Highness is away in Fimle."

"You know the queen?" Rugen couldn't help but laugh. "You've been inside the palace?"

"Been there? My dear boy, I built it. And lived there for many good years."

Rugen nearly dropped the coin pouch. Was that possible? The palace in Náklav was ancient, several hundred years old. He had never bothered to find out just how many.

"So, what happened?"

Nafraím's eyes took on a faraway look, as if he were looking at something a world away. He sighed.

"Peace. I gave it up for peace."

THE OCEAN TAKES

Juva had never seen a longer funeral procession. She glanced over her shoulder but couldn't see the end of it, just an infinitely long train of lanterns in the drizzle. A death in the Seida Guild always drew people, and Mother was a leader who had not made it to the age of fifty.

Juva recognized some of the mourners, folks who had worn down her mother's doorstep for years and spent Muune knows how much money making sure that they were not nearing their deaths. Others were here because this was an important place to be seen. Or maybe because they believed the myth that blood readers could pass on their powers before they vanished into the ocean.

Solde walked by Juva's side, the death horn dangling from her arm. She wore the same red theatrical number she'd been wearing when she turned up at Hidehall. The rain-drenched veil had started to stick to her face. Veils left the world feeling dreamlike, so Juva had decided to walk without one. She'd had enough of fuzzy, illusory things, more than enough of riddles. She wanted to see everything knife-sharply that evening, the very last thing she needed to do for Lagalune Sannseyr.

Náklav's persisting twilight had begun to recede. The spring melt was right around the corner, the month that ended with the spring equinox and the Yra Race. Soon enough the sun, which everyone missed, would keep them up all night. New light, new life.

It should have given her a feeling of freedom, but it had been poisoned by the vardari. Nafraím had taken Mother's life, and there was no indication that he would be called to answer for it. That thought burned like embers in her chest. Dangerous to dwell on, but impossible to overlook.

The procession wound its way along the old city wall on the south side of Skodda up toward Corpse Bay. The death drums rumbled behind her every time she managed to forget them. They lured curious people to their windows to peer down at Mother, who lay in the frontmost carriage, pulled by four men.

They had to finesse their way through the gate and then proceed down the slope along the outside of the cliffs. It was steep and Juva hoped the men were strong enough to hold the carriage. That thought felt strangely familiar, as if it had passed through her head before. Maybe when she was seven, on her way to her father's sepulture. Maybe no one had ever walked here without thinking that same thing. But the men held on and got the carriage all the way down to the sea.

They opened a door in the carriage and pulled out the bier. It was meant to evoke a boat, since people used to burn the dead on ships in the past. Now it was just a sort of pod of starched linen, stiff at both ends, like a pupa containing a larva, pregnant with Mother. The opening was a small tear, as if she were about to break her way out. Maybe emerge as someone other than she had been. Her body was wrapped in a shroud, so it could have been anyone at all lying in there.

Juva put her hand on Solde's arm, but she pulled away.

Of course. Never let them see a weak blood reader.

The bier was pushed over into the boat, which would take them to Kleft, the Skerry of the Dead. It stuck up from the ocean like a fang, bathed in the glow of the bonfire that kept ships at a safe distance. But not this one. This longship had been traveling back and forth for as long as she could remember, with the same, yellow-painted keel. To frighten Gaula, they said. Gaula feared fire.

Juva climbed aboard along with Solde and those the Seida Guild felt were closest to Mother. There were at least forty of them. Solde seemed to know them all. To Juva, they were strangers. At least she had Broddmar. He was there for her. The rest of the entourage stayed on shore.

The others found seats on the thwarts, and Juva spotted Maruska leaning over to Solde and whispering something to her. Solde looked around and shook her head. She had seemed unusually nervous the last several days. More anxious than mournful. Had it dawned on her yet that the Seida Guild would be demanding? Or was it just her age that now caused her to fear the position she had always wished for?

Juva sat down on one side, grabbed the oar with both hands, and started rowing in rhythm with the others. After a few strokes, the sweet pain began to burn in her shoulders, and she wished they could just keep rowing, hour after hour. But the boat dug into the beach a short while later. Solde sat in the bow and clutched the horn in her lap. Had she forgotten that she was supposed to fill it?

Juva gave her a little signal. Solde leaned over the side and filled the horn with seawater. Then they carried Mother up the slope, past the lighthouse, and out on the cliff where the rocks leaned out over the sea. The bier was placed on the first of the three ramps. This place had been used for sepultures for generations. The strong currents carried people all the way until Gaula took them to Drukna. Even if a person had died by drowning, they needed to drown once more in the realm of the dead. Become a part of Gaula's tentacles and pull others to their deaths. *Horrific*, Hanuk had said once on a hunt. They had been sitting around the campfire and comparing gods and rituals. Competing for the worst. Hanuk was from Aure, and he thought something must be wrong with people's heads if they thought death was worse than life.

Maybe he was right. All of Náklav was a madhouse.

So how long would Mother need to drown for? Would she get extra time for all the lies she had made her living off of her whole life? And where would she end up afterward, once Gaula was done with her? The Seida Guild claimed that all blood readers ended up with Muune to spend eternity whispering truths to the blood readers who were still alive. That belief ran deep enough that they still ate the tongues of their dead, a fact that was grotesque enough to secure Juva the victory in the competition with Hanuk.

Ogny lifted a corner of the cloth and revealed Mother's face. It seemed cold and artificial, and there was something unfamiliar and hollow about her cheeks, which revealed that her tongue was gone. Solde came over to the bier and poured seawater from the horn into Mother's blue mouth. Then it was done. Mother had taken the water, for the third and final time.

The onlookers pulled back a bit, and Solde touched the torch to the bier. The clothes had been sprinkled with oil of fire kelp, so it caught quickly and burned a sparking yellow. Soon, the whole funeral ship was in flames.

The bearers arrived and raised the head end of the ramp. For a second it looked as if Mother wouldn't go. As if her boat was stuck. One of the men gave it a discreet push. The burning bier slid off and dove down into the waves below. Juva couldn't see her hit the surface, just the yellow fire that spat out sparks in the depths, in that eerie way that only fire kelp did. Then everything became black again.

Those assembled broke up and walked back to the ship in scattered groups. Juva followed them, hesitating, feeling like she should have done something more. But all that remained was the wake at Jólshov. She could make out the fortress on the tip of Skodda, and it struck her that you only got to see Náklav from here when someone died.

In the jumble of lights atop the steep cliffs, she could roughly locate their house. Just above where the old wharves had been, and she remembered the stories about her great grandmother, Síla Sannseyr, who had hated the smell of smoked whale so intensely that she had demanded the wharves be relocated. Even though she was a blood reader, the city council had at first refused, but then they had faced the worst storm in a lifetime. What a woman she must have been, the woman who painted the wolf on the wall and who got the sailors to believe she could summon a storm when all she could do was read weather signs. Maybe you could inherit a gift for swindling people?

Was I born to be a liar?

Ogny came up beside Juva, pulling up her hood against the rain that had started afresh, and tried to make eye contact.

"She was never meant to inherit the position, was she?" Ogny said.

Juva suddenly felt colder. Her heart beat a warning, and she didn't dare respond. She kept walking as if she hadn't heard.

"Juva, this isn't something you can run away from. Solde doesn't know what she's supposed to know. She doesn't have something that Lagalune should have given to her, a proof she doesn't even know exists. But I believe you do . . ."

She knows I took the card.

Juva put her hand to her ear, as if the weather were making it difficult to hear.

"Who? What proof?" she said.

Part of her wanted to stop and ask her outright whether she meant the devil. As if that was proof of cooperation with the vardari. Warow drug pushers didn't care that people came down with wolf-sickness. But if she broke down now, she would lose her chance to let it disappear forever. She should burn it, like Mother had said. And worst of all: She would be forced to admit what Mother's final wishes had actually been.

That is never going to happen.

The ship was full and waiting only for Juva and Ogny.

The old woman asked Juva for help climbing aboard and used that opportunity to whisper, "We'll discuss this later. At the wake."

Juva climbed aboard after Ogny and looked at Solde who sat in the bow as pale as a corpse. The hem of her skirt was soaked, and her nearly white hair was plastered to her head. She stared out into the darkness, as if she were waiting for Gaula to break through the surface of the ocean at any moment. Solde's eyes met Juva's, and the emotion vanished in an instant. A stony face that she pulled down her veil to hide.

What in the world was going on between Solde and the guild? Juva wished she didn't care enough to wonder. The blood readers weren't her problem anymore. Hopefully the card being missing would keep Solde away from the problems, too. Away from blood use and Nafraím at any rate.

Juva sat on the thwart and moved her hand to rest discreetly below her breasts. She felt the edges of the card, which sat wedged under her corset. She had lived with the wolf her whole life but had never had him so close. The devil lay against her skin, following every move she made, like a lover.

BLOOD-SURE

Juva regretted having sat down. Everyone would notice when she stood up, and the need for that was already urgent. How long did a person have to stay at their own mother's wake? Could she get away soon?

It wasn't that she didn't feel sadness, because that was there. It just didn't feel the way it should. It was watered down with so many other things. Despair about the murder that no one would acknowledge, fear of what was to come. But the worst was the bitterness she struggled to keep a lid on. A stifling feeling that the murder robbed her of the right to be angry at Lagalune over everything that had happened. Muune had taken Mother in a gruesome way, and that was the final whitewashing, divine forgiveness. What kind of person could rage against someone who had been murdered?

But the grief clung around her on the outside, like a shroud, and threatened to constrict when she least expected it. She didn't want to be *here* when it happened. There were too many people here, and she knew almost none of them. They came, offered their condolences, ate, and left. There were so many, but there was room for them all since Muune's Hall was the biggest of all the many halls in Jólshov. And the most distinctive. It was all made of wood, built like a vaulted ship without any straight walls. But since it was so tall and narrow, it was known for its resemblance to a vagina. Lok had said it best when he got married here: A massive troll vagina.

The red lanterns just made the impression worse. They hung high, from a narrow balcony that Juva used to hide on, long before she was old enough to see the resemblance. Back then, she had been obsessed with the carved double doors, covered in wolves and snakes fighting for space, but captured forever in the detailed woodwork.

The Seida Guild itself sat at the end of the hall, in front of a stone wall with openings shaped like the phases of the moon. An enormous fireplace behind the wall made it look as though the symbols glowed. Solde sat under a burning waning moon and smiled stiffly, flanked by Ogny and Maruska. They hovered over her and hadn't given her a second's peace apart from when Ogny had given a speech about Mother during the Muune ceremony.

What if they don't accept her? What if they know what Mother actually wanted?

The beer horn rang through the room and helped settle everyone down. Cured meats, pickled herring, blood cookies, and beer were carried in and placed on the long tables. Juva looked up at Solde and the rest of the Seida Guild, who had each received their little piece of Mother's tongue. Hardly more than a pea, but it was madness all the same. Mother had been poisoned, and they knew it. At least Solde did.

Either the whole thing was an act with ox tongue or they were risking their lives. Juva stared at her own bowl of pickled herring and set down her fork. Even wolves couldn't have gotten her to eat anything.

Her heart started quivering in her chest, a sudden, nascent alarm. *No! Not now!*

She was surrounded by people, many of whom were looking her way and nodding their condolences. The worst conceivable time to lose your sense of reality.

Maybe she was imagining it? She so rarely had panic attacks when she was out. Juva pulled her hands over her face and felt them shaking. She forced herself to breathe more calmly, but her heart was beating double time. She felt hot and sweaty. The beer had softened people and they had started mingling between the long tables.

I survived the last time. I'll survive now, too.

She stood up, repeating the words in her mind over and over again as she looked for a way out. Her eyes were drawn up to the balcony, but there were other people up there already. A figure in the shadows, with his hands on his back.

Nafraím . . .

Juva stepped backward and nearly smacked into the door to the kitchen hallway, which was ajar.

Mother's murderer. At Mother's death rite. Her heart pounded and she could swear that it was beating its way higher and higher up her chest. The blood roared in her ears. She needed hoggthorn!

Nafraím noticed her and cocked his head to the side. A look of surprise crossed his face, as if he hadn't expected to see her there. It was so grotesquely backward! *He* was the one who had no business there. Hadn't he done enough damage?

The warow gave her a nod, a perverse offer of condolence from a killer, then he walked calmly down the stairs and left the room. Everything went quiet. It was as if he took all the sounds from the room with him and left her underwater.

Juva looked around and realized that no one else had noticed him and the sounds were still there. Small talk, clinking glasses, a bench scraping on the floor as someone stood up . . . But the sounds *inside* her were gone. They had vanished with him, and she could no longer hear her blood roaring.

She could hear Mother whispering from Drukna.

You're the blood reader. You've known it your whole life.

"Is everything all right?"

Juva heard someone speaking, but it didn't concern her. It came from another world. The front door was closed again, as if the warow had never been there. Had she imagined it?

No! I know what I saw!

Even Mother had admitted it as she was dying, that there wasn't anything wrong with Juva. These weren't the imaginings of a fretful child. She had felt or seen *something*. An animal, or someone with wolf-sickness. But she needed to think clearly and hold on to what was real, otherwise she would perish.

If blood readers could sense evil, like in the fairy tale, then every single member of the Seida Guild would have felt the same thing she just had, and none of them seemed even remotely frightened.

No, her panic had nothing to do with the vardari. It had always been there, and it could come over her at any time. A thousand different things could take her breath away and send her heart into a tizzy. Nafraím. Lying underneath a wolf that was trying to bite her. Being home in that damned house. Even Rugen, sometimes.

"Juva? Is everything all right?" Rugen's voice snapped her out of her trance.

For a second, she thought she was imagining him, too, but he stroked her arm, alive enough.

"What are you doing here?" she asked, and then realized that that wasn't such a nice thing to say. But Rugen had his own ability to disregard her insults.

"It's a wake, Juva. Probably the crappiest day in your life, and you thought I would let you go through it alone?" He spoke calmly and quietly, as if it had never been a matter of life and death, for him or for her.

His hand slid down around her waist and he pulled her into the kitchen hallway with him.

"Come on. Wakes are best when you're alone with someone." He held up a beer glass and looked at her. "Or would you rather hang out in there with the old people?"

She responded with a brief laugh and followed him. They quickly made their way through the hectic kitchen, as if they just needed to get something. It was a wake, where anything could happen, so no one stopped them. They climbed up a ladder and into an attic room with exposed timbers, which was packed with stored food. Large hams and smoked sausages dangled from overhead, and they had to wriggle their way between sacks of flour, wine barrels, and jars of pickled herring and jam. Juva hadn't thought she would ever feel hungry again, but the smell of smoke and lard made her stomach rumble.

They lay down on a pile of grain sacks. Rugen suddenly grabbed his jaw, as if something had stabbed him. He looked at her and shook his head. "A little stiff, that's all." The double entendre played at the corner of his mouth. He took a huge smoked sausage from a trough and held it in front of his crotch. "Sausage?"

Juva burst out laughing, and it was exceptionally wonderful even though she felt like she was betraying herself. Rugen was an idiot. He had stolen from her and run off without a word. People like that never changed. She mustn't forget.

Reading people, seeing them for what they were, wasn't much help if you had a strong desire to see something else.

But the beer was good and they were surrounded by abundance, away from the Seida Guild and the warow.

Rugen dug around in his pocket and handed her four coins. Twenty-two runes.

"That's the rest of what I owe you, plus a little more. Because I was an idiot. Because I *am* an idiot."

"You're an idiot if you think I'm going to argue with that," she replied and took the money.

It bothered her that she hesitated. She would receive a good bit of compensation even though Solde was taking the house and everything else, so Rugen needed the money more than her. But he didn't deserve that degree of consideration, and she felt weak to have even thought it.

He took her beer glass. "You were the only one who could drink me under the table, do you know that? I used to dream that we would travel, you and I. Eat and drink everything the world had to offer. In Kreknabork or wherever. Where you guys used to be."

"The beer is better here than in Kreknabork."

Juva made herself more comfortable, prepared for an argument that never came. She was also prepared for him to make a pass at her, but he didn't do that, either. Rugen was calmer than he had been when they were together before, and he was curious about her in a completely different way. They lay among the grain sacks and talked about Kreknabork and Skippalun, about places she had visited as a child, about Jólshov and all the hundreds of rooms there, and he listened and asked questions. They emptied the beer glass and he filled it with wine from one of the wine barrels. Left a coin on the top, as payment, even.

She asked what he was running away from, and in his tipsiness, he became warm and honest. Said he hadn't touched blood pearls in forever, that he had quit, but that there were people out there who didn't like that. People he would prefer to avoid.

When they finally climbed back down from the attic, she felt like it was possible for people to change. Or maybe she only hoped so? They were among the last to leave Jólshov, and there was no sign of either Solde or the Seida Guild.

Rugen was right. He couldn't handle his liquor as well as she could, and she had to support him most of the way home as he muttered apologies for everything he had been saying all night. It had stopped raining. Mother's sepulture was completed. Juva had run off and there she was, dragging back a drunken fool who had left her.

What is wrong with me?

She helped him up the front steps and into the foyer. He laughed and fell backward into the wall as she untied his shoes. The house was deathly quiet, so Solde was probably already in bed. The servants had gone home, and the corpsewood in the fireplace was giving off its final glow.

Juva helped Rugen to the stairs and glanced down the hallway. The door to her mother's room stood open and a faint light flickered inside. That familiar flutter returned to her heart. A vague uneasiness.

Juva walked over to the doorway and looked in. Solde sat snuffling on the floor without any clothes on with her back resting against Mother's black four-poster bed, as if someone had just flung her off it. In Svartna, she must be even drunker than Rugen!

"Solde?!" Juva went in, stepping in something wet and disgusting.

Blood pearls . . .

Mother's glass flask lay on the floor by the edge of the carpet, and it was empty. Blood pearls lay scattered about like pale red hailstones.

"Solde, what have you done?!"

Juva knelt beside her, pulled the blanket off the bed, and covered her.

Solde smiled lethargically, with blood between her teeth. "Juva . . . They asked. They asked the whole time; they asked about the weirdest things. The blood answers, doesn't it, Juva? That's what they always said, that the answers are in the blood and I know all the answers. Ask me anything at all, I know. But it got so hot."

She rested her head on the bed. Her eyes rolled, like a wild animal.

179

I've seen that before. White eyes.

Rugen came in, suddenly scared sober. "I thought you hated blood use?"

"Does it look like I'm the one with a problem here?!" Juva hissed back. "The pearls were Mother's. The blood readers use them. Tell me what to do!"

"How much did she take? Fuck, there's a fortune's worth of blood pearls here." Rugen stared at the floor.

He came over to her, careful about where he put his feet, and helped her lift Solde onto the bed. Not that that was necessary, she didn't weigh much, as thin as she was.

Solde pointed to Rugen as if she had just noticed him and smiled flirtatiously.

"You . . . Do you know what Lorn Selver offered if he could de-flower me? Three hundred runes! Do you have three hundred runes? You're not a jarl or anything, but you can have me if you've got that much."

Juva grasped her chin and turned her face toward her. "How many did you take?" she demanded.

"None, really!" Solde slurred. "I'm not like you, Juva, someone who'll sleep with anyone."

"Blood pearls, Solde! How many blood pearls did you take?" Juva's cheeks burned. "It's not true, what she's saying," she told Rugen. "You were my second, in my whole life."

She hated that she felt like she had to say that, as if it were any of his business.

"So what?" Rugen shrugged. "You weren't my first, second, or third, but you were the best."

"How sweet," Solde said with a scornful laugh. "It's because you haven't had someone who was unused yet. Do you want to try? You don't need three hundred runes, you can have me. All I want in exchange is the devil." The look in her eyes faded, and she seemed to forget her desire just as fast as it had come over her. "Juva, they asked for the devil, and that's so strange, because who walks around with a devil? He's missing, Ogny said. She's missing the devil, and I didn't know what to say."

Her eyes lit up again, full of answers. Blood-sure.

"You can draw one for me!" Solde said. "You draw devils, and I know you don't need them all. We're sisters, you have to give me one!"

Juva put a pillow under Solde's head. She felt sick to her stomach. This was her fault. She had passed the inheritance to Solde, but she'd apparently also rendered it useless even though she couldn't fathom why. But if she had given Ogny the card, they wouldn't be pressuring Solde for it.

Solde's head sank down into the pillow and she murmured her pleasure. Juva placed a hand on her forehead and realized that she hadn't done that for many years. Closeness was a rare commodity in the Sannseyr home.

"Rugen, how dangerous is this? Can she die from this?"

Rugen sat down on the edge of the bed. The look in his eyes was answer enough, but he mumbled anyway, "Maybe not right now, but . . . "

Juva felt despair washing through her body.

Wolf-sickness.

Stupid Solde! This was suicide. How could she have taken such a risk? She knew what could happen, and now she had consumed half a flask of blood pearls as if she were invincible. She didn't have a chance. Solde was going to become one of the ones Broddmar had to kill, one of the ones she had been fighting to be allowed to kill.

Juva squatted down and swept the pearls on the floor together. Her hands were shaking. The house felt alive and demanding around her. It sucked away her vital energy. This day had been too much, she needed hoggthorn.

Mother knew. She knew that Solde wouldn't be able to cope with blood pearls. I should have done more than take the devil. I should have gotten rid of the pearls. I should have . . .

"Juva," Rugen grasped her arm and looked at her. "Leave them. We have time. She's going to sleep for a long time."

Juva nodded. She got up, went to the kitchen, and heard Rugen following her. The hearth was still hot under the cook plate, thank goodness for corpsewood. She pulled the kettle over.

Rugen sat down at the table and pulled his hand through his brown curls.

"What are *they* going to do with blood pearls?" he asked. "Have visions? Zone out? What's the point?"

Juva let out a snort. "You're older than I am, Rugen, you should have understood this ages ago."

"Seriously, Juva. I've never seen a blood reader on drugs."

She sighed. "Listen, they don't get high; that's not why they take it. Mother used to take *one* single pearl before she met her most important clients. The wolf blood heightens their awareness. She could smell when people were lying, see when their pulse sped up and their pupils dilated. Pure gold when you make your living off of reading people, right? And not just anyone can get their hands on it, only the Seida Guild, as far as I know. Maybe they mix other stuff into it, I have no idea. But they get that filth from . . ." Juva gulped. She couldn't make herself say the name she had thought. "From the vardari."

She took the tea caddy down from the shelf and sprinkled crushed hoggthorn into a mug.

"But then why did Solde do it?" Rugen asked. "I mean, she must know that she can get wolf-sickness?"

"She hasn't used them before. She's no slave, not like you."

Juva had no idea why she wanted to pick a fight, but she felt wrung out like a rag, pressured, on the verge of unraveling.

"Like me . . . What about you, then?" he asked, without a trace of anger.

"What are you talking about?" Juva took a sip of her tea.

He nodded at her mug. "Haven't you been making tea from those berries your whole life? There's not a fucking bit of difference. We're both slaves. We do what we do to avoid feeling, no matter what that requires. Don't you go around thinking you're somehow different from me, Juva."

He had made that accusation before, the day she had knocked him down. It made the tea unbearably bitter in her mouth. He was right. She used hoggthorn to control her anxiety, and she couldn't live without it. She had made herself into a slave. The truth forced its way into her, even though there was no more room. She was already full up, full of misery, of Solde, blood pearls, vardari, Mother, the devil, Nafraím the murderer, and the whole damned Seida Guild.

Something broke inside her, and she threw her mug so it smashed into the wall behind Rugen. The shards rained across the table. He hardly reacted. Just gathered up the shards without a word. As if she had done the same thing many times before.

SIEGE

Juva's fingers slid over the book spines as she climbed higher on the stepladder. This was the third time she had checked this same shelf, and she needed to accept that the book she was looking for was gone. When she was little, she had believed that the library ate books, and that she only had a short time to read them before they disappeared. Now it seemed like she'd been right.

Maybe it doesn't exist?

The doubt came spontaneously, like always. The incessant fear that what she was experiencing might not be real. It had taken her many years to understand that this wasn't something she had been born with, but a wound that had been inflicted on her. Mother had done many things wrong but had never admitted a single one of them. Every confrontation had ended with her accusing Juva of having an overactive imagination, a shoddy memory, or worse: of outright lying.

Juva had scarcely been able to sleep or breathe when things were at their worst, and now Mother had admitted she had been manipulating her, lying to her, and ridiculing her. A life of self-recriminations and confusion that had been created on purpose.

I saw someone with wolf-sickness kill Father.

It was by no means a clear memory, more a fuzzy sense that it had happened. She remembered the iron wolf, a beast in a cage, claws, and the whites of its eyes. But as soon as she began examining the memory, her heart started racing, so it felt like she never got close enough. She was doomed to think in circles about the harmless things that lay in the margins of a dream. Father in his sickbed, so then maybe he hadn't been killed after all—or was she confusing that with a different occasion?

What if Father had wolf-sickness? What if he killed someone?

Juva pulled out a book on mythology. It wasn't the right one, but it would have to do. She climbed down and sat on the sofa in front of a pile of books she doubted would give her the answers she longed for.

The house was dead quiet. It was the first sun-day, so she had given the staff the day off for sun-free and made sure that the red lamp outside was turned off. Someone had knocked anyway, of course, but Rugen had sent them away. Solde had woken up sporadically from her blood fog, dazed and with a headache, and asked for the devil. It would pass, Rugen had promised, but Juva wasn't so sure. At least she had thrown away the rest of the blood pearls.

Would she have been driven to the blood pearls if I hadn't taken the card?

Juva forced herself to breathe. Her thoughts went to the hogg-thorn, a bitter reminder of how dependent she was. *Never again.*

Rugen's words kept running through her mind. His conviction when he had said that they were both slaves. She took a sip of tea. Plain tea, without hoggthorn.

It drained her willpower to quit. Her heart was constantly anxious, and she knew that at any time it could start booming heavily and violently, like it wanted to beat its way out of her chest. The fear that came with that was something she had never been able to explain to herself. She had never been afraid of dying, apart from those occasions when it was extremely, viscerally real, in the form of a snarling wolf. It was more the feeling that the world was unraveling and that she wasn't alone in her own body.

Stop thinking about that!

Juva flipped through the mythology book, from the new gods to the old, from all of Slokna. Muune, the moon goddess, the blood readers' favorite. Gaula, the queen of Drukna, who grew the dead into tentacles. Jól, the all-mother, whom Jólshov was named for. Fylja, who was actually a goddess from Fimle. Some believed she was a protector who followed those in danger, but who wanted a goddess glued to them day and night? That seemed more like dubious over-supervision. Virriveg was a creature Juva had loved as a child. No ordinary god, but a fairy, who had become the companion of travelers, because he brought luck.

And nowhere in the world did people travel as much as in Náklav. The stone circle had weakened the gods, they said, robbed them of their power over daily life and faded them to stories on paper.

Then she found Vitnir, the god she was looking for. He wasn't a normal god, but the greatest of all-father Votn's wolves. Vitnir, who could alternate between wolf and man, and who would one day devour the world. People had believed that long before Undst had spread the concept of the devil. They had come to Slokna with thoughts about an ancient wickedness. Their myths had blended with Slokna's myths, and in that way, the devil and the wolf had merged together in the stories.

And in my dreams.

Juva studied the drawing of Vitnir. It was an expensive book, beautifully illustrated. She looked around to make sure she was alone in the library, then she pulled the card out from underneath her top and set it next to Vitnir. They were very different in style. Vitnir was an extremely detailed charcoal drawing with light and shading. The card was primitive, with simple lines, burn markings on whale cartilage. But he was drawn like a god in both, strong and muscular, with a wolf head and canine teeth. Had they believed wolf-sickness was a deity in the olden days?

She wished she understood why the wolf had pursued her her entire life, and why he was so important now. What was she supposed to do with him?

Juva flipped the pale card in her hand over. Was it the whale cartilage itself that was so important, or was it something in the drawing? She poked at the edge, but it didn't seem like multiple layers had been glued together, the way you would do if you were hiding something inside it. Maybe it was just ancient and valuable? But then her mother wouldn't have asked her to burn it, would she?

The drawing on the card was just as pompous and ostentatiously mysterious as all the others in a blood reader's deck, so it was impossible to tell if there was supposed to be some hidden message in the symbolism.

No, it was probably what she'd first thought, something as basic as a membership card to the Seida Guild. The passport that secured them the blood pearls through steady deliveries from the city's criminal rulers.

She ran her fingers over the wolf's face. Sometimes that made her heart beat with panic, other times it beat for completely different reasons. She got goosebumps on her arm and a yearning tugged down toward her groin.

She slammed the book shut again. It was Rugen's fault, she had to get him out of the house, otherwise she was going to give in and sleep with him, like before.

Would that matter so much?

The front door banged out in the foyer. Juva hurriedly wedged the card back into place under her corset and put the most revealing of the books away. Denying any dealings with the devil wasn't going to do much good if she was caught reading about Vitnir, wolf anatomy, and theories of evil.

Ogny and Maruska came marching into the library, with Liv and Myrna in tow, their daughters who would inherit their seats, just as

Solde had inherited Mother's. They hadn't even shaken the snow off themselves, merely handed their winter coats to Rugen, who had to support the pile with his chin.

Liv, Ogny's daughter, darted out into the foyer again and up the stairs, as if this were her house. Maruska strode right into the blood reader room and Myrna vanished into the dining room.

"Where's Solde?" Ogny asked.

Juva must have given herself away with her eyes, because the old woman proceeded straight into her mother's room. The whole thing happened so quickly and matter-of-factly that it gave Juva chills. She noticed a couple of suitcases in the foyer.

What the Gaula are they up to?!

Juva followed Ogny into her mother's room. "What is going on here?" she asked, without hiding the sharpness.

Ogny pretended not to hear but sat down on the edge of the bed and whispered into Solde's ear. Solde struggled up into a sitting position, with sweaty hair and bags under her otherwise youthful eyes.

"Solde isn't well, Ogny. What do you want?" Juva asked again.

"We're here to find something that belongs to the Seida Guild," the old woman said, waving her hand dismissively. "Something Lagalune didn't have a chance to take care of. I'm sure you understand."

"There's nothing here that belongs to anyone but us, and I'm going to have to ask you to leave." Juva stepped aside in the doorway to make room, but Ogny showed no sign of budging.

Solde's tired eyes roamed between them before she seemed to find her normal mask. "Juva, stop! They left something here that Mother forgot to return. Let them find it. Don't be so rude!"

Juva stared at Solde, suddenly realizing that she would let them burn down the whole house if they asked, as long as that strengthened her chances of becoming one of them.

"That's very generous and wise of you, Solde. We won't forget it." Ogny placed a wrinkled hand over Solde's.

"I'm sending Rugen to fetch the guard." Juva turned in the doorway and started to walk away.

Ogny came after her at a speed she would have thought impossible for such an old woman. She caught up to her in the foyer and grabbed her arm. She was about to say something, but Maruska came out of the blood reader room with Mother's deck of cards in her hand.

"It's gone . . ." Her face was nearly bloodless.

"Find it!" Ogny barked, pulling Juva down onto the black skeleton bench. The old woman's knees touched Juva's and the intimacy felt like a comical contrast to the situation as a whole.

Ogny closed her eyes for a while and placed her hand on her forehead. Her hand was shaking and that was clearly intentional. The small medallions on her headband jingled. She looked up at Juva again, with feigned calm.

"Juva, you are a completely different person than your mother. We see that. You never wanted a life in the Seida Guild. We see that, too. It's not for you, all this nonsense with . . . " She waved at the shelves of curiosities, as if that underscored her point. "Fates, cards, blood, and death. It's not your path, and I respect that. The Seida Guild is led by three, we've always been three, and we will always be three, each of us with our own heir. It would never occur to me to force you, so you needn't fear us."

"I've never feared you," Juva lied.

Ogny's upper lip trembled, and Juva could vividly imagine what an ordeal it was to have to coax, negotiate. The old woman was not used to hearing no.

"Juva, this is not a game anymore. Lagalune should have given Solde something, but she didn't receive it, and without that we know she's not prepared to assume this position. Only Muune knows if that means that your mother wanted *you* to have it, or neither of you. It matters less than you think, but that doesn't change our need to have it. We need it, and it's a matter of life and death. You must give it to us. Do you understand?"

Juva was painfully aware that she was face-to-face with an experienced blood reader, far better trained at reading people than she was herself. Convincing her would be a feat.

Juva remained calm, without exaggerating her gestures, but reminded herself not to hide her anger. She had reason to be furious, so if that was not evident, it was as good as an admission. She looked Ogny in the eye, but not so intently that it would seem forced. She leaned toward her slightly, not away.

Then she let loose a torrent of lies:

"I have no idea what you're talking about! What are you even looking for?"

"The devil. We're looking for the devil."

Juva laughed, the way she assumed any random normal person would have laughed to hear that the house had been overrun by fortune tellers hunting for the devil. Ogny seemed to wilt and leaned back on the sofa. She made a sign over her chest, a Muune's moon, which struck Juva as surprisingly pious.

She's scared.

"Maybe I've underestimated how strongly you despise us," Ogny said. "You might want to punish us, the way a child would, but then you need to know that this is no obstacle. It won't stop us. It will just take a little longer. And the card is worthless to you."

"The card? What kind of card? What do you want it for if it's worthless?" Juva asked, knowing she had passed another test.

For the first time, Ogny seemed to doubt herself. Her gaze was colored by what Juva could swear was fear. "We need it because it's deadly in the wrong hands. That's why I hope you have it. If you have the devil, then give him to us. After that, you can do what you want, Juva Sannseyr."

What I want . . .

Ogny had struck a nerve. This could all be over in an instant if they got the card. And why not, it was just a card after all. She could give it up now and be left in peace.

But what about Solde?

Solde would become one of them. Use more blood pearls and end up wolf-sick, that was what was going to happen. And what if the scope of this was bigger than Juva thought? What if this was about all the blood pearls in this whole damn city?

Her hesitation made Ogny narrow her eyes.

"Has anyone been here since Lagalune died?" Ogny asked.

"Half the city," Juva replied with a shrug.

"You know who I mean."

"You mean the old man?" Juva afforded herself a smile. "The really old man, who looks a good bit younger than you?" Ogny's eyes widened, and Juva continued, enjoying the unexpected intoxication of having the upper hand. "Tall, slim, ridiculously nicely dressed? Or what was nice a hundred years ago, I suppose."

"Empty your pockets, girl!" Ogny abruptly stood up.

Juva laughed, even though she knew she'd been caught. It didn't matter. They would never get anything from her anyway. She hoped it hurt them, hoped it destroyed the whole guild, and that they would never get even one more blood pearl.

"What the fuck?" Rugen came over to them, clearly having caught Ogny's last command.

"It's all right, Rugen," Juva said, turning out her pockets with a smile.

Ogny came closer, as if she wanted to check for herself, but Rugen stepped between them. Again, the peculiar look on the old woman's face revealed that this was the first time anyone had ever stopped her from doing anything.

"You can't protect her against the devil, boy," Ogny said, scowling at Rugen. "And certainly not forever."

"Hardly," Rugen replied. "But I can protect her from you, right now."

Juva felt exhausted, torn between laughing and crying. As if she needed *him* to deal with this. What a joke.

He put his arm around her waist.

"Come on. Being here isn't good for you," he said, and he wasn't wrong.

They crossed the foyer toward the front door. They could hear laughter and hollering from the street where people were celebrating sun-day.

"Wait," Juva whispered. "I have to get my things."

She went upstairs, looked down at Ogny and smiled wryly, while the devil burned against her skin, just below her breast.

BREAKERS

Nafraím buttoned his coat at the neck and withdrew to the after-deck. The sails flapped above him as the ship swung out of Nyhavn and around the northern tip of Kviskre. He couldn't see Domnik, who owned this exceptional four-master. None of the other warow either, which meant that they were in place, waiting for him in the stateroom.

The gulls shrieked and circled around him, an omen of what was to come. The questions that would arise in the wake of Lagalune's death would be numerous and critical. There would be conflicting opinions and impossible demands. Some would demand blood, out of fear of the coming shortage. Or that the Witness should be torn down, as an assurance. Some would fear more blood readers now that the Might was back. They would doubt each other, and the old alliance was threatened.

He certainly understood them, which only made his task more difficult, maybe impossible. His statement needed to both reassure and distract. But there was hope, as long as he could keep them focused on the wolf-sickness and not on blood readers and the devil.

It was a beautiful day. Náklav's rocky shoreline towered over the black waves in the rare light one got just before the first sun-day. The rime frost sparkled on the gunwale and the woodwork creaked. He filled his lungs with fresh marine air and hoped it would sustain him through the meeting. Then he went below and into the stateroom.

Twenty-one warow waited around the long table. It made the room feel cramped, even on a ship of that size. They were silent as tradition dictated, but Seire gave him a barely visible nod. Both she and Faun knew what was at stake. Did any of the others suspect it? Would any of them be willing to sacrifice their long life for a greater cause?

He looked at them. Young Storm, with the haunted eyes, a thin cigar in her trembling fingers. She probably wouldn't have cared, if she knew. Yrgen, self-indulgent and depraved, would prefer not to put up any resistance as long as he could go down high. Domnik was worse. The banker was able to separate fact from emotion. He sat straight-backed, groomed to perfection, his strawberry-blond hair combed back into a ponytail. He wouldn't have hesitated to declare war, had he known. Vippa would have dithered until the indecision killed her. But Eydala . . . She would be the most difficult.

She sat with her back to the windows, the breakers behind her. No one had sat close to her. Her eyes were lazily inspecting him from above her sharp cheekbones. The tips of her fingers were discolored, almost black, a result of her obsession. Her life's work, which at one time had drawn him to her.

Eydala was shy of two hundred years old, young for a vardari, but the wrinkles on her neck revealed that she had been over fifty when he had given her the gift. She was his second biggest mistake, in all his years. The proof that not everyone possessed the ability to maintain both immortality and humanity.

Nafraím hung up his coat and sat down in the captain's chair. The box of questions sat on the table in front of him, and the silence would last at least until he had read them all. He opened the lid and picked a random card.

Who killed Lagalune Sannseyr?

Not a good start, even if he hoped to subdue the panic with his statement afterward. He set it aside and took out another.

Who killed Lagalune Sannseyr?

The card grew heavy in his hand, like the weight of all the eyes watching him. He tried to smile but it amounted only to a twitch at the corner of his mouth. The ship heeled and creaked, but the heavy chest of questions stayed put. He flipped through the cards, and everyone had the same question in one form or another. Aside from one.

Take the devil back.

It wasn't a question. It was a command. He looked at Eydala. She shrugged, almost imperceptibly, as if it went without saying that she should make demands of him, even a demand that would mean the end to a several-hundred-year-old peace treaty between the warow.

Nafraím rested his elbows on the table and rubbed his knuckles. He had believed he'd have more time, but the next few days took shape before him in his mind, dreadfully clear.

This meeting would never dip below the surface. They would all pretend they accepted Lagalune's death as natural, but none of them would believe it. And they would leave the ship secretly hostile.

Then they would go after the other blood readers. Break the treaty and start their own private hunts for the devil. The only way to stop them was to make sure they didn't have anyone to interrogate. He had to kill the initiated blood readers. Every single one of them.

WEAK LIPS

The streets were so full that it was a challenge to reach Hidehall. First sun-day was almost as hectic as the spring run. Everyone was out to soak up what little sun they could. The ice melted off the roofs, strangers hugged each other like old acquaintances, bakers handed out overbaked sun kringles to ecstatic children, and the girls at the silversmithy danced in the doorway with sheer joy.

The mood did not manage to uplift Juva. She was still seething and couldn't understand why. The Seida Guild had besieged the house, and so what? She hated that house and had planned to leave as soon as Mother was buried, anyway. What did she care who took it over?

The courtyard outside Hidehall was packed full of people singing Solsulla, the sun song, in multiple languages. Juva squeezed through them and let herself in the back way with Rugen on her heels. He was just as shaken as she was by Ogny and the others.

"It's just pure looting!" he said, for once putting precise words on how she was feeling.

"They haven't taken anything yet," she replied, and felt a touch of schadenfreude that the only thing they wanted sat nestled under her corset.

She asked Rugen to wipe off his feet, then she went into the common room and put a couple of logs onto the embers in the fireplace. The room smelled of smoke and blood. There were three fox hides stretched over a wooden pole drying against the wall, maybe Nolan's or one of the other guys'. She suddenly missed them so much; the feeling settled in her gut. She needed them, all of them. She missed the dead woods, the snow, the hunt, missed having the world's easiest conversations around the campfire. Just being back in Hidehall again made her chest lighter and her heart steadier.

The flames rose on the hearth. The antlers along the railing above filled the room with pointy shadows that mirrored her thoughts. A forest of stabbing spikes. One for Mother, one for the doctor's cowardly cause of death, one for Nafraím, one for the hoggthorn she struggled to quit, one for Solde, who may have given herself wolf-sickness through her drug use, and one for the Seida Guild and their pursuit of the devil.

Juva sank into the chair closest to the fire and heard the Dead Man's Horn sound in the distance. The effect was immediate. Rugen stiffened where he stood, and the hollering in the courtyard subsided. Even the room grew darker, a sign that the first glimpse of the sun outside was over.

What am I going to do?

The slow, sad sound was the call for the bleeder. Soon Broddmar would be standing in the courtyard dressed in red. He'd said they could discuss her hunting with him. Should she go find him? The mere thought of it felt heavy.

"So," Rugen clapped his hands as if to put a final note to the Dead Man's Horn. "Do you have anything to drink?"

"No."

He disappeared into the kitchen anyway and returned with a bottle of Ruvian red wine. "How about this?" he said. "There are five of them on the table!"

Juva squinted at the bottle. It wasn't hers and very few of the guys were dumb enough to leave wine there, much less such expensive wine.

Ester.

"Find a corkscrew." Juva smiled.

Rugen's stupid grin confirmed that drinking with him was a bad idea, especially now that her body was simmering and all she wanted was to forget. But he had apologized, many times. He had paid her back, which she never would have believed a few weeks ago. He'd been there for her at her mother's wake and when she found Solde in a blood fog. He had even stood in between her and Ogny, and that said a lot.

Maybe he deserved better than distrust? After all, she didn't know anything about what he'd been through. Yes, he had hinted, overtly at times, but she had kept him at arm's length. And still he was there. He wouldn't be if he didn't care.

Juva felt weak, far too aware that reality was not always as it appeared. It was possible that she had treated him unfairly.

Rugen came back with an open bottle, and a slightly more open shirt. He started tossing pillows onto the carpet in front of the fireplace, the look on his face making it seem like it was the most natural thing to do.

"So, what are they looking for?" he asked casually.

Juva felt the card itching against her skin, as if it knew it was being talked about. She had an inexplicable urge to show it to him, tell him everything. But she didn't want to drag anyone into the affairs of the vardari. Besides, she didn't have any explanation of what it was. She didn't even know for sure why she had taken it. A good person would have taken it to stop the blood pearl trade, and to fulfill her mother's last wish. But was she a good person? Maybe she had taken it just as much to sabotage things.

"I don't know," she shrugged. "But I wouldn't give it to them if I knew."

"Ha! You were really born into the wrong family."

"You can say that again," Juva chuckled. "I think my dad was the only normal one."

"He died when you were little?"

Rugen lay down on the carpet, on his side, apparently to show that there was room for her, too. Juva lay down next to him on her stomach and took a sip of wine. The bottle wasn't full, so he had obviously helped himself to some in the kitchen.

"I was seven and it was my fault."

Rugen took a bigger swig than she had and wiped his mouth with the back of his hand. "If I'm remembering right, you used to think that *everything* was your fault."

Juva looked at him, thick brown hair lying in waves around his ears, his full lips, and his eyes, which always looked studiedly innocent. Or was she the ruined one, because she had been raised with blood readers? Did she see falseness everywhere? How would she ever get close to someone if she never started with a clean slate?

Give him a chance.

"You don't know what it's like," she said. "Growing up with a blood reader. People believe them, believe they can tell you how long you have left to live, whether you have enemies around you. People will pay anything to know, and the blood readers will do whatever it takes to pretend they know. My father wasn't one of them. He was a hunter, a totally normal hunter. They said he was bitten by a wolf, and that it killed him, but . . . I conjured up the wolf."

"That's stupid, Juva." Rugen's eyes began to glaze over. "No one can conjure up wolves."

"Oh, I know! I know it can't be done. I mean, I know that now. But I didn't know it when I was seven. Mother told me *I* did it. That the wolf was because of me, because I had drawn him, drawn the devil."

"Wait . . ." He looked comically confused. "You drew a picture of a wolf, and they said *that's* why your dad died?"

"No, I . . . I saw someone with wolf-sickness and got scared out of my wits. Afterward, I drew him, I think. I don't know, Rugen! I don't remember, it was a long time ago, and . . . I just know that I need to draw him when things get . . . tough. I draw the devil and burn the paper."

She knew that sounded crazy, but everything had been crazy for last several days now—no time like the present. Besides, she wanted to test him, check his limits to see if he would distance himself and run off when she put up resistance.

He took another swig of wine. "So, you're a little damaged," he teased. "Welcome to the exclusive club. Everyone in this city is afraid of wolves."

That was true. He made it sound inconsequential, and she liked that. She had never talked to anyone about her father before, or about anything at all that was bothering her. It felt like she had been sitting in a cage, but now Mother had undone the lock and taken it with her to Drukna. Lagalune was no more. She couldn't laugh, rage, or impose silence.

"I hate them," she whispered, picking at a pillow seam.

"Who, the wolves?"

"The blood readers. They get the blood pearls from the vardari. I know that. They're the ones who supply or sell that shit. A lot of people think they're only a legend, but they just use that to their advantage. They're running the show from the shadows. They killed my mother, Rugen. You saw it, you were there."

Rugen ran his hand over her back. He didn't answer, but he didn't look like he thought she was crazy either. That encouraged her to continue.

"I think I can feel them. The warow."

"What do you mean, feel them?" Rugen emptied the wine bottle and got up. "Wait, don't go anywhere," he said flippantly, and vanished into the kitchen.

Juva heard him rummaging around while she stared into the flames. Red embers spat at the black fire screen, and she felt warm and open. Even so, she couldn't shake her sense of being in danger.

Rugen returned with another bottle of wine and crawled up beside her. "Feel them: explain."

Juva turned to face him. "Like in the fairy tale about the sisters and the wolf. You must have heard that one. Everyone's heard it."

Rugen handed her the bottle. She took a swig while he twined her hair between his fingers.

"Maybe I just like to hear your voice," he said.

Juva pretended she hadn't heard that but leaned closer and began the tale:

"Three sisters were out wolf hunting, and they caught the devil in wolf's clothing. He said that if they set him free, they would receive the gift of always knowing where he was, where there was death and evil. The sisters would never again need to wonder if someone wanted to hurt them. They would know it for certain. So they said yes."

Rugen smiled lazily and said, "That's not what I would have done. It's got to be better, not knowing."

"Listen. The sisters, they said yes. He gave them some of his blood to drink and that's how they got their ability to see. They were the first blood readers."

"But didn't they die?"

"Yes, two of them. One saw that she herself was evil and took her own life. The second saw that the man she loved was evil, and when she attacked him, he killed her. But the third, she saw that the devil was everywhere, that everyone could perpetrate evil. She survived, and since that time the blood readers have always known where the devil is."

"And the vardari are the evil that you can feel, because you're descended from blood readers?"

"I didn't write the fairy tale." Juva shrugged.

Rugen leaned toward her. His eyes were hungry with desire and dulled by the wine. "So maybe that was real once upon a time and now it's become real again, that people can perceive them, I mean.

That wouldn't be the strangest thing that's happened. Just think about that tower in Nákla Henge that started ticking all on its own. There is actually more between heaven and earth than we suspect, Juva. But so what? It's the first sun-day; why not just live and be happy?"

She knew what he was up to, but she couldn't work up the will to resist. He was right, after all. Why not just be happy if everything was going to Drukna anyway?

Rugen brought his lips to hers, softly and tentatively. It bothered her. If she was about to give in, then he could at least do this properly. There was no resistance in his kiss, as if someone had taught him to be soft.

Juva pushed him away and wrestled him down onto his back. She straddled him and kissed him the way she wanted him to kiss her. She wanted him to be like Vitnir, like the wolf in the myth. She was going to show him what she needed.

His response was immediate and hard underneath her. Her tongue tickled at his teeth, and she could have sworn that one of them wiggled.

Juva sat up and stared at him. He smiled, as if that were also a part of the game. A thousand thoughts kindled like sparks in her head and then gathered into a fire. He had been a blood user, might still be. He had come to her, desperate for help and couldn't say why. He had clutched his jaw, in pain. And now, a loose tooth?

Rugen has wolf-sickness!

He tried to pull her back down, but she stood up and backed away. Possible explanations fought for space in her head, each one more useless than the one before it.

Maybe he didn't know? Of course he knew. How could he not know he was losing his canine teeth? Maybe the tooth got knocked loose in a fight? Father had knocked out no less than six of Broddmar's teeth.

Rugen propped himself up on his elbows and looked at her, mystified. She needed to buy herself some time while she considered whether she ought to ask him point blank.

"Get another bottle of wine," she said.

Rugen got to his feet and looked at her. For a second, she thought he was going to get mad, but he played along and went off into the kitchen.

The front door's hinges creaked. Broddmar came in with Skarr padding after him. He pulled down the red mask and regarded Juva with a look she had never seen from him before. Steely gray and near bursting. His face was pale and drawn. His upper lip sank inward like an old man's where his teeth should have been.

"Jufa . . ."

He came toward her and threw his arms around her, holding her tight. Juva felt so unsteady that she thought she would fall if he let go of her. She knew that something awful had happened, but she couldn't get a word out.

Rugen returned from the kitchen. He let out a guttural sound and dropped the wine bottle. It rolled across the floor, glugging out wine.

Through the fog of raw, naked fear, Juva realized that he did know. Rugen knew he was wolf-sick, and he thought the bleeder had come for him. But Broddmar didn't even glance at him.

This wasn't about Rugen. This was about something completely different, and Juva was afraid she knew what. She grabbed her jacket and set off running.

THE DOLLS

Juva bumped into people but didn't take time to apologize. Her jacket flapped around her as she ran down the street. The red lights dangled like blood pearls over the crowd of merrymakers.

She took the stairs two at a time and yanked open the wrought iron front door, which had never been heavier. A complete stranger stood just inside, blocking the way. A mountain of a man, bearded, and dressed in black, with a ring of white dots on his chest. The Ring Guard. In deepest Drukna, the Ring Guard was in her house!

He grabbed her arm. "I'm sorry, no one can come—"

"Let me in! I live here!"

Juva stormed into the foyer without hearing what the man yelled after her. Gomm sat sobbing on the skeleton bench, where she herself had sat with Ogny earlier. He was talking to two Ring Guardians. They flanked him on either side, as if they were afraid the cook might make a run for it.

The house was full of them. Men and women dressed in black tromping in and out of the rooms in their slush-soaked shoes. One of them was carefully inspecting the shelf of rarities. He picked up a jar of teeth and looked around, as if he were in Drukna.

Juva's skin crawled. Tingling as if from millions of little pinpricks and every single poke made her more afraid.

Below the gallery, the flames flickered in the fireplace, and through the open arches on either side of the chimney, she saw several figures wandering around the library. Juva walked toward them, feeling as if she were sleepwalking, dreaming.

Five women sat around the tea table in the middle of the library. Motionless. Lifeless. Ogny and Maruska sat side by side on the leather sofa, both with their heads tipped as if they had fallen asleep in the middle of a conversation. Their daughters sat, each in her own chair, Liv with her head lolling back and Myrna slumped over the armrest. And Solde . . .

Solde sat looking down at her cup with her eyes half-open, as if she were bored. But she was dead. They were all dead. They looked like dolls, carefully arranged at a tea party.

Juva wilted. The tingling in her body sank down to her feet and took all her warmth with it. She was chilled to the bone. The glow behind the fire screen cast lattice-like shadows over them, like a living fishnet. They were a picture, a painting of a whole life. Solde, only sixteen. Ogny, over seventy, and the others, every age in between. Myrna Auste, delicate and dressed in lace. Liv, Ogny's daughter, with a tight bun and a flawless part.

Juva felt unbearably confused. She should do something, but she didn't know what, and it seemed ridiculous. The room was trying to push the most insignificant details at her. Dust on the breakfront bookcase. A missing nail on the armrest on the sofa. The case of beetles on the shelf, insects from all over the world, in shimmering colors. Chestnut-brown. Greenish-black.

Living people from the Ring Guard observed this tableau of the dead, walking around and taking notes as they mumbled to each other and sniffed the teacups. One of the men looked up and came running toward her. Juva didn't understand why until she felt the edge of something against her back. A corner. Had she fallen? She turned and looked up, into the eye of that shabby raven in Mother's silly fortune-telling cabinet. For some reason, she felt the bird had failed.

The man came over and got her on her feet, supported her out of the library, and helped her down onto one of the steps in the foyer. She could hear him speaking, but thought he was talking to the others, over by the door.

It was Broddmar, with Skarr on a leash, and he was shown into the library. Juva could hear the wolf's claws as he padded across the floor, and she followed him with her eyes. A wild animal, inside the foyer of the Sannseyr home, what would Mother say?

Past tense. What would Mother have said?

Who would say anything now? There was no one left. Juva wrapped her arms around herself to warm up. This was her fault. Everyone was dead because of her.

She had said that Solde could die since she was eating blood pearls, and now that had happened. She had always wished the Seida Guild would go to Drukna, and now that had happened, just like with father. Why? Juva stared over at the skeleton bench, where she had sat with Ogny.

The Seida Guild is led by three, we've always been three, and we will always be three, each of us with our own heir.

The realization was beginning to churn in her head, merciless, like an ice drill. The vardari had killed them because they were the leaders of the Seida Guild, inextricably tied to warow affairs. They were heirs to a troika of families: Sannseyr, Volsung, and Auste. The only ones who knew what the devil meant, and she should have been one of them.

Solde was dead because she had been given the spot that Mother had wanted to give Juva. Solde wasn't supposed to be sitting motionless in the library. She was.

It's cold here. Why is it so cold here?

She heard Skarr growl, a sure sign that someone present had wolf-sickness. A lie. Just as much a lie as that her mother had died of food poisoning. Nothing was real.

She heard someone go past, out on the street, bawling sun songs in broken Norran.

An old man from the Ring Guard handed her a cup of water, and she took it, even though it seemed pointless. This was the devil's house; people died here. What difference was water going to make?

Juva peered up at him and realized that she had seen him before. In Smalfaret, by the body. He was the one who had asked to see her hunting license.

"Do you know him?" the man asked, pointing to the front door, where the bearded giant was restraining Rugen.

Juva nodded, and Rugen was admitted. He didn't notice her but ran straight to the library. She should have called out to him, warned him. He was going to be shocked. Cursed, lost Rugen, who didn't love her, and whom she didn't love, either.

You're going crazy.

Her heart pounded in her chest, so violently that she wanted to hit back, but she didn't have hoggthorn anymore. She no longer owned her own body, not even her thoughts. Was that the house's revenge? Ghosts had taken up residence in her brain, and they were talking at the same time, a chorus of memories, lies, and accusations, some as old as she was. They were wearing themselves out and becoming fewer and fewer, decreasing until only one was left. Mother's.

What have I always said about the devil?

That he was always there. That she had been a difficult child. Juva, the devil child, with shameful thoughts and drawings. Mother had said that she had the devil in her. She had the devil in her heart, and nowhere else did it pound like it did at home.

That realization clawed its way into her, like a drowning rat, clinging, desperate, and insistent, until she became one with the animal, and understood.

This wasn't about some blood reader's card. This was about something that could show the way to the real devil. The iron wolf. She had seen him as a child. He had killed her father, and that was anything but imaginary.

The devil was real, and he was here, somewhere in the house.

THE MISTAKE

Rugen fought his nausea. Five dead women. Five! Damn, Juva's pretty younger sister was barely old enough to fuck, and the oldest lady from the Seida Guild was probably pushing a hundred. And before them there was Lagalune.

Nafraím is insane!

The warow had said a lot was going to happen, but this was atrocious. He should have received a warning, at least. An opportunity to prepare himself. *Fuck.*

He lifted the lid of the lacquer box and found the cigars he had been looking for. Put one between his lips and stuck a handful in his pocket. What about a light? Lagalune had smoked like a bonfire. She must surely have had some kind of lighter in here? He looked around the gloomy bedroom. What kind of person had a black four-poster bed when she could afford anything?

A blood reader, of course.

It fucking sucked that Juva had thrown away the blood pearls. She must not have had any idea what that stuff was worth! He found a lighter on the nightstand and lit the cigar. His hands shook like crazy. Then he took a blessedly delicious drag and glanced out into the corridor.

The Ring Guard was still here, but the worst of the fuss had subsided, and an eerie calm had settled over the residence. They were finished with their investigations and now they were just waiting for the hearses. There had been too many people out on the streets earlier, but by now the festivities had settled down enough that the hearses might be able to get through.

Rugen scooted past the library and went upstairs. He leaned over the railing and looked down as he smoked.

The fat cook had been allowed to leave, apparently. He was the one who had discovered the bodies when he returned from the sun festivities, but he had been cleared of suspicion since the fucking wolf had picked up the scent of wolf-sickness.

The animal was still down in the study on the other side of the gallery. Rugen kept a good distance, but he could see it through the open doors. It was lying on a carpet by the desk with its eyes closed. Every now and then, it pricked up its ears and Rugen had to remind himself that it would have caught him already if it had smelled something on him.

Juva had collapsed on a deep chair in the study, and the red hunter was squatting in front of her. Why hadn't she ever mentioned that she knew the man who gave all blood users nightmares? More than knew him, they were hunting buddies. Friends! It was nuts. The man he had feared, and was old enough to be her grandfather, was holding Juva's hands in his, pretending he cared, when obviously all he wanted was to get between her thighs.

Barf! A toothless old man hunting pussy with five corpses in the house? That was so fucking sick.

Rugen blew smoke out of the corner of his mouth as he sized up the guy. What was his name again? Broddmar? The name of the bleeder had to be worth something to Nafraím—or did he know it already? It was impossible to guess; Nafraím seemed to know most things and be able to cope with most things. After all, he must have walked right in here, confidently in the middle of the chaos with everyone off work for sun-free, and just . . . Well, what had he done, actually? There wasn't a drop of blood in the library. The women looked like they had bored one another to death. The wolf had been tricked into smelling the wolf-sickness, but people with wolf-sickness didn't fucking talk people to death, they ripped people to shreds if they got the chance.

Rugen rubbed his jaw, prepared for a new jolt of pain that didn't come.

Did wolf-sick people like it? Killing? Were they lucid enough in their heads to enjoy tearing people down from their pedestals and eating them?

Broddmar stood, and Rugen ducked into Solde's bedroom to be out of sight. It smelled like nauseatingly sweet perfume. The smell of a young dead girl. He ran over to the window to make sure the old man actually left the house. The hearses had arrived, and people started gathering outside. Broddmar and his wolf came out, and the whole crowd steered clear as they followed him with their eyes. An old woman put her hand over her mouth, apparently the first to understand the inconceivable, that someone with wolf-sickness had killed a blood reader.

Imagine what they were going to say when they found out that it wasn't just one dead, but five. Six, including Lagalune, every last one of the top figures in the Seida Guild. It was outrageous.

Rugen knew he ought to say something, talk to the Ring Guard about Nafraím, but what the fuck would he say? That he was positive who the murderer was, and that he was probably an immortal? The few who might consider believing him would never look into it, not as long as the vardari were involved.

I'm also involved. I can't say a word.

Rugen put his cigar out on the windowsill and left the sentimental bedroom. He went into the study, where Juva was on her feet now. She stood looking for something on the mantle, between what must surely be rat skulls or something. Was there a single normal room in this house? A place without morbid decorations and tired antiques?

Juva opened a box of matches. She seemed sluggish and disoriented. What was she holding between her fingers? A playing card?

He walked over to her.

"What are you doing?" he asked.

She looked up at him in confusion, as if she had forgotten he existed. "I need to burn him," she said and knelt in front of the fireplace.

Her face was sallow, almost green.

She's in shock.

"Burn who?" Rugen sat down on the floor next to her.

She took out a match but couldn't get it lit. She pulled it across the striking surface over and over again, but her fingers were shaking too much. He understood her well. He'd had the same problem, although not as bad as this.

Suddenly, the match caught, and she dropped it on the birch bark, which started to burn. She held the card out toward the flame, and now he understood what it was. A blood reader card with the devil on it.

Poor, poor girl!

This was what she had told him about in Hidehall. They had scared the wits out of her as a little girl, told her she had to burn the devil so he wouldn't become real.

Rugen pulled her hand to him. She dropped the card on the floor and her whole body started trembling.

"You're in shock, Juva. Something horrific has happened and you're in shock. You need to relax." Rugen had no idea what else to say. What did you say when people were dying like flies? "Juva, you hated these old women, remember that. And Solde . . . She was going to come down with wolf-sickness anyway, and that would have been worse."

She looked up at him as if she were really studying his face. Then she raised her hand and ran her thumb over his upper lip. It was almost as if she knew. His tongue moved over to his canine tooth out of sheer reflex, and he imagined that it was looser than the last time.

"You don't understand," she said. "It's my fault. Terrible things are happening because of me, because I didn't burn him."

"Juva, terrible things happen all the time for no reason."

She reached for the card again, but he held her back. The gods knew he hadn't had the easiest childhood, but this seemed downright perverse. What kind of sick people told a kid that she needed to burn drawings of wolves and devils so the world wouldn't end?

He cupped her cheeks and tried to force her to look at him, but she resisted.

"Juva, listen to me. This isn't your fault." The words just tumbled out of him, but they sounded right.

Juva pulled free and wriggled away from him. "You don't understand anything, Rugen! It should have been me!"

"What should have been you?"

"Down there where Solde's sitting, it should have been me. Mother wanted me to take over for her, do you understand? Me, not her! It was never supposed to be her. I should be dead, and she should be alive."

Rugen felt like he was going to belch. It became a cough that contained both smoke and blood. What in Gaula was she saying?! Was she lying? No, that wasn't Juva's style. But that sure was an outrageous claim. This house was worth an inconceivable amount. Why in Gaula would she give away her inheritance?

Because she hated it.

She was telling the truth. Solde wasn't supposed to inherit the house or the blood reader position, Juva was. And all the main figures in the Seida Guild were sitting down there in the library, stone dead.

Nafraím had killed the wrong sister.

Rugen stared at Juva. She was so damned fine. Her blond hair was darker underneath and hung in tangles down her back. Those narrow, catlike, cold blue-gray eyes, which always seemed a little tired, ready for bed. That soft body, which was a dream to have on top of you. What would Nafraím do if he found out? Surely even he couldn't kill something so beautiful. Fuck, what a thought.

He didn't want to see her dead; he wanted to see her naked. So, what the fuck should he do? He had to tell Nafraím, of course. He didn't have any choice about that anymore. But surely, even the warow had sex, so he'd have to understand, wouldn't he, and it would be possible to negotiate a little? This information was definitely worth a lot, so the least Nafraím could do was let him have this girl.

Rugen pulled Juva into his arms and let her cry. They were surrounded by death. There were hearses outside, the bleeder had just been there, and five corpses sat in the library having a tea party. Even the mantle above him was decorated with animal skulls. And for all he knew, death would come to Juva as well, and to him.

It felt inconceivably morbid, but his dick wasn't lying. He had never been more turned on.

DEATH RITES

Five wrapped bodies lay along the edge of the cliff, each in its own boat-shaped pod. Two of them lay in the frost-whitened grass because there were only three sepulture ramps.

Kleft was packed with people. Still more had wanted to come, but the chief steward at Jólshov had been forced to limit the ritual to family members. Two extra shuttles were still required to transport people out to the sloped skerry. Five dead blood readers left a lot of surviving relatives behind.

Everyone who wasn't family remained onshore, spread along the city walls and down the road to Corpse Bay. An enormous turnout, even though notice of the sepulture ceremony hadn't been posted in Jólshov or in the squares. The plan had been to avoid crowds and prevent panic, but they had already failed at that. Ester had mentioned riots at the rafts, the Ring Guard had stationed extra security around Nákla Henge, and the city council had held crisis meetings. An attack on the Seida Guild meant that no one was safe.

Fear held Náklav in its iron grip. People had even started informing on each other. All it took was vaguely pointy teeth, an angry outburst, or someone acting strange.

It was even worse in the Seida Guild, to the extent that there even was any guild left to speak of. The killings indicated that someone had it out for blood readers. Several had been frightened into turning off their lanterns, and there was no leadership anymore. The next in line refused to take over, and Juva couldn't blame them. She should have been among the dead, but there she stood as the sole survivor.

The Sannseyr family was small, but a couple of souls had come whom Juva hadn't seen in many years. Semde, whose father had been Mother's brother before he died young, along with her husband and two little kids. They lived in the country outside Naar, and that was about all Juva knew about them. Juva had steered clear of everyone, not just her mother and Solde. That awareness weighed on her shoulders now. It wasn't their fault that they had been born into a blood reader family. They bore no blame for that, no more than she did herself.

The only people Juva would call family were standing back onshore. Broddmar, Hanuk, Nolan, and Muggen. And Lok and Embla, with their newborn son, who would soon take the water for the first time. But first she would give the water to Solde for the last time.

Juva clutched the horn of salt water, the same one Solde had used at Mother's sepulture. Solde lay on the nearest ramp, which creaked in the wind. Anasolt from the Seida Guild nodded to Juva. She was young enough to be brave and had taken it upon herself to lead this day, to guide the five blood readers to Drukna. Juva walked over to Solde and raised the shroud to reveal her white face. Her cheeks were hollow, and Juva felt an ominous prickling in her mouth, as if she was going to throw up. Five dead meant five tongues. Who was going to eat them all?

Juva opened Solde's mouth, a blueish-black opening with a meat-like stump where her tongue should have been. The tongue that had mastered so incredibly many bad words.

It should have been me.

She poured salt water into Solde's mouth and closed it again. Her skin was ice cold and waxy against Juva's fingers. No one should need to take the water for the last time at the age of sixteen.

The oil in the cloth caught in her nose and Juva took an unsteady step back. She held out the horn to the next person, who would give the water to Maruska and her daughter, but no one took it.

Juva looked around, perplexed. People stood, silent and motionless, colorless in the twilight. Undead. Some stared at her vacantly, others stared at the ground. No one came over to her outstretched hand. What was wrong? Had they not agreed on who would give the water to their people?

They're afraid.

Juva felt her feet fading and supported herself against the ramp. She realized that no one was going to step forward. Giving water to a deceased blood reader fell to the heir, and that was a role no one wanted anymore. They believed it was a death sentence. The Seida Guild had been decimated.

Juva stared at them in disbelief. The wind cut through the wool and leather and snatched at her hair. She let it carry her onward to the next body, to Maruska. What else was she going to do? Someone had to.

She used the salt water sparingly, making it last, as she moved from woman to woman in anguish. Maruska, Myrna, Ogny, Liv. She could hear someone breaking down. Deep sobs were stifled against someone's chest, as if the grief was a greater disgrace than the betrayal they were committing against the dead.

Juva took the torch from Anasolt and set fire to the three bundles that lay on the ramps. Solde, Maruska, and Myrna. As soon as that was done, more people came. They pushed at each other to claim space to help tilt the biers. There was no responsibility tied to the sepulture itself. Juva felt her lips tighten in an unpleasant sneer she couldn't control.

Wasn't this what she had always hoped for? No one wanting to become a blood reader. The guild dissolved. It was a wish granted, a prophecy that fell into line—but it was only causing pain.

One after the other, the burning bundles toppled down into the black ocean, a fall that seemed as short as their lives, before they were extinguished again. Juva could vividly imagine being one of them. Throwing herself over the edge and disappearing into the cold and dark.

She would have been down there already if she had done what Mother had ordered and kept Solde away from the inheritance. What if she *had* burned the devil, would that have changed anything?

The card rested like a cold hand against her skin. It would have been lost forever if Rugen had let her burn it. For her part, she could barely remember having tried. But she remembered her insight.

She had a guide to the devil. He wasn't a fairy tale, not some spiritual force, but rather a living creature she had seen as a child. And all the others who had known the same thing had been killed by the vardari. She could hear Mother whispering from Drukna.

Do you remember? You called him the iron wolf.

Juva looked up and realized she was about to be left behind. The group had thinned out and was walking back down to the boats. Some looked back in stolen glances. Some whispered together, but no one came over to her. Was she imagining it? Or had she done something wrong when she gave water to all the dead? What should she have done—let them go through their sepulture without receiving their final water?

Juva walked the whole way to the boats alone, not able to shake the feeling that they were all talking about her. Her uneasiness grew and wove its way into her grief, until she didn't know what she was feeling anymore.

She put her hands on the edge of the boat to climb aboard, but it was jerked out of her grasp; she got wet stepping into the water's edge to avoid stumbling. They had pushed off with the pole before she could climb aboard, but there was still room in the boat. Juva gulped and walked over to one of the smaller shuttles. One of the men there helped her aboard, and tears welled up in her throat.

She sat down in the stern, next to a girl who looked a little younger than Solde. The girl had a fist full of little shells that she was pouring from hand to hand, as if to see how many would be left once they'd crossed.

She looked up at Juva. "I don't believe a word of it," she said.

The boat pushed off from shore with a jerk.

"Of what?" Juva asked.

"Of what they say. I told them so, that it wasn't you. You left home because you wanted to be a hunter! You would never have killed anyone. You didn't even want to be a blood reader, so why would you?"

Juva stared at the girl, unsure of what she was trying to say. Was she not right in the head?

The girl suddenly looked scared, as if she had realized how crazy what she'd just said had sounded. The shells slipped from her hands.

"I mean, not everyone! Not everyone's saying that, just . . . some people said it. You were the only one brave enough to water the dead, right? You weren't scared, and they said that proved that it was . . ."

Juva was going to throw up. She leaned over the gunwale and closed her eyes. She felt the girl's hand on her back.

"Don't worry about it!" the girl said, not understanding how impossible that request was. "People say such fucking stup—sorry, very stupid things. Don't listen to them."

"Thanks," Juva mumbled, and it seemed subservient, a vile submissiveness.

She had buried her mother, buried Solde. The vardari had killed them both, and people thought it was her. And now there she sat, thanking a girl on the boundary between childhood and adulthood because the girl didn't believe she was a murderer.

Juva could feel the edges of the card chafing under her breast as she clung to the side of the boat. Nafraím wanted it, the Seida Guild wanted it. Everyone wanted the devil, but it was becoming painfully clear that the devil had chosen her.

NAFRAÍM'S MERCY

Ester's guesthouse was everything the Sannseyr house had never been: colorful and full of light and life. Juva felt like she was in another country, maybe Thervia, or somewhere in Ruv. It was as if the old lady had decided to bring the whole world home in a refined celebration of greens and blues. The walls were painted like flowering fruit trees with birds in abundance, a motif that recurred on the pillows, exquisite vases, and embroidered seat covers. Empty cages dangled from the ceiling, overflowing with dried flowers that had never grown in Slokna.

Juva felt like a traitor being there at all, but being at home had been hopeless. She had given the staff time off indefinitely, and she fled, fled from the certainty of what the house was hiding and from the unstoppable flow of people.

The hassle had already begun on the sepulture day. Crazy clients pounding on the door, runners bringing condolences, and cryptic invitations she had no inkling how to deal with. Someone had broken the blood reader lantern, but at least that sent a clear message. The Ring Guard had also been by to hear how it was that she had been at the scenes of two murders, both at home and on Smalfaret. Juva had said they should question the vardari, not her. After that, she hadn't seen or heard anything from them.

The suspicions against her were so surreal that she couldn't even manage to fear them. They were just white foam on an already stormy sea, and she couldn't do anything but ride the waves, try to stay away from Drukna. At least until Ester came back with whatever it was she had decided the table was lacking.

Juva looked down at the street. Myntslaget consisted of shops people only entered if they could afford it. Agan Askran was one of them, the legendary armorer located kitty-corner across the street. Juva had had her eye on a crossbow of his for a long time, but she hadn't been able to afford it. Until now.

Money was not a problem anymore. As the sole heir, money was suddenly something she had enough of, in the worst conceivable way. And at the same time, now she had a reason to use it.

She ought to kill Nafraím, end the disgustingly long life of the murderer no one dared to confront. Her simmering rage against everything he represented frightened her. The vardari were a powerful, shady elite who would never have to answer for their crimes, Gaula knew how many. Would they come after her, too?

Juva didn't doubt that she could also be a murder target. Even so, Broddmar and Hanuk had offered her a place to stay because they didn't think she should be alone. Lok also, and he had put it bluntly, his eyes moist: he was terrified of putting his kids in danger, but she was welcome. Juva had declined. They were her chosen family. The thought of anything happening to them turned her stomach.

Ester, on the other hand, had not taken no for an answer. She had insisted on putting Juva up in her fancy guesthouse.

It was called Vinterhagen, "the conservatory," and at any given time it housed about twenty travelers who were used to being well looked after. Juva could hear some of them chatting in the room that had given the place its name, an old public square, now interiorized below a wood-framed glass roof. The abundance of lush, green plants made it impossible to tell if she was inside or outside, and wherever she went in the guesthouse, she could hear the twittering of little birds, flying around freely.

The ladies were discussing the Witness, the sculpture up at Nákla Henge, the security measures which had been stepped up, and how preposterous it was that they were no longer allowed to bring their dogs with them. A deplorable new rule, as if dogs had ever given people wolf-sickness. They gave each other tips about blood readers, too, but had heard that there was some sort of crisis on that front, and that was an insufferable inconvenience in Náklav.

A young man sat in the corner embroidering. He had a faded bruise underneath one eye, but he seemed far from the type to get in fights. Juva got the impression that he had been staying there for a long time.

In the other sitting room, she could make out Rugen, who had brought her things. He was playing *Last Warrior.* The wooden pieces wouldn't stand up properly in the holes on the board. They tipped over frequently and that seemed to irritate him more than it should. He hopped over and removed pieces, hoping to be left with only one, but apparently defeating himself was a challenge for Rugen. He was on his second or third glass of whiskey, so presumably he had drunk too much to think clearly.

How long would it take before the wolf-sickness became conspicuous and he started spitting blood? Before he was drenched in a fever sweat and went crazy? How long before he tried to rip out her throat with his fresh canines?

Juva hadn't asked him about it. Wolf-sickness was a death sentence, and it was up to him to decide when he wanted to share the truth. She was almost certain that he knew, but there was still a small chance that he didn't, and if so, it would be heartless to ruin the time he had left. After all, he had been there for her in spite of everything, pretty unconditionally.

Ester came back and planted a bottle on the table between the dainty teacups, which were decorated on the inside with butterflies. She opened the bottle and diluted Juva's tea with liquor.

"There. Now you'll see it start to look like something," she said once she had made the tea clear enough to see the butterflies in the bottom. Then she continued where she had left off. "You don't owe it to the Sannseyr house to live there, Juva. It's a house, not a creature."

Juva would have laughed if she could. She was anything but superstitious, but if there was a house in Náklav that could be said to be alive, it was hers. The Sannseyr home was hiding the devil.

"I owe it to myself," Juva replied, not sure what she meant.

"Do you know what I like about you, Juva?" Ester took a generous gulp of the tea and studied her.

"My bubbly personality?" Juva quipped dryly.

If Ester understood the joke, she hid it well. "That, too. But what I like about you is that you're afraid of wolves."

"How can I be afraid of wolves? I'm a wolf hunter!"

"Exactly!" Ester pursed her brown-painted lips in a secretive smile. "You'll see; you'll understand one day."

"I don't mean that I'm never afraid." Juva felt a sting of shame at denying it.

"No, I understand that, and you don't need to tell me. I know what fear looks like, and it's not the way people think. I was slower on the uptake than you, so it took quite a blow before I'd had enough and decided to stand up for myself."

Juva glanced at her cane, sensing that these cryptic words had to do with it.

Ester fondled the fist-shaped handle and looked at her. "So, you've heard the rumor, too?" Ester asked.

Juva wanted to respond that she didn't listen to rumors, but that seemed cowardly, so she took a sip of tea instead. Although it was more like tea-flavored liquor at that point.

Ester looked over at the young man sitting in the corner doing embroidery. He met her gaze and a wordless conversation between them made him get up and join Rugen. Ester helped herself to another slice of blueberry cake and pulled her chair in closer to the table.

"Let me tell you something that I've only told two other people in my life. You've heard that I murdered my husband with the cane, is that right?"

"Yes," Juva replied. "But I don't believe it."

"Well, it's true."

Juva's tea went down the wrong way, but Ester continued as if she were talking about the weather.

"I've heard the most unbelievable rumors: that he contracted wolf-sickness, that he took a lover, that he threatened to throw me out. But they all end with me murdering him and that's the only true thing I've heard. And if I had the chance, I'd do it again. This cane has left more marks on me than you can count, but I counted every single blow he gave me. And when the day came when I was lying at the bottom of the stairs and he stumbled after me, then I gave them right back, every single one, until that brute wasn't breathing anymore. I wasn't much older than you."

Juva stared at her in disbelief. Ester, who enjoyed life to its fullest, who never allowed herself to be picked on.

"So maybe you think now that I'm not the type of person to kill someone?" Ester said and took a bite of cake.

"No, I think you're not the type to . . . be beaten?"

"My girl," Ester chortled, "no one is the type to be beaten. I was never a victim, not even in my twenties. I saw myself as strong enough to live with a difficult man. Gradually I forgot what it felt like to be loved. Time wore down my threshold until it was low enough for him."

Her words hit Juva in the gut. Juva's eyes were drawn to Rugen, and she was sure Ester noticed that reflex. But this was about more than him. How much crap had she taken from her mother, because that threshold had been broken down? How much crap had all of Náklav taken from the vardari, because no one expected any better?

"Juva, sometimes life sends us to the foot of the stairs and then the choice is both the simplest and the hardest you can imagine. Do you get up or do you go under? And I believe that you got up already, even though you were a child, you just don't know it yet. So have a little cake, girl!"

Juva took a slice of blueberry cake and gave a bit of it to a blue finch that flew in under the table. The front desk manager called from down below, and Ester excused herself. Juva was left sitting with a fire in her chest that threatened to flare up for no reason. If she opened her mouth, the embers would get air, and the flames would break out, explode into a storm of sparks.

Do I get up or go under?

Juva pushed the cake away and went in to Rugen. "Do you want to come with me to buy something ridiculously expensive?" she asked.

Rugen looked up at her, confused at first, but then, with a growing grin, leapt to his feet. She walked down the stairs, threw on her jacket, and crossed the street with Rugen in hot pursuit.

Agan Askran's shop was protected as if it were Náklabank. The deep green storefront was iron-clad, like an enormous treasure chest, and the windows were covered with a black grating. A sign hung beside the door that said, *"no weapons permitted,"* which was of course comical.

Juva walked in to the jingling of a little bell, and was suddenly surrounded by daggers and swords. They filled all the walls, displayed in the shape of fans or in a herringbone pattern. A long counter stretched along the back wall, which consisted of narrow drawers in green and brown. The smell of steel oil blended with smoke from large lamps under the ceiling.

Juva walked over to the crossbow that she hadn't been able to forget. It was lovely but built for someone bigger than her.

A broad-shouldered man with thinning hair came over to her side. "The young lady has impeccable taste. That one is . . . expensive."

His words were intended to size her up, but she wasn't there for appearances.

"It's mostly too big," she replied.

The man smiled and waved for her to follow him. He took a crossbow of the same type down from the wall and set it on the counter.

"I think you'll like this one. It has a smaller stock, and it can . . ." He glanced over at Rugen, who was juggling a dagger poorly. He cleared his throat loudly, and Rugen set the knife down. "As I was saying, it has a shorter stock, and it can be cocked with one hand."

Juva felt it and gave it back. "No, I need something better. Do you have anything that's lighter to carry, but still effective?"

"Effective against what, reindeer or grouse?" he asked. His eyes lingered on hers, as no answer was forthcoming. "Ah," he said finally. "If you have a license, then I have exactly what you need."

He unlocked a cabinet, took out a glossy wooden box, and opened it on the counter. The crossbow inside was only slightly longer than her forearm. It lay on a black velvet cushion, and she quickly realized why.

Each part was made of steel, richly cut-out to lighten its weight. The mechanism was protected from the wind and weather. He tugged on a bolt on the bottom and the bow cracked in two with a slight click. Juva bit her lip. It was collapsible. And light. She could fit the whole crossbow in her backpack.

"Agan Askran made it himself. It can fit in a trouser leg, and it can bring down a . . . wolf from a couple of paces away. It never fails, not even in wet weather. You could use it underwater if you wanted to. The price is one stave, eighty runes."

Juva brought her knuckles to her lips. Holy Jól. A hundred and eighty runes—she could buy a longship for that much! But she had no use for either a longship or the money. What she needed was something that could kill a warow.

The thought sent a quiver through her heart, as if it were waking back up after several days of rest. Its beats came heavier and faster, followed by a nascent anxiety. The thought of hoggthorn came instantaneously, but then she remembered that her runaway heart didn't mean she was dying, it meant something worse.

Juva turned around and saw a tall figure outside. It was too dark to see the face, but she didn't need to see him to know. She could recognize him, just as surely as if he had been standing next to her. The smoldering light from a lantern across the street drew the outline of the old-fashioned coat with the collar.

Nafraím entered the shop. The bell over the door shook, and then he locked the door. Juva backed away and collided with the counter. Nafraím unbuttoned his coat at the neck.

"I need a small, handheld grindstone," Nafraím said, looking at the merchant. "Could you fetch one for me? You have them in the cellar, I seem to remember."

The merchant's eyes wandered back and forth between Juva and Nafraím before he nodded and ducked into the back room. He closed the door behind him.

Juva patted her hand along the counter, feeling for one of the daggers she had seen there, anything at all that she could use. It felt as if the room were closing in around her. She wanted to run but no longer had control over her feet. Mother's murderer stood before her, Mother's and Solde's. The man had brought the Seida Guild's leaders to their ends and now he was there to get what Mother hadn't wanted to give him.

She could feel the card so clearly under her shirt that she was sure he could see it. But Nafraím didn't do anything. He merely stood there studying her for what felt like forever. There was something hunted about the look in his eyes, sleepless.

"You can sense me," he finally said. It didn't sound like a question.

He came over to her and leaned forward, a hair's breadth from touching her cheek with his own. His breath smelled sweetly rotten, like overripe berries.

"Do you know why? Can you feel it in your veins, the power that binds the worlds together?"

He's insane.

Juva glanced over his shoulder, at Rugen, but he looked more helpless than she had ever remembered seeing him, pale and drenched in sweat. He knew who this was, knew what she was dealing with, and was not in any condition to help her.

Nafraím placed his hands on her cheeks, cold leather gloves against her skin, and stared into her eyes.

"You know where the devil is, don't you?" he said.

She wanted to scream *no*, but she knew that her whole body would give her away if she tried. That was why he was holding her, to see if she lied. Nothing she had learned would help against an immortal. Cold fear constricted her throat and choked her words. The only thing that could save her now was the truth.

Juva nodded.

Nafraím closed his eyes in a surprisingly pained expression and whispered, "Where? Where is he?"

He doesn't know . . .

His ignorance was a straw on the edge of chaos. This was a test. He hadn't been sure if she knew, like the others, the ones who were dead. Nafraím wanted the devil, but he had no idea where he was. No one had any idea where the devil was. Only her.

"Where is he?!" he yelled, so close to her ear that she jumped.

That sudden rage sucked the energy out of her. Mother's words pushed their way forward through her panic.

Don't let them get him.

Juva had to give him something. A piece of truth, but not everything. If she gave him the real devil, or said where he was hidden, that would be the last thing she did. She would be sent to Drukna, buried at sea like the others. Her hope was to give him the truth as it had been only a few days ago, when all she had was a blood reader card.

Juva fumbled under her shirt and handed him the card. Nafraím took it. Turned it over in his hand, as if he was confused. The pulse pounded in her neck, dangerously uneven, clear that the next few moments would determine whether she would live or not.

"Take him," she said, her voice faltering. "The cards were Mother's, her most cherished possession, but take him! Do what you want with the devil, I don't care!"

Nafraím stared at her. His rage seemed to melt from his eyes, and she could swear that he was relieved.

"A blood reader card?" he scoffed and tossed the card aside onto the counter. "You actually have no idea what I'm talking about, do you?"

Juva knew. She knew that the devil was real, and she thought the card could show the way to him, but she had no idea how. And the card didn't seem to mean anything to Nafraím at all.

They kept it hidden from him.

She had to maintain the mask, think like a blood reader. What would she have said if she had nothing to hide? Asked him to leave? No, that was too cowardly and too little, he would see that. She needed to say what she was burning to say. She needed to confront him. She summoned her scorn, and it was not hard to find.

"You're a murderer," she said through clenched teeth.

"It would be both delusional and self-delusional to deny it," Nafraím said, straightening his collar. "I've taken many lives, Juva, but never out of anything but necessity. I can't stand death and I protect life more than you think. Why else would I choose to live so extraordinarily much of it?"

That admission left Juva speechless. It was unexpected and perverse how easily he stood there confirming both murder and ancient myths. As if she didn't mean a thing in the bigger picture.

I am nothing in an eternal life.

Nafraím lowered his chin and looked at his own hands, one oddly stiff, like on a doll.

"I can't blame you for doubting, but I choose to save your life anyway, Juva Sannseyr. That's the least I can do."

He turned his gaze to Rugen, who recoiled at the attention and looked downright sick.

"The boy here has wolf-sickness," Nafraím said. "So, if I were you, I would turn him in or steer clear. Before it escalates."

The silence in the shop was suffocating. The walls gleamed with steel and sword blades. Rugen's chin quivered.

"Ah," Nafraím said, looking at her again. "You knew that already? Well, then I still owe you."

He walked over to the door and placed his stiff hand on the handle. Then he turned back toward Juva.

"My deepest condolences for all you've lost."

His words made the nausea tingle in her throat. They were disgusting coming from his mouth, and he had no right. He walked out and shut the door behind him.

The emotions slowly returned to her body. She was afraid, but her pulse was normal. Her arm hurt where it had been pressed up against the counter. Relief would have to wait. This was only the beginning. She had a secret, and it was going to cost her her life.

Why? Was this about money? Control of the blood readers and the blood pearls? What was it about, the cooperation the warow had had with Mother and the Seida Guild?

And what did it have to do with the damned devil?

Rugen came over to her with the searching look she knew too well. The one that meant he was testing the mood so he could find the right lie. Which one would he choose? That he hadn't known he was sick? Or that he knew, but he wanted to protect her? Or that Nafraím had made up the whole thing?

"Juva, I was going to tell you, but . . ."

Something in her eyes must have warned him not to try anything other than some approximation of the truth.

She abruptly cut short her own laughter and said, "Rugen, I need you to leave now."

"I'm serious, Juva. I was going to tell you, but people were dying, for fuck's sake!"

She shoved her fists into his chest so he stumbled toward the door.

"You're pushing me away?" He assumed his wounded puppy look. "Now, when my life is in danger and I need you the most?"

She wanted to respond but had far too many things to say. She wanted to say that he was one to talk since he'd always run off when she'd needed him the most, that he had put her life at risk, too, by keeping quiet. Plus, it's not like he had lifted a finger against Nafraím.

How did Nafraím know he was sick? Can he smell it?

Most of all, she wanted to tell him to go to Drukna so she could have some peace and quiet and find the devil, find the creature who had triggered a war between the vardari and the blood readers.

Rugen backed away like a pouting child and left the shop.

Juva stood there, her arms shaking, staring down at the crossbow. She heard the door to the back room creak but didn't look up. She could sense the salesman approaching.

"I'll take it," she said.

BONE

Juva waited until evening before she crept through Lykteløkka with her hood pulled down well over her face. A month until spring equinox, and the city lay as if it had been beaten, in a bluish-purple light.

There wasn't a single red lantern to see, just a few yellow ones, which were surely now regarded as safer since they didn't have anything to do with the Seida Guild. She had never seen the place so colorless before. The blood readers' street had bled out.

The anxiety welled up in her as soon as she saw the house, but it was hazy, drowsy. Maybe it was just nerves or warow in the distance. She looked over her shoulder but couldn't see anyone following her.

The Sannseyr home looked like a haunted house. Dark and lifeless, without any lights behind the narrow windows or smoke from the chimneys. The blood reader lantern had been torn down and lay discarded on the landing.

A fragile layer of ice crunched under her feet as she climbed the front steps. She hurriedly let herself in before her courage failed her. The door clanged shut behind her, the way it always had, an ominous song reverberating through the dark foyer.

The squeezing feeling around her heart did not wait, but now she knew where it came from. It was one reason she had never felt at home there, never found peace, not even as a child. She was sharing a house with the devil.

Or was she losing her mind? There'd been so much death. Mother's body, huddled on the floor. The lifeless blood readers around the table in the library. Solde's lolling head, as if even death bored her. Was her mind vulnerable enough to break down and give her a devil to blame?

No. I know what I saw.

She was done doubting her own senses. No one could punish her anymore, nor could they twist reality. She was alone. What did she have other than her own instincts?

A stack of letters lay on the floor inside the mail slot. One of them was embossed with the city council's seal and her name. She reluctantly opened it. The words stood out in the darkness, cool and formal. A request that she report to city councilmember Drogg Valsvik to clear up and sign an agreement as guild master. The other blood readers had designated her the new leader of the Seida Guild.

Juva tossed the letter aside with a bitter laugh.

They want me dead.

From time immemorial, the blood readers had competed for the powerful position of guild master, and now they didn't want it. Now that leadership meant death, they wanted to foist it off on her. To be leader of a guild she would prefer to see drown with Gaula? It was downright laughable, and it wasn't going to happen. But clearing that up with the city council would have to wait. Right now, she had other things to attend to.

Juva set her bag on the skeleton bench and took out her crossbow, prepared for the worst. She should at least be able to defend herself if Nafraím or any other vardari showed up. Or the devil.

As if the devil could be killed by a crossbow bolt.

Should she light a fire in the fireplace? No, then people would know that she was home. Nafraím could find out. She would have to make do with the lamps and lanterns and keep the curtains drawn.

She lit a storm lantern and headed down to the kitchen to put away the food she had brought with her. The house was stuffy: no one had been there since the sepulture. She went into the cold storage room and hummed to chase away her jitters as she unloaded cheese, eggs, bread, and the Vinterhagen Guesthouse's original lavender marmalade.

The basement was the most obvious place to start, so she cocked her crossbow and started searching the rooms. She moved old wooden wine shelves, pushed aside boxes of jam, roots, salted bones, and dried fish, but the only thing she found were the worn stone slabs on the floor. She rapped on the walls with her knuckles. Everything sounded solid. Besides, surely no one would hide something important in a place where the staff rummaged around every single day?

She went back upstairs and thoroughly examined the foyer, the dining room, the bathroom . . . It seemed as if the house changed as she worked since she was seeing it with new eyes. Everything became a potential hiding place. Wide drawers and cupboards, the bases of bookshelves, paintings that were large enough to hide doors.

Is this what it feels like to dissociate? Searching for something you don't actually want to find?

And what would she do if she did find something? Was the devil like the wolf in the fairy tale, or was he like they believed in Undst, a monster that ate people's souls? The thought made her skin crawl. Nafraím was the worst she could imagine, so what if she found something even worse than him? Would the evening end with her beseeching the warow to come take the devil?

Juva moved from room to room, fully aware that she was putting off the library. It was as if her whole body remembered what she had seen in there and was holding her back. She checked the roof, too, a muddle of angles due to the turret-like additions. But there was a flat section in the middle, surrounded by an old stone wall. The only thing she found up there was a broken flowerpot and a wooden stool.

She went back downstairs again and forced herself to go into the library, steeling herself against some sort of reaction to the memory, but the room was asleep in the blue semi-darkness. There was no indication that anything unpleasant had happened in there other than the staring raven in the glass box.

The bookshelves had never been moved, as far as she could remember, so there could be something hidden behind them or possibly in them. But there were corridors running along the outside of the room on both sides, and the walls were too thin to be able to hide anything. She felt with her hands along the open fireplace. She found ashes and dust, nothing else.

Juva wiped her hands on her pants and walked back into the blood reader room. She needed to think. The house was big, it wouldn't do any good to search at random. The wolf glared at her from the wall painting, as if to tell her where he was, but she had already searched along the whole wall without finding anything resembling cracks or secret doors. She had the feeling that her great-grandmother was laughing at her from the hereafter.

Síla Sannseyr. She was the one who had painted the picture. Had she bought this house because there was something devilish in it, or had she brought something devilish later on? Someone with wolf-sickness? Or perhaps a warow, who had cost Father his life. Why?

The devil is the blood.

That's what Mother had said. Did that mean the vardari and the Seida Guild were working on the blood pearls together, and had been ever since her great-grandmother's time? For money and blood-reader-power? And where did the devil card fit into the picture? Those cards had belonged to her great-grandmother as well . . .

Juva sat down at the table where each client had sacrificed one drop, one after the other until a rust color had soaked into the woodwork in the middle. She retrieved the card from inside her

235

corset. Nafraím hadn't understood its significance either, so maybe only the Seida Guild knew its secret. Or was she on a wild goose chase? She took the other cards out of the box and spread them on the table. It left a bad taste, knowing that her mother had done the same so many times.

Juva stared at the cards. None of them made her any wiser. If the symbolism and significance of the cards had something to tell her, then she was going to be sitting there until her hair turned gray. Aside from the pictures, the cards were identical. The same style with the same borders, apart from . . .

The corners.

The devil card was different from the other ones! All the cards had the same borders, with four little dots in the corners, like the dots on dice, but none of the corners on the devil were the same. Some of the dots were completely black while the others were not filled in, just outlined. That detail was nearly impossible to notice. You had to be looking for it. Could that be from wear? No—true, the card was old, but they all were, and none of the other cards had similar flaws. It seemed intentional.

She got goosebumps on her arms. The burn-marked picture seemed alive in the scant light from the storm lantern. She rubbed her thumb over the dots to make sure she wasn't imagining it, but they were real. The reality she had always striven to grasp felt more solid than ever.

Thoughts and memories fought for space in her head, too many to control. Things Mother had said, the iron wolf she had seen, her heart fluttering, blood pearls, and true-sight. Juva put her hand to her chest and felt the hard, irregular rhythm. Her whole life the devil had followed her.

Pull yourself together! You don't believe in the devil!

The Dead Man's Horn resounded in the distance. A signal of a far more palpable evil, but she needed to get to the bottom of this.

She had to stow away her fear and think clearly, or succumb to the superstition that had always surrounded her. She was searching for something or someone, and she had seen him. In a cupboard, or a cage, out in the hall. It was a long time ago, so if it was someone with wolf-sickness, he would be dead by now. But it could be a warow . . . a man who attacked her heart, the way Nafraím did. No matter what, it was a living creature that needed air, water, food . . .

Who had taken care of it? Mother?

That thought was downright laughable. Mother had hardly been able to take care of herself. If she had been responsible for Ester's guesthouse, every single plant would have withered overnight. Juva exhaled, her body lighter. Of course there wasn't anyone there. If the devil existed, and he had been dependent on Mother, then more's the pity for the poor thing. Lagalune had never been anything but impulsive, fickle, and lazy.

Mother was lazy.

So lazy that she would have made it easy to get to a hidden room!

Juva leapt to her feet and ran into her mother's bedroom. She checked under the bed one more time, around the fireplace, and in the cupboards. No loose tiles, nothing that could be pushed. The chest of drawers wouldn't budge. She opened its drawers and rummaged through the corsets, jewelry, and cigars. The bottom drawer was locked, but what kind of devil could you fit in a drawer? All the same . . .

Juva found the key in the nightstand, twisted it in the lock, and pulled out the bottom drawer. She stared down at neatly organized stacks of lace underwear, obviously never used since the drawer contents were the only tidy thing she had seen in her search. And why was it locked? Mother had never been the shy type, had she? Her room had been generally strewn with intimate undergarments.

Juva ran her hand over the bottom. There was nothing there, but the edges seemed thicker than in the other drawers.

It had a false bottom!

She tugged on the handle, but the drawer refused to come all the way out of the dresser. She positioned her hands inside and lifted. The entire contents of the draw followed. Juva tossed aside the insert containing the underwear and stared down at what had been so painstakingly hidden.

A coiled rope and an empty hemp sack.

She sighed in disappointment. Why were they hidden? The rope had hooks on both ends. One was secured to the solid wooden front of the dresser. The sack was completely ordinary, but she opened it anyway. Breadcrumbs. And the smell of rancid fat.

Food.

Fear washed through her body and her fingers stiffened, but she felt along the edges of the drawer anyway. She had to find what she was looking for, because it was more than the devil. She was looking for herself, and a truth she had been waiting for far too long. The house had shrunk to this one room, to this one drawer. Nothing else existed.

There was a joint in the bottom, and it felt loose.

It's a magic trick! A magic box!

The shops around Nákla Henge had loads of them! Boxes you could put little trinkets in, and when you opened them again, the items were gone, because you pushed them down into a secret space when you closed the box.

Juva stood up and walked back down to the cold storage room as if in a trance. She took down a piece of young goat meat that was hanging from the ceiling to age, painfully aware that she was acting bizarrely. This was without a doubt the stupidest thing she had done.

She went back up to her mother's room again, put the goat meat in the hemp sack, and secured it to the hook on the rope. Then she closed the drawer. She heard a click, followed by the unmistakable sound of the rope uncoiling as it fell. The front of the drawer gave a jerk, and then it was quiet.

How far had the sack fallen? The height of four or five men, maybe more?

Juva stared at her hands, which were shaking against her thighs. She felt nauseated, dizzy. Her heart was prickling as she breathed, and she heard an echo from the cook's stuttering self-defense from when her mother had died.

What hasn't she eaten. She . . . she eats like a bear.

But nothing happened, of course not. If the devil had actually been in the house, then he would have starved to death by now. No one had fed him since Mother had died.

You've lost your mind, Juva. It's over.

She was a child again. The little girl who had imagined that she had seen a devil and drew it. Mother had beaten her, laughed, raged, threatened, called her devil child, and said that she needed to shut up so she didn't conjure him up again, the beast that killed Father.

Enough. It was enough now.

There was no devil. She had been destroyed by this house, by blood readers and warow. She had become mixed up in a war over blood pearls that did not concern her. She had to get out of there. Sell the house or burn it down. Move to Fimle, or Skaug, and finally be free.

Yes, that's what she would do.

She felt nearly weightless with relief. She opened the drawer a crack and saw that the bottom was hinged at the joint. The rope dangled down into a darkness she couldn't see the end of, and she pulled it up again, imagining that it felt easier than it should.

Juva lifted the sack out of the drawer and opened it. The goat meat was gone. All that was left was a cluster of bones that had been picked clean. She dropped the bag. Crawled backward until she hit the wall and threw up.

IRON WOLF

Juva pressed her back to the wall. Fear tightened like a band of ice around her chest. She groped for her crossbow and aimed it at the dresser, as if Gaula were going to crawl out of it. Her arm started shaking and she had to brace it against her knee.

We've been living with the devil.

She had been steeped in superstition and mysticism from an early age. In all its unpleasant forms and from every corner of the world—banned books, decorated skulls, plague masks, entrails in jars, dried tongues from necromancers and gruesome illustrations of blood sacrifices. But this . . .

This was the worst. A baby goat carcass with no meat left on it. A hemp sack of pale bones picked so clean they could have been ancient. She could picture the conversation with the guys around the campfire in the woods.

"What's the scariest thing you've ever seen?"

"Food scraps."

Juva laughed. Her fear abated and became a familiar amazement that she hadn't lost her mind. Her thoughts were jumbled in her head, small rafts on a stormy sea. Had she imagined it? Had it not happened? Had she made it happen? Had someone tricked her? One last drama from Lagalune, tailor-made to drive the devil child insane. It could be the warow, revenge for Mother's having defied them. And now they'd made her crazy.

No! I was never the one who was crazy.

The proof was right in front of her, in an open dresser drawer. All the times she had felt her heart racing, lost her footing, and asked herself what was real . . . There was a reason for it. She had seen something she was never supposed to have seen, something her mother had tormented her about to make sure she'd forgotten it—but it was still here.

Three metallic bangs on the front door ripped Juva from her trance. Her flock of worries narrowed into one single question.

What the hell am I going to do?!

What if it was Nafraím? She was alive because she didn't know anything. Solde had taken her place and died for it. She would never be able to hide what she knew now, and that would be the end of it.

Never let them see a weak blood reader.

For once, her mother's teachings were welcome. Juva got up and walked out to the foyer. She set her crossbow on the stairs, lowered her shoulders, and wiped her sweaty hands off on her pants. Then she opened the door.

A boy stood outside, a little older than a typical delivery boy, and considerably better dressed.

"Mrs. Sannseyr, pardon me for disturbing you in your grief, but I represent a client whose name must remain unspoken at present. She sends her deepest condolences."

"Thank you," Juva replied. She tried to close the door again, but the young representative stuck his foot in the way.

"She knew your mother and would, of course, very much like to continue her relationship as a customer."

"Convey my greetings to her and thank her, but I don't have any customers. There are no longer any blood readers residing in this house."

"No, we understand that it's . . . complicated, and we can assure you that we will keep our contact both lucrative and confidential."

Juva would have laughed at his choice of words if the whole situation hadn't been so tragic. So, they understood that the blood readers were afraid after the murders, but they still wanted advice on their own fates?

"I don't have any customers," Juva repeated. "Neither above board nor under the table. But thank you all the same."

She closed the door and there was another knock, almost immediately. She opened it a crack and peeked out. Another errand boy, this one more normally dressed. How in Drukna could they know she was there? Had somebody hung up a damn flyer at Brenntorget or something?

"Juva Sannseyr? I have a message from city councilman Valsvik. He has been trying to get ahold of you. It pertains to the leadership position in the Seida Guild, which needs—"

"Tell the councilman that if he wants to speak to me, he can come here on his own two feet," Juva said, feeling confident that that would never happen, because Drogg Valsvik was the most out-of-shape man in Náklav.

She closed the door and stood listening to be sure that the messenger departed. He did, but not long after that, footsteps came back up the stairs. Juva yanked open the door and found herself staring at Broddmar, dressed in red.

The Dead Man's Horn.

Someone with wolf-sickness was loose again, but she was glad to see him anyway. Broddmar would understand. She could talk to him.

No . . . Not about this.

The weight of what she knew couldn't be shared with anyone. To know was to die.

Broddmar walked past her into the foyer with the wolf at his heels. He pulled down his red mask and looked over at the crossbow on the stairs.

"Good thing I stopped by, I see," he said.

Juva bit her lip as she searched for an explanation, but Broddmar didn't ask for one.

"No weapon and no contact," he began to rattle off brusquely. "Keep your distance, both from me and from the sick person until he's dead. You're observing, that's all, and you'll do what I say. Got that?"

He wants me to come!

Juva nodded. She couldn't say no. Then he would know something was wrong. She had been whining to get this chance for a year. The timing couldn't be worse, but she still felt relieved to get out of the house.

She wanted to ask why he had backed down, but she knew the answer. The murders gave her the right. As long as he believed someone with wolf-sickness had killed Solde and the others, he couldn't deny her a shot at revenge.

Juva didn't have any hunting clothes with her, but they were in a hurry, so what she had would have to do. Pants she could easily run in, and a warm jersey with a hood. Not made for blood work, but she would just be watching. She double checked the front door as they left. The lock had never failed, as long as she could remember, but now suddenly it seemed meager. It would surely be an easy undertaking for someone who was determined to get in.

Or out.

Skarr circled her once, even though he had met her before. This time, she was the newbie. His wary, yellow eyes met her own, and she could imagine what the wolf was thinking.

You hunt mine, now I hunt yours.

Broddmar clicked his tongue and then he and the wolf hurried off in the lead. They didn't hesitate, so they knew where they were going. She followed them up to Ringmark, the oldest part of the city, around Nákla Henge. The Dead Man's Horn had chased most people indoors, but not there. People strolled past Broddmar and pretended not to notice him. People in Ringmark had a blasé attitude, as if no misery could ever reach them.

But wolf-sickness didn't discriminate, and blood users could be found in every stratum of society.

Up by Brenntorget, the Ring Guard had hung two dead wolves from the gallows. Flayed and hoisted up by their hind legs. People glared at the carcasses and avoided coming too close. Juva felt a distaste she knew she had no right to, but this was no hunt. This was a meaningless attempt to pretend that something beneficial was being done against the sickness.

Broddmar continued up Kistestikk and then took a detour, to where the Ring Guard stood at the ready outside an old-style tenement building, richly decorated with stone figures. Weathered tentacles writhed around the windows, as if Gaula was about to personally eat the building. The residents had been drawn out onto the street, thinly dressed and sensitive to the cold. A hysterical woman fought to get back inside, but the Ring Guard restrained her.

Juva approached to hear Broddmar and the guards talking. The wolf-sick individual was a long-term resident housekeeper, who had killed her husband in a bedroom in the basement. Now she had moved to the second floor, to the parlor of the family she worked for. The hysterical woman was a member of this family. Her husband and nine-year-old daughter were still inside. No one knew if they were alive.

Broddmar left his wolf with a nervous and reluctant watchman, and waved Juva into the house with him. She followed him up the stairs until he stopped outside an oak door with polished brass fittings. Someone had pulled a chair in front of it to keep the infected person inside. Creepy noises could be heard through the door. A sort of feverish scraping and furious shrieks. Then silence.

Juva felt its heart quiver, tentative and uncertain. This was neither wolf nor vardari, but it was *something*, and she could feel it.

Was this what lived in her house? Had she just fed a furious, bloodthirsty monster? Juva hid her hands behind her back so Broddmar wouldn't notice that she was shaking.

A man yelled and pounded on something persistently. Then the screaming and scraping started again, several times. The noise was muffled, from some room other than the one just inside the door. Juva clenched her fists, trying to chase away the worst-case-scenario images of what was going on.

Broddmar cautiously moved the chair. He pulled one of the knives from his belt and handed it to Juva.

"Second choice," he whispered.

Juva grasped the knife greedily. She'd felt completely naked without it.

"What's the first choice?"

"Run."

Juva stared at his toothless smile and reminded herself that he had done this many times before. He put his hand on the doorknob, waited until the screaming began again, and opened the door a crack. He raised his hand flat, a hunting signal that told her to stay calm. Then he pulled another knife and stepped inside. The door remained ajar.

They stepped into a living room in pale pink and yellow. There was an open door at the far end of the room next to a fireplace of veinstone. The veins were pink, to harmonize with the walls. It would have looked regal if it hadn't been for the bloodstains. There were smeared stripes of blood as if someone had failed to claw their way into the chimney.

The fireplace sat dead, aside from the ash drizzling down from the chimney. Juva squinted, but the ash rain ended just as quickly as it had begun.

Broddmar moved like a cat on a fence, placing his feet slowly and deliberately. The flat, red bloodskins lay strapped to his back, and made it look like he was hiding wings under his outfit.

The screaming stopped again. Footsteps approached. Broddmar threw himself around the corner of a glass-front bookcase, just in time to hide from the woman who came in. She waddled toward the fireplace as if she had injured herself. Her fingers were bloody and injured, and she was touching her face and hair. And her stomach . . . Juva stiffened. The woman was expecting a child, and she had seen her before. In the waiting room at home, the day she had returned home.

Vera.

No wonder she had been afraid of giving birth. She was a blood user!

And I told her it would go well.

Juva felt her cheeks tingle, as if she were going to be sick. Broddmar peeked around the corner of the book cabinet at the woman, who stood with her back to him, clawing at the chimney as she had apparently done many times before. Then the pounding began again. Panicked shouts came from a man in the room Vera had just come from. Vera stopped clawing and looked up.

The man . . . The girl! The chimney!

Suddenly Juva realized what was going on. The girl had climbed up inside the chimney, and her father had barricaded himself in another room. He was making noise to attract her attention so she wouldn't find the girl.

Juva clutched the doorframe and breathed to keep her nausea at bay. The woman turned toward the racket in the neighboring room. She wrinkled up her nose like a wolf. Her eyes were cold and wild, stripped of their humanity. Even so, she still had a hand on her belly, as if she still had an instinct to protect the life of the unborn child.

Broddmar lunged forward, raising his knife for the kill, but stopped short, hesitating. He was staring at the woman's belly, and his arm fell back down, powerless.

No!

Juva rushed in with her knife out in front of her, and the sick creature came at her in fearless bounds. She would have run right into the blade had Broddmar not caught up with her. The woman stopped short and stretched up her neck. Her throat made a gurgling sound. A jerk of her body revealed when Broddmar pulled his knife out of her back. She knelt and then fell over onto her side. The murmuring in Juva's heart was doused.

Broddmar stood mesmerized. His eyes drilled their way into Juva, like a prayer, but there was nothing more she could do to help him. The shouts from the man grew more desperate.

"Go in there and talk to him," Juva prodded Broddmar. "Tell him what happened."

Broddmar snapped out of it and ran into the room next door. Juva walked over to the fireplace. She was about to bend over and peer up but guessed that she would take a stone to the head if her theory was correct.

"You can come out now," she said instead. "Vera's dead. Your mom and dad are waiting for you."

There was a scraping in the chimney, and a pair of bare legs appeared. A black-haired girl landed between charred stumps, filthy all over. Her face had clean grooves where her tears had washed off the ash. She was wearing a nightgown that had surely been clean before the evening had turned into a nightmare.

Juva squatted down. The girl flung her thin arms around Juva's neck, and her little body trembled. The price of wolf blood had never seemed higher. Juva squeezed her eyes shut. She couldn't break down now, she had to keep it together, show Broddmar that she was worthy. No more wolf blood, never. She should quit hunting. The damned stone circle could rot, it didn't matter to her. People could sail on ships like they did in Undst. They had no traveling stones and they got by. Nothing could be worth this.

She felt a strange urge to say that this would pass, but Juva knew that the girl would never forget.

"My name is Juva," she mumbled into the girl's hair. "Juva Sannseyr. And if anyone tries to tell you that you didn't see what you saw tonight, then come find me."

She felt the girl nod energetically against her chest.

Broddmar came in with a man whose face was just as streaked from crying as the girl's. Juva wriggled out of the girl's grasp and the father embraced her with an agonized expression. Broddmar walked over to the window and made a sign. A second later the room was full of Ring Guardians, watchmen, and the girl's sobbing mother.

Juva stared at the bloody marks on the chimney.

The chimney. The best place to hide something.

She had checked all the chimneys at home without finding anything resembling cracks or openings. Maybe they had bricked them over?

Juva headed for the door, but heard Broddmar say from behind her, "We're not done."

The Ring Guard went through the house and made sure that everything was all right before they left the building. They left the body lying there. Juva remembered what that meant and felt so infinitely tired.

The blood. She will be fed to the stones.

Broddmar provided the instructions and Juva obeyed. They carried Vera into the bathroom and lay her in the tub. Broddmar snapped out her canines. Then he grabbed her around her legs and pulled her up as high as he had the strength to do.

"Take the skins," he grunted, and Juva loosened the two bloodskins from his back. They were bigger than the ones they used on their wolf hunts. She handed them to him, but he shook his head. This was her job now.

I thought I was just going to observe?

Juva wanted to throw down the skins and leave. She couldn't remember what she was doing there anymore. She wanted to go. Home. Even home to a wolf-sick devil or a rotten warow. Anything was better than this. But she had bled so many wolves that her hands obeyed all on their own. She opened the stopper and placed the pouring spout to Vera's throat. Then she hit it, giving it a sturdy blow, and the knife-sharp spout sank into Vera's neck. Right away, the red skin began to swell.

"Hurry up," said Broddmar, who had begun to sweat. He shifted the woman's limp legs to get a better hold.

Juva pulled out the spout, which made a macabre kissing sound. She screwed the plug into the swollen skin while the blood continued to flow down into the tub. She swapped out the skins as quickly as she could. It was always gross to swap them out. Driving something into an open wound felt inhumane. And it was almost impossible not to spill.

The woman grew pale, and the skins full. Juva strapped them back on to Broddmar's back, and he hustled her out of the room. The Ring Guard would come back to clean it up.

Outside, it had started raining. The drops froze into ice the minute they hit anything and formed little needles that broke beneath her feet. They clung to her hair and her clothes.

They left without a word. Skarr padded along in front, as far ahead as his leash permitted, but he kept having to wait for them. The ice decorated his fur, and she could smell it, wild and wet. She wished she could take him home with her to feel safer. But why would a wolf want to be with a hunter like her?

They stopped outside the Sannseyr home.

Broddmar gave her shoulder a couple of helpless pats. Ice pearls glittered in the stubble of his beard. "I wasn't planning to—"

"No."

"Do you want me to—"

"No."

"Fine." He nodded. "Think it over for a few days. I'll stop by."

Juva walked up the front steps and let herself in. The dark foyer with its glistening black staircase felt unexpectedly safe. An illusion thanks to what she had just seen and done. The sudden presence in her heart told her that the devil was still in the house.

In the woods, it was often ravens that led the way to wolves, and Juva knew just which raven to follow.

She slipped off her shoes and walked right into the library. The stuffed poultry seemed to have more of a glint in its eye than usual.

The overdecorated cabinet the raven sat in was taller than she was and too heavy to budge. There was also no wear on the floor to suggest that it had ever been moved much. But maybe there was something inside of it, in its base?

Juva went and fetched what she thought was the right key from the drawer of the nightstand in her mother's room. It was small and golden, like a piece of jewelry, and she stared at it with disgust. As if it had forced her to do this searching. She turned it and opened the door in the base of the raven cabinet. The cashbox was attached on top. There were a few coins in it, from visitors who had amused themselves with the fortune-teller. Otherwise, it was empty.

No. There must be something here.

The food hatch in the bedroom had been a clever, well-hidden arrangement. The raven cabinet could be something similar, something no one was meant to find. She got the storm lantern and knelt down in front of the door. She felt around the inside with her hand. There was a lever on the inside of the wall, but it didn't move. She propped her feet against the cabinet and pulled the lever toward her with both hands. The cabinet made a barking sound and jerked. A thump came from the chimney.

Juva stood up. There was a narrow gap underneath the cabinet now and she could just barely make out little brass wheels under the corners. She raised her arms and wrapped them around her head. Looked around, as if someone would suddenly be there in the room. Holy Jól and cursed Gaula, had she contracted wolf-sickness and lost her wits? Her heart beat double-time, as if in confirmation.

She stared at the cabinet. It wasn't too late. She could push the lever back again, sell the house, and move to Kreknabork somewhere, leaving all of this behind her. What was the worst that could happen?

Nafraím would find the devil, that's what. The monster Mother hadn't wanted to give him. The wolf blood would flow, blood use would increase, and the nightmare she had experienced tonight would continue for all eternity. And the vardari would get away with it.

Juva put her hands on the side of the cabinet and pushed. It started rolling, but not by itself. The wall went with it. She kept pushing as she goggled at the opening that grew into a gaping hole in the chimney. Juva stuck her head into it and stared down into a cool, black abyss.

Rust-stained steel tracks gleamed in the four corners, with tooth-like notches. There had been some sort of elevator a long time ago. A narrow iron ladder was bolted to the wall just below her. She couldn't see the bottom of it. Juva turned up the wick in the storm lantern with trembling fingers. The flame grew, but the abyss remained just as vast.

The answers she had never gotten were somewhere down there—even horrifying answers were better than none. There was something in the house, something people had died for. She got to her feet and retrieved her crossbow from the foyer, cocking it anew. She hung the lantern from the same arm, so she had one free hand to climb with.

She put her feet on the top rung, tentatively at first and then adding more weight. The ladder creaked but seemed solid. She started climbing. The temperature dropped quickly. The shaft went far deeper than the basement. What in Drukna could be underneath the basement?

The wharves!

The stories about her great-grandmother spun through her head. Síla Sannseyr, the woman who had bought this house from an old harbormaster and forced the city council to relocate the wharves. Why? Because she hated the smell of smoked whale.

He's in the smoke shafts.

This was where the ships had moored, sailing right into the cliff walls to unload their catches. Enormous whales had been gutted and smoked right here. For crying out loud, she could still see the old dark dock pilings from her bedroom window at low tide!

Her feet found solid ground. A tunnel with a high ceiling sloped diagonally down toward the water.

Underneath Mother's room and the wine cellar.

Juva held the crossbow and lantern out in front of her and hesitantly made her way forward. The end of the tunnel didn't look like anything but a black wall. But there was something in it, over to the right. She walked all the way to the end and stood in front of a door. A rusty iron door with a small window hatch covered by a grating.

That door . . . She had experienced this before, seen it before, forgotten it before.

The closet with the wolf, the iron wolf.

Her heart thundered in her chest as if it were two hearts—violently, spasmodic and rhythmless, completely unable to define the danger. Her breath caught in her throat and her crossbow was on the verge of sliding out of her sweaty grip. She put her hand on the rusty iron door. It was ancient, a grotesque, mechanical device with levers and gears. Two rows of bolts ran across the door underneath the hatch, each bolt just barely stuck up from the surface.

There was a metallic smell and the faint odor of smoke and ocean. The lantern light flickered. Juva had been only seven when she first came down the stairs and saw the iron wolf, the monster in the iron closet. She got up on her tiptoes and peered in through the narrow hatch. There wasn't just one hatch, but two, she saw now. Because the device was a closet, an iron closet, with a door on each side. Like a little room, bricked in by the stone walls.

She held up the lantern and tried to see what was in the space inside the iron closet. It was dark. Empty. Then the silhouette of a form emerged, a pale, naked man with black hair. Juva's heart beat against the rusty iron, throbbing against the door. Not just her own, but two, two hearts beating against one another. Was this what it felt like to die?

The devil lifted his head and looked at her with milky-white, blind eyes. The ones she had only seen in nightmares. The lantern slid out of her hand. It shattered on the stone floor and left her in an unbearable darkness.

TRAITOR

Nafraím turned the card over in his hand, even though he knew what would be on the other side: a seemingly innocent invitation from Eydala, issued to select warow, as if she had ever been in a position to summon them together. At worst it was a trap, at best a declaration of war. But he had known that it would come now that the devil appeared to be lost to them all. They were desperate.

He crumpled the card in his hand, tossed it onto the floor, and looked at Rugen. The exhausted man stood by the door, drenched from the rain, his nerves clearly frayed, as he rattled off what little he had to convey.

"... and, anyway, I would have gotten her to talk if you had given me more time! If you hadn't said I was sick, I would have gotten more, so what was the point?"

Nafraím stood up. "The point?"

Rugen looked like he was trying to back away, but there was no space behind him.

Nafraím went over to him. He put a finger under Rugen's chin and lifted his face. Forced the boy to look him in the eye. "I have taken many lives, few with joy. The point was to give her a chance. An opportunity to let go of you and save herself."

Nafraím heard the sorrow in his own words but doubted that Rugen was able to notice the difference. He turned his back to the boy and walked over to the window.

Rugen came darting after him. "But listen to what I'm saying, would you? You took the wrong life! The sister was never supposed to be the heir—it should have been Juva."

Nafraím struggled to control his irritation. The boy was like a horsefly, a true nuisance, wolf-sick and desperate.

"Juva doesn't know anything," Nafraím said. "Come to your senses and leave her alone. I don't need you anymore."

"But she must know *something*! She's always been secretive, and I don't know what devil you're looking for, but she's been drawing him her whole life. That's got to mean something."

"Drawing him?" Nafraím turned toward him.

"Always!" The hunger grew in Rugen's eyes. "Since she was little. I can find out more, but for fuck's sake, look at me—I'm done! I taste blood."

His hands shook and he was sweating. It wouldn't take long. Soon his new teeth would grow in, the madness would flourish, and his life would be lost.

"I see that. The safest thing you can do is stay indoors."

Nafraím felt an unfamiliar agitation. Drawing the devil? That wasn't exactly common subject matter for little girls. But then, people discussed the devil in so many contexts, and he could be so varied. Still, doubt lodged in his thoughts like a thorn.

"Have you seen these drawings?" he asked.

"No, but she never lies." Rugen chuckled.

"And how little was she?"

"How the fuck should I know? Seven? Eight? She said she'd seen him and been scared out of her wits."

Nafraím dug through his memories, trying to remember what had happened when he'd forced Lagalune to move the devil. It must have been about ten to twelve years ago, when he had first suspected that the Might was on its way back. He had bluffed, saying the source was threatened, that it would be revealed by other vardari, and so needed to be moved. Lagalune had promised to discuss it with the Seida Guild, and a few days later, she had informed him that the job was done.

He had hoped that they would react by panicking and giving away the hiding spot. But he had kept an eye on them and hadn't detected any indication of where the devil was.

Could Lagalune have seen through his ruse? She was a smarter woman then she'd appeared to be. What if she'd had him moved that very night and used her own home as an interim location? Juva had been little at the time, and she could have seen him, as Rugen claimed.

An uneasy agitation settled in his chest, and he knew it wouldn't let go until he figured this out.

"I'm right, aren't I?" Rugen elbowed him as if they were old friends.

Nafraím eyed him without hiding his disgust. What was it that made betrayal come so easily to some people?

"Right about what?"

"Juva saw him, the one you're looking for. I know that's worth something, man. I need more, for the pain. You promised!"

Nafraím clenched and unclenched his fist, feeling that ancient numbness in his muscles.

"Boy, I never promised you anything at all. You squandered the chances you were given and nothing I can give you is going to help. Now, run along."

Rugen stared at him in disbelief. An angry look crossed his face, but he caught himself. He wasn't so slow on the uptake, that was something. Nafraím stared out at the ocean and heard the youngster cursing as he ran up the stairs.

Could it be true that the devil had been in Náklav? That seemed unlikely. All the evidence, for centuries, led to Kreknabork. It was a favorite destination for Lagalune and the others. It could also be somewhere in Fimle, possibly a place of worship. There had been rumors about a monastic order that kept him in subterranean burial chambers. How in Jól's name would they get him out of there and through the stone gates? Impossible. Had he come by ship? Hidden from the crew for the whole voyage?

No. If Rugen was right, and Juva had actually seen him, that meant he had *always* been in Náklav—and still was.

Nafraím's fingers felt warm, as if the blood had suddenly started flowing to his half-dead hand. Could multiple generations of blood readers have been so reckless as to hide something from the vardari *in the vardari's own hometown*, a place he had almost unlimited control over?

That would be downright idiotic.

But wasn't that what he himself had done? The door in the wall at Nákla Henge was hidden in full public view, right in the middle of a bunch of other doors.

Nafraím turned and looked at the floor, cocking his head to the side. He had crumpled up the invitation from Eydala and tossed it aside. Now it was gone.

Rugen.

Gaula's coward! That boy was going to find Eydala and share the same information with her. A chill crept down his spine and Nafraím felt repulsively alive, vulnerable and exposed. This was a race he couldn't afford to lose.

GRÍF

Pain shot through her knee and snapped Juva out of her shock. She had fallen on the stairs in the foyer. She couldn't remember having climbed back up the shaft, just the panic that had propelled her.

She got up, took a seat on a stairstep, and rubbed her temples with her fingers. Her head ached, as if she had gasped in salt water.

The devil is down there.

He was no wolf, nor any normal man. But she had seen him before, and he was just as real as the throbbing in her knee. She got up on wobbly feet and looked down at the floor in the foyer, the way she remembered having done that time, as a child. She closed her eyes and summoned forth the memory she had hidden away and forgotten for so long.

There's a thunderstorm. Ice needles whip against the windowpane, and I sit up in bed. Why? Am I scared? No, I'm never afraid of the weather. The fear comes later.

It's something else, something I hear. My feet don't reach all the way to the floor, so I wriggle off the side of my bed. I walk down the corridor, following the angry voices from below, Mother and Father.

I start down the stairs, one step at a time because they're so steep. I can barely see over the railing. It's dark, but there's a . . . cupboard, a huge standing chest that I've never seen before. Light shivers on the floor, from the library, where Mother and Father are arguing. I think maybe they're fighting about the cupboard.

I walk around it, touch it. It's made of cold iron and has two doors, with an opening at the top. But I can't reach up there. The doors are strange, without handles. Just a wheel, like on a ship. There's a chair under the stairs, one I have never seen since, and I move it over to the cupboard. I climb up and peek in the opening.

Juva opened her eyes and stared at the floor where the cupboard had stood. The iron cage, which was now bricked into the wall down in the shaft. She squeezed her hands around her head because she knew it would get worse. She'd remember things she didn't want to remember, but she didn't have a choice, because what she had seen had shaped her life.

She walked down the stairs and positioned herself as if the iron cage still stood there on the floor. She had climbed up onto the chair, holding on to the bars in front of the window opening, and looked at him. Black haired, white eyed, sharp canine teeth. He had touched her hand with his claws.

Father . . .

Father had come into the foyer and seen her. His cry was genuine, she could hear it still. He had grabbed her and started attacking the iron closet with the fireplace poker, jabbing it between the bars. She had become hysterical, kicking and crying while she dangled in her father's grasp. Red rain over her nightgown. *Why?*

Juva looked at her pants, as if the blood would grow from her memory.

The wound. The gaping wound on his forearm.

The beast in the cage had injured her father. She had always known that it wasn't a hunting injury. He had stayed in his bed afterward, before he died. She had no idea for how long. Mother had been the only one allowed to be with him. Juva had stood outside, sneaking peeks and knowing it was her fault.

Nothing had been the same since. Everything had been lost that night. The closet. Father. And her sense of safety.

The way a child would, she had given him a name of his own, a creature with canine teeth and claws in an iron closet. The iron wolf. She had drawn him and shown it to Mother. Mother had gone berserk and hit her. Juva could remember how the shock had taken her breath away, and she had felt as if she would never be able to catch it again.

Mother had said it was the devil and thrown the drawing in the fire.

Do you want him to become real?

She could hear the question so clearly now, as if it had happened yesterday. She had believed that she had conjured up the devil, that she was the one who had brought him. And most importantly of all: she needed to burn him, so he wouldn't become real again. And she could never, ever speak of him.

Slowly but surely, she had begun to doubt her own senses. She had lost her grasp on reality. Drawing him in secret and burning him so more people wouldn't die, so more horrible things wouldn't happen. The obsession had ridden her, relentlessly.

Why? Because it had been more important to hide the creature than for her to grow up feeling safe. And now that everyone else was gone, she was left with this legacy, the world's most dangerous secret.

Juva wiped her nose on her sleeve, and she realized she was crying. She had found a man, a monster, and she was the only one who knew where he was, but the relief washed through her all the same, purifying, clarifying. She had found proof that she knew what was true and what wasn't, proof that she wasn't a devil child. She was Juva. And she had seen him.

Juva lifted her chin and took strength from this certainty. She could be relieved later, furious later. And she could sleep later. Right now, she needed to confront the most real thing she had experienced in this house.

She fetched a new storm lantern from by the front door and double checked that she had locked the door. She threw on a thick shawl and stuck her feet into a pair of slippers. Then she walked back to the library and opened the bar cabinet. The first thing she saw was the whiskey that Ester had brought to Mother's wake. She filled a glass and drank it. It burned going down into her chest, but there were limits to how clear-headed you wanted to be when you were about to confront the devil.

She took a deep breath and began the long climb down through the massive rock layer that all of Náklav sat atop.

The walls were smooth near the top, but rougher for the last portion, presumably the part that was deeper than the cellar. Her feet touched the bottom and she raised the lantern. The tunnel seemed shorter. She could see the crossbow and the smashed lantern in a dim light that hadn't been there before.

He lit a lamp.

The whiskey wasn't strong enough, and her courage threatened to fail. The iron door lay at the end of the tunnel, but if it had just been straight ahead and not to the right . . . she wouldn't have needed to get so uncomfortably close to it to see.

She crept forward, her back to the wall, until she stood facing the door. It was bleak and didn't look like anything she had seen elsewhere. Reddish-brown rust had eaten its way along the seams of the door and around the hinges. The turning wheel and levers must have been an opening mechanism, but the two rows of bolts made no sense.

Someone had carted him here, in this closet, which must be unbelievably heavy, and bricked that into the wall, like a little vestibule to the room within. Not to mention all the work of hollowing out the tunnel.

What in Drukna was worth doing something like that?

Through the bars in the two layers of doors she could see the room, but not him. It would be easier if she opened the outermost door, but the very idea gave her goosebumps. Two doors between her and the devil was barely enough.

A shadow moved. It crept forward and stood before the hatch. Two doors, but only one step away.

Juva gasped, but the air felt empty. Her pulse rushed in her ears as if her whole body was one enormous, beating heart, and it was pounding so hard that she knew each beat must be the last. She backed away and bumped into the wall.

"Breathe in."

The voice began suddenly, deep and husky, and made her stiffen. She stared at those white eyes, completely devoid of pupils or color, but they were obviously anything but blind. He had spoken to her.

"Breathe out."

The command was so simple that she found herself obeying. She was lured in, enchanted and surrounded by bedrock, with the devil. And he was asking her to breathe.

"Slowly," he added. He moved so she couldn't see him anymore.

She let the air leak slowly out between her lips and felt her panic abating.

"You don't need to say anything," he said. "Just listen. You're not going to die. It's not your heart that you're feeling, it's mine."

His words seemed foreign, even though she understood them. They were enunciated crisply, sharp around the edges, and every now and then *du* became *thu*, like in Old Norran. The meaning of what he said sank into her. She put her hand to her chest and found her wild, unruly heart.

Juva closed her eyes and listened. What she had always believed was chaos could be divided into two tidy rhythms: her own and a slower, heavier one, which was his.

He was right. She had known him her whole life.

"How?" she asked, unable to formulate a better question.

"You're a blood reader."

He's crazy. That's why he's here.

The ground felt firmer beneath her feet and the serenity came drifting in. His heart became a vague ache. Juva walked up to the opening in the door but couldn't see him. The room inside the doors was almost bare, just stone and wood. She had expected something more primitive, a sort of cave, but the black stone walls were straight. Reddish-brown woodwork created a warm glow on the floor and on a partition wall at the far end, with an opening into another small room. She glimpsed the corner of a low bed, with a long-haired, furry gray hide. A pale gash in the darkness by the ceiling hinted at a fissure that led out to the open air. She could hear water trickling and his breathing.

"I presume you're not actually supposed to be here?" he said.

His voice gave her the shivers. She still couldn't see him, but it sounded as if he were standing right by the inner door, as close as he could get.

Juva nodded, but realized that he couldn't see her either, so she forced herself to reply. "No."

"So, you're not the next in succession?"

Juva bit her lip. You weren't supposed to talk to the devil, every-one knew that. He was the father of lies, that's how it was in all the fairy tales. She held tightly to the grating bars in the opening, as she had when she was little, but this time he couldn't reach her because he wasn't in the closet anymore.

She swallowed. "You're the iron wolf."

His face came into view again. Black smoke swirled in his eyes, like ink in milk, darker and darker, until his gaze was as black as his hair. It felt as if she would never see anything else.

"I'm Grif."

Grif. His name is Grif.

She felt a prickling in her chest and caught herself smiling. The creature who had turned life in this house into a nightmare had a name.

Suddenly, she realized that he had been trapped there all these years while she had been living up above. What did he do there, and why did they keep him imprisoned? It was possible he was crazy, but she had certainly seen free men who were crazier.

"I'm Juva," she said.

He smiled wryly, revealing a canine tooth. His face was impossible to look away from. Compelling and frightening. His lips were narrow, not like Rugen's. Not pouty and soft, they seemed . . . strong. He had high cheekbones and a strong jaw. His black hair hung in front of his face in unruly tufts.

"What are you doing here?" she asked, her voice unsteady.

It took a second before he answered.

"You mean why am I voluntarily choosing to be right here, when I can obviously go wherever I want?"

Juva's cheeks flushed with heat, and she felt embarrassed by her own question. She felt oddly intoxicated. "They're keeping you captive because you're the source, right? You're where it comes from, the blood that heightens the blood readers' senses and causes wolf-sickness?"

"They really haven't prepared you at all, have they?"

Juva let out a bitter laugh, not having any other answer. It sounded as if he were moving around restlessly in there.

"Does this mean that—" he began.

Juva completed his sentence. "They're dead."

"Ah."

He didn't sound sympathetic, more like he was just acknowledging what had happened before he continued. "And no one told you how to open these doors, either?"

"No," she admitted.

Silence. Juva turned her back to him and leaned against the iron door. It sounded as if he did the same. Her pulse beat more calmly. She had so many questions, but she couldn't think of a single one. It was like being out hunting in Svartna and trying to focus on just one of the charred trees that surrounded her.

"No," he said, breaking the silence. "I'm not the source of . . . what was it you called it, wolfishness?"

"Wolfishness?"

"Wolfishness, wolf-sickness? The blood high and what you call wolf-sickness have never come from me. That comes from them."

Juva pulled her hand over her face. New questions arose in her already full head. "Who is *them*?"

A new pause, as if he were weighing his words before he answered.

"If the three in the Seida Guild are dead, and you lost your way and ended up here, that means something has gone appallingly wrong, so under the circumstances, I'd have thought you would have heard from them."

The vardari.

"Oh, them . . . Yes, I've heard from them. I thought you were one of them."

"Do I look like a vardari?"

That question sounded so bitter that she realized they had found some common ground, which made her a little more confident.

"No," she replied. "You don't look like anyone I've ever seen."

She had the feeling that he was smiling. "Murderers," he said. That dark voice was both creepy and alluring, like a dream you couldn't quite pin down. "They have dirty blood, which makes people sick. No, I'm not the source of the wolf-sickness. I'm the source of *them*."

The source of . . . This is a dream. I'm asleep.

Juva was grasping for reality, anything concrete to hold on to. The iron door that cooled her back. The draft of air that whispered through the tunnel. Her heart, always her heart. She was tired to the bone, but awake, and the meaning of what he said was greater than she was able to bear.

"You mean . . . you're the source of the warow?"

"Not a fate anyone would have chosen voluntarily, right?"

Juva slumped to the floor and sat. She had inherited a devil, and he was the source of the vardari, the source of eternal life. No wonder Nafraím wanted him! No wonder the Seida Guild hadn't wanted to give him up. A secret they had kept and used for generations.

"How long?" she whispered.

"What year is it?"

"Fourteen forty-seven."

"Then six hundred and sixty years, give or take."

Juva stared at the stone wall. The storm lantern glowed in her lap. It was woefully insufficient, no more than a flicker in an infinitely deep darkness. The silence rushed, a distorted hint of ocean, and from inside his shaft she could hear rain trickling in.

"But that's not what you should be asking," he said. It occurred to her that he had given her time to digest.

She let out a half-stifled laugh. She had so many questions, she would have knelt before anyone who could tell her which one was most important. He probably knew that because he didn't wait for her to respond.

"The most important question isn't how long I've been held captive. The most important is how much longer will I need to stay?"

CONFIDENCES

Juva pounded on the frame until the ice was knocked off and she was able to open the window. The ocean wind blew into the library in gusts and fed the flames in the open fireplace. The walls of the house were bearded with frost as far as she could see, dazzlingly beautiful, but fiendishly cold. A wretched way to start Smelta.

She hauled the carpet over the windowsill and started beating it as if her life depended on it. She hadn't made any headway on the big question, the same question she had fallen asleep thinking about.

What am I going to do?

That morning, the answer had been obvious. She needed to sell the house. That's what she would have done under normal circumstances, gotten rid of it, left, so that she never needed to see the place again. And the best protection from Nafraím and the vardari was for everything to seem normal.

But nothing was normal anymore. She had bled out a woman who should have given birth before midsummer. Mother and Solde had been murdered, someone was trying to eradicate the Seida Guild, Rugen was wolf-sick, and she had a black-eyed, immortal devil in her basement. Definitely an undisclosed defect.

But even a false rumor about the Sannseyr home being for sale could help her, buy her time without drawing suspicion, time to figure out what she should do with Gríf.

Juva scrubbed the floor until her knuckles were red and sweat dripped from her chin, but it became increasingly clear that the filth she was fighting wasn't the sort that could be washed away. She was carrying a swelling rage she didn't have room for before.

If she hadn't known better, she would have thought it had replaced her fear, but she was still very much afraid. She was afraid of wolf-sickness, the creature in the basement, and the warow who were hunting for him. She was afraid of people who believed she was a murderer, the ones who had broken the lantern. But those were reasonable things to be afraid of—anyone would have felt the same. That was rational fear.

What was gone now was any shame about feeling afraid.

Everything she had believed was imaginary, some flaw within her, was demonstrably real. Even the palpitations in her chest came from a man made of flesh and blood! One she knew as well as her own heart, but whom she didn't know anything about at all, not even what he was or where he came from.

Should I set him free?

Every nerve in her body told her that he was dangerous—but to whom? She wavered between fear of what he would do if she managed to open the doors and guilt that she hadn't already tried. She had atoned for her guilty conscience that morning by sending half the pantry down to him. Bread, duck pâté, smoked eel, roulade sausage, and the blood cookies that were left over from Mother's wake. Whatever she could do to procrastinate. But sooner or later, she was would have to talk to him again.

Juva got up and wiped her sweat on her sleeve. The most used rooms were spik-and-span. Mother's room as well. She had cut up the mattress and burned it in the kitchen fireplace. Then she dragged a new mattress down from the guest room, for the sake of appearances. Mother's room looked as if it had never been used. She had put the broken blood reader lantern in the storeroom. The only thing left to wash was herself, and the water should have been hot long ago.

She went into the bathroom, a steam-filled sanctuary lined with blue tiles from Ohrad with a big wooden tub. The firebox glowed and the light played against the copper piping that snaked its way down the wall. Mother had been one of the first in the city to have water piped in.

Juva wiped the condensation from the mirror and stared at her own face. She had blue circles under her eyes, and her blond hair had lost all its luster. Grief and anger came at a price.

She loosened her corset. The devil card fell onto the floor. She had almost forgotten about it now that she had found him. She took it with her into the tub. Sank down into the warm water as she stared at the card. The devil stared back, burned onto the yellowed whale cartilage.

What was it that she'd overlooked? Ogny had been desperate to find it, had even tried to steal it, and Mother had told her she needed to burn it. But there wasn't anything special about it, aside from the pattern in the corner. Four dots, in four corners. Some sort of code?

The bolts!

Juva sat upright in the tub. Sixteen dots on the card, sixteen bolts in the iron door. This was the key to opening it! That's why they had needed it. Those initiated into the Seida Guild had known where the devil was, but not how to move him. Ogny had said so herself when they were sitting on the skeleton bench in the foyer.

It won't stop us. It will just take a little longer.

Juva's joy at solving the riddle was short-lived. If she was right, she could no longer blame the locked door. She could release him if she wanted to and if she dared.

She scrubbed her skin red, but the peace she had hoped for remained elusive. Every time she closed her eyes, she saw a different bathtub with a lifeless figure dangling from Broddmar's arms.

She climbed out of the tub, dried herself, and put on clean clothes. She combed her hair with a couple of drops of oil of røyksnelle. That distinctive smoky scent of the burned herbs was a reminder of how long it had been since she had taken care of herself properly. She wedged the card into place beneath her corset, walked straight to the lacquered cabinet in the library, and took a good stiff swig of whiskey. She poured the rest of the whiskey into Father's hip flask and stuck it in her pocket. She was going to need it.

Nothing would make her feel safe down there, not even her crossbow, but she brought it with her anyway and hung the storm lantern on her arm. Then she opened the hidden door and started her descent. She had a bone to pick with the devil.

The air grew denser as she walked through the tunnel with what she hoped sounded like decisive footsteps. The sensation of his heart grew stronger. It was absurd, but so perceptible that it was impossible to deny. Her relief at finally knowing what she was feeling was drowned out by her anger. All these years wasted on fear and shame. Dr. Emelstein's feebleness, all the vague talk about nerves, countless pots of hoggthorn tea . . . all to deal with something that had never been about her.

Gríf stood right in front of the opening, as if he had been waiting for her.

"Thank you for the food. That was what I wanted second most of all," he said dryly.

"Shut up, Gríf." Juva put her finger in front of her lips. "I have something to say."

His white eyes filled with ink until his eyes were black as the night.

"Back up," she said, squeezing her crossbow, ready to run if necessary.

His upper lip twitched and she glimpsed a canine. It looked like he was going to snarl, but he did as she said, backing away several paces to stand against the wall. A blend of delight and fear darted down the nape of her neck.

An ordinary man would have fallen apart in captivity, but there was nothing ordinary about this man. The cold clearly wasn't a problem since he walked around with his torso bare and loose linen trousers that were far too thin—see-through, even—to provide any warmth. There was next to no fat on his body. Chiseled, like those laughable sculptures around the castle in Thervia. The clearly delineated muscles revealed something unfamiliar about his jaw and shoulders.

He must have cut his black hair in the dark. Wild and wispy, like wet fur. And his claws . . . They didn't look like anything she had ever seen on an animal, short and powerful, and they were a continuation of his fingers. It almost looked like the claws were *under* the skin. A scar ran diagonally down one forearm, a dark hollow in his pale skin.

He lifted his chin, clearly aware that he was being evaluated.

What is he?

Juva took a long drink from her pocket flask and studied the iron cabinet that stood between them. The locking mechanism was visible along the walls and showed the way to the linked lever. It was as she had thought: the cabinet was a small security vestibule, and its doors could be opened one at a time.

She pulled out the card and started pushing in the bolts that corresponded to the black dots. The rhythm of his heartbeat increased in her chest, until it was as fast as her own. A day ago, she wouldn't have had any explanation for that, only panic.

"So you've . . ." he began, but she shot him a look, as a warning.

He looked somewhere else, suppressing a smile that made her feel naked. He knew that she was drunk, maybe more so from having the upper hand than from the whiskey.

She held her breath and pulled down one lever. Iron yowled against iron. She turned the wheel and opened the nearest door. Rust and dust sprinkled down onto the bottom of the closet. Gríf stood there, reluctantly, his hand twitching.

Juva backed up against the wall of the tunnel and wriggled down onto the floor.

"Come," she said.

Gríf appeared in the opening again. He seemed eerily much closer now that there was only one closed door between them. She had to remind herself that the distance was the same, as she downed a couple of swigs from the flask. She swallowed the alcohol along with the fear she had brooded over for twelve years.

"I was seven when I did my first and last blood reading," she began, sure that she would fall apart. "Up in the study with Father. He reached out his hand to me, as if I should make it bleed, the way Mother did with the customers, a silly game. 'How old will I live to be?' he asked. I mean, seriously. What a stupid thing to ask a kid! Death didn't exist for a man like my dad, so I said . . ." She gulped. "I said: 'Dad, you'll never get old.'"

Juva stifled a pained laugh. She had never repeated those words aloud and they burned in her chest along with the liquor and the devil's beating heart.

"I thought he would live forever. That's what I meant, you know? But I was right. He never grew old because that night you killed him."

That charge was preposterous, she knew that. Her father had feared for her life and had gone on the attack. If she had been the one in the cage, she would have defended herself, too. Gríf apparently also knew that because he stared at her without blinking.

She shook the flask, significantly emptier now, and studied his face through the bars.

"I drew you, afterward. It didn't look like you at all, I see that now. Only . . ." She pushed on her own tooth with a lazy motion that indicated that she had drunk more than she should. "Just the teeth, right? And the claws. I called you the iron wolf. Isn't that clever? I just fused the two things I had seen, a wolf and an iron cage."

Juva chuckled and leaned her head back against the cold stone wall.

"I gave the picture of the iron wolf to my mother, and she . . . Well, I understand now that she must have been pretty freaked out, right? It's no good to have a kid who mopes around drawing the devil if you're taking care of the vardari's secret pet."

Gríf narrowed his eyes and the corner of his mouth took on a dangerous wrinkle. Juva took another swig and waved her hand at him, as if to brush aside any insult, just as her mother used to do.

"Anyway, Mother got all irritated. She slapped me until I was dizzy, that Gaula-bitch, and threw my drawing in the fireplace. It was the devil, she said, and if I talked about him, he might become real. And I believed her. I believed I had created you with my imagination and that terrible things were going to happen if I didn't burn you. Like what happened to my father. Would it have been so hard for her to say that it wasn't my fault, just once?"

Gríf gave no indication that he was going to respond, not like Rugen would have. He would have comforted her and sweet-talked her, with nothing to gain from it but the sex. The creature who was staring at her now had everything to gain but nothing to say.

"Then I became afraid of hurting people. I stuck to Broddmar and the guys on the hunting team. And Ester. Older people have always made me feel calmer. I felt like I couldn't hurt them in any way. I mean older as in sixty or seventy, though, right? Not like, 'hey, look at me, I'm almost a thousand years old. So, do you come here often?' Not that kind of old."

Gríf gave her a new smile, smug but genuine. Juva pointed at him and chuckled again. She felt like she had accomplished something by drawing that out of him.

"You're not like Rugen, are you? The worst part is that I didn't even *like* him. He was just suddenly there one day, and he meddled so little that it felt safe. You can't hurt someone who doesn't care, right?"

Her mouth felt dry, and she tasted smoke.

"No, that was far from the worst thing. The fear was the worst, always. Even when I wasn't scared, I was scared of becoming scared. Because I couldn't trust myself, trust my own senses. Damn it, I lived with a blood reader who lied like crazy, for payment! Unscrupulously doling out years of life and fates to people. I hated it, hated her, the house, the blood pearls that tricked people into believing that she was wise and clairvoyant. I hated the vardari, who gave them to her, without any regard to wolf-sickness. Sometimes I hoped she would . . . well, that she would come down with it, that she would get sick."

Juva looked him in the eyes. She found no judgment in those black depths. He was impossible to read, which gave her a dangerous sense of freedom. He was captive and open-minded, two traits that helped him break open doors she had sealed tightly shut, and already he knew more about her than anyone she'd met in her life.

"I used to think that my heart was punishing me, that that was why I had these episodes. Have you ever tasted hoggthorn? To Drukna, it's bad, but I lived on the stuff, to calm the rhythm, because they claimed I was a nervous child. And now you tell me it's 'blood reading,' that it's real." She flung up her arms. "What am I supposed to do with that?"

The weak light where Gríf was had grown warmer, from a sunset that wasn't visible. Half his face glowed, the rest was in shadows, and it made his high cheekbones jut out. The devil was animal-like and fascinating. Like in the myths.

In the fairy tale, the sisters let him go in exchange for the ability to see. Juva felt dizzy at the thought of how close to the truth that actually was. The fairy tale was a warped representation of something that actually happened. Gríf had been caught, and his blood had created the vardari, giving eternal life to the worst of the worst. And the blood pearls the Seida Guild had used to see came from the vardari. So, the blood readers' powers came from the devil, but they had never set him free.

The shame came creeping back. He had been waiting for an eternity, and here she sat whining about her miserable childhood. But she looked him in the eye without backing down.

"I've been afraid of you, drawn you, burned you, fantasized about you, and repudiated you. You've made my life an abyss."

She took the last swig of whiskey, and the flask banged against the floor.

"So, what are you thinking now, devil?"

Gríf braced his arm against the window opening and rested his forehead on it.

"I think you're more of a prisoner than I am."

His answer paralyzed her. Those unexpected words left her powerless, and she fought against a traitorous burning in her eyes. She didn't know for sure what he was, whether he was more animal than human, but one thing was certain: He wasn't stupid.

"What kind of creature are you to be kept captive?" she asked.

"You have a marvelous ability to wonder about the wrong thing, don't you?" His husky voice made her body tingle. "The question is what kind of creature *you* are, to keep a man in captivity."

Juva closed her eyes a moment. It felt as if she had already lost, but she wasn't going to let herself be manipulated. Never again.

"Don't you dare," she said. "You'd have done exactly the same as me if you were sitting here, and you know it."

"There, you see? We're both on our way to freedom."

Gríf smiled, revealing a canine. It was just a tiny bit longer than his other teeth, but sharp. You'd feel that against your tongue . . .

You're drunk, Juva.

She quickly looked away and let him talk.

"I came here through the stones," he said, "from a place you've never seen, and which doesn't exist on any map you own."

"Liar," she said, sure of her facts. "The stones in Nákla Henge only go to places that are on the map. Even the two dead stones, the ones people used to think went to Drukna, only go to a place that's underwater."

"If you think I would lie, why are we having this conversation?"

"Because what people lie about says more about them than the truths."

Gríf cocked his head, as if that were the first thing she'd said that interested him. She caught herself wishing that was her own wisdom, but it was elementary for any child who'd grown up with blood readers.

"I'm not lying," he said. "You're talking about the outermost ring. I'm talking about the stones in the middle."

"There aren't any stones in the middle, Iron Wolf. The only thing that's there is the Witness, a sculpture with gears and things."

"Three stones!" He took on a hounded expression and grabbed the bars. "Three stones in the middle, I know they're there."

"If you're talking about Nákla Henge, then you're wrong. There's a couple of walls, like a tower. With three sculptures on top, a raven, a wolf, and a stag. They're made of copper. They're bright green."

"*Jólsyngel. Thei e skandika deim . . .* " Gríf turned his back to her and put his arms behind his head.

Juva got chills. His words were entirely foreign, but their grave power was impossible to misconstrue. He turned to face her again.

"We don't have time for this, so let me make it as simple as possible. The stones are there, and they were powered by the Might, a force that disappeared over a thousand years ago. You'll never

276

understand what it could be or do, but I'm guessing that you can still see traces of it . . . a black scar in the forests."

"Svartna." Juva nodded dully. "I know the woods. But the stones are driven by wolf blood, they don't need any . . . might."

"Not these. Even the wolves were weakened when the Might disappeared. It takes more than death to travel to where I come from."

"So, why did you come here?" Juva asked, pulling up her knees and resting her chin on them.

"War. Isn't that where all misery begins? You all didn't have a chance, of course. The Might made us stronger. But when it vanished and the gates no longer worked, we were trapped here. Hunted and slaughtered here. I was one of the last, and the ones who captured me knew what they were doing. They had learned what our blood could do for them, and they used it to cheat death, which you all so easily fall victim to. The first three shared the secret and called themselves the vardari, the guardians."

Juva didn't want to interrupt. She wanted to fall asleep to his voice and let it ride her in her nightmares until she woke up again, but she had too many questions.

"Where did the blood readers come into the picture?"

"War. I did say that that's where everything starts. There got to be so many warow, and, well, let's say that they didn't always agree on who should control access to the blood."

"They went to war over *you*? For control over you?"

He growled. "I've been many places, and with many warow. I was waiting for them to annihilate each other, since you people lack the ability to think long—what's it called—long-sighted?"

"Long-term?"

"Precisely. And it was a Nifla's bloodbath. Eventually, they would have all destroyed one another, but then something happened after a couple hundred years or so. Wolves only know how, but they managed to make peace by giving me to another party, the one you know as the Seida Guild. They've been my guardians ever since."

Juva felt her old doubts weighing on her. Was she imagining this? Was this real?

"Why the Seida Guild?"

He drummed his claws on the door. "Because the women in the Seida Guild were a common enemy. Blood readers could sense the vardari back then, perceive my blood in them, like you can. And the best of them, they could do infinitely more. They were hunters back then, warriors. It was completely different from today. The Seida Guild became the new guardians, but never more than three initiates. There were three who knew, each with her heir. They kept giving the vardari my blood and getting the vardari's own blood back in return, contaminated and rotten. That's why people get sick."

"So, wolf-sickness never had anything to do with wolves? Is that what you're saying?"

"That is exactly what I'm saying."

Juva felt queasy. The wolf blood had been the perfect cover, since it was used for the stones anyway. She had killed gods knew how many wolves for blood, teeth, and hides. Because people feared them. When all along, it was the warow they should have been afraid of.

"Why did you give them blood at all? Couldn't you just . . . ?" She regretted the question before she had finished asking it. Her eyes settled on his scars. Of course he hadn't given it voluntarily.

His eyes narrowed, and he tilted his claws back and forth as if he were sharpening them.

"I could tell you things that would keep you awake for the rest of your brief life," he said in his throaty voice. "I gave nothing. They took. But eventually I gave so as not to starve to death, as I watched them destroy themselves. I'll gladly give blood to watch them bleed."

His heart squeezed around hers, heavier and more stifling. She swallowed her shame and tried not to picture what they had done to him.

"But why keep you captive when they already had eternal life?"

Gríf hesitated before he responded.

"To make more of them, to be able to choose who would become one of them. Eternal life is a very intense gift to give someone you really like, do you understand?"

He's hiding something.

Juva studied him. His eyes were more expressive than she had thought at first. She had merely been put off by the all-black thing. But there were shades in the darkness that gave away where he was looking and when his gaze strayed.

"No, you don't understand," he said, shaking his head. "You don't even want to live the brief life you've been granted, do you?"

He attacks to avoid answering.

"Enough to be scared, devil. So, tell me, if the warow voluntarily handed you over to the Seida Guild hundreds of years ago, why do they want you back now?"

Gríf pressed up against the door again.

"Now you're asking the right questions. Because the Might is back! I feel it with every nerve in my body. You won't believe me, because you humans have never been able to feel it, but it's here. It's in the woods and in the ocean—if they haven't sucked out all of it, that is. The Might is life! It has been seeping in slowly but surely, for almost as long as you are old. The Might is back, and now the vardari are panicking."

"Panicking about what?"

"Everything. They're afraid that we'll come back, my people, now that the stones are working again. And they're afraid of blood readers and the wolf-sickness spreading. They smell their own doom, and it's not going to be pretty. The world as they know it will collapse, so let's assume that they're . . . nervous. Listen, girl: not to make you hysterical or anything, but we don't have time to sit here chatting. The vardari will come after you, and they will come after the Seida Guild. They'll come after everyone who might conceivably know where I am or who could be a genuine blood reader."

"Genuine?"

"It's quite possible that the ability to sense blood will awaken in those who have an aptitude for it, especially those who were born after the Might returned. Being able to feel my people's blood, either in me or in the warow, is a rare gift, but not one vardari are particularly happy about. Except for when they used blood readers as slaves and weapons against other warow. Which is exactly what they will do with you."

Juva squeezed her knees and mumbled, "They don't know that I know anything . . ."

Grif grabbed the bars in the opening, and she could hear him take a deep breath as if he were struggling to control himself.

"Think it through. If everyone who knew where I am is dead, then no one can give them blood anymore. They've surely attacked each other already. A war over who will be the first to find me. If you were one of them, what would you do?"

Juva gulped. "I would go after anyone who could conceivably know."

He flung out his arms as if he had finally gotten her to understand.

"Do you think they know that I've found you?" She felt fear take root again.

"They would be here if they did, and you would be dead."

"Like my mother and Solde. I know who killed them. He was here before they died, and before I found you, when I was a child. He has always been here, like an evil spirit. His name is—"

"Nafraím."

Gríf spat out the name at the same time she did, as if it were a curse. He rubbed the scars on his arm. "Nafraím was one of the original three, the ones who captured me. I know him far too well, and believe me, he's not the one who killed the blood readers. The initiated blood readers were wiped out by someone who wants me to be forgotten, someone who hopes that I will starve to death and never be found, someone who wants to eliminate the vardari. So, either Nafraím suddenly changed his mind after six hundred years, or . . ."

"Or what?"

"Or he already knows where I am but wants to stop others from finding out. If that's the case, then you are the only thing standing in his way."

Juva pinched the bridge of her nose between her fingers. She felt woozy and drunk and knew she wasn't up to digesting everything he had said. She was *sure* that Nafraím was the one who had killed them. But had he done it because he already knew how to find Gríf— because he didn't need the Seida Guild anymore?

"Juva . . ." She jumped to hear him say her name. "Juva, if you're the only one who knows where I am, and you die, then I die, too. Can you let me out, damn it, so I don't need to depend on a child?!"

She got to her feet, anything but steady. Profoundly disappointed at being seen as a child. "What would you do in my position? Blindly trust a prisoner? For all I know, you're dangerous, so I need to find out what the vardari want first. Preferably I'd kill them all, but I need to know. That's what it comes down to."

"No, this is not about the vardari. Whether you let me out or not depends on who you are."

"No," she said and shook her head. "It depends on who *you* are. And I know you're hiding something. You said they needed you to be able to make new vardari, but people rarely think about anyone but themselves. So why are they panicking? What is it that they *actually* need you for?"

Gríf slammed his fist into the door and turned his back to her. She could almost smell his frustration, and she couldn't blame him. He turned back toward her again and slowly exhaled.

"They need me because nothing lasts forever. They need new blood, at least annually, otherwise they start to rot. Organs that have never functioned properly will begin to shrivel. If they endure the pain, they will age like most people, but . . ."

Juva gaped at him. "But they'll die like most people, too. They're panicking because they're dying."

Gríf closed his eyes, and Juva understood why he had kept that from her. Without him, the vardari would die. All she needed to do was keep him here, or kill him, and she would win.

DEAD LANTERNS

Juva woke up at dawn to an avalanche of thoughts that chased away any hope of more sleep. Her crossbow lay on the pillow beside her, in a bed she had never slept in before—Mother's—big and gloomy with black curtains.

Lagalune's chamber had always seemed as sacred as the blood reader room, and now she knew why. She peered over at the chest of drawers that hid the shaft, with a vague sense that that was why she had slept here. To be closer to Gríf. To be in control.

Juva still had her clothes on, and a dull ache in her thigh revealed that her flask was still in her pocket. It took her a moment to remember that her life was in danger.

Juva stumbled over to the window and looked out into a boundless sea of fog. She couldn't even see across to Skodda. Jólshov lay hidden, which suddenly seemed painfully poetic since all the blood readers were as well. If Gríf was right, they were free game to the vardari now, divided and desperate.

She wrapped her arms around herself, colder at the thought of what that meant.

More blood readers could be killed because the vardari were afraid that this *Might* Gríf spoke of would turn the in-name-only blood readers into *genuine* blood readers. That the Might would awaken in the blood readers a dormant ability to sense the vardari. And Nafraím already knew that Juva could, because he had seen her do it.

Gríf had been talking about a completely different Seida Guild than the one she knew. Hunters and warriors of old. Sensers, used as a weapon by the warow against one another, in a battle over who had the right to use Gríf's blood.

And I have him. I have the vardaris' eternal life in my hands.

She should kill him. She should have done it already. One shot with her new crossbow and Gríf would be gone. His blood had created a contagion, a long chain of misery, which would gradually break down. The vardari would die out, no hearts would flutter, no blood pearls of warow blood, and never any more wolf-sickness.

No resounding Dead Man's Horn, no bodies with bloodskins pounded into their throats. Killing him was a small price to pay in comparison. So why couldn't she climb down there right now and shoot him?

Was it because she knew that he was telling the truth, even about the most inconceivable things? Was it compassion, because he had been held prisoner for as long as the vardari had lived? Or was it because he didn't look like a monster? The source of the warow ought to look horrifying, arousing fear, like Gaula. Evil should be repulsive and ghastly, with tentacles, not . . .

Not like him.

She should never have gone down there. They had talked to each other. He was already under her skin and preventing her from doing what she should. It was too late. She couldn't kill him, and she couldn't set him free. She could only hope that he still had a home and that it was possible to get him back there.

If we can get past the Ring Guard. If the stones he's talking about work. And if the vardari don't kill me first.

Juva shuddered. It was too big, too heavy to bear. She felt like the middle of an hourglass, that slender neck that stood between everything that had been and all that was to come. What if she broke?

Gríf was right. She couldn't sit there waiting to die. She had to do the most important thing first: warn the remaining members of the Seida Guild. There could be more sensers out there, both inside and outside the guild, young women who were living just like she had been, with fear and palpitating hearts. They had no idea that anything was wrong, or that everyone in the Seida Guild was in danger. She couldn't fail.

Juva went out into the hall and double checked that the front door was locked. It felt shockingly insufficient. She should bolt the windows, too, and ask Broddmar and the rest of the hunting team for help.

No! Knowing about Gríf would put them in harm's way, too.

Besides, it would be suicide to turn the Sannseyr home into a manned fort. She might as well put a sign on the front door saying "The source of eternal life lives here."

She brought the stack of unopened letters into the library and flipped through them as she ate. The oldest were condolences to her and Solde, then just to her. Most of them came from her mother's wealthy clients. One of the letters could have been written by Mother herself, dripping with drama. A red envelope, secured with an unfamiliar, white seal. Juva opened it and pulled out an invitation written in an ornate hand. It was to her, "on behalf of well-wishers," who wanted to protect her life at "this difficult time." The name of the so-called well-wisher was conspicuously absent. The only name was that of a middleman at Náklabank.

Vardari. And so the wooing begins.

Juva tossed the letter aside, uncomfortably aware that the politeness was far more short-lived than the sender. She needed to get Gríf back to his home as quickly as she could, if it was even possible.

She threw on her jacket and walked out into the fog, which was reassuringly thick. If she couldn't see other people clearly, then they couldn't see her. The bakery across the street had just been sold, so she hurried past just in case the new owner was vardari, someone who wanted to keep an eye on her.

She stopped by Náklabank and dropped off a card saying she was considering selling the Sannseyr house. Then she set out for Nákla Henge. The increased security was noticeable even from Bodsrabben, the street that ran along the old city wall. Guards from the city watch wandered along Brenntorget. The western gate in the actual ring wall, Vestporten, was usually open, but wolf-sickness had changed the routines there as well. People were being let through one at a time, through the enormous bright green doors.

Juva followed the sparse morning line and paid an outrageous fifty skár for admission without travel. A gruff Ring Guardian checked her teeth and hustled her into the dim light under the grooved wooden dome. Daylight shone in through the opening in the top along with dancing fog, and it reminded her of Gríf's eyes. The pale smoke sank in swirls as if it were being sucked down by the three-edged tower that went by so many names—the Witness, the Pathfinder, the wolf walls.

The sounds of conversations blended with the mechanical scraping of the gears that brought the bright green walls to life. She could almost hear Gríf laugh. His power was authentic; this was obvious to her now that she was seeing everything with fresh eyes. The Pathfinder had woken up on its own, driven by a force none of the scholars understood.

Juva pulled back into the shadows under the balcony and studied the Witness from a distance. A wolf, a raven, and a stag sat on the outermost end of the three walls, one on each. The walls met in the middle, so people couldn't actually walk between them like they could the other stones. If they tried, they'd be standing in a corner.

Or disappear before they got that far.

If Gríf was right, the Witness was traveling stones as well, a gateway that led to worlds beyond this one. But could they be used? And did only she and the warow know that?

She raised her eyes. The arrow slits at the top of the ring wall had gained crossbows since her last visit. Big assault munitions mounted in position and pointing inward, facing the stones, and she could see guards moving around. The last time she'd been there, with Ester, she had thought how odd it was to have arrow slits that faced inward. That was before Gríf, before she had learned the enemies that people had feared in the past hadn't come from outside. They had come from the Witness, in the middle of the stone circle. Did that mean that the Ring Guard was also under warow influence? Did they know that the Witness was a doorway to new threats, or was it a natural defensive reaction because it had started moving?

Sixteen men guarded the stones, two for each pair. No one was admitted without a travel card, and anyone who had one was shown to the proper stone depending on their destination. You could make a run for the middle, but probably not without being shot or captured. If Gríf even made it through the gates to try, he would end up with a bolt in his back. Or ten. It was useless.

Around the entire stone circle there were blood runes, etched in the ground. The intricately carved stone lid hid the wolf blood that ran through gutters underneath, which powered the stones. She felt faint thinking of all the time she had devoted to trying to figure out how the blood was being stolen, when it had never had anything to do with wolves at all. The blood pearls contained warow blood, an addictive and corrupt product that originated with Gríf.

Juva felt a distant tickle in her heart and backed into the shadows. It was foolish to have gone there. If any vardari saw her studying the Witness, it could give her away . . .

She followed the balcony back around to the Vestporten gate, turned in her visitor's card, and walked back to Lykteløkka. She would have to solve the Nákla Henge problem later. Right now, she needed to talk to the blood readers.

Ogny's and Maruska's heirs were the most exposed and the ones she dreaded the most. It was completely surreal for her, of all people, to knock on the doors of people she had been avoiding her whole life to keep them united in a guild she had always despised. Blood readers had lived well for generations by lying to people about how long they would live, and now it was up to her to tell them that death was near.

What should she say?

Hi, I inherited a stunningly gorgeous devil in my basement, and the vardari desperately need him. I'm sorry if they think you're also involved and kill you for it. Plus, there's an other-worldly force that can make blood reading real, so, yeah, maybe we ought to get together for tea?

The buildings on the narrow street hid in the fog, ghostly in sunlight that never quite penetrated. Juva climbed the steps and knocked on Spegill's door. She was surely the oldest blood reader of them all.

A young girl opened the door, nicely dressed with tired eyes. She yelled for Spegill right away, as if she knew who Juva was. Spegill came shuffling to the door.

"Ah, it's you," she squeaked.

A typical blood reader trick to give the impression that she had sensed the visit in advance. Juva struggled to find the words she had memorized.

"Spegill, I'm here to say that the blood readers are in danger. The whole Seida Guild, and we need to stick together against—"

"Child, I'm almost a hundred. Do you think I'm a fool?"

"No! No, of course not. I just wanted—"

"Six blood readers are dead! Even a Jól goat understands that

288

there's an act of war, and you want to keep us together so we'll be an even easier target. I think you're out of your mind!"

The old woman spoked without any pauses, and Juva didn't see an opportunity to jump in.

"No! You don't understand. Other things can happen besides murder, Spegill! The vardari fear us. They think . . ." She searched for a way to explain it without mentioning sensing. "They believe that we've become a hazard to them, and if we each go it on our own, we don't stand a chance."

"Ha!" Spegill chuckled. "Child, we didn't stand a chance when we were unified, and we don't stand a chance now."

"So what do we do then?" Juva flung up her arms. "Should we hide until they forget about us? That's not going to happen. We can gather together and be stronger or we can die, each behind our own door."

Spegill chewed on her wrinkled lip and said, "We'll die either way."

Then she closed the door.

Juva felt like she'd been slapped in the face. She wondered if she should knock again, but it seemed pointless. Spegill was old and done fighting. Hopefully there were others who would understand. Maybe she should remind them that, on paper, they had designated her as the new head of the Seida Guild?

Or maybe not. After all, that was a title they had foisted off on her because they feared for their lives.

The next house belonged to Ilja, a blood reader who was her mother's age. The red light was gone there, too. The only traces of it left were the wrought iron fasteners in the wall, which had been snapped off at odd angles.

Juva knocked. A skinny, gray-haired man opened the door. "Yes?" he said distractedly as he half-heartedly kicked at a cat that darted between his legs.

Juva was about to ask for Ilja when she saw her. The jewelry-laden blood reader picked up the cat and then spotted Juva. There was no mistaking the shock in her eyes. She rushed toward the door, which was abruptly slammed shut. For a second, Juva thought it had been done by mistake, but then she heard heated whispering inside. The word "murder" made her back away.

Disbelief grew in her throat, prickling and nauseating. She put her hand to her chest on impulse, even though she knew now that her heart wouldn't rupture. It was beating quickly, but it was still just hers, an even and solitary rhythm.

She was gripped by a feeling she never expected to feel: homesickness. What was the point of saving these people? What was she doing there? She could go home, where her heart wouldn't be so utterly alone, where she would be able to feel him.

Spegill is right. I've lost my mind.

One more house, she could handle that. She had to warn Ogny's heirs. They were probably the first ones the vardari would go after. Juva climbed the steps to the magnificent home that had belonged to Ogny Volsung. She knocked, more cautiously than before. A girl in an apron opened the door, and Juva asked for the closest heir to Ogny and her daughter.

"That's Haane. Wait a moment." The girl vanished back inside while the door remained ajar.

Juva had a familiar feeling in her chest. A hint of agitation, a rhythm that didn't come from her.

Vardari.

The fog seemed to thicken around her, and she clutched the railing. What should she do? She could run and reveal that she knew they were there or stay put and risk her life. It seemed like an impossible choice.

After a long time, Haane came shuffling back to the door. She was somewhere in her thirties with stooped shoulders, wearing a sweater that rolled up at the edge. Her eyes looked nervous and run-down.

Juva took charge of her own breathing and tried to feel the other rhythm, which grew stronger in her chest. The feeling reminded her of Nafraím, but it was still unfamiliar, so she doubted it was him. But no matter who it was, they were in the house and Hanne knew it.

Why? Were they there to kill Haane, or to recruit her to fight a coming war? Or were they trying to threaten her into talking about a devil she didn't know anything about?

Juva realized that Haane's fate lay in her hands. She had to make the warow in there understand that Haane didn't know anything and do so without giving away her own ability to sense.

"Haane, I . . . I'm Juva Sannseyr, Lagalune's heir. And Solde's. We have suffered the same fate, you and I."

Haane nodded without looking her in the eye.

Juva hurriedly continued. In spite of everything, it was the most encouraging reaction she had received thus far.

"The murders were an attack on the entire Seida Guild, and I appreciate that you're scared. Everyone is scared. But I'm here to say that we need to stick together. We can't let the guild be destroyed."

Haane hesitated but seemed to realize that she needed to say something. She shrugged her heavy shoulders and that seemed to cost her all the energy she had. "I don't suppose there's much that can be done about it," Haane said.

"But there is. We can stick together and stand against those who killed Ogny and the others. And I know it was the vardari. They want something. I can't say what, but . . . we need to talk."

Juva could almost taste the anticipation from inside the house, like an eager pulse in her throat. She desperately searched for words that could buy her time.

"Haane, I think both Jólshov and my house are being watched; could we meet here and try to gather the Seida Guild again?"

"What do the others say? Have you talked to Spegill?" Haane stared at the floor.

"Not yet," Juva lied, "but I'm going to. And I'll send a runner with the date and time. Are you in?"

Haane swallowed and nodded. Juva forced herself to smile before leaving. She had to stop herself from breaking into a run. She felt like she was balancing on a sword blade, with no inkling of whether she would emerge alive. Had she just talked her way into her own death sentence? She had as good as admitted that she was hiding something . . .

But she had won some time, both for herself and for Haane, because one thing was for sure: the warow who had been listening wasn't going to lift a finger until the Seida Guild meeting. They believed that Juva had something to say, and they would be there to hear it.

The only problem was that she had no idea what to tell them. But now she had an opportunity to plant lies with the vardari. What she told the Seida Guild didn't matter. They had given up. There was nothing left of the warriors Gríf remembered.

MEASURED

"She needs it roomy around the knees." Broddmar's voice sounded muffled through the heavy curtain.

"Of course." Savill squatted down in front of Juva and placed the measuring tape to the inside of her thigh.

He was surprisingly limber for a portly man of over sixty. Popping up and down into a kneel without any complaint.

"And the shoulders," Broddmar said. "Good flexibility at the shoulders."

Savill rolled his eyes. "Noted," he replied, but the only thing he wrote down in his notebook were her measurements.

Juva was sweating even though she was standing there in only her underwear. "It's hot in here," she apologized.

"We're burning corpsewood. We need steady light," the tailor mumbled. "We're used to it. Straighten your back."

Juva obeyed. Her shoulders made a clicking sound, stiff from worries and secrets. She had spent many hours down with Gríf over the last few days. He had grown more restless, which she had no trouble understanding, but she didn't dare trust him, didn't dare set him free, not yet.

"The jacket needs to be light," Broddmar said. "No longer than halfway down her thi—"

Savill turned toward the curtain and said, "Perhaps you should go to someone who does this *professionally*?"

Broddmar grunted and continued trawling around the shop. Everyone knew that Savill was the best, not just in Sakseveita, but in all of Náklav, and, as a rule, whoever was best in Náklav was best in the world. His people had made the Ring Guard uniforms, so you certainly couldn't complain that they lacked experience. Juva knew that Broddmar's anxiety stemmed from his caring. He knew better than most how important the red suit was.

That thought sent a wave of shame through her. Broddmar believed she could handle this, that she had it in her to become a bleeder, but people with wolf-sickness weren't what she wanted to hunt, not anymore. She wanted to hunt the vardari, the source of the rot.

Savill came around to stand behind her and handed her the end of the measuring tape.

"Could you? Right over the bosom," he said.

Juva pulled the tape around her breasts and handed him the end again.

"Good," he said, tugging at her corset. "It's not too tight. Is this the type you usually wear?"

"Yes." She felt like she was in safe hands, like she was nothing but one of the many wooden dummies that stood along the wall in half-finished garments.

Savill hung the measuring tape around his neck. "I have two types of red leather for you, thick and strong, able to resist cuts and . . ." He cleared his throat. "Bites. But we're putting the collar snug to your neck, with tracks for steel rails. You'll be able to pull the collar up over your nose and mouth, like a mask. You've seen Broddmar's suit, haven't you?"

Juva nodded.

Savill pulled out one of the small drawers in the massive tailor's cabinet that occupied an entire wall of the shop. "You need maximum mobility, so we'll put woven fabric into the critical seams. What do you think of these?" He handed her two swatches of red leather.

One was even and lifeless, the other was a deep red and had a mottled surface, as if it had already been worn. Savill ran his thumb over it.

"It's been washed and scrubbed with salt water, so it will be just as nice even if you should . . ."

Juva realized that he wasn't going to finish his sentence, so she did: "Spill blood?"

He looked as if he was trying not to respond but failed. "You're too young for this," he said with a sigh.

She didn't respond. He was right. She could have been something else. A tailor, for example. She could have spent her life in this lovely shop, surrounded by dark woodwork, leather samples, and drawers full of spools of thread. The years would go by, marked by more gouges in the workbench.

But she had grown up with a hunter and a blood reader. And she had seen something she shouldn't have as a child, linking her fate to the wolf.

Gríf.

"She's nineteen. She's not a child," Broddmar said. "When can you have it finished?"

Juva got dressed, and Savill pulled the curtain aside.

"We have about twenty orders for the spring run," he said.

"The spring run?" Broddar said, sticking his head in. "This is a bleeder suit, Savill. We hunt the people who have come down with wolf-sickness, and you're prioritizing overpriced costumes for the Yra Race?"

"I did not say that." Savill stuck up his nose.

The Yra Race.

Even something as ordinary as the spring run in Náklav was associated with Gríf. Every year, on the spring equinox, people got dressed up to race through the streets. They might dress like anything at all, but originally it had been a race for wolves. People in animal furs with fake claws and canine teeth. What if the tradition was born out of memories and not fairy tales? The thought was dizzying. As if the world hadn't even existed before Gríf.

Savill promised to have the suit ready to try on in ten days. Broddmar was going to push, but then the bell above the door rang and a woman came in. Juva thrust her feet into her shoes and shivered mid-motion, an uncomfortable prickling in her heart.

Vardari!

Juva tied her shoes as she snuck a little peek at the woman. She had an unusual smell, like vinegar, and an unmistakable aura of nobility. Knee-high lace-up boots and a dark coat lined with patterned silk. Her eyes roamed lazily over the shelves and lingered for a second on Juva, before Savill walked over to serve her.

"Are you coming?" Broddmar opened the door and Juva followed him out.

He kept talking, but Juva didn't catch a word, engrossed with the little stings in her heart, which abated as they walked. Her whole life, with these attacks of inexplicable fear, how many times had it been due to some warow, begotten from Gríf's blood?

How many of them were there? Ten or ten thousand? And were they only in Náklav, or had the blood traveled around the world? Juva was going to war against something she had no sense of the scope of, and that thought was paralyzing.

Broddmar stopped walking and she realized she was home. He patted her on the back of the head the way he always did, and she watched him go. If only she could have told him everything. But that wasn't possible. Not without putting him in danger.

Juva stomped the slush off her shoes and unlocked the door. Her heart started fluttering again, but she could tell right away it wasn't Gríf. Someone walked up behind her and grabbed the doorknob.

"Allow me," Nafraím said.

Fear tore through her, cold and sharp as steel. She stifled a gasp. Nafraím put his arm around her back and guided her inside, as if he understood that she would run away if she got the chance. The door reverberated closed behind them.

Juva fought her panic. Her heartbeat raced, now against two others. One was Gríf's, the other was a murderer's, and they were squeezing the air out of her lungs. Heavy, old hearts.

"I heard a rumor that you were thinking of selling the place." Nafraím looked around as if he had never been there before, considering the purchase.

Juva had nearly forgotten about that. Náklabank hadn't even started the work, so he must have friends who were informing him. Either way, he must be completely insane. Did he really think she would sell to the man who had left six bodies there? Or was he living under the delusion that she didn't know it was him?

There was a third alternative as well, the worst of them all.

It's a pretense. He knows about Gríf.

Juva did her best to breathe calmly as her thoughts raced. Had she properly closed the opening in the chimney? Was the dresser drawer in the bedroom closed? Would he find traces? Was that why he was there, or was it her turn to die? Could she make it to her crossbow on the bed?

Nafraím took off his gloves, folded them, and stuck them in his pocket in a motion that seemed rehearsed because of his stiff left hand. He took off his coat and held it out to her. Juva didn't move. She clenched her teeth to hide the trembling in her jaw. He seemed to realize that she wasn't going to take it, so he hung it over the stair railing post. His shirt was white as snow, and he wore a brown vest over it, closed with golden clasps. Not the sort of clothes you chose when you were going to kill someone, right?

"My deepest condolences," he said. "This must have been a difficult time for you. Shall we begin with a cup of tea?"

297

Juva didn't know if she should laugh or scream. Mother's and Solde's murderer was asking for tea. He smiled and she jumped. He had fangs!

Juva turned her back to hide her shock. Had she lost her mind? He had never had fangs before, she was positive about that. They were short, but sharp.

This is a game to see if I react. He was hiding them before.

She walked into the corridor, down to the kitchen, and heard him following. She let her gaze fly through the room, hunting for anything that could help her. Could she poison him? The bottle of bolt toxin was in her bag, or had she left it at Hidehall? She wasn't sure and, either way, she couldn't get to her backpack up in Mother's room.

Maybe she could crush his skull with the pot? No, he was taller than her, thin, but strong. His motions suggested that he had good bodily control. The knives? They were in the drawer under the butcher's block, too far behind her.

She pulled the kettle over the cook plate and blew life into the corpsewood, which still had embers from that morning. Nafraím strolled around, considering the room with his hands behind his back.

"They have a charm of their own, these old basement kitchens," he said, walking into the wine cellar. No one had touched that since her mother had died. He emerged again with a condescending smile, as if none of the wines were worthy of his visit. "Lots of exciting rooms, aren't there? You could hide anything at all in a house like this."

Juva pretended she hadn't heard him and poured the water over the tea. If she hadn't gotten rid of all her hoggthorn, she would have finished the box by now. She passed him the teacup, surprised that she managed to keep her hands steady.

He walked into the pantry, and Juva hurried toward the stairs. If she made it upstairs before him, she could get to the crossbow. But he quickly came back out and didn't let her get a head start. He followed her into the library. He set his cup down on the table, where the dead had sat. Juva was painfully aware of how quickly her eyes could give her away. One little glance at the chimney and it would be obvious where he should search.

He walked over to the raven cabinet, even though she hadn't even glanced at it.

"Do you remember when these came out?" he smiled. "No . . . No, of course you wouldn't." He pulled a coin from his pocket and put it in the slot. Nothing happened.

Juva gulped. "You have to turn the crank," she said in a hoarse voice and realized that was the first thing she had said since they came in.

Nafraím turned the crank, and the awful bird opened its beak. It turned from side to side in a choppy motion. Nafraím laughed and Juva could swear there was an eerily authentic joy there. The tray in front of the raven jumped and threw the many-sided rune dice. Nafraím leaned forward and squinted into the glass cabinet to see the symbols.

"Broken heart, blood, and ocean," he read. "What do you think that means?"

That I'm going to break you, kill you, and send you to Drukna.

"I'm not a blood reader," she said with a shrug.

"No?" He looked at her with those intense brown eyes that seldom blinked. "I hear you're the next head of the Seida Guild. That managed to surprise even me, I must admit."

He took a sip of his tea with that strangely curious expression that made it seem like everything was a new experience to him. Maybe that was a trait he needed to cope with living for so long? His mouth looked pained, and he pushed away the cup and took a lozenge from the pocket in his vest. Then he nodded for her to follow and walked into the blood reader room. Juva followed him, relieved that he was done with the library.

Nafraím flung up his arms when he saw the mural.

"Síla Sannseyr!" he exclaimed. "She was a storm of a woman, your great-grandmother. Impossible to forget, if I might be so bold."

Juva clutched her cup to stop herself from smashing it against the wall. The intimacy he was insinuating was unbearable. He was a monster, and he was talking to her like they were old friends. Old as in hundreds-of-years old and that made her rage stronger than her fear.

"Are you done?" she spat.

"Of course, I didn't intend to take up much of your time."

He walked out again and into the corridor where the door to her mother's room stood open. Juva hurried after him. Her crossbow lay on the bed, giving away how sleepless she had been. He looked at her with a concern that was reminiscent of the tailor's alarm at her choice of profession. It was so out of place that it turned her stomach.

He walked over to the nightstand and picked up her sketchbook.

No!

"Do you draw a lot?" he asked. It struck her as an odd leap. Wouldn't it be more natural to assume she kept a diary?

"My whole life."

"I've done a lot of drawing myself," he smiled. "Do you mind if I . . . ?"

She nodded, fully aware that it didn't matter how she answered, because he already knew what he was going to find, even though Rugen was the only one she had told about her drawings. Well, Rugen and Broddmar. And neither of them knew Nafraím.

He opened the book with his stiff hand and browsed through her drawings of wolves and men, sometimes both in the same figure. He stopped at the one she had hoped he wouldn't find, a naked wolfman with a flagrant erection.

Nafraím raised one eyebrow at her, unexpectedly bothered.

"There's plenty of Síla Sannseyr in you, too, I see." He set the book down on the bed. "Unusual subject matter, isn't it?"

He knows. I have to be as honest as I can afford to be.

"I've had nightmares, always have. I saw someone with wolf-sickness when I was a child."

Nafraím came over to her and she had to fight to remain on her feet. Three hearts pounded in her throat, and she caught herself wondering if Gríf could feel them as well. Did he know that the man who had kept him prisoner for almost seven hundred years was here right now?

"Someone with wolf-sickness?" Nafraím asked. "Well, that's nothing to be embarrassed about. Or are you worried for some other reason?"

Juva clung to her rage, the only thing that would save her. "I'm not embarrassed, and you don't scare me. I hate you. You're a murderer, you and everyone like you. I don't want anything to do with you abominations!"

She stormed out of the bedroom and into the library, with Nafraím on her heels. She flipped feverishly through the condolence letters until she found what she was looking for, the red envelope.

"Here! This came from one of you, too, and you can tell them that I'm not interested. I'm done with blood reading, and the Sannseyr house is done with vardari!"

Nafraím glanced at the envelope and nodded as if he understood where it had come from. Juva immediately regretted it. Maybe she had given away someone who really wanted to help her.

"That's a relief to hear," he said and walked out into the foyer.

For a second, she considered rushing in to get the crossbow, but he was about to put his coat back on, so she followed him instead. She clenched her fists and said a silent prayer for him to hurry. He stopped with his hand on the doorknob.

"You think you know me, Juva Sannseyr," he said in a low voice. "But I am far more than the sum of my sins."

He walked out and the door slammed shut behind him. Juva turned the key in the lock and sank to the floor. Her eyes began to burn, and she couldn't stop the flood of tears. She had thought she was safe from him since she had shown him the card. He had said as much himself, that she didn't know anything at all.

Why had he started wondering again? And what would have happened if he had killed her just now? Gríf would have been left sitting in the shaft until he starved to death. He would have rotted in captivity, and it would have been her fault.

Nafraím thought he owned her, the way he had owned her mother and her mother's mother. The vardari had controlled the blood readers with blood pearls and power ever since they had made the agreement to guard Gríf. It was madness. And if there were more who could sense them, then things were going to get significantly worse.

Juva rubbed at her traitorous tears until her cheeks burned. Then she got up and went back into the library. She had lived in fear her whole life without knowing why. And now that she knew, was she supposed to just replace the old fear with something new to be afraid of? No, never again.

She opened the letter from the city council. The Sannseyr home would not be sold, it would be protected. Neither she nor any other blood reader would be slaves to the warow anymore. Even if that meant she had to become what she had always detested.

RUST

Juva combed her hair and considered braiding it, but she decided against that. If she was too dressed up, the city councilman would realize that she wanted the job and not agree to her demands. She needed to think like a blood reader and let him sell himself first. He was the one who needed her, not the other way around. He lacked a guild master for the Seida Guild, and the job had become about as appealing as being stricken with wolf-sickness.

She threw an extra log on the fire and tried to go over what she would say, but her thoughts revolved relentlessly around Gríf.

It had been eight days since she had found him, eight days without her setting him free. They had talked through the rusty iron door, but she always had a pathetic excuse for not opening it, and it was eating away at her, keeping her awake at night. What was she afraid of?

At worst, he was an actual devil, a monster who would tear her to shreds as soon as he got the chance. At best, he had told her the truth and he was an innocent prisoner of war. Although *innocent* was the last word she would use to describe him.

Her ability to read people crumbled whenever she saw him, but no matter how much she mulled it over, she did know one thing for sure: being unsure of her next move did not give her any right to hold a man prisoner. Every day that passed was a fresh injustice, an even bigger reason for him to wreak havoc the day he was free. And she did not want to see Gríf wreak havoc.

The very thought made her shudder. Ester's husband had beaten her up until the day she fought back. Had she known what he was capable of when she married him?

The door knocker banged in the foyer, and she ran to open it, relieved to hear it for once. The city councilman towered outside, wide as a mountain. She could barely see the two young men behind him, their arms filled with books. A glossy carriage took up almost the full width of the street, a rare sight in Náklav's narrow alleys.

"Juva Sannseyr, and really not a moment too soon!" The councilman pushed his way in the door, a hair's breadth from getting stuck.

The two porters followed, and Juva pointed them into the library.

"You asked for books," the councilman panted. "And books you shall definitely receive. Here's everything we could round up on the Seida Guild and the myth of the warow, more fairy tales than you could make your way through in a lifetime!"

The two men heaped the books onto the table and the councilman waved them out again. Then he flopped onto the sofa with very little room to spare. He did not extend his hand, nor did he introduce himself, but she knew that his name was Drogg Valsvik, and he probably figured that the rest of the world knew that, too.

Juva opened the lacquered cabinet and took out a bottle of whiskey.

"No, thank you. I don't drink," Drogg said.

Juva sat down in the chair across from him, leaned back, and crossed her legs. She left it to him to begin.

"Do you know how many people succeed in getting me to come see them these days?" he said, mopping off his sweat with a floral handkerchief. "None, Frú Sannseyr. It has cost me many footsteps and probably a year off my life, which tells you something about how serious the issue is." He watched her with an unexpected glint in his eye. His dirty-blond hair was thinning on top, and a different type of man would have tried to comb it over.

"Can I expect that you will show me the courtesy of telling me precisely how much time I've wasted once we're done with today's undertaking?" He stuffed his handkerchief back in his pocket.

Juva did her best to hide her confusion, but he saw enough of it to proceed.

"Your mother shared the secret with me—oh, my condolences, naturally—and may Gaula eat me if I haven't kept it. I presume that you, as her heir, can assist me now."

Juva ignored the touch of dismay. It was unlikely that he was talking about Gríf. "My mother had many secrets. Which one of them do you mean?"

"I mean that the length of one's life lies in the heart." He ran a plump finger along his shirt collar, as if it fit too snugly.

That seemed obvious, and Juva had no idea what he was getting at, so she kept her mouth shut.

"In the number of heartbeats?" he tried.

Juva shrugged.

"You are not a woman for small talk. I can appreciate that. I am referring to the length of a life being predetermined, having to do with how many heartbeats one has been granted. Your mother was generous enough to calculate how long I had left when I visited her. It varied, based on how many heartbeats I had used up. Now that I have wasted a significant number getting myself over here, I suppose I might be permitted to expect that you will provide me the same service?"

Juva tensed her jaw. She had nearly let it drop.

"You mean . . . You minimize your travel in order to . . . ?"

"Save heartbeats, that's right," he completed.

Juva stared at him, but there was no indication that he was joking. Mother had found an open wound and kept it open, had fed his anxiety until he no longer dared move. The man before her would have been half as large if he were fearless.

Gaula's heartless woman!

Drogg eyed her expectantly. He seemed like a practical man, far from the type to succumb to superstition. So what should she say? That her mother had lied? He would hardly believe that, and might take it as an insult or a rejection.

"How much did it cost you to find out how long you had left?"

"Fifty runes. I'm not here to haggle over the price, Frú Sannseyr."

"Fifty runes each time? And you were never skeptical?"

Drogg hesitated. He had most definitely been skeptical, but he wouldn't dare admit that to a blood reader. She realized that the question would need time to ripen, so she leaned across the table.

"Drogg Valsvik," she said, "we'll discuss that afterward. Let's deal with the other matters first."

"Of course!" he said, clearly relieved. "As I'm sure you probably know, our beloved city is not at its healthiest at the moment. More people with wolf-sickness, fewer travelers, less money in circulation . . . And in the wake of that, there's unrest, riots on the rafts—and not just in the poorest neighborhoods, either. We've had upsetting incidents at the best addresses! It's in everyone's interest, yours included, that we maintain a certain stability, right? I will be the first to admit that there is unrest tied to the Seida Guild after these . . . unexpected deaths."

"The murders."

"Yes. The murders, let's say it like it is." His smile was genuine. "I like you, Juva Sannseyr. Where was I? Yes, the murders have cast a sad damper on our spiritual life, if you will. The Seida Guild might as well not have existed! The daily operations in Jólshov proceed, for there are many on the staff, but none of them wants a title. No one wants to lead. The city council handles many weddings and sepultures, but quite a few for . . . let's say peculiar faiths from the gods only know where: fanatics from Undst, necromancers from Au-Gok. It is not a sustainable situation. We need a guild master."

He caught his wheezing breath before he continued.

"We have the Yra Race soon, the spring run, Frú Sannseyr, and before then we need a guild master for the Seida Guild, even if only on paper. We can't release half the city to run around Nákla Henge without the guild master's speech. People need their traditions!"

Around Nákla Henge . . .

It was as if his words untied a knot. The spring run! The Yra Race on the spring equinox was the only day of the year when no one was checked at the gates. It simply wasn't possible since hordes of people would be racing through the city, in around the stones, and back out again. People dressed like all the wild animals of the world. No one checked for fangs during the Yra Race because there were so many of them, made of bone or clay, glued on or painted on, and everything you could imagine in the way of furs and claws.

If they had any chance of getting Gríf home, it would be during the Yra Race.

Juva bit her lip to hide her smile. She needed to tell Gríf about this as soon as the councilman was out of the house. But she couldn't say yes too soon. She had terms that he needed to agree to. She leaned back in her chair and sighed.

"My dear councilman, the challenge is clear, but I'm not the type to give speeches. Besides, I already have two jobs. I hunt wolves and I also hunt the wolf-sick with the red hunter. I'm going to be a bleeder."

Drogg pulled his handkerchief across his brow again and said, "That strikes me as a morbid job for a . . . well, for anyone at all."

"Someone has to do it."

"That is true, and it's an attitude I know to appreciate, Frú Sannseyr. But being the guild master doesn't need to mean anything more than being the spokesperson. No one intends to drown you in work. What we need is a leader, and the members have indicated you. You can gather them using your name. You will be handsomely remunerated, of course, and you'll have the opportunity to shape the Seida Guild the way you want it. That is a rare privilege, Frú Sannseyr. What you wish the blood readers to be and the laws you would like to have in force, we will leave it up to you. Your fellow countrymen need you. The queen needs you. So, what if I said that this job was even more important than hunting the wolf-sick, but that you're free to do both?"

Juva pulled her hand over her mouth to hide another smile. She had him right where she wanted him.

"You mean I'm free to do both jobs until someone breaks in here at night and murders me in my sleep?"

"There is no indication that that will happen," Drogg said, his eyes roaming, searching, "but of course we will take steps to prevent that. What do you need?"

Juva pretended to contemplate this, even though she had her next words ready.

"I need security outside the house, at least in the beginning. Two guards, around the clock. And more frequent patrols all over Lykteløkka, so the blood readers can feel safe."

"I can have them here this afternoon."

"And since the blood readers feel like sitting ducks, I would like them to be allowed to carry weapons if they feel threatened."

Drogg blinked as if he didn't understand her request. "No one in Náklav is allowed to carry weapons in the streets," he said. "That's—"

"I am. I have a hunting license. We need more."

"I'll see what I can do." He pulled a couple of papers out of his case and set them in front of him on the table. It was the contract.

"One more thing," Juva said. "I want a license to hunt vardari."

The silence grew denser around them. She knew that she was asking for the impossible, but if Nafraím came back, she wanted to kill him. She couldn't risk the aftermath or going to jail for defending herself.

"Frú Sannseyr, the so-called vardari are . . . Well, the city council does not recognize any such organization, and neither does the Ring Guard or any lawmen in Náklav. No one can give you a license to hunt something that doesn't exist."

Juva pushed the contract away a little and leaned toward him.

"No," she said, "but you could give me a license to hunt anything that has fangs."

Drogg studied her. "So," he said, "you want to expand the wording on the license you already have for wolves and the wolf-sick?"

"Correct. If vardari don't exist, then it won't matter to you if they can be hunted or not. You don't get involved in the wolf blood or the teeth from the wolf-sick. The Ring Guard is in charge of that."

Drogg picked up a fountain pen and made a note on a piece of paper as he repeated to himself, "entitled to hunt anything with fangs."

"Is that possible?" Juva smiled.

"I believe that could be done, Frú Sannseyr."

He pushed the contract toward her. She read through it in its astonishing simplicity and signed.

I run the Seida Guild.

She had gotten what she needed, but it felt like anything but a victory. For her whole life, she had believed that blood readers should kick the bucket, every last one of them, but now she had signed on to lead them. Had she just signed her own death warrant?

Hardly. Her death warrant sat imprisoned under the house. It didn't matter whether she led the Seida Guild or not. The vardari were going to come no matter what.

Her signature was shiny. It slowly dried and, ultimately, it looked as if it had always been there.

Drogg also signed, and his massive shoulders relaxed right away. "You've done the only right thing, Frú Sannseyr. It really feels like I've saved heartbeats here after all." He watched her with poorly concealed expectancy.

All she needed to do was lie. Puncture his hand with her mother's blood reader claw. Maybe set out a couple of cards and rattle off what he wanted to hear. But what he wanted wasn't what he needed.

How many people had her mother kept imprisoned? Gríf, in the shaft, and her daughters, in fear. And the city councilman, in his own body. Lagalune had rendered him immobile for fear of dying, afraid of his own heartbeats, and Juva knew all too well how that felt. She owed him his freedom.

Juva stood up.

"Let me tell you one thing my mother neglected to say, councilor. No one can know how many heartbeats you have left, absolutely no one. She made quite a good living off that lie."

He opened his mouth as if to protest but glanced at the contract which was sticking out of his briefcase and kept his mouth shut. She held her hand out to him and helped him to his feet.

"Councilman, no one is born with a fixed number of heartbeats. Fate is far more playful that that. Come on."

She pulled him into the foyer with her, until he was visibly winded. Then she lifted his hand and helped him put it against his own throat.

"Can you feel that?" she asked eagerly.

"The beats, they're running out . . ." Drogg's eyes widened in alarm as his fingers shook against his neck.

"No, councilman! They not running out, they're running in! What my mother didn't know is that for every beat you use, you earn an extra one. If you use many of them, often enough, then you'll gain heartbeats much faster than you have time to use them. That's why I love to go hunting, to run in the woods."

Drogg let his arm fall. "Are you saying . . . are you saying that it doesn't matter what I do?"

"I'm saying that no one can tell you when you're going to die, or what will ultimately send you to Drukna. But if you earn more heartbeats, then at least you won't die because you ran out. I swear to that."

The councilman seemed to ponder her words without revealing what he thought, but then she hadn't expected that either. He had kept a lid on the truth and himself for many years. It would take him time to scrape the rust off.

He hoisted his bag over his shoulder and looked at her.

"Guild Master Sannseyr, you are very different from your mother and your sister."

Juva held back the thank you which was on the verge of escaping her lips. She walked him out and stood there until the runners, two strong men, had gotten the carriage moving.

The spring run! Gríf!

Juva locked the door and darted back into the library. She opened the hatch in the raven cabinet and pulled the lever. The bolts thumped inside the chimney. She pushed the door aside and climbed down the cool shaft. She had so much to tell him that she forgot the light and had to follow the tunnel wall with her fingers.

The sound of running water made her walk more slowly toward the iron closet. The closest door was still open. The second was safely locked. A flickering light fell through the bars in the window opening, drawing pale patches on the rusted walls. Juva tiptoed up to the door without making a sound and peered in the opening.

Gríf stood with his back to her, in a niche in the stone wall. Water trickled down from the ceiling over his naked body, which aroused feelings in her that were anything but virginal. He combed his claws through his hair, pausing for a brief instant with his head cocked as if he were listening.

He knows. He notices me.

Maybe he could hear her or smell her, like an animal? Or could he feel her heart, too, the way she felt his? Heavy, sucking, in time with her own. Traces of soapsuds slipped down his spine, which sat deep between his muscles.

Juva pressed her knuckles to her lips and that did nothing to quell her sudden urge to bite him. Would he have let her do that? Would he have mocked her for trying or would he just have broken her neck? That would be easy enough. Surely he could do it with just one arm.

He turned around and emerged from the niche, completely naked. Juva could see his penis swaying as he moved.

Look away!

But her eyes refused to obey. She pressed her forehead against the iron door, smelling rust and salt. He came closer and shook himself off like a wet dog. She felt a couple of drops rain against her lips.

What am I doing?! He's the iron wolf, the devil, the source of eternal life, and the man who killed my father.

Juva pulled away and stole back through the tunnel, feeling like she were drunk. Had he drugged her? She didn't know anything about him other than what he had told her himself, and why would that be more than the tip of the iceberg? Sure, the man could pass as human as long as he was dressed, but those all-black eyes, the fangs . . . And he could ingest food through his claws! She had seen it herself. It was sick, and Gaula knew what else he could do.

She couldn't set something like that free. He was dangerous.

Juva climbed up the chimney shaft and pushed the wall into place. She pulled her hands across her face and slowly exhaled. She'd known he'd wondered what was keeping her from releasing him. What if it wasn't fear that he would hurt her or anyone else but fear of losing him? She sank down onto the sofa.

Jól help me, I want him . . .

This was the last thing she needed. She needed to think clearly, and see him clearly, not through some ridiculous veil of lust. She had always felt like an outsider, and now she was engrossed in something that was even more foreign than herself, that was the explanation, plain and simple. Not to mention that Gríf was the one who had explained to her about her heart. It was like he had plucked out the panic and made her strong. But that wasn't true, he was also the cause of it as well. She couldn't afford to forget that.

Desire tied itself in a knot in her chest and turned into a feeling of being in immediate danger. She could say a lot of things about Rugen, but at least with him she had never felt like anything was at risk.

FANGS

Will any of them come?

Juva dared not hope. She had sent runners to the whole board of the Seida Guild about the meeting with Haane but doubted she would see a single blood reader. The only one she knew for sure would be there was the warow she had sensed the last time.

The preparations had taken several days, but she now knew more about the Seida Guild than she had ever wanted to know, more than Mother had known and probably more than Ogny and Maruska. The books lay strewn around her, open to the most important pages, with bookmarks where the history matched what Gríf had told her.

They were warriors.

Rarely with swords or crossbows, according to the books, but with ingenuity and skill. Sensing, it was called in some places. In other places, it was a whisper from the dead. Only in one place had she found any reference to hearts, and that was one person who had said that she could feel the wolf in her heart. It did not say anything about what that entailed. A gift, and a curse, that slowly but surely had been forgotten. Until now.

She lived in a city with hundreds of thousands of people and none of them understood what was about to happen. The vardari were denied, avoided, or flattered. And blood reading was nothing but prophecy and fabrication, as far from the source as you could get.

But that wasn't going to stop the vardari from ripping them to shreds—torturing, murdering, or using them as weapons in a war no one suspected was imminent. There were no means they would shy away from in their pursuit of the source of their abominably long lives.

It was up to her to create a new Seida Guild that would dare to stand united against them. And even if no blood readers dared to come to the gathering, then at least she would get Haane out of the warow's claws and send the rest of the vardari a signal that they needed to stay away.

Juva strapped on her hunting gear, hooked the crossbow onto her back, and tossed a cape over it so she wouldn't stand out on the street.

She locked the front door and stepped out into the drizzle. The Smelta storms weren't far off, and then everything would likely freeze over again. Two tall Ring Guardians stood on either corner of her residence, just as she had requested. They nodded to her, but she pretended not to notice, encumbered by the thought that she might not see them again. She had no idea what she was in for and knew nothing about the warow who seemed to be manipulating Haane.

Juva caught a runner and sent him to Broddmar with a message that she knew of a potentially wolf-sick person and that he should stake out the Volsung home. That was a meager security measure, but better than nothing. Then she headed straight for Ogny's house, which now belonged to Haane and a handful of other heirs.

She knocked. Haane answered the door herself, dressed in the same curled sweater as last time and looking significantly more nervous. Juva walked in and felt the flutter in her heart right away.

There were five blood readers sitting in the living room, more than she had dared hope. Anasolt was one of them, but she had expected that. She was reliable and looked like she had been born from a tree, with rootlike tangles in her red hair. Laleika was also there, which was more surprising. She was about fifty and a blood reader right down to her fingertips. She wore black makeup, her delicate body weighed down by jewelry. She sat with her feet folded underneath her, like a child.

"Pardon my hunting clothes," Juva said, taking off her cape. "I'm training to become a bleeder and have a meeting later."

The others exchanged meaningful looks. Haane started biting her nails.

The room was small and dark, overloaded with old-fashioned decorations and a very visible layer of dust. There was a bearskin rug on the floor with a gaping mouth. The only place the warow could be was behind a faded, red double door at the far end of the room.

Juva's eyes wandered among the women, who were all significantly older than her. She put her hands on her hips.

"All right," she said. "Raise your hand if you've never used the blood."

Haane, who had never worked as a blood reader, raised her hand tentatively but then looked around at the others and let it fall again. She probably had no idea what this was about.

Juva started moseying among them, slowly making her way toward the red doors.

"Mother, Ogny, and Maruska led the Seida Guild with blood pearls," Juva said. "They received them from the vardari and distributed them to you. Some of you would resell them, knowing full well that they could cause wolf-sickness, and I'm here to say that will never happen again. I personally bled someone who was affected. If any of you are here in the hopes that I'll continue where my mother let off, then you might as well leave right now."

Laleika rolled her eyes. A couple of the others suddenly looked uncomfortable in their seats, but they did not get up. Juva was nearing the doors.

"You are brave to be here. You know that someone is out to destroy the Seida Guild, and yet you're here anyway. Maybe you know

316

that it's necessary in order to survive. But you wouldn't be here if you thought I had murdered my own family. So, what makes you so sure?" Juva unhooked the crossbow from her back and didn't wait for anyone to answer. "You're sure because there's not a soul here who doesn't know who was behind it. The warow have used us, for generations, controlling us with the blood. And it ends now."

She opened the folded lath on the crossbow and nodded toward the door to signal that there was someone there. Haane sat on the edge of her chair, chewing her nails. Juva pulled a bolt from her thigh belt and put it in the groove.

"There was a time when you were the hope against the vardari, and now for generations you have been fawning over them. You should be ashamed of yourselves. The women who were supposed to protect people from the wolf-sickness were the ones spreading it. Under the vardari's control! You've failed the fairy tale you love to tell. The devil gave us the ability to see where the evil was, and we fought it. I'm going to be a red hunter, and I'm a blood reader, but once upon a time those were both the same job. It was all about the fight against bad blood." She stood in front of the red doors now and spanned her bow with a scarcely audible click. "We can carry on that fight. There are genuine blood readers out there. Not fortune-tellers or interpreters of tea leaves, but blood readers who can sense warow. They have the real gift, from the fairy tale. And I'm going to find them."

"Juva, darling." Anasolt was the first who dared to say anything. "I know this has been difficult for you, but I believe that if this were true, we would all have heard of them. So how can you—"

Juva interrupted her: "I know, because I'm one of them."

She yanked open the closest of the doors. A man inside backed away with his arms raised and his eyes locked on the crossbow. He was a good deal taller than her, with short, blond hair that was combed back.

From behind her, she heard the blood readers gasp and a chair tip over. Juva stared at the man through her crossbow sight as she approached. She forced him back until he stumbled on the base of the white spiral staircase and ended up sitting on a step.

"Who are you?" Juva asked. Her mouth was so dry that it sounded like a growl.

His gaze moved to a point behind her and out of the corner of her eye, she saw Haane approach. The warow gave her an unobtrusive nod.

"Juva, what are you doing?" Haane asked, her voice unsteady. "This is Nantes Retta, from Kreknabork, a very highly esteemed antiques dealer. You can't—"

Juva interrupted her without letting him out of her sight.

"She means an extremely old antiques dealer, right?" Juva said.

Nantes adopted a shaken expression, and, looking at Haane, said, "I can't imagine what this crazy young woman is talking about. Haane, could you help me up?"

"Do not approach him." Juva stopped her.

His heart beat faster against her own, as if he had only just grasped that she knew and that she meant business. A hunting high washed through her. She had him. She had one of them! She searched for the right words, unsure where she should begin. She wanted to know how many of them there were, what sort of groupings they had, and whether they were actually at war. But first she needed to vent her seething rage.

"Nantes Retta, I don't give a damn about your antiques business, but you will never buy blood from us. The next vardari to approach a blood reader is a dead vardari."

Nantes narrowed his gaze at Haane, who took a hesitant step toward them.

"Haane, freeze!" Juva instructed, taking a step closer to her. "He wants to use you as a shield so he can get out of here without answering any questions. If you come any closer, I'll shoot him."

Haane's eyes, shiny with tears, roved back and forth between them.

"He has no power over you anymore. We are standing together against them now!"

Juva could hear the others whispering behind her about how he had normal teeth, that she had lost her mind. Haane took a couple of steps toward Nantes. Suddenly he was on his feet and grabbing at her. Haane screamed.

Juva pulled the trigger. Nantes tossed his head and tipped backward. He lay on the white spiral staircase, with the bolt sticking out of the base of his throat. His head fell forward until his chin was resting on the bolt.

Juva still had him in her sight, which made her realize she was shaking. She could not afford that now. It was not supposed to end like this, but she couldn't let them see her having doubts. She was there to unite them, show that they were strong together.

Never let them see a weak blood reader.

Haane collapsed onto a chair with her arms folded over her stomach. She rocked back and forth, breathing in short bursts.

"Haane, I need a handkerchief."

Haane's eyes wandered until the simplicity of the task sank in. She stood up and left the room. The other blood readers had clearly decided to argue their way through the shock, panicking and at a loss for what to do.

"You aren't going to do anything at all," Juva said, folding up her crossbow and hooking it onto her back. "The Ring Guard is on its way. They'll clean up."

Haane came back with the handkerchief, which trembled as she held it out to her. Juva took it, walked over to Nantes, and tilted his head back. His wound glugged blood. She pulled the pliers out of her belt, opened his jaw, and broke out the fangs. The blood readers went silent. A couple of them sank back down onto their seats again.

"You see?" Juva held out her hand to them and showed them the teeth in the bloody handkerchief. "They had been filed down."

Finally, reality seemed to catch up with Haane. She slumped down onto her knees and started crying in deep sobs.

"He . . . He just came to the door one day, and . . . He was so strong, and I couldn't answer any of his questions. I have no idea where the blood came from!"

"Did he do anything to you?" Juva asked, squatting down beside her.

Haane was sobbing uncontrollably. Juva put her arm around her and looked at the others.

"Have they been to see you, too?" she asked.

"I can't be sure," Anasolt said with a nod, "but someone has been following me ever since the sepulture."

"They've been keeping an eye on all of us," Juva said, standing up and letting Flo attend to Haane.

"But why?" Anasolt's question hung in the air as every eye turned to Juva.

She couldn't tell them about Grríf. Couldn't say that they were searching for the source of eternal life—and that he was in her basement.

"Because they know that blood reading is real. I can sense them, and there may be more like me. So we can shut ourselves in and wait for death, individually. Or we can rebuild the Seida Guild as it once was: the opposition to the warow."

There was a loud, persistent knock on the door. The others jumped, terrified. Juva went to the front hall and let Broddmar and two Ring Guardians in.

"Are you all right?" Broddmar followed Juva into the living room, with Skarr slinking after him.

"Yes, thank you for coming," Juva said shakily, leading him to Nantes while the Ring Guard spoke to the blood readers.

Skarr bared his teeth at the body, growling, the hackles up on the back of his neck.

Juva held the teeth out to Broddmar. He stared at them, and she knew what he was thinking.

"Juva . . ."

"These are fangs!" she said.

"I can see that! What have you done?"

Juva gulped, clutching the teeth in her clenched fist.

"He threatened Haane," Juva said. "He attacked her, he had fangs, and Skarr growls at him. What the fuck more do you want?"

Broddmar grabbed her by the shoulders. "You know what I'm talking about! This wasn't someone with wolf-sickness. He's one of *them!*"

Juva didn't respond.

His eyes searched her face, and his fear gave way to anger. "You knew," he said. "You killed a warow, and you did it knowingly."

"They murdered Mother and Solde! And all the Seida Guild leaders. They're murderers."

"But for Gaula's sake, Juva!" Broddmar pulled his hands across his face and stared at the ceiling. "Was it *him*? Was *this* the man who did it? Or are you going to kill them all?"

"If I have to." Juva clenched her teeth.

"You started a war, without me. Without . . . Fuck!" Broddmar paced in a circle.

"It's me or them!"

Juva fought against her tears, which had formed a lump in her throat. She had believed Broddmar would help, that he would understand. She had even wanted to tell him the truth about Gríf. She should have known better. If there was one thing she could be sure of, it was that she was alone.

She walked over to Nantes's body and pulled the bolt out of his neck. The blood ran down, following his shirt collar, like a piece of jewelry. She wiped the bolt off on his jacket. Broddmar placed his hand on the back of her head.

"Juva, go home now and stay there. Do you understand? Don't let anyone in."

"Broddmar, I'm not a child. I'm guild master of the Seida Guild. The contract is signed. My house is protected by the Ring Guard. I know what I'm doing."

Juva felt anything but confident about her words, but they seemed to surprise Broddmar. He nodded a couple of times.

"We'll clean up here," he said. "Don't leave your house, and I'll come as soon as I can. Do you understand?"

Juva smiled, but it felt like a sneer. She went into the living room where the other blood readers sat huddled together, relaying their accounts to the Ring Guard. The room grew quiet when she entered.

"Hang the lanterns up again," she said, her voice hoarse.

Then she walked out onto the street. It was raining harder now. Broddmar's words burned in her head.

You started a war, without me.

She hadn't intended to kill. All she had wanted was to prevent more blood readers from being used by the warow, living in fear of them the way she did of Nafraím. He was the one who had started the war, not her. So why did she feel so sick to her stomach?

Juva ignored the looks from the guards who flanked her house, fully aware of how she looked. She walked into the storeroom and retrieved the blood reader lantern. It was dirty, and one of the red glass panes had been shattered. She wiped it off with a rag, cleaning the glass and putting it together as best she could.

She carried it out and hung it up outside. The door to the waiting room was still bolted—she was no fortune-teller and clients were the last thing she wanted. But she would show the others that the Seida Guild was alive. Even if hers was the only red lantern on the street.

THE BETRAYAL

"Against the wall," Juva ordered, watching Gríf through the opening.

Those milky eyes blackened, but he backed up to the end of the room and sat down on the floor. He pulled one foot toward his body and rested an outstretched arm on his knee, his fingers toward her, as if to show his claws.

He was barely ten paces away, both too many and too few, but here went nothing. She was bitter and bloody, worn down, with little to lose.

Juva set down her crossbow and pulled down the lever that unlocked the inner door. It hadn't been moved in the gods knew how long and groaned ominously. She walked into the cage and pushed the door ajar while she checked that he remained seated. Then she opened it all the way, until there was no longer anything between them other than distance.

It was the first time she had seen him not behind bars.

Gríf didn't move, other than his chest, which rose and sank with each slow breath. Every third heartbeat she felt was his, an inhumanly slow pulse, quiet before the storm.

Juva leaned against the doorframe. The ceiling was higher than she had realized, with strong beams supporting it, full of gashes and gouges from where they had once tied up the catch for smoking. The twilight seeped through a fissure in the rock wall, but she couldn't see anything outside, neither ocean nor sky. The black wall was too thick and the opening too narrow.

He had frequently paced in a circle, judging from the worn marks on the wooden floor. Water trickled in along the wall where he had showered. In the inner room, there was a bed, if you could call it that, a wide platform with a long-haired sheepskin.

There was a stool by the door and a simple wooden table with books that tugged at her memory. And they weren't the only thing she recognized. She saw a wool blanket that they used to keep in the library and a lantern from the pantry.

"Everything that disappeared ended up here, didn't it?" she said with a scathing laugh. "The books Mother said I'd dreamt I had . . ."

Gríf shrugged, but she saw that he was tense. Was he waiting for the best time to attack? To rush past her and out to freedom?

"I just killed one of them," she said.

She backed up and leaned against the wall of the tunnel. The doors were wide open, and the iron closet was just a rusty frame between them now, but there was no room for fear. She was too full of failure. It felt worse than coming back from hunting empty-handed in deep snow that clung to her calves. She had done the job but failed all the same.

"What are you waiting for? Congratulations?"

His apathy penetrated her tired body, right to the bone. She had gotten to know his eyes, hot and cold, and their nuances, which revealed what he was looking at. There was no indication of joy or sympathy.

"It was an accident," she muttered.

"I see. You made a mistake, so now you've come down here to make another one." His gaze settled on the crossbow that lay by her feet. "*Ik thaurir*. What's wrong with you, human? There are three bounds between us, and you have nothing to defend yourself with. Because you don't dare hold the weapon you just used to kill with?

You made a mistake, which leads to another, which will lead to still another. What a life."

"You've been imprisoned here for seven centuries, you fool!" Juva slid down onto the floor. "And every day you talk like you've had a better life than me."

He leaned his head against the wall and revealed his fangs as he gave a husky laugh.

"I've seen the basements under Jólshov," he said. "The labyrinth under Náklaborg, the top of the Widow's Tower in Ankri, and the bottom of Skollgap in Kreknabork. I have seen the hole in the earth at Nidauge and gone down with a sinking ship. All that, as a prisoner." He nodded to the rusty frame between them. "Even that damned iron closet has seen more of the world than you. You think I've been blind and deaf, but I have seen and heard generations of blood readers. Quiet, chatty, horny, and—what's the word?—sadistic."

Juva glanced at his scars, dark depressions by his elbow.

"No," he said, shaking his head. "No blood reader gave me these. I got them from a . . . mutual friend."

"Nafraím."

The bitter expression of his mouth left no doubt. Juva pulled down her sleeves, cold from the rock wall. She had no idea what he had been through, but she couldn't shake the thought that no matter what he might decide to do as a free man, the world had it coming. Maybe she did, too.

He lowered his chin and looked up at her, between the black tufts of his bangs.

"So, you haven't heard anything at all of what I've told you? You have no pack, no one to rely on, and yet you've killed one of them without setting me free first. You could have bled out in a ditch by now, and I would have been left to rot here as the result. Your folly could have cost me my life. And I still have something to lose, unlike you."

325

Juva looked down. His sharp accent suited his harsh words. He was right. All she had to lose was him. Her whole life had been about him, both before and after she had found him. But to him she was nothing. A random, hopeless girl in a long line of blood readers.

Gríf put his hands behind his head and took a deep breath, which made his chest rise.

"Listen," he said, "I understand that you were thrown into this. No one prepared you, and you've been lied to your whole life. It's smart to be wary, that keeps you alive. But I've given you more time than we have, and you're not going to trust me any more tomorrow than you do today. There's nothing I can say that will make you feel safe enough."

"How nice that you know that," Juva scoffed, "given that you haven't even tried."

"Good point," Gríf laughed so his whole face softened. "Fine, I just want my freedom back. I promise that I won't hurt you or demolish the house. Does that help?"

"Or hurt anyone else, or destroy the city?" She knew it sounded like she was joking, but she meant every word.

"I think you're asking a lot now . . ." He gave a smile that weakened her.

"So you want me to believe that you're just going to stroll out of here after everything they've done to you?"

"I want to go home, nothing else."

"Nothing else?" Juva rolled her eyes. "You're just going to traipse through the biggest city in the world, with fangs and claws? Stroll up to a massive, round wall, crawling with Ring Guardians armed with crossbows searching for people with wolf-sickness? Maybe that was possible when you got here, but a lot has happened in six hundred and sixty years, you know?"

"You don't mince words, do you?" He wrinkled up his nose in jest. "What about the three openings in the wall?"

"Doors. Heavy metal doors, green with patina." She flung out her arms. "Big ones. Picture an enormous door and I can guarantee you that these are bigger. But I'm sure you can just knock, show them your fangs, and ask if you can go home again, right?"

Gríf smiled, and Juva felt an aching need to get him to do that more often.

"But I have a plan," she said, far more bravely than she felt.

"Good. You have no idea what a relief that is to hear, because I've never had a single plan myself."

He looked into her eyes, and she could see that they were both on the verge of laughter. Her body softened and it felt as if the hopelessness had dissolved.

"Good for you to say that," she said, pointing to him teasingly. "I had been meaning to ask, but it seemed impolite—"

He cut her short with a raised hand, cocked his head to the side, and listened. Seriousness cooled his face again.

"We're no longer alone."

Juva was going to laugh, but then she heard a distant clang as the front door banged shut and someone called her name.

"Shit! Rugen."

She leapt to her feet and raced up the tunnel, cold with stress. It wasn't possible. The door was locked, how could he . . . ? The wall in the chimney was wide open! She climbed up, hit her knee on the top rung, and stumbled into the library. Out in the front hall, Rugen yelled again. She ran to him, ready to chew him out, but she could see right away that something was wrong. He was sweaty and looked groggy. Drunk, but she didn't think he'd been drinking.

It's the wolf-sickness. He's getting worse.

"Rugen, what are you doing here? How did you get in?"

He came closer and dangled a key in front of her.

"I winked and showed this to the two statues outside," he explained. "They get that we're lovers. It was laughably easy."

He was grinning, but his eyes were eerily cold, which gave her reason to be cautious.

"I never gave you a key," she gulped.

"No, but Heimilla did. And since you threw out the entire staff, she doesn't need it anymore."

He stuck the key in his pocket and came right up to her, ran his hand over her cheek.

"Rugen, you need to leave," Juva said, pulling away. "Now's not a good time."

"It's always a good time for us, you know that. I knew you would be difficult, but I came over here anyway. That tells you something, doesn't it? I need you, Juva. I need help and it'll cost you nothing. Come with me and you'll see."

Juva snuck a peek at the front door. She had to get outside and yell for the guards. Rugen wrapped his hand around the back of her head and leaned in to kiss her. His mouth tasted like blood. Was that blood pearls or was he losing his canines?

"Where? You want me to come with you where?" She darted around him and backed toward the front door.

"You're trying to run off, you . . ." His smile took on a scornful and nasty twist.

Juva lunged for the door. Rugen grabbed her neck and pushed her up against the cold wrought iron, with more force than she would have thought he had.

The wolf-sickness is making him stronger!

Fear amassed in her heart, pumping cold blood through her body.

"You're so damned demanding, Juva." Rugen's gaze grew heady with power. "You got your money back. You got to hear everything you wanted to hear. Does that mean nothing? Plus, I haven't even laid a hand on anyone you care about. Do you think you're immortal because you have the devil?" He took a step back, as if to study the effect his words had on her. "I know, Juva. I know you have him, and that you've been keeping him hidden from me, when I need him the most."

"You're sick, Rugen."

"Fuck that! You're worse than Kefla, that guildless girl up in Herad who plays at being a blood reader! I'm not sick. This is the beginning of my eternal life! With the best of the best." He flung out his arms.

A sickening assurance grew in her stomach.

"Nafraím," she whispered. "You've been with Nafraím."

For how long?

She searched back through her memories for the answer. Nafraím had known that Rugen had wolf-sickness. He knew about her drawings. The money that had been returned to her, that had come from him, from a vardari. All the questions from Rugen and his sudden interest in her life. How he had comforted her when her mother died. It had all been a job to him. Had it been like that from the beginning, when they were first together?

"Always," Rugen replied, as if he had read her mind. "Powerful friends to have."

"You . . . You told him about my drawings of the devil."

"Where is he? Answer me?!" Rugen pressed against her again.

She turned her foot, hoping to jam her knee into his crotch, but he shoved his own leg in between her feet.

He's going to kill me.

"You can't do this, Rugen! The red hunter will find you," she forced the words out as he tightened his hold.

"Ha! Broddmar? You stupid girl. He won't touch me. I'm protected now. Who do you think pays for the wolf-sick to be killed? The money comes from them, Juva. It's warow money. The Ring Guard takes the blood and the teeth, but the vardari run the hunt."

Broddmar works for the vardari?

Rugen pulled his hand through his sweaty, brown hair. It was the only chance she'd had. Juva twisted free and shoved him as hard as she could.

"You're lying! Broddmar would never work for them!"

Juva felt sick. It couldn't be true. If wolf-sickness really was the beginning of an eternal life and something survivable, why would they kill their own? Had they no limits? Did Broddmar know who he was working for?

He's lying!

"You'll have the same outfit soon," Rugen said, rubbing his jaw, clearly in pain but sneering anyway. "Then you'll do it, too. If you live that long, that is."

Juva stared at him. He looked like himself, but at the same time he didn't. The wolf-sickness had strengthened everything ugly, both on the inside and the outside. He believed he would live forever, believed the vardari had a place for him, and it had turned him into a grotesque version of himself.

"Oh, Rugen . . . you poor idiot." She shook her head.

Rage contorted his face and he pulled something out of his pocket. A jackknife.

Juva blocked his arm with her elbow and brought up her knee to kick, but Rugen suddenly slowed, held back by a figure behind him. Grif.

I left the door open!

With one hand, Grif tightened his grip around Rugen's neck and dug his claws into his neck. Rugen gasped and jabbed behind him with his knife, blindly. He slashed Grif's arm before his eyes glazed over. His arms fell heavily to his sides and his knife clattered to the floor. Grif threw him at the wall, from several paces away. Rugen's body slumped to the floor and lay there.

Juva pressed herself against the door and stared at Grif. The iron wolf from her sketches stood before her now, alive, a black-haired devil from countless nightmares, his rib cage naked and alien in the dim light, the hint of fangs in his half-open grimace.

He was so animal-like that she suddenly wondered if she had imagined all her conversations with him. The ones she'd had without letting him out.

He's going to kill me.

She glanced at Rugen, who lay motionless over by the wall, a chilling reminder of his violent abilities. Her heart pounded in her chest, and it wasn't alone. Grif's slow rhythm supplanted her own and she realized she had forgotten to breathe.

He watched her with all-black eyes. A twitch in his upper lip made it look like he was snarling, like that wolf in Svartna, who had stood over her as she floundered in the snow. Only this time she had nothing to defend herself with.

His forearm was bleeding, where Rugen had cut him. The blood ran down between his fingers and dripped onto the floor. Slower and slower until it stopped altogether. Juva stared at the cut, which had closed completely. The wound might as well have never been there. There wasn't even a drop to trickle down anymore.

Grif turned to the wall and walked back into the library. She could hear him climbing down the chimney.

This isn't real. This isn't happening.

Juva took a breath after what felt like an eternity. Grif was free, after nearly seven hundred years, and he was climbing back down to his cage? And he had healed himself, like a god! She stared at the red drops on the floor, the blood the warow had coveted and lived on.

The drops looked deceitfully ordinary, like any other blood. Nothing revealed that these specific stains had enormous ripple effects that had shaped the world. Everything from the blood readers' alertness to a network of addicts, plus people with wolf-sickness in all the ring cities.

Rugen!

She had to do something about Rugen. Was he dead? She walked over to him and put her hand to his throat. His pulse was only just barely palpable under her fingers. Sooner or later that asshole would wake up, even angrier than before. But she couldn't walk outside and yell for the Ring Guard, not while Gríf's door was wide open.

Pull yourself together, Juva. You're a hunter.

She grabbed hold of Rugen under his arms and dragged him into the little bathroom next to her mother's room. All the other rooms downstairs either had windows or more than one door. Rugen was heavy and hung from her arms as if he were dead—but he was alive.

Not for long. He'll be fair game when his teeth come in.

The most compassionate thing would be to kill him, to save the lives he'd be doomed to take. She left him sitting on the floor propped up against the tub and ran out to grab the jackknife he had dropped. It lay half-folded on the floor. He hadn't even had time to open it all the way before he had fainted. She returned to him and knelt on the floor beside him. She straightened out the knife and held the blade to his throat.

Come on, Juva. This will be over fast.

She stared at his sweaty face. His mouth was half open and his teeth still looked normal, nothing she could pull to use as evidence of wolf-sickness. But maybe the new ones were there in his gums?

She tightened her hold on the knife. It was new, shiny and pristine, with a carved handle. Had Nafraím paid for it? To kill her?

She smelled a faint whiff of urine under the heavy odor of stale smoke from her mother's years of smoking. Rugen made a half-smothered snore and chewed his lethargic lips. Her hand started shaking and she let go. She folded the knife and stood up.

She felt cowardly, weak. He deserved to be killed. He deserved what was coming, but it would have to come later.

She locked him in the bathroom and went into the library. The gap in the chimney was still open. Maybe she could just close it and hope that Gríf wouldn't come up again? That hope was laughable after what she'd just seen him do. She climbed down with the storm lantern dangling on her arm. It warmed her with light through the dark tunnel.

Gríf sat on the floor with his back against the wall and one arm draped over his knee, as if he hadn't moved. He stared at her with fire in that black gaze, but she could feel from his heartbeats that he was restless.

Juva put her hand on the handle of the iron door, as if she were going to close it. Gríf didn't move, but she saw his fingers twitch. The muscles in his neck tensed, like a wolf sensing danger. If he had had fur, his hackles would be up.

She could shut him in again. He wouldn't be able to stop her, no matter how fast and strong he was. But she didn't.

Jól help me.

She took a couple of hesitant steps and was inside. Inside the shaft, with him. His heart beat more strongly than her own—or had she started confusing them? She wasn't sure anymore where she ended and he began.

Juva knelt on the wood floor and crawled closer, on all fours. Every thought was blown away and the only clear thing that remained was him. They were both animals, wolves in the woods. She could smell him, burned bark and animal pelt, like hunting in Svartna.

She crawled forward until she was kneeling by his legs. He was barefoot, and it struck her that he didn't have claws on his toes. Had she expected that? She reached out and put her fingers on his wrist, where the cut had been. She could feel a twitch, but he didn't move. His skin was cool, and more than anything else, she wanted to feel it grow warmer.

His mouth curled into a cautious smile. She felt his claws, hard and cold, like rocks at the seashore. Worn down by the ocean for thousands of years. He splayed out his fingers, as if to make it easier for her to feel them, and that was all the confirmation she needed. She braced a hand against his bare chest and leaned forward until her forehead touched his. She could feel his breath against her lips. Longing rushed through her. Her blood poured down between the apex of her thighs, gathering into a pulse, throbbing like a third heart.

She pressed his head back against the wall and opened her mouth to kiss him. Gríf brought his hand to her breast and stopped her. She swallowed and looked into the night sky of his gaze as they breathed in unison.

"Why?" he whispered, his voice hoarse. "Why should I give you that power as well?"

Juva pulled back and knelt before him, with a burning heat in her cheeks.

"You kept *me* as a prisoner and *him* as a partner?" He chuckled. "That says something about your . . . ." He glanced up and seemed to be searching until he found the word. "Judgment." He exaggerated the pronunciation of the word, as if he had never said it before.

He looked into her eyes again.

"You've held me here for more years than you can fathom, human, and still you want more? You come to me as if we were equals, as if we were both wild and running free in the woods. Look around!" His outburst startled her, but he continued, just as callously. "You interrogate me, secretly study me, and size me up as if freedom is something I should make myself deserving of. Should I become someone else in the hopes of getting out? No. I am not part of that game, Juva Sannseyr. Save your mercy for a man who needs it."

She turned her gaze to the floor, unable to face his anger, justified as it was.

"Look at me," he commanded. "Look at me and tell me: If it were you sitting here and I came through those iron doors, what would you have done? Embraced me? Would you have opened yourself to me, spread your legs in the hopes of being set free? Or would you have refused to give yourself to the beast who kept you imprisoned?"

"That's not the same," she said, a lump in her throat from the shame. "You just threw an adult man across the room! I have every reason to be cautious, while you know you have nothing to fear from me."

He let out a brief laugh. "Then you don't know yourself very well, girl."

Juva didn't know what he meant, but the words left her feeling oddly content. Silence fell over them, letting in the murmur of the ocean. Water dripped from the deep niche in the wall, without any rhythm. Why was he just sitting there? He could be a free man, after more time than she could bear to think of, yet . . . it wasn't to lure her in, he had just proved that to her. He wasn't a wild animal.

He's afraid!

That realization clarified her thoughts, and she saw her mistake.

"Everyone wanted the devil," Juva said, standing up. "I thought I had found him, the wolf from the fairy tale, the source of the warow and a monster in captivity, not a man. You were so real and unreal at the same time that I wasn't able to see beyond the myths, but now I see."

"I can hardly wait. What do you see, human?" He gazed up at her.

"You talk big, Gríf, but I'm not the one keeping you here anymore. You're the one who doesn't dare to be free. I've lived with fear long enough to recognize it when I see it, and you . . . you're afraid."

Juva knew she was speculating, but she also knew that he would hate her assumption enough to leave the room, if only to prove her wrong. She turned her back on him and walked out without closing the door.

WHALEHEART

Juva flopped onto the sofa and took a swig of Gaula water. It was just as disgusting as she remembered, but she was out of whiskey. This rubbish was brewed from the same seaweed that was used to oil the dead, and there was probably no difference in the taste.

In the twilight, the library was like a painting in blue. The rain had turned to slush, which spat on the windows. She was so tired her eyes hurt, but she managed to keep them open. There was far too much death to see. Mother, Solde, wolf-sickness . . . And the murder she had committed herself, the warow at Haane's place.

That was going to cost her. Punishment awaited her, even if Nafraím was the one who had started the war. All she had done was give notice that she was aware of it—probably a mistake. Chances were good that she had just made a bad situation worse for them all by daring to fight back.

All she had wanted to do was show the blood readers that they could stand together, that they could say no to the warow and to the blood that made people sick. Instead, she had ended up taking a life, a life that had maybe been as long as ten lives.

None of the others had sensed him, that was for sure. So if there *were* more sensers, then they were outside the guild. Not surprising, since the Seida Guild had pushed away anyone who wasn't good for the group's bottom line or who didn't agree to the rules. They had failed the task they had been founded for. They had knelt down

336

before the evil they were intended to combat, in exchange for blood pearls and wealth.

An ocean of time had eaten away all knowledge of authentic blood reading and no one could recognize it anymore. Náklav might be full of young girls who lived as she had, in fear and confusion over why their hearts bolted when they least expected it. Who would believe her if she tried to explain?

She took another sip from her glass to the hollow sound of climbing from the chimney.

And now I've set the devil free, a creature I have no control over whatsoever.

Gríf pulled himself up out of the black opening and started walking along the bookshelves, as if he had never seen a library before. Juva reluctantly got up and followed him, uncertain of where they stood after their argument. She took a gamble at elevating the mood.

"There's something about captivity you haven't understood," she said. "You're supposed to be gaunt, filthy, and have a beard. And cold. And you're supposed to have missing teeth."

Gríf grinned, displaying his fangs. "Like you?"

"Very funny . . . You're not supposed to be funny, either."

His claws opened wide, grazing the spines of the books as he walked.

"I am Vitnir. We're not like you humans. You're useless. You freeze to death, just like that, and need to eat everything with skin and hair for nourishment. If you had claws, you could simply filter the most useful bits out of the food."

"We're civilized. It's not nice to eat through your fingertips. But since you do anyway, one might wonder why you have a mouth, since it seems fairly superfluous."

He clearly struggled to suppress a smile.

"I can eat with my mouth if I so desire," he said. "But then I won't know what's in the food I'm eating. Go ahead and call me an animal, but I like to know what I'm consuming. Three people have tried to poison me."

"Couldn't they just have starved you to death?"

He continued out into the hall where he ran his hand along the banister, as if enthralled by all the new things he could now touch.

"Oh yes, they punished me with hunger as well, but they weren't poisoning me to kill me. I suppose they just wanted to knock me out for a while."

Juva swallowed. She could hear scars of seriousness in his light-heartedness.

"Why?" she asked.

He smiled wryly and unambiguously. "To be able to ride me safely, I would think."

Juva felt her stomach contract. Who would poison a man and then have sex with him in secret? That was an outrageous thought. All the same, shame burned in her chest. She had tried to kiss him, and it had never occurred to her that for centuries, multiple blood readers had felt the same urge.

Was he the source of the bawdy fairy tales, too? The titillating versions of the sisters and the wolf? The thought made her feel insignificant, and she didn't want to ask.

"What did you do to Rugen?" she asked instead.

"Nothing that lasts. He'll wake up when the night is through." Gríf walked over to the shelves and picked up the carved skull. "Unless this is him."

"No," Juva chuckled. "I locked him in the bathroom."

She felt like an idiot to have trusted Rugen at all despite her instincts. All the things he had rattled off before he attacked her came tumbling into her tired head.

"He said wolf-sickness was the beginning of eternal life, but that's not true, is it?"

338

She looked at Gríf and silently prayed that he would say no. She had too much to bear already. What if Rugen was telling the truth? What if all the dead wolf-sick people could have survived? They had been hunted, bled out, and fed to the stones for as long as anyone could remember. Their teeth had been yanked out, and she had participated in that personally.

Gríf didn't seem to have heard her, his hands wandered over the rib bones on the skeleton bench, as if he had never seen anything like it.

"Gríf, can you stand still just for a minute?"

"You're releasing me from captivity and asking me to stand still?"

"Could we sit down in here?" Juva said, opening the door to the blood reader room. "Just so I can get the answers I need."

Gríf followed her in and stopped in front of the mural, his head tilted.

"That's my great-grandmother's work," Juva said. "Síla Sannseyr."

"Síla Sannseyr," he said, eying her with playful smoke in his white eyes. "I knew she liked me more than she let on."

Juva sat down at the table. Gríf sat down across from her, where her mother used to sit, and looked down into the box of cards. He picked up the blood reader claw and turned it over like a curious child, his actual claws with the blood readers' fake one, the one they used to draw a drop of blood from their customers.

Had it been inspired by him as well? The scope of what he meant threatened to break her. She was too tired to fight. Her fingers found the grooves in the woodwork and she clung to the delicate feel of something real. Gríf had lived longer than any creature should. He had blood in his veins that imparted eternal life. His wounds closed all on their own, and he anesthetized people with his claws.

"What would you like to know?" he asked.

She took a breath and dove in. "Rugen said wolf-sickness is survivable. Is that true?"

"Yes, it's not impossible. If he receives enough of my blood, he will become one of them."

"A warow?"

"Perhaps. It depends on how strong he is and how far the rot has progressed. Why do you ask? Do you want to reward him with immortality?" The scornful turn to his lips left little doubt about what he thought of the matter.

"Of course not. No one should live forever."

"Then he's doomed to die," Gríf said with a shrug. "Unless he becomes a varig and then stops taking the blood."

Juva rubbed her eyes. She tried to find something to fix her gaze on besides him. "What happens if he stops?" she asked.

"I told you that before. It's exactly what the vardari are afraid of now. Without fresh blood, their bodies will rot. If you haven't been a warow for long, then you *can* survive it. But I doubt that he has it in him. Few do. The pain would drive him to the wall, and the longer you've been a warow, the worse it is. Why do you think I've let them drink it?"

His smile became dangerous, and it dawned on her what had kept him alive for so long.

He has been hoping to gain his freedom, just so he can watch them all rot.

She made an effort to think clearly.

"But . . ." she said, "Rugen said the vardari are paying Broddmar for the teeth and the blood, that they're the ones hunting people with wolf-sickness. That doesn't make sense! Wolf-sickness is a result of their blood pearls, a sort of newborn warow, and if that's the case—"

"If that's the case, they're killing their own." Gríf put his hand on the table, ready to stand up.

"But that's like killing your own children," Juva said, a chill creeping down her spine. "That's sick! Why?"

"I have no idea, and I'm not planning to be here long enough to find out. Where's the exit?" He got up and walked back out into the foyer.

Panic roused her and she set after him, grabbing his arm. "Wait!" she pleaded. "You can't just go. They're going to kill you or take you prisoner again. And then we've lost!"

"Just let them try."

"Gríf, damn it! This city isn't the same as you remember it!"

He stopped as she grasped at straws.

"Look," she said, "I have no idea how things looked six hundred years ago, but I know that it's not the same as now. You can't just stroll up to the stones or stand out on the street and call out to Nafraím like some confused caveman!"

He appeared to contemplate the meaning of that word while she struggled to come up with some way of explaining that he would understand.

The roof! I can show him!

Juva reached for his hand to pull him along and felt his claws graze her palm. She pulled her arm back again, his rejection still vivid in her memory.

"If you want out, then we'll go out," she said. "Come on, you'll see."

He followed her up to the attic, in between the chests, junk, and an old loom. The warp yarns were fuzzy with dust. Juva doubted that any Sannseyr had ever had use for a loom, so it must have been there since her great-grandmother had bought the house.

Gríf stopped by a rusty fox trap and the look in his eyes darkened.

"It's old. Come on." Juva opened the door and the wind off the ocean grabbed it right away. "Be careful near the edges so that no one sees you," she said over her shoulder.

She thrust her feet into a pair of leather slippers and stepped out onto the roof.

The rain had worsened into a snowy slush that had built up into mounds along the dilapidated edge wall that surrounded her. Gríf had to bend down to come out. His bare feet slapped against the cracked flagstones. He stopped in the middle of the roof space and looked up at the sky.

Juva realized that for her this was just a visit to the roof. For him, it was his first time outdoors in hundreds of years.

Wet snowflakes kissed his back and melted on his skin, as if encountering him had made them cry. He closed his eyes and took a breath so deep and genuine that his heart grew in her chest. It swelled out with every beat until she thought she would burst.

How big could a heart get? She had seen a whale heart at the wharves, many years ago, and it was as tall as she was, a bloody knot of meat with arteries that were big enough to crawl into.

What if Gríf's heart had already swallowed her, crowded out her own? When had she allowed that to happen? She bit her lip, worn out, tired to the bone, and with a dawning fear of the space he was taking up within her.

Get a grip, Juva.

She snuck into the corner, where the wall was taller than she was, so she could hide them from view. Through a collapsed section of stones, she could see out over the city. Náklav lay chilly and bruised in the blue night light. Gríf came over beside her.

She pointed and whispered, "The roof right here belongs to the bakery. It was sold recently, definitely to a warow or someone who's keeping an eye out for them. Lykteløkka continues all the way up to the old city wall, which you can just barely see over there. The wall is falling to pieces in many places, but it runs along the entire damned Ringmark, you understand? Tunga and Skodda, too, whole sections of the city. That big gate leads into Brenntorget, and if you keep going straight, you'll get to Nákla Henge. The wall is enormous, Gríf. And it's well guarded. The three gates are never open at the same time, and no one enters or exits without a visitor's card. Right now, you also need to show your teeth to prove that you don't have wolf-sickness. If you go out onto the street, people will freak out and you'll be a dead man. If we can get you to the wall unseen, you'll be stopped at the gates, and you'll be a dead man. If you manage to break in and get to the stones, you'd have a back full of crossbow bolts and—"

"I'll be a dead man?"

"Ah, so you *can* learn?" she said.

He gave her a smile that could just as easily have been a snarl. Náklav's thousands of lights reflected in his eyes, and she could see that his gaze was wandering. Subtle nuances she had taken the time to understand. She leaned her head against the wall and for a moment she thought she was asleep.

"You people have been busy," he said. "I could cross the whole city on the roofs. What happened to all the trees?"

Juva struggled to open her eyes but couldn't answer. There had never been room for trees in Náklav, not in her lifetime. She pulled her sleeves down over her hands, but her sweater was cold and already wet.

"You're right," he suddenly said.

Juva smiled sluggishly and put her hand to her chest. "Ouch, that must have hurt to say!" she teased.

"Don't get used to it."

"But we'll get you home, Gríf." Juva wrapped her arms around herself against the cold. "We just need to wait until the Yra Race. When the spring run is underway, no one will—"

"Are you kidding? You people still do that? Run through the streets dressed like wolves?"

Juva would have laughed if she'd had the strength. Apparently, the race had been going on longer than she had imagined.

"Of course we do. And it's the only day you can go home. Think about it, Gríf. No one will notice teeth and claws on someone like

343

you and the gate to Nákla Henge will be open so people can run around. But they stop the blood gutter that feeds the stones, so they won't work."

"I don't need blood to make them work. I have the Might."

"Good. Then we've won." Juva let out a relieved sigh.

"You call that winning?"

"If we get you home, the vardari will rot. Maybe it will take time, but they won't be eternal anymore. And they won't have blood to sell, so no one else will come down with wolf-sickness. So, yes, I call that winning, in the long run."

"The long run?" He looked at her in surprise. "What will you do while you're waiting for them to die out? What's the point of winning in the long run if they kill you in the short run?"

"Not if I kill him first."

"Him?"

Juva didn't respond. He knew who she meant. She leaned her forehead against the wall and fought to keep her eyes open.

Gríf moved to stand behind her and shelter her from the wind.

"So, if I disappeared," he said, "you will have won because the vardari will die out? And the world will magically become everything you want it to be?"

Juva thought she nodded. She could feel the heat of his body against her back. Or had she fallen asleep? Was she dreaming? Maybe she was freezing to death?

No, his voice was real, deep in her ear.

"You get that the easiest way to win would be to just let me starve to death behind the iron doors?" he said.

"If that's what you want," Juva said with a shrug, "then it's fine by me, wolf mouth. Hide yourself away in the shaft where it reeks of smoke and fish."

She smiled sleepily and had a strong sense that he was doing the same. His arm lay across her chest, so hot that her skin began to tingle. The scent of him salted a wound in her heart that was rawer than she had suspected.

Yes. This is a dream.

She glanced down at his scars.

"Why do you have scars when you can heal yourself?" she murmured.

"It happened at the wrong time," he said and pulled her to him. "Come, Juva. You people aren't made for being outside."

She slumped and was out.

THE SECRET

Juva stared at her own reflection and saw a straight-backed stranger in red. The collar hugged her neck; its stays would protect against bites. The jacket fit snugly around her waist, molded like a corset, and the washed leather gave the erroneous impression of having been in use for a lifetime. She looked like the girl with the wolf in her great-grandmother's mural.

The sister who survived.

Savill bustled around Juva with a critical eye. Something told her that he always did that, no matter how good the workmanship was and no matter how busy he was.

The Yra Race was only a month away, which was obvious in this shop. The shelves bulged with goods and wicker baskets, marked with cryptic abbreviations that only a tailor could understand. Wadmal lay like a tablecloth over the worktable, covered in paper pattern pieces—back, side pieces, sleeves . . . A carved-up carcass, like an animal at the butcher's. The difference between a stag and a man suddenly seemed smaller.

What about Gríf?

How would the pattern pieces have looked if the jacket were for him? Broader over the shoulders, narrower at the waist. The high collar would suit him. Gloves to hide his claws. No one would suspect that he was anything other than human if he kept his eyes and mouth shut. Or would people be able to sense that they were passing a predator? A man who could heal his own wound in mere moments, who had eternal life flowing in his veins? A pleasurable chill ran down Juva's neck.

She wished Savill would hurry up. Broddmar was guaranteed to be on his way, and she still didn't know how she'd figure out the truth about him. Did he really work for the vardari? And if he did, did he know it? If so, he had hired her to do the same thing, and that thought made her queasy.

She needed to get home, too. Gríf was free and alone in the house. What if he broke his promise and left? Or, for that matter, just looked out the front door? It wouldn't take any more than that to lose this battle. But he didn't seem like the type to break his promises, unlike Rugen, who was now in Gríf's former spot in the shaft. It was grotesque, but what else was she supposed to do? He had threatened her life and was too sick to release. For now, he was in the safest place he could be. At least he had never had a chance to see Gríf.

"Stand up straight," Savill mumbled.

Juva obeyed and realized that her body was an open book. Just the thought of Rugen had caused her to slump.

"Try this," Savill said, handing her the mask. "It's a slightly different type than Broddmar's."

Juva put the mask on her face and secured it around her neck. It hid the lower part of her face, like a muzzle. The leather was shaped over the bridge of her nose with an opening underneath her nostrils and holes over her mouth. She pulled the red hood over her head. The mirror didn't show the girl from the fairy tale anymore. Not a victim, but a hunter.

The bell over the door jingled. Broddmar came in and spotted her. His eyes left no doubt that he still had something to say about the mayhem at Haane's house. He stopped at the half-opened curtain. A subtle touch to her heart revealed that Skarr was waiting outside.

347

Why do I sense both wolves and warow?

"She carries it really well," Savill said, pointing out the details, completely oblivious to the mood. The plump tailor threw his hands together. "Oh, I almost forgot! I have a sample of those . . . what do you call them? The back flasks? Wait a minute!" He disappeared into the back room.

Broddmar came into the dressing room, which suddenly felt far too crowded. He towered over her, a good head taller.

"You think you're cut out to wear this outfit?" Broddmar asked. "After the craziness at the Volsung house?"

"What craziness?" Juva said, pulling the mask down under her chin. "The craziness you didn't witness?"

"You killed one of *them*, Juva!"

"They've killed six of us! Mother, Solde, Ogny, Maruska, their daughters . . . And that's just since our last wolf hunt!"

"Stop!" Broddmar pulled his hand across his face. "No one knows who carried out those killings, and you can't run around conducting your own revenge raids in Náklav, no matter what you—"

Savill returned and Broddmar shut up again. The tailor held a flat bloodskin up to Juva's back and looked at her in the mirror.

"There will be two of them, naturally," he said. "We won't be able to deliver those for a couple more days. We rely on someone in Naar who makes spouts and stoppers, but you can get an idea of what it will look like."

The bloodskin sat on her back like a horsefly's wings.

"It's easy to hook on and off up here by the shoulder blades, but they'll need to be strapped down, too, once they're . . . full." Savill swallowed that last word and seemed to pick up on the tension in the room. He chewed his lips and politely guided Broddmar out of the changing room.

Juva closed the curtain and changed out of the outfit while the other two discussed the price. The bleeders were under the Ring

Guard, so they paid. It struck her that if Rugen was right, warow money was paying for her clothing.

Never!

She pulled the curtain aside.

"I'll pay for this myself," she said, setting her outfit on the counter.

Broddmar turned his back to her and hurried out onto the street.

Savill meticulously folded the outfit and slid it into a linen bag. "You can pay when the blood flasks arrive," he said. "And if you need shoes, we recommend Kastor just across the way. A couple of red knee boots would look exceptional, and he'll get a good price on the leather. Think that over a little for next time." He smiled sincerely.

Juva thanked him and turned to leave. She spotted a wooden bust in a black shirt, and hesitated. It was rounded at the neck and narrow at the waist. With a hood.

Savill came up beside her and lifted the cloth.

"You have good taste," he said. "It looks simple, but this is of the finest quality. We've been making them since I was a little boy. Feel the fabric! Soft and comfortable but wears incredibly well. Is this a gift? What size?" he asked with a knowing smile.

Size? Devil sized. Seven hundred years old and immortal sized.

"I don't know," she mumbled. "A bit bigger than Broddmar?"

"This, I would think." Savill pulled a black shirt off a shelf and held it up.

"Yes, thank you."

What are you doing, Juva?

"Wonderful!" Savill darted behind the counter again and expertly folded the shirt. "I'll add that to your tab, and I can all but guarantee that an offer of marriage will be forthcoming." He winked and handed her the shirt.

An offer of marriage?

The thought was thoroughly ridiculous, but the word squeezed her heart dangerously. Juva put the shirt in the bag and went out to join Broddmar, who stood waiting under Savill's store sign, shaped like an enormous pair of black scissors, which would cut off his head if it fell.

Broddmar laid into her right away. "The rules don't just change because you pay yourself. That doesn't give you permission to do what you want."

He wants to control me. Is he protecting the warow?

Juva swallowed her anger and replied calmly, "Vardari murdered my family and you're mad because I was forced to shoot one of them? Whose side are you on, Broddmar?"

Broddmar shook his head and untied Skarr from the lamp post. "Juva, I know what you've been through, and I'm not blaming you for being angry. But you might as well be fighting fog! You're lashing out without knowing what you're aiming at, and it's going to cost you your life!"

Juva turned her back on him and started walking. He yelled and hurried after her, but if she talked to him now, she would say something she regretted.

She crossed Ringgata and walked into the food halls, a cool labyrinth of underground passages that ran through Kingshill. He would hardly follow her in with the wolf. The tunnels were crammed full of stalls and people as far as you could see in the hazy gleam from the corpsewood lights. The rock walls echoed, and every conversation became part of one nonstop echo.

"Juva!"

Her name sang between the walls. Broddmar caught up to her in a narrow corridor of cheese stalls and grabbed hold of her.

"Jufa, I'm trying to protect you!"

Juva walked into Broddmar and stared up at his toothless upper jaw, which had been given to him by her father and which deformed her name when he got stressed.

"Me? You're trying to protect yourself because you work for them!" She looked around and lowered her voice until she was hissing like a cat. "You slaughter the wolf-sick for the warow! You're worse than them. You clean up after them, help them get rid of their trash after the blood usage they themselves spread, and that is damned pathetic! You should be ashamed!"

Broddmar's face completely crumbled, clearly in shock that she knew.

It's true.

Juva pulled free and walked on. If she stayed there, she was going to pummel him. The cheese tunnel opened out into the fish hall, and she heard Broddmar behind her.

"The vardari aren't highway robbers, Juva. People like us can't fight them off. You find them in Náklabank, on the city council, in the Ring Guard, even on the Queen's council! You're not going to get the fair fight you're dreaming of, and you can't go after all of them for something one of them did. You need to trust me, Juva."

"Why? Why in Gaula should I trust you, Broddmar?" she asked without looking back.

"Because I was one of them!"

Juva stopped. The jumble of sounds grew more distant, as if she were drowning. People drifted by, some in bloody aprons, and she was surrounded by dead fish. Tubs of ice with eels, octopus, and fish roe that looked like little blood pearls.

She turned to face Broddmar and stared at him without finding a single word to say.

He flung up his arms. "Because I was one of them," he repeated, like a weaker echo of himself.

Liar. Traitor. Sharp words swelled on her tongue.

"Was?"

That was the only question she could get out. Either you had eternal life, or you didn't. What was he talking about? And Broddmar wasn't a vardari, he had very plainly aged with the years.

He rubbed his hands across his brow and squeezed his eyes shut for a moment.

"I was one of them," he said. "For almost a year. Until I stopped taking the blood." His voice was unsteady, and she moved closer.

Skarr wagged around a mountain of crabs. A stout woman leaned over the gutting bench and pointed with trembling indignation. "Hey! You can't bring that animal in here. You should know that!"

Juva pulled Broddmar with her into a nearby grotto containing empty crates and pushed him down onto a barrel.

"Talk!" she ordered.

"Your father knew, and we spoke about it often," Broddmar said, unwilling to look her in the eye. "About the shadow over the Seida Guild and the warow who kept the pressure on you. He wanted to know more, but I couldn't help him. I didn't know anything and never got far enough to be on the inside. I was just a damned fool who bumped into the wrong people and let myself be enticed into something I didn't actually want. I wanted to get old, Jufa. Shrivel up and die like everyone else, but . . . The vardari, they're not an organization you can resign from."

Juva paced back and forth between the crates, nauseated by the fishy smell and the truth as she sorted her thoughts.

"Your teeth," she said. "That's why you don't have . . ."

"Your father took them for me, because I asked him to."

"Was he also . . . Did he work for . . . ?"

"No, no! Valjar was . . . In Drukna, how I loved that man, Juva. Your father was everything. He helped me out of it, but at a cost."

"That's why you're a red hunter." Juva stared at him.

He nodded heavily. "That was the price. Nafraím let me go free in exchange for me hunting down the wolf-sick. It's a bloody job that no one has chosen voluntarily. Except for you."

"And you let me do it! You would have let me work for the man who murdered my mother and Solde!"

"I work for the whole city, not for him. I haven't seen Nafraím since he hired me. All the blood goes to the Ring Guard. That's what I've been trying to tell you: there are many warow. Some are lawless, some deal in money, others in blood, but many of them live like you and I do. And the city council's position is that they don't exist, so you can't start a blood feud here just because you believe someone is a warow."

Juva smiled but knew there was no warmth in it. She put her hands on his thighs and leaned toward him.

"I don't need to believe, Broddmar. I can sense them! I know where they are and who they are. They can't come near me without my knowing. The vardaris' pulse pumps in me like my own heart. They can't hide anymore." She could see his immediate skepticism, but she didn't give him a chance to respond. "Like in the fairy tales, Broddmar. The blood readers could sense them in the past, and now those abilities are coming back. I know, because . . ." She paused, unsure how much Broddmar knew about the devil.

"How did you become one of them?" she asked him. "Do you know what you drank?"

"I drank off of one of them, a brute of a lady," Broddmar said with a nod.

Juva studied him. His face was strained from tension, not from lying.

He believes he's telling the truth. He doesn't know.

"But it doesn't matter who it was, I'm chained to the job anyway." He stood up and the wolf did the same. "At least I'm doing the city a service. After all, it has to be done. The wolf-sick are insane and doomed to die."

He doesn't know that they can survive.

Juva looked down at the black shirt in her linen bag. Now was the time. She needed help, a crew, and she couldn't be the only one who knew about Gríf. If anything happened to her, someone else would have to get him home.

"Come on," she said. "I have something to show you."

They walked in silence through the food halls and out the other side of Kingshill. Lykteløkka was nearby, but it seemed farther than ever. She nodded to the guards outside the house, who took a couple of steps away from Skarr. Then she let herself in while talking more loudly to Broddmar than she needed to, in the hope that Gríf would stay out of sight. His heart quivered against hers, as if to tell her that he understood.

She helped Broddmar off with his jacket. He was pale, a ghost in the black foyer, surrounded by Lagalune's macabre curiosities. Skarr started whining and tugged at his leash.

He smells him.

Juva took a deep breath.

"Broddmar," she began, "you didn't drink from vardari to become one of them. You drank from something completely different. And it's not true that the wolf-sick are doomed to die. Some of them could have survived by doing the same thing, drinking from the same source as you."

"That's wishful thinking, Juva," Broddmar said shaking his head. "There's no cure."

"Yes, there is, although the cure may not be any better than the disease. They can become warow like you did and then quit drinking the blood. Then they have a chance. It's small and it's painful, but some manage it. Like you did."

His eyes swept around her as he was clearly wrestling with that thought.

"No," he mumbled. "No, if that were true, they wouldn't hunt them. Why kill the wolf-sick if they could become . . ."

"Why kill your own monstrosities? I'd like to know that, too."

"Your own? Because the vardari sell the wolf blood, you mean?"

Oh, Gaula, he still thinks it's the wolf blood!

"Listen to me, Broddmar," Juva caught his eye. "It's not wolf blood in the pearls. It never had anything to do with wolves. It was their own blood. Rotten warow blood can give people wolf-sickness, but it has never stopped people from aging. Eternal life comes from somewhere else, and I can show you where. Don't move."

A pained look came over Broddmar. As if he either hadn't heard her or was unable to comprehend. He petted Skarr's neck and chatted to him, but the wolf would not be soothed.

Juva let them comfort each other and went into the library. Grif stood just inside and had obviously been listening. The smoke in his eyes silently asked if she was sure about this. She wasn't, not by any means, but it couldn't just be her against the world anymore.

Should she ask him to put on the shirt first? No. Broddmar should see him the way she herself had that first time, in linen pants with a naked torso.

She nodded to Grif, and he followed her into the foyer. Broddmar looked up. His face turned from confusion to fear in a fraction of a second. He backed away while fumbling with his hand at his hip, searching for the knife he wasn't wearing. Skarr whined and cowered, his ears completely flat.

Juva raised her hands in an awkward attempt to show that there was no danger.

"Grif, this is Broddmar, the head of my hunting team and my friend. Broddmar, this is Grif, the source of eternal life and the vardaris' prisoner for the last six hundred and sixty years."

Broddmar stared at Grif. His eyes ran down Grif's body until they stopped at the claws.

"There was . . . There was a myth . . . about a wolf." He stumbled over to the wrought iron bench and sat down as if frozen to death against the rib bones that formed the back of the bench. Skarr slunk underneath the bench and lay whimpering.

"They called him the devil," Juva said. "And he's been guarded by initiated members of the Seida Guild at all times. The vardari don't know where he is, but I can promise you that they want to know, because without him, they're going to die. Gríf's blood has kept every single warow in the world alive, and it created you as well."

Broddmar stared at the floor while making clucking sounds with his tongue against the roof of his mouth. He usually did that when he was thinking, but now it sounded more like a crazy man engaging in self-soothing. He was quiet for a long time before he looked up again.

"And he can also turn people with wolf-sickness into warow?" Broddmar asked.

"He says so. And then they have a small chance of survival."

Broddmar clutched the bench until his knuckles were white, and she knew what he was struggling with. He had been slaughtering people with wolf-sickness all these years—young, old, men, women—in the belief that death was the only way out.

He bent forward so she couldn't see his face anymore. He didn't say anything. She wanted to go over to him, but Gríf carefully held her back.

Broddmar's broad shoulders began to jerk. She thought he was throwing up, but then she realized that the shaking stemmed from deep, silent sobs.

KEFLA

The fire crackled on the hearth in the library and the wind tugged at the windows. It struck Juva that this could have been blissfully idyllic for a normal family, but nothing in the Sannseyr home was normal.

A nearly toothless man in his sixties sat on the sofa with his third glass of seaweed liquor, and a half-naked immortal sat on the floor running his claws through the fur of a wolf who had accepted his own complete subservience. And they were all being observed by a stuffed raven with a penchant for lying about the future using rune dice.

But it must have felt unreal to Broddmar. He had recovered from his shock and, between swigs, he bravely tried to carry on a conversation with Gríf, but there was too much between them for the words to flow easily.

Broddmar had asked how Father had lost his life, and Gríf had laid it all out there. She suspected that Gríf wanted to penalize Broddmar, even though he hadn't known where the blood came from during his brief time as a warow. The nascent trust was fragile, also for her. But she couldn't fault Broddmar for keeping secrets when she had been keeping the biggest of them all.

It felt good to have an ally, even though that knowledge put his life in danger. But could she trust him? It hurt to even think that maybe she couldn't. She had always felt that she could trust Broddmar with her life, but she had every reason to be cautious. Rugen was proof of that.

What in Drukna am I going to do with Rugen?

She couldn't just leave him lying in the shaft until he was dead. But if she were to let him out, it would have to be worth it. Could he lead her to Nafraím? And what about that girl Rugen had mentioned? His words were still bothering her.

You're worse than Kefla, that guildless girl up in Herad who plays at being a blood reader!

Kefla, who had known that he was sick. How? Was the girl one of the ones she had been searching for, a senser?

Juva rested her gaze on Gríf and felt the quivering in her heart. The explanation had seemed so simple in the beginning. She was a blood reader. She could feel Gríf and everyone who had traces of him in them, the warow and the wolf-sick. But why could she feel wolves, too? Not anywhere near as strongly, but like a breeze on her heart that couldn't be explained away.

Gríf shifted and Skarr sidled up to him again as if he couldn't get close enough. The fondness was clearly mutual. She'd never seen a bond like they had. She had two wolves in the library, not one.

Her heart grew and beat more heavily. It beat slower, as if it would melt into Gríf's, and she looked away. There was no point in feeling something that could never be hers. Something she was doomed to lose and grieve.

Juva stood up. Skarr pricked up his ears but remained lying down.

"Where are you going?" Broddmar asked instantly, clearly uncomfortable at the thought of being left alone with Gríf.

"I need to go find a girl, someone Rugen mentioned who I think can sense warow, too."

Broddmar set down his seaweed liquor and looked as if he was going to get up.

"No," Juva said. "Stay here with Gríf. There's still a lot you need to know."

"It's starting to get dark . . ."

"We're in the middle of Smelta, Broddmar. It won't get any darker than this. I'll be careful, but I need to find this girl before the vardari do."

Broddmar looked to Gríf to back him up, but to no avail.

"She knows what she's doing," Gríf said with a shrug.

He's free now. He doesn't need to fear for my life anymore.

It had grown colder; there were fewer people out than she would have thought. The wind came through the streets in unpredictable gusts, a premonition of the Smelta storms. She didn't make it any farther than Skjepnasnaret before she felt a revealing flutter in her heart.

A warow, but not Nafraím.

This was a new heart, an unfamiliar impression inside her own chest, and it was close. She suppressed the impulse to turn around and continued resolutely but without running. Revealing her sensing ability would be idiocy.

She crossed Steinleia and ducked into the food halls. The flutter abated, but she knew she wasn't safe. Whoever it was, they would run around Kingshill and watch her come out of the halls on the other side of the hill. She waited a while, then she went back out the same way she had come in and ran straight up the road to Herad.

But how would she find the girl? Herad was a big neighborhood.

Florian's Parlors.

If she remembered correctly, Rugen used to work there, so it probably wasn't far from there. She walked past Myntslaget and felt a pang of guilt. She had sent a runner to Ester, but hadn't talked to her since she bought the crossbow from Agan Askran. Her thoughts had been elsewhere.

Juva popped into all the alehouses she came across, and in the fourth one she found a hostess who had heard of Kefla. The woman sent her to "Lykksalige Runas Vei or somewhere near there." She found another alehouse up there that only sold boiling wort, an unlikely place for Rugen to visit, but she went inside anyway. The host was very familiar with Kefla, her place was right around the corner. But he hadn't seen her around for a while. That wasn't a good sign.

Juva walked around onto the narrow side street and peered up at what the host had so generously called "an addition." So crooked and tumbledown, it was a wonder it remained suspended over the street. It was sort of a glorified, interiorized catwalk with a couple of small window openings, but no lights and no smoke from the little chimney.

Nor was any light shining from what was surely meant to represent a blood reader light: a ball of yarn painted yellow, dangling in the net by the door.

Juva knocked and waited. Nothing happened, so she knocked again. "Kefla?" She looked around. She was alone in the alley and didn't feel any warow, so she took the opportunity to be more forthcoming.

"Kefla, I'm Juva Sannseyr from the Seida Guild and I need to talk to you. It's important."

The only response was the wind whistling through the cracks in the bricks. Was she in the right place? She detected some movement out of the corner of her eye, but if there was anyone there, they didn't want to be seen. The safest thing would be to try again tomorrow.

Juva left, but after a short while, she became aware of footsteps some distance behind her, revealingly cautious ones. She turned into a narrow passage and continued, but the footsteps still followed her. Her heart beat faster, but entirely on its own, so it wasn't a warow. And it also wasn't a big, heavy man. It sounded more like . . .

A child.

Juva smiled and turned around. The girl froze a few steps away and quickly looked in another direction before accepting that the game was up.

"What do you want with me?" the girl asked with a boyish voice.

She was young, maybe twelve or thirteen, with unkempt black hair and a scrape on her nose. No, it wasn't a scrape; it was a stripe of freckles on her golden-brown skin. Was she from Ruv? Juva caught herself wondering if her parents had abandoned her here during a visit, but she spoke fluent Norran.

Juva came a couple of steps closer.

The girl backed away and said, "Stop, or I'll stab you!"

"You're Kefla? The blood reader?" Juva raised her hands disarmingly.

"I'm not in the Seida Guild." The girl laughed.

"I'm the new guild master of the Seida Guild," Juva said. It felt unreal to say. "And I think you belong there."

"I think you smoked something that didn't agree with you," the girl replied. "I'm not pale, rich, or talentless."

Juva bit her lip to conceal her smile. That was a fair and accurate summary.

"You're not dumb, either," she replied.

The girl folded her arms in front of her chest and gave her a look that essentially said *no shit*. A string of white sheets fluttered in the wind from the clotheslines above her, a slightly overoptimistic sign of spring as they were sure to freeze.

"Kefla, I know what you're thinking, and you're right. I had nothing left for them but contempt. But that was before . . ."

"Was that your family?" The girl asked, cocking her head to the side. "The murdered ones?"

"Two of them," Juva said with a nod. "My mother and my sister."

"Sad." The girl kicked a pebble as if to hide that it bothered her.

"That destroyed the Seida Guild." Juva took another step closer. "People were scared out of their minds and the guild is nothing but a name now. But that's going to change."

"Doesn't matter. The Seida Guild is a bunch of moth-eaten ladies who make up destinies, and that's not my style."

"It's not mine, either."

"So why do you want to be part of that?" Kefla looked around, wary and alert.

Juva studied her.

Young, unkempt, and in threadbare clothes. Bone tough, probably on her own.

"Were you thrown out of where you were living?" Juva asked.

"Screw that," Kefla spat. "Why do you want to hang around with the Seida Guild?"

Big mouth, but full of feelings. A fighter.

"I want to be part of it because it used to be something else. It used to be about protecting people from wolf-sickness. And that is something you can do, right? You can tell if people are sick or not?"

Kefla backed away a couple of steps. Juva realized that she had been too open, too soon. For all she knew, Kefla might think she was there on behalf of the warow.

"You don't have anything to fear from me, Kefla. I'm here because we're on the same side. We blood readers need each other. There are others out there who will be looking to take advantage of what you can do. We won't survive alone."

"I've made it this far," she replied, shaking her bangs off her face.

"That's because no one knows what you can do. Kefla, how do you know that people are wolf-sick?"

The girl grinned as if she had just won the Yra Race. "If I made it this far because no one knows, why would I start talking about it now?"

Juva smiled. The girl was beautiful. And smart, well above the norm, but not enough to make it on her own against the vardari, if she could sense.

"It's in the blood," Kefla said, rewarding her smile with a shrug. "Easy to notice if you know what to look for. You ought to know that, shouldn't you, since you're in the Seida Guild?" She turned her back and started walking away.

No!

"I know you have more than one heart!" Juva yelled.

Kefla slowed. The white sheets flapped above her in the wind and it sounded like cracking whips. She glanced back over her shoulder at Juva, hesitating, but then she kept walking.

"Good luck," Kefla said.

She can sense!

Juva wilted to see her disappear around the corner. The girl was not in the habit of trusting people, and Juva could certainly relate to that. She would have done exactly the same thing. She *had* done the same thing, kept the fear and the panic to herself, avoided people, especially the Seida Guild. It was as if she had been talking to a younger version of herself, and that told her all she needed to know about what it was going to take to win over that young heart.

It was going to take time, time she didn't have. Unless she managed to put an end to Nafraím before he found the girl.

THE CURE

Rugen paced back and forth within the shaft's stone walls. He pushed off with his fists, turned, and walked back, over and over again. This cursed prison was cold as an aristocrat's twat and significantly tighter. It stank of men, too, so fuck only knew how many she had ridden down here.

I'm going to kill her.

How long had he been there now, three nights? That Gaula's whore had caged him and fed him, like an animal, through a shaft in the ceiling. And she'd had the devil the whole time, probably down here! The source of eternal life and she wanted to cheat him out of that?

That thought made him sick with rage. All the days he had wasted listening to her talking rubbish. All the arrogance he had endured without so much as a single dip of his dick, and now she was going to let him die even though she was sitting on the cure.

His fury thickened in his throat, and he clenched his fist, triggering his toothache again and, with it, the taste of rot. Oh, once he got out of there, she was going to get it all right, in an insane way. He leaned against the wall and closed his eyes. Let his imagination run wild about everything he would do to her.

A sound made him jump. Scraping. Footsteps.

Juva!

Rugen ran over to the rusty door and squinted through the bars of the grating. A light was approaching down the tunnel. Then her face appeared. He clenched his teeth to keep from snapping. He had to warm her up by talking to her and get out of there.

"Juva." He smiled.

Was that contempt that flashed over her face? He felt his smile fade.

"You lied, Juva. You have the devil, and you've had him the whole time."

"Yes," she replied, very simply.

Rugen howled and slammed his fist into the iron door, then licked the blood off his knuckles as he watched her.

"You screwed him here? He's slept in this bed?"

"No," Juva said, shaking her head. "This is . . . Mother had lovers."

Lovers? A little fuck room in the basement?

Wild! He had always known that Lagalune was the type. Cold on the surface, but sharp with her eyes.

Rugen tossed his hair and pulled his tongue over his teeth. "So hot," he mumbled, and then stood right up against the door, where he knew she couldn't see as he unlaced his pants. He was so hard it hurt. "Aren't you going to come in here with me, then?"

She didn't respond, but he would get her to respond, one day. Fuck, was she going to respond.

"So where do you have him?" he asked.

"In Hidehall." It looked like she was going to cry.

"In Hidehall?!" Rugen let go of his dick and grabbed the bars. "What the fuck, Juva! Don't you get that I'm dying here? I need his blood, and you owe me that!"

"What are you going to do with it, Rugen? It's not going to help you."

She doesn't understand.

He needed to pull himself together, calm down, and explain his way out of this.

"Juva, damned cute Juva . . . I told you, the devil's blood will give me eternal life, cure my wolf-sickness. You don't want to be a murderer, do you?"

"But what if the opposite is true, Rugen?" She pulled her hands over her face. "What if it hurts you? I don't dare try it, I can't. I don't want anything to happen to you."

I still have her.

He grinned and lowered his shoulders a bit, more confident that he was going to succeed.

"Listen, Juva, nothing's going to happen to me. I'm going to live forever and we're going to have a damned good time. Don't you remember?"

"Rugen, I can't take it anymore." She started to cry.

"What? You can't take what?"

"The devil, the warow, wolf-sickness . . . All of it! I found out from my mother that he's in Hidehall, but I don't want him! I just want this to be over. I wish I could just give him to Nafraím!"

The knot of pain and anger in his chest loosened. Had he heard that correctly? She had the devil and she wanted to get rid of him? Rugen clenched his teeth and felt his canines move. He had to play his cards right so that wolf-twat would release him.

"Yes, I know! I understand, and it can be like that, Juva. I can help you! I can give him the devil for you. Just get me out of here, then we'll finish this. Together. You and me, Juva."

"No," she said, shaking her head. "You can't help me. No, that won't work." She turned to go.

"Wait! Juva! Don't go, damn it! I can help you . . . with what?"

She looked at him again. Embarrassingly hopeful, the damn fool.

"Could you tell Nafraím that I have him?" she asked.

"Yes, I absolutely fucking can! I know where to find that grumpy old bag of bones. I'll say you've got the devil in Hidehall, and that he can go pick him up. No problem, Juva. This is going to work out. We need each other."

She nodded, tentatively.

Nafraím . . . This was going to be a problem. Nafraím had betrayed him. Thrown him to the wolves, refused to help. Which had forced him to look elsewhere for help, and Nafraím wasn't going to like that. They were like night and day, he and Eydala. That old lady was a creepy bitch, but at least she had welcomed him with open arms and shared the truth about the blood and the devil, all the juicy secrets Nafraím had kept to himself. Eydala had never forced him to grovel or apologize the way Nafraím had. Eydala understood him. And all she'd asked for in return was Juva.

"But I get his blood first, right?" Rugen licked his lips.

"You can have a little," she said. "A little up front, so we know if it works. Then you'll get the rest afterward, once you've given Nafraím the message and he's gotten him, right?"

Rugen nodded. He was closer to eternal life than ever. His body itched, his fingers, his teeth, his dick . . . All those barbs about breaking ties. So much good awaited him and gods knew he deserved it.

Juva stuck a glass flask between the bars. The same type Lagalune had kept blood pearls in. It was red at the bottom. It took him a second to realize that it was the blood he craved.

Rugen yanked the flask from her and emptied the far too few drops into his jaw. He smacked his lips. It was like licking metal. The pains died away and only now did he realize how awful they had truly been. Unbearable, now that they were gone. A strange feeling of shame came over him and he laced his pants back up, thinking clearly for the first time in several days.

"I feel immortal already," he said and smiled at Juva. "Even the damned toothache is gone."

Juva seemed to hesitate. What more would she demand? What more could he say?

Rugen pressed himself against the door and stuck out his fingers.

"Thank you, Juva. I'll help you, I promise. Can you let me out now?"

Juva took a breath and nodded. Then she opened the door.

THE TRAP

Juva bent into the wind that raced down the deserted streets with a nagging feeling that she was going toward her own death. Every step felt momentous, and she was starting to doubt that she had done the right thing. She consoled herself that she felt this way because of the storm. Every spring and fall, it tore off a roof or two, and it was easy to be tricked into thinking the end was near.

But it is, for Nafraím.

Soon Rugen would tell him that she was keeping the devil hidden in Hidehall, and she knew that Nafraím wouldn't hesitate to react.

What have I done?

Her crossbow felt dismally light on her back, far from the comforting heaviness of the old one. She had to remind herself that it was better in every way—lighter, faster, stronger, not to mention collapsible and possible to hide. That had never been important in the woods but had suddenly become invaluable.

The red hunter outfit felt foreign on her body, but it provided a safe shell against the surrounding world. She felt more alone than ever, a lone wolf, without a pack. The Sannseyr family no longer existed. The Seida Guild lay shattered and might never rise again. Broddmar had promised to help during the Yra Race, but she couldn't share this, not even with him. He had been a warow. He would never understand. He would stop her and tell her she was risking her life for pointless revenge.

This is more than revenge.

Gríf had asked what the point to winning in the long run was if you lost in the short term. His point had been terrifyingly clear when Rugen came to threaten her. Nafraím had started a blood feud, and he had no intention of ending it. Now that Broddmar knew, his life was also in danger.

As well as all the genuine blood readers out there. Like Kefla.

After tonight, they would have one less murderer to worry about, and they would make it safely to the spring run in thirteen days.

The hardest part had been keeping the plan from Gríf, but what else could she do? He had lost more than half a millennium and been through Gaula knows how many torments. He would never have let her go alone to meet the man who had captured him. He would have ruined everything, set off in blind rage and been shot by the guards before he got anywhere near Hidehall.

Blind rage . . .

Juva couldn't shake the look on his face when she had asked him to offer blood to Rugen. That an inky black gaze could contain so much contempt and disappointment. She struggled to explain, but it was impossible without also explaining what she intended to do.

If I lose my life tonight, he'll never know why.

Broddmar would get Gríf home during the Yra Race, and Gríf would always believe she had asked him to save Rugen's life and let him go because she felt something for Rugen, even after the assault. A certainty that ached in her heart.

She leaned into the gusts in Taakedraget, trudging up against the walls the whole way to Hidehall, where the ship's lanterns by the door had been tethered against the wind. Judging from the sounds from inside, people drank during storms, too.

Juva let herself in the back way. The door hinges creaked, and it hit her how long it had been since she was last there. The scents of leather and salt filled her nose, and a wave of longing formed a lump in her throat. This was home. If everything had been different, she could have brought Gríf here. Shown him how safe and pleasant life could be, taken him hunting . . .

The thought tormented her with glimpses into an impossible fairy tale. His skin against the snow, the crackling of the campfire. Blood, pelts, and sweat.

Juva took a deep breath, pulled herself together, and walked into the living room. The whole hunting team was in there drinking in front of the fireplace. Broddmar, Hanuk, Muggen, Nolan, and Lok. She stopped, gaping. She had no idea what to say. The odds of finding them all there on a night like this was vanishingly small.

Broddmar stood up, and suddenly she had a disturbing suspicion. The guys were uncommonly quiet, and she could see it in their eyes, that combination of agitation and conviction they only had when things got serious, when it really mattered.

They know about Gríf.

"You blabbed," Juva stared at Broddmar.

"Of course," he replied without any trace of shame.

"You promised," she said, staring in disbelief. "You said you understood. You knew you weren't supposed to—"

"Juva, we're hunters." Broddmar walked over to her.

She dropped her bag on the floor and pushed him away with both hands.

"It doesn't matter what we are! This is dangerous to know, and you promised!"

"Jufa?" Broddmar caught her hands and held them at a safe distance. "What's rule number one in the forest if you get injured? Answer me. The very first rule!"

"The first rule is to say it." Juva clenched her teeth.

"Why?" He caught her eye, and she reluctantly looked into his, knowing where he was going with this. "Why do you need to say it, Juva?"

371

She sighed and said, "Because the team is never stronger than its weakest member. It's not one person who's injured, it's the team."

"You're in danger, then we're in danger." Broddmar patted the back of her head, as if the matter were settled. "This is what we do to survive."

"Cheers," Muggen said, and everyone raised their beer mugs as if they had been secretly practicing the move.

Her feeling of betrayal eased, melted away into an unbearable tenderness. Juva squeezed her eyes closed to keep from crying. Once she started, she'd never be able to stop. She would keep sobbing until she died for lack of water.

"But how did you know I would come here?"

"I followed . . . What's his name? That numbskull of a nincompoop you set free?" Broddmar led her over to the table.

"Rugen," she muttered.

Muggen scooted over to make room for her on the bench.

"You don't understand, guys," Juva said, sitting down next to him. "Six blood readers have been murdered because of him, because of the devil. The warow are desperate to find him and now that you know, your lives are in danger. Lok, think about your kids."

Lok pulled his hand through his thick, red beard. His eyes filled with tears. "You thought I was going to wait until you died before I got involved?" he said.

"No, I didn't think you were going to get involved at all! If anything happens to you guys, it'll be my fault, and I can't—"

"If it were one of us," Muggen said, "you'd have gotten involved."

Muggen wrapped a heavy arm around her shoulder. Juva opened her mouth to respond but found herself at a loss for words. Muggen could be slow sometimes, but he was right about this. Of course she would have been there for them. Why was it so difficult to live with their being there for her?

"So, tell us all about him, then!" Hanuk slapped the table with both palms, displaying his dimples. "Broddmar says he's got eyes as black as coals. And claws, real claws, is that true?"

"Yes, that's true," Juva said, blushing. "His eyes can be white, too, but they fill up with a sort of smoke depending on what he's feeling, I think. He's . . . indescribable."

"I have to see him!" Hanuk chortled like a magpie out of childlike glee mixed with fear. He looked around at the others. "Don't you?"

"No one is going to see him!" Juva exclaimed. "Have you guys lost your minds? He's . . . It's not safe."

"Why do they call him the devil? What if he's a god? Then we're really in trouble!" Hanuk continued, even more enthusiastically than usual, and she guessed it was due to the beer. He had an extremely low tolerance.

Nolan and Lok started talking over each other and suddenly the whole table was debating the man she had managed to keep a secret up until then. Juva stared at Broddmar with a silent *now look what you've done*, which he ignored.

"Isn't anyone going to ask the obvious here?" Nolan said, raising his hands to calm everyone. "If it's true that the vardari will die if this creature dies . . . Why is he still alive?"

Everyone around the table went quiet.

"Oh, in Ur's name, man," Hanuk looked at him in disbelief. "He's been locked up for centuries. What's wrong with you?"

The others mumbled their support and Nolan looked to her for help.

"I'm just saying!" Nolan said. "We don't know what we're dealing with. He sounds like an animal if you ask me. What the heck's the difference between him and a wolf? Surely that's a question it's all right to ask?"

"He's not an animal. He's a prisoner of war," Broddmar said.

"From what war?" Nolan said.

"Ugh, you big whale dick!" Hanuk slapped the table again, his eyes agog. "He's from the wolf wars!"

"Doesn't ring any bells," Nolan said with a shrug.

"The wolf wars? You know, the myth? At least where I come from."

"Everything's a myth where you come from, Hanuk."

The guys clashed again, hot from the beer and being together.

Broddmar interrupted, "It doesn't matter where he comes from. What's most important now is getting him home."

"I thought the most important thing was catching the guy who's coming after Juva?" Muggen said.

The room went quiet, the mood darkened by the anticipated violence. Broddmar clicked his tongue against his palate, lost in thought.

"We'll see," he said finally. "If he comes then he comes, and we'll do what we need to do. I'm more worried about him bringing someone with him."

"If he comes, he'll come alone," Juva said. She was sure and less afraid since the guys were there. "He's not the type to rely on anyone and he's not coming to kill me. He's coming because he thinks I want to give him the devil."

Muggen nervously chewed his lip and said, "He's not coming to celebrate."

"No," Juva said. "He's coming to die. If he had gotten ahold of Gríf, he would have killed me to keep the secret hidden. The way he killed my mother and Solde and the gods only know how many others up through the ages."

"That's why we're here," Nolan said.

"But what about the law? Aren't we going to . . ." Muggen furrowed his troll-like brow.

"No," Nolan interrupted and nodded to Broddmar. "Both he and Juva have permits to hunt the wolf-sick, and the man has fangs, right? No one could tell the difference."

Broddmar looked into her eyes over his beer mug. Juva swallowed. Nafraím was a murderer, and he was a danger to her life. But even so, this conversation left a bitter taste.

The door of the tavern opened, and the guys jumped, but it was only Rut. She sailed in, with full mugs in her hands, and served them.

"You all are so quiet, you'd think you were talking about *me*!" she winked.

The guys chuckled uncomfortably but didn't say anything else until she left again and the door closed behind her.

"So, what are you thinking, Juva?" Lok asked. "We're planning to lie up in the gallery, each on a different side, and when he comes in, we'll be ready for him."

"If anyone's going to take him, it's me," Juva said, shaking her head. "There's a lot I want answers to first, and I'll only get them if he thinks I'm alone. He has every reason to be cautious, and he likes to have the upper hand." She thought of the dead blood readers, like dolls in the library, and stared down into her beer. "He liked to come close . . ."

"Fuck," Muggen took her hand, drowning it in his own.

"So, you're just going to stand down here all by yourself and wait for him? Unarmed?" Broddmar looked anything but satisfied.

"No, I'll wait for him with the crossbow, but he won't realize that I have it."

"How?"

"Because I'll be sitting in the bathtub."

Nolan nodded with an appreciative smile.

"But . . . You can't sit in the tub all night," Muggen said, rubbing his smooth head. "You'll get all wrinkly!"

"She's not going to sit there, Muggen," Nolan said, as if he were reading her mind. "She's going to climb into the tub when he arrives, like an innocent nymph. That's brilliant. He won't know what hit him when she shoots. Ideally, he'll die instantaneously without even suspecting that we're here. In a worst-case scenario, he'll be injured, and then we'll be there in a flash. And we can keep an eye on the doors and warn her when he shows up."

Juva peeked at Broddmar, glad that he hadn't also shared the secret that she could sense. Her heart would let her know the instant Nafraím arrived, but a signal from the guys was also reassuring.

"But I have no idea how long we'll have to wait," she said.

"At least four more beers." Nolan grinned over his mug.

Juva took another swig and felt the seriousness ease up. This was going to work out. She wasn't alone anymore. She had the guys, and soon Nafraím would be dead. The vardari would suddenly have other things to think about besides her, and they would be able to get Gríf safely home.

The guys were arguing about the best way to alert her, and they ended up locking the door that led into the tavern so Nafraím would be forced to use the back door. Its hinges squeaked loudly enough that she would hear it herself. They tested it to make sure, but the varying noise level from the tavern and the wind outside left them with some doubts. The solution was to place Hanuk at the back of the gallery, near the stairs, where he could see the door and warn Juva with a short piece of rope that he would shoot down so it landed in front of the bathroom door.

They each took up their positions, in silence, just like in the woods. Juva could see them through the bars of the gallery railing as they hid. Hanuk, Muggen, and Lok to the left, Broddmar and Nolan to the right.

Juva went into the bathroom. She pumped water into the tub and fired up the woodstove. Then she took off the red outfit and sat down on the bench to wait, with the crossbow on her naked lap, cold against her thighs.

MONSTER

Juva bit her nails and stared intently at the doorway, afraid that Nafraím would suddenly be standing there. Her neck was stiff from waiting. She jumped at every little noise—muffled laughter from the tavern, a bottle breaking in the alley, the wind tugging at the walls.

The reassuring whispers between Hanuk and Muggen had quieted. The room grew warmer and steamier as the tub filled. She made more soap bubbles in the water, so she had something to hide both herself and the crossbow under.

She was going to kill a man.

Not a man, a warow!

A wooden soap dish sat on the bench opposite her, impaled by sharp shadows from a huge rack of antlers on the wall. Nothing looked right. Everything was distorted by darkness, steam, and fear. Little drops beaded up on the woodwork in the tub and dripped down, forming tiny ripples where the foam had opened up. Her hair grew heavy and stuck to her chest.

She checked her crossbow yet again—bolt in the track, trigger, stirrup, a couple of extra bolts just in case. If she could have found the bottle, she would have gladly used poison as well. And wasn't the track a little rough? Of course not, she was imagining things. The noises from the tavern faded. All she could hear was the ocean boiling against the cliffs and the wind buffeting the shutters and her own shaky breaths.

Her heart beat, without company.

What if he didn't come? What if he had figured out that he'd been tricked? Several hours must have passed by then—should she go back out to the others? They had agreed to wait all night, but—

The door in the hallway squealed and Juva stiffened. Her heart began its double dance, egged on by the wave of fear that washed through her body.

He's here!

Juva fought the paralysis. There was something she was supposed to do, but she couldn't remember what.

The tub! She had to get into the tub, fast!

She slid silently into the water and pressed the crossbow against her thighs. The crossbow was impossible to see under the soap bubbles, and she said a silent prayer that it had been worth the money.

Why hadn't Hanuk warned her? Where was his rope? He must have seen Nafraím? She stared at the door. The floor creaked as he approached. Cautiously, but it didn't sound like he was trying to sneak up on her. Not at all. It was late—maybe he thought she was asleep?

The plan, which had been so clear, suddenly became impossible to follow. She had thought of everything, or so she had believed, but unexpected details were turning up faster than she could grasp them. Should she shoot right away when she saw him in the doorway? Wait until he came in? Should she pretend she had known he was coming? Should she say something? Should she assume he would surrender and tell her everything she wanted to know? Would he overpower her? Was he armed, too? Would she hit him better if she stood up?

She held her breath until she had it under control.

You're taking a bath. Do what people do in the bathtub.

She submerged her hair and sat up again. She soaped her shoulder with one hand and clutched the crossbow with the other, sliding the extra bolts under her knee.

His shadow grew on the floor, then he was standing in the doorway. Juva jumped and covered her breasts with her hands out of sheer reflex, even though he couldn't see them under the soapy water. He looked down, like a timid young boy. His coat draped over his arm as if he were just coming over for a visit.

She tightened her grip on the crossbow. Why wasn't he looking at her? She couldn't shoot a man who wasn't looking at her!

"I'm sorry to barge in," he said, still without looking up. "But it's time for us to talk, Juva Sannseyr. It has become clear to me that you have something in your possession that you cannot possibly comprehend the scope of."

Juva's eyes swept over the doorframe, but there was no piece of rope to be seen. No hint of a warning from Hanuk. It was so quiet that she might as well have been alone. Apprehension exploded in her chest. Nafraím glanced up at the gallery, as if he had realized what she was missing. Then he finally looked her in the eye and took a step toward her. His smile was flimsy, abominably polite.

"Do you think I've gotten to be more than six hundred years old by being a fool?"

No! The others. What has he done with them?

Her panic roused her instincts, and her arms acted of their own accord. She raised the crossbow out of the water and fired. The bolt flew into his shoulder. Nafraím jerked and stumbled against the wall. Juva groped for another bolt, pushed it down into the wet track, and spanned the bow. She stepped out of the tub. The water poured off her, flowing across the floor.

Nafraím held on to the doorframe and grabbed at the bolt, as if he couldn't quite comprehend that it was real. His hand found it and sat there just below the wound.

Juva aimed the crossbow at him, aware of her own nakedness, but what did that mean anymore? The man was going to die anyway. Blood emerged in his linen shirt, spreading in a checkered pattern along the threads in the fabric. He turned to her with a look that she struggled to interpret—fearless and incomprehensibly peaceful, as if he had been longing for the pain.

"Broddmar! Hanuk!" She screamed their names, but no one answered. "What have you done to them?! Answer me, you rat prick! What did you do?!"

"They're asleep, Juva. They're asleep. Don't be scared." He dropped his coat on the floor and held up a hand to calm her.

"Asleep?! You're lying, they would never—"

"The beer," he interrupted. "Drugs in the beer." He rested his forehead on the doorframe, clenching his teeth at that slight motion.

"Lies! I drank the beer, too."

"You drank what Rut gave you, right?" He bent forward and supported himself against the bench. "Would it be all right if I sat down?"

Juva dug through her memories. He was right: Rut had served their beers individually. She had taken the mug she had been given.

Nafraím sank down onto the bench, knocking over the soap dish. The soap cakes sailed away, sliding across the soaking wet floor.

"I promise," he moaned. "They'll wake up in the morning, barely hungover. I'm a man of my word, but check on them if you must." He leaned forward with a gasp of pain.

Blood dripped from the bolt onto the floor.

"A man of your word?" Juva laughed, not recognizing her own laughter. "You're a murderer! You sell blood pearls of warow blood, giving people wolf-sickness. Then you use bleeders, like Broddmar, to hunt them. You kill your own spawn. You're not a man of your word, you're a monster!"

His blood swirled in the water around her feet without truly mixing in. As if it had a heavy essence that held it together. She stepped aside in distaste, just before it reached her toes.

"A disdain that even a blood reader cannot hide." Nafraím gave her a tired smile.

Juva glanced at the towel that hung from a hook by the antlers above him. She couldn't access it without losing the upper hand. He followed her eyes and reached for the towel, in obvious pain. He got it down and handed it to her.

"You're young, ruled by the heart rather than the head. I knew that, but I didn't think you had this in you. I'll explain if you can pacify your blood-thirst for a bit?"

Juva hesitated, staring at the towel he held out to her. He averted his gaze again, and she snatched it. "Thank you," she mumbled, hating herself for it. She covered herself as best she could without lowering the crossbow.

His injury wasn't fatal. Unless she let him slowly bleed to death.

He laughed as if he could tell what she was thinking.

"You think I go spreading around blood pearls for money and chasing the wolf-sick for fun? Yes, warow blood is the source of the wolf-sickness, that's true. But it lives a life of its own out there, without our help. We make them. We release them. Then they bleed into the stream of greed and addiction that is all of Náklav, bought and sold like everything else. What you believe to be a path to superficial wealth is a necessary evil. We need wolf-sickness for the stone gates. Nákla Henge wouldn't work without it."

Juva wanted to protest but didn't know where to start.

Nafraím limply raised his hand, like a promise of an answer, but now he was winded.

"Wolf blood ran the stones for generations, for centuries. Up until . . . either it was the stones or it was the wolves, Jól knows. But Nákla Henge became greedier, thirstier, and required more to open. We saw the same thing spread all around the world, to all the ring cities. Without a few cases of wolf-sickness every year, they stop working. Wolf blood wasn't enough anymore."

Her head was bursting with questions, but the only thing she wanted to express was disgust.

"So, you knowingly and intentionally spread wolf-sickness for business reasons, to be able to travel from city to city quickly? Do you really think that improves things?"

He gritted his teeth in pain, feeling around in his mouth with his tongue, troubled by something. He spat a hollow tooth out into his hand.

"You think money is about how many snuff boxes people can buy, or how often one can sunbathe in Ruv? No," he said. "The gates are more than travel and more than money. The stone circles created the world as you know it, safer than you can comprehend, with less disease and fewer living in poverty. Poor girl, you've never seen a bloody battle. Closing the gates means sending all the world's people into wretchedness, chaos. Do you even understand the meaning of the word? What do you think I've spent all these years doing, Juva? Wealth for wealth's sake is a weak man's goal. I've hired the best of the best to build a civilization! Call me a monster if you will, but know that this monster cured the Black Plague, founded the schools, and put in power the people who gave you the freedoms you were born with. I've seen battles and misery such as you could never imagine. I've seen tyrants come and go, and here I sit, bleeding out in front of a girl who thinks she knows better."

Juva backed away and dropped down onto the bench. She felt empty, fighting the feeling of shame she knew was his goal.

"You hate me with a vengeance," he moaned. "But *you're* the one who believes eternal life is a reward, not me. Eternal life turned out to be the biggest sacrifice of all. I wouldn't wish it on anyone . . . getting used to seeing things go to pot. But one learns to forget the individual person and instead to care about humanity. The big, bird's-eye view. I wanted to see the world become a place to be proud of."

Juva's arm burned from the weight of her crossbow, and she let it rest against her thigh, still at the ready in case he tried anything. But she had a feeling that he was done with games.

"Silver tongue," she mumbled. "If it's such an enormous sacrifice to be a warow, then why do you need the devil? Why this desperate hunt for the source that can give you even more centuries?"

The pain seemed to melt from his face.

"So, it's true? You know what he is and where he is?" His eyes took on an uncomfortably vulnerable look, and he seemed more naked than her. He closed his eyes. "But that's where you make your biggest mistake, Juva Sannseyr. I'm not hunting for the devil so I can live forever. I'm hunting for him because I want to kill him."

"Kill him? Why in Gaula would you kill him? That would mean—"

"That would mean the end of the vardari, the end of all warow life, forever." He nodded, exhausted, and then he opened his eyes again and looked at her. "So, you see, Juva . . . We share the same goal, you and I."

Juva felt dizzy. Her thoughts weighed down by looking for lies. His words fell into place with everything that had happened, opening a secret space in her head, like a magical compartment.

"That's why," she whispered. "That's why you killed everyone who knew, because you wanted him to be forgotten."

"Everyone except Lagalune. I didn't kill your mother," he said.

"Liar!" Juva bared her teeth and raised her crossbow again. "You wanted to kill me, too. You sent Rugen to do the job, which is so ridiculously cowardly!"

Nafraím had begun to droop on the bench. He struggled back up again and swallowed, plucked out another hollow tooth to reveal the fang it had been hiding.

"Rugen?" He laughed briefly with evident pain. "Dear child, that lout can barely put one foot in front of the other. He gathered information for me about who knew, but it would never occur to me to dispatch him to kill anyone. If I wanted you dead, I would just have shown you the respect of doing it myself. No, child. Rugen's in a wretched state, so much so that I found it best to lock him up.

Rugen has betrayed us both, I'm afraid. He fell into bad company. No matter how hard it must be for you to believe, there are far worse vardari than I.

"Could you spare a bandage?" He glanced at the bolt. "I'm afraid that this is bleeding faster than I can talk."

Juva got up and walked in an arc around him to the door with her crossbow at the ready.

"Move and you're a dead man!" she said. But she doubted that he would be able to do anything more, and she caught herself feeling scared that he would bleed to death.

She walked out into the parlor and dared to set down the crossbow while she put on socks and a shirt. Up in the gallery, she heard Broddmar snoring, a whistling sound from the gap where his teeth had been. Nafraím was telling the truth. He hadn't hurt them. He had just realized what she was planning.

And yet he came anyway.

She got the medical kit and handed it to Nafraím. Then she sat back down on the bench with the crossbow in her lap. He opened the kit and took out a container of salve.

"Ringborre," he said, relieved. "Who knows, maybe I'll survive the night."

He ripped open his shirt around the bolt. Juva knew that was difficult, but she refused to lift a finger for him. He took a firm hold around the bolt and hesitated. "I would have asked you to help, but it strikes me that that would be significantly more painful," he smiled. Then he yanked out the bolt, choking back a shriek.

He deserved every single fit of pain he experienced. Juva looked away.

"So, why?" she asked. "Why do you want to end the vardari?"

"It was never meant to belong to us," he mumbled as he staunched the bleeding and tended the wound. "The blood, I mean. Capturing the devil was a mistake, my fault, a mistake that changed the world, and—even if it was for the better—we'll never know how it would have been without him. Do you understand?"

Juva nodded. She didn't need to accuse him anymore; he was obviously more than clear on what he'd done.

He took out a bandage and awkwardly wrapped it around his chest without moving his shoulder.

"But the most important reason to kill him and end the vardari is that we don't need the wolf-sickness anymore. Something has happened to the stones. I wish I had time to explain, but there was a force that ran them."

Juva knew he was talking about the Might, but she didn't say anything.

"So I want to end the vardari for many reasons. I want to fix an almost seven-hundred-year-old error. I want to stop the spread of wolf-sickness, which the power I mentioned makes worse. And I haven't made a single blood pearl since I received proof that it's back."

"How noble of you," she said bitterly. "And it only cost a few blood readers their lives."

He gave up on getting the bandage in place and let his arm drop. She reluctantly stood up and set down her crossbow. The man was in no condition to hurt her anymore. She wrapped the bandage around the wound and secured it over his shoulder.

"Have you never put on a bandage before?" Nafraím looked at it and started to laugh dully.

"I prefer not to get worked up into blood vengeance," Juva said with a shrug. "That seems simpler."

Nafraím looked her in the eye, and she realized that that wasn't true.

"You think it was an easy choice, to kill those blood readers? It was them or everyone else, Juva."

"Everyone else?"

"The stones are awake and some of them go to places I hope you'll never need to see. Where do you think the devil comes from? Imagine a whole world of devils and imagine the revenge they would take on us if they knew what we . . . what *I* have done. Believe me, Juva, that's a war neither you nor I want to see. If you had known anything at all about him, about his people, then you would have gladly given him to me or killed him yourself. Killing the blood readers who guarded him was the price I paid to save Náklav."

"Killing him doesn't prevent his people from using the stones."

"No." Nafraím smiled tentatively. "But it prevents them from finding out that they have something to avenge. And it will stop *my* people from attacking each other in order to find him. I'm sorry to have to say that most vardari do not view things my way."

"They don't know what you're trying to do?" Juva felt sympathy for him, reluctantly.

"All they know is that the blood readers are dead, and they're accusing each other. Everyone needs him, everyone wants control of the blood. Quite frankly, I don't think it will occur to any of them that one of us is trying to end the vardaris' eternality. It makes me . . . anxious to think of what would happen if they knew. I don't expect you to understand."

Juva looked at him. He seemed incredibly tired, and the only familiar emotion she found in his eyes was the fear. He was a warow who wanted to die, and he claimed it was to save lives, but there was more to it than that. The fear of revenge, both from Gríf's people and from other vardari.

"You're wrong," she said. "I understand fear better than anyone. I've lived with it my whole life. Because I didn't understand what was happening inside my heart when you were near me."

"Yes." His eyes woke up and he smiled again. "The first real blood reader in half a millennium. The evidence that you saw him as a child. Tell me: did you ever know what he was?"

"What do you mean, the evidence?" Juva cocked her head.

"You can sense me, sense vardari. They say that genuine blood readers can be born from the Might, and for a long time, I thought that was what had happened with you. But think of how infinitesimally small the odds were that specifically you would receive that gift. Would the first blood reader in five hundred years randomly be born into one of three families who guarded the devil? No. The blood readers were originally created by the wolves, by his people. And you, Juva, will be a living legend. He created you, bound you to his blood and gave you the ability to sense his blood."

Juva felt her body wilt until her back was resting against the wall. It wasn't true. He had no idea what he was talking about. It *couldn't* be true. She'd had her troublesome heart her whole life, ever since . . .

Ever since I met him. The iron wolf.

Nafraím leaned forward cautiously and folded his hands in his lap.

"They have something in their claws," he said, "the devils. They can do unbelievable things. He touched you, back then. When you saw him as a child, didn't he?"

Juva nodded, swallowing her nausea. Grif had created her. A whole life, faded into fear, into the struggle between confusion and episodes. Her fluttering heart was his fault. And he hadn't said one word about it to her.

She stared at the floor. Her socks were wet. The water in the tub had stopped steaming a long time ago. Nafraím struggled to his feet.

"Sit down!" She grabbed her crossbow and aimed it at him.

Nafraím remained standing.

"You've seen him since then, too?" He looked as if he had had a revelation. "You've talked to him, and you didn't know that?"

Juva fought back her tears. This night be damned. Everything had been ruined, distorted. She had no idea anymore who to believe, herself or the man she had gone there to kill. Nafraím came closer and sat down next to her.

"Juva Sannseyr . . . There's a reason we called him the devil. His folk share blood with the wolves, and they can become one with them. I don't mean in a spiritual sense, believe me. They can literally assume the wolf's form. It was a wolf that I captured, a snarling beast, gray, furry, four-legged. We caught him in a wolf trap. I was a hunter, just like you, and the wolves used Slokna as their hunting grounds. They killed and ate people for food, for fun. I could tell you stories from the wolf wars that would leave you sleepless."

Nafraím pulled up his shirt sleeve to reveal his forearm. He had always hidden it and it had always seemed stiff. Now she understood why. A piece of it was missing, almost down to the bone. New skin had grown over it in a crooked pattern, like wax in water.

"A gift from the devil," he said, pulling his sleeve back down.

Juva got up and leaned on the tub. She felt like a child again. Unable to tell what was real and what wasn't. Nafraím had the same goal she did, to end the vardari. And everything she had thought about him was wrong. Everything she had thought about Gríf was also wrong.

He's used me. He created me.

Why? Had he understood that she was a potential route to freedom even when he had seen her as a child? And was Nafraím telling the truth? He had told the truth about Broddmar and the others, after all; they weren't dead, just asleep in the gallery. And that Gríf's people could take the form of wolves . . . Wasn't that what the fairy tale had always said? And she herself had called him the iron wolf, seen the kinship between him and Skarr.

That's why I can feel both him and the wolves. . .

Juva didn't know what to think. Would she be able to read it in Nafraím if he were lying? He had lied about her mother, after all, hadn't he?

She straightened up and took the crossbow but let it hang by her thigh.

"So, if it's true that you killed the blood readers, but not my mother, then who did kill her?"

"That is an extremely good question, and I've been pondering it since it happened. Lagalune's death created waves among my people. Who would dare to kill one of the initiated, one who guarded the devil? I thought it might be a warow who shared my goal, but I quickly rejected that. Then I thought it was an outsider who had caught wind of the secret and wanted to kill the guards to exterminate us. But no one touched the other members of the Seida Guild, so I rejected that as well. Apparently, your mother was murdered by someone who didn't know about us or the devil. My best guess is that it was your sister."

Juva started laughing, but her laughter quickly got stuck in her throat. Solde? She couldn't have . . . She *wouldn't* have . . .

Memories of old conversations with her mother and Solde forced their way into her head. Mother who, with absolute certainty, had declared that Solde was a sadist. Solde's fear of losing the inheritance. The desperation for Mother's seat in the Seida Guild, so strong that she nearly killed herself with blood pearls to get the answers she thought they were seeking. But would she . . . ?

Gaula eat me, it's possible . . .

"Are you all right?" Nafraím asked, a look in his eyes that seemed genuinely concerned. "It's just a guess," he added, but she knew that they were both thinking the same thing.

"You would have killed her," Juva said. "If someone else hadn't done it. I heard you with mother and you asked her to turn him over, but she refused. You would have killed them all to take the devil's life."

"Yes. I'm sorry about that, more than you realize. But yes, I would have." Nafraím looked down. "I don't expect that it will make any difference to you, but they had no idea. They fell asleep without any pain, all of them. I planted the blood of someone with wolf-sickness under a skirt waistband so Broddmar's wolf would react. Of course it would have been far more convincing if the murders had been more . . . beastly, a bloody tableau, right? But I thought about how you might be the one to discover it, so I . . ."

He hesitated. Juva longed for him to continue with this feat of creating empathy for the way he had committed the murders. It was perverse and if he tried, she would hit him.

"It had to be done," he said, cheating her out of the punch. "There was no other way out. The devil had to die."

Juva let out a brief, pained laugh.

"Well, then we finally agree on something," she said and straightened her back. "I know where he is, Nafraím, and you will get him. There's something I need to do first, but you will get the devil you are seeking."

Nafraím's shoulders lowered without any signs of pain. The salves had done what they were meant to. But if he was happy to hear this, then he hid it well. He looked half-dead, and she was sure she herself must look even worse.

"How do I find you again?" she asked, a question she had never thought she would ask him.

"Florian's Parlors," he said, leaning his head back against the wall. "Don't ask for me. Just go in and sit down at the table they give you; I'll find you. But Juva . . . Do what you need to do quickly, because there's every reason to believe that I wasn't the first one Rugen ran to with the information."

Juva stood there, feeling like there was something she ought to do, something she ought to say.

"I'll be fine," Nafraím finally said.

Juva nodded, picked up her bolts, and left him. She had known she'd be killing someone that night, but it appeared that she had been wrong about whom.

PULSE

Juva went up the stairs between two sleepy guards who did their best not to look at her. Her crossbow was heavy in her hand, and she realized that she had been walking with it out in front of her the whole way home, as if in a trance. If there had been anyone out, they would have thought she was insane, a red hunter who had contracted wolf-sickness herself.

She let herself in. The wind almost yanked the door out of her hand. She barely had the strength to hold on to it. She untied her shoes, fumbling with the laces. Her hair fell over her face. It had dried in a tangled mess, leaving it looking damp and frozen.

There wasn't a sound to be heard in the foyer apart from the weather battering the building. But her heart beat uneasily, so she knew he was here.

She walked straight into Mother's room and started searching through her things. She checked the drawers, the pockets of her bag, everything, but the vial of poison she used for her bolts was gone. It hadn't been in Hidehall either.

Her feet carried her out into the foyer again, as if by their own free will, and up the stairs into Solde's room. She had only been in there once since they had died, to draw the curtains. The room felt dry and dead. It still smelled like Solde's perfume, a cloyingly sweet floral scent. Juva didn't want to think about what she was doing in here. She didn't want to find anything, but she couldn't not look, propelled by her anger at having been betrayed—by Mother, by Solde, by Rugen, by Nafraím.

And by Gríf.

She tossed her crossbow on the bed and cautiously opened the first dresser drawer. She flipped through corsets and lace with the sense that she was doing something forbidden. But once she got started, it became easier. Her hands didn't ask for permission, they started digging, searching, seeking. She tossed skirts and stockings onto the bed, pulled out entire drawers and emptied them onto the floor.

The jewelry box was locked. Juva pulled her knife out of her hunting belt and broke the lock. She opened the box and pushed the top drawers aside. There was something there, wrapped in a hand-kerchief. Juva unwrapped it and stared at the empty poison vial.

Solde, what have you done?

Her throat constricted, as if she had drunk the poison herself. She sank down on to the bed. Every word Nafraím had said was true. Solde had poisoned Mother . . . and saved the vial. Why?

It was insurance. In case things went wrong.

Solde had kept the poison vial as insurance, in case anyone became suspicious. Dr. Emelstein could have reacted or the Seida Guild. The plan could have gone straight to Drukna, and then she would have been able to plant the evidence on someone else.

On me. Everyone knew it was mine.

Had it been an accident? Solde couldn't have known what effect the poison would have. She could have thought it was something else, she was anything but a hunter.

Hunter . . . Hidehall!

Juva remembered Solde sweeping into Hidehall to say that Mother was ill. She had wrinkled her nose and toyed with the things on the table, had touched the poison. Juva had stopped her.

Don't touch that—unless you feel like throwing up your own lungs.

What if that's when she got the idea? Juva clutched the vial in her hand. Maybe she had inspired Solde to murder. Lagalune's alleged illness just made it easier to do.

Why? It was utter madness! Little Solde, barely sixteen . . .

She knew Mother was going to give me the inheritance.

Juva spanned a bolt into her crossbow and got up. She felt like she hadn't slept in days. The only thing keeping her on her feet was a burning rage that cut right to her bones. She was done doubting, done being an idiot, done being used by other people. And now she had to kill the creature she had released. The devil had ruined her heart.

But where was he? Not on the roof in this weather . . .

Juva went into the library, feeling her way along using the heart-beats like the hunter she was. The chimney wall was pushed aside, and the shaft gaped at her. What was he doing down there when he was finally free of that place? It seemed inconceivably macabre; he should avoid it like the wolf-sickness.

Juva lit the storm lantern and climbed down. She remembered the first time, how terrified she had been. How little she had known. If only she had shot him then, right away, and spared herself a sea of pain.

At the end of the tunnel, the hinges of the open iron doors creaked in the wind. Gríf sat on the floor the way he always used to when they talked. The difference was the black shirt he was wearing, the one she had bought him.

He looked up at her and she could see they both knew that the storm had reached them.

"I couldn't sleep," he said in the husky voice she knew she would never forget.

Juva stepped in. The crossbow weighed heavily at her side, and she caught herself doubting she would even be able to raise it at all. He had folded up his sleeves, and she could see the scars on his forearm. Now she knew for sure where they had come from. A wolf trap.

That was why he hadn't healed them himself, the way he obviously could. He had suffered them while he was in wolf form. What was it he'd said up on the roof?

It happened at the wrong time.

Gríf followed her gaze to his arm, and it seemed to dawn on him what she was looking at. He smiled coolly. "Ah . . . he told you," he said with certainty.

Juva set the storm lantern on the floor and pointed the crossbow at him. The weight forced her backward, and she leaned against the wall next to the iron door. She was going to need all the support she could get. Her eyes felt swollen, and she blinked away a telltale burning.

"You're a wolf," she said, her voice failing her, "just a wolf, and I've killed many of them."

"And you don't have the sense to be ashamed of it," he replied.

His voice was frozen, as if *she* was the one who had let *him* down, not the other way around. Just one shot, that was all it would take, then both the vardari and wolf-sickness would die out and her heart would be at peace.

Her arm threatened to fail her, and she used her other hand to support it.

"I've lived my whole life with this wild heart, in fear, and it's your fault. You did this to me."

Gríf flicked his claws against each other, in time with his heart: *Flick. Flick. Flick.* His eyes were devastatingly black, like the ocean outside.

"Yes, right? Everything's been done *to* you. You've never done anything at all other than be let down, used. Is that how it is?"

"You created a blood reader! Out of a child!"

"What would *you* have done?!" He snarled and then spat.

394

She jumped at his sudden anger. The crossbow shook in front of her, and she fought to keep the bolt aimed at his chest. He got up into a squat, ready to leap at her like the wolf he was.

"Answer me! What would you have done, Juva? After many men's lifetimes in captivity, I had a chance and there haven't been many of those. A child, a girl who had no idea what she was dealing with, and she came to me, fearless, open. And I thought maybe you had the gift, and that was what made you come. But I couldn't be sure. So, when you came close enough . . ."

Juva gulped, "You put your claws in me."

"I opened you to the Might. That was the only way I could be sure."

"Sure of what?"

"That you would grow up and know that I was near, so you could find me. And you did. So really, spare me from your grief at having lived in fear, because at least you've lived in freedom and with a gift many would kill to obtain. Forgive me for not crying over that."

Is he even capable of crying?

The shaft felt infinitely empty and cold. The wind came in violent gusts off the ocean and whistled though the narrow gap in the wall.

"You lied to me," she whispered. "Both about this and wolf-sickness."

"I have never lied to you!" He clenched his fists so his claws scraped on the floor.

"Yes, you did. The wolf-sick *were* necessary. They used the blood to run the gates, and you didn't mention that."

"Ah . . ." Grif looked away and chuckled. "Yes, that explains a lot. And if I had known that, I would have said that."

She stared at him, the iron wolf. She had drawn him and burned him so many times that it ought to be easy to put an end to him one last time. If only he weren't wearing the shirt, which made him so human, that and those wisps of hair on his forehead, those strong lips. She inhaled in shaky bursts.

"You lied about Nafraím. He didn't want you for your blood. He killed the blood readers to put an end to you, to put an end to the vardari."

"And you believe him?!" Gríf snarled. "You set me free and now you're choosing to trust the man who's lived off of holding me prisoner? A murderer!"

"You're a murderer, too." Juva's voice faltered. Her arm burned. "You killed my father. That time he tried to protect me from you, which he had reason to do!"

Gríf closed his eyes. His heart stopped in her chest, and for a second, she was inexplicably afraid he was dying.

She kept talking, testing, unsteady.

"You're both murderers. And the gods only know what you did as a wolf. That's what he's afraid of, that you'll come back with an army of . . . wolves, of your people, and take revenge on all of Slokna."

Gríf opened his eyes again and she felt his heart wake up. "So, he's convinced you that he wants to end his own life to save everyone else's? How noble. No, Juva. If he finally wants to kill himself, then it's because he's tired of living. Few people have it in them to endure eternity."

Juva couldn't take anymore. Her legs failed and she sank to the floor. She sat there with the crossbow pointed at him, propped on her knees.

"I don't know what drives him," she admitted tiredly. "But I know we have the same goal. We both want to end the vardari."

"You've always known that you could end the vardari by killing me." Gríf crawled one threatening step closer, unfamiliar, like an animal. "But you haven't done it. Why?"

Juva put her hand on her chest but his words squeezed around her heart as completely as a claw. She thought he knew why. That's what hurt the most. She let her arm fall and pushed the crossbow away. It was over.

Suddenly, he was in front of her, faster than she would have been able to react if she had still been aiming at him. He snatched the crossbow and held it up in front of her face.

"I'm sick and tired of talking to you with this facing me. You ask for the truth while I'm locked up. For trust, while I'm staring at the business end of a crossbow. I doubt you even know what those words mean!" He tossed the crossbow into the corner. "You think a weapon gives you power over me? Your bolts would hardly harm me."

He grasped her chin. His veins were sharply outlined as they ran up his forearm and disappeared under his shirt.

"The gift I've given you is greater than you suspect," he said, his breath caressing her cheek. "You can sense my blood—in me, in the vardari, and in those with wolf-sickness. You can even sense the wolves, my brothers and sisters. But what you can feel, you can also learn to rule."

"Rule?" Juva tried not to stare at his lips, so incredibly close.

He leaned forward and braced his arm against the wall behind her. His cheek touched hers as he whispered into her ear, "a heart you can feel, you can control."

She wanted to say he was crazy, that that wasn't possible, but her body betrayed her. Her heart began to race, together with his—faster, heavier, chased by excitement, and by something she didn't have the ability to understand or control.

"Do you understand?" he whispered.

Blood readers can control hearts!

She heard the blood gushing through her head, a pumping pulse in her ear, which increased and increased. Her cheek was clammy with sweat. Her chest burned, as if she were being squeezed beneath him, but he was only close, incredibly close. The pressure she felt was coming from within. She was going to die!

"Stop . . . STOP!" Juva tensed herself against him.

She gasped for breath and felt him do the same. He pulled a hair's breadth away but remained standing over her, like a predator. The feeling of running uphill vanished, just as quickly as it had come. He rested his forehead on the arm he was using to lean on the wall. His chest rose and fell, in time with hers. He breathed with his mouth half open, his fangs white and sharp against the darkness.

"So you see," he said breathlessly, "no iron doors will be thick enough. I've been free since the first time you climbed down here. Where did you think all the sayings about broken hearts came from? I could do as I pleased and could have left, if I wanted to."

The howling of the wind quieted. The chaos in her thoughts quieted. The pain became delightfully fuzzy, as if she had sunken into the ocean. The only response she found was his own.

"But you didn't. Why not?"

His eyes flickered in shades of black. A gleam of uncertainty, which gave her an intoxicating feeling of being invincible. Her body was tense, like the crossbow, a vibrating string, stretched to the breaking point. He was the devil, the wolf.

And she wanted him. That was perverse, she knew that. No matter how close he was, there were seven hundred years of injustice between them. Her rage. His. And everything they had done to each other was just the beginning. They didn't even belong to the same world. He was perilous, but Jól save her, she wanted to feel his teeth against her tongue.

Gríf growled. Suddenly, he got her to her feet and twisted her up against the iron door. She caught herself with her hands, her palms hitting the rust. The door screeched and banged against the wall. He came up against her back, smelled her.

"You stink of him," he said, his voice hoarse against the back of her neck. "You come here, wrapped in his scent, the man who did this to me."

His arm touched hers, and against her tailbone she felt the pressure of an unmistakable hardness that chased the blood to her groin. He pulled away again, as if to hide it.

"No, I haven't left yet," he continued. "But now I will."

The weight of him was gone, and she heard him leave. Juva let out a muffled sob against the rusty iron door. Her feet shook and she grabbed the bars in the door's window grating to hold herself up. The storm lantern flickered its last, bringing the crossbow in the corner to life. Then it went out.

GONE

Juva rested her arms on the railing, heavy as a dead body. The roof was chilly after the storm. The rainwater soaked into her shirt, but she couldn't find the energy to stand upright.

The city lay before her, waterlogged and sad under a heavy sky. Gudebro Bridge looked like a snake on stilts. A magical beast eating itself from the peak of Kingshill. Náklaborg, even uglier than usual, seemed abandoned by everything but the unruly ravens riding the gusty wind. There had gotten to be so many of them lately, as if they expected a mass die-off.

He's gone.

Her heart beat so cursedly, evenly, solitarily. It was unbearable. Every beat a cry in the darkness. Was this what it'd be like when he was gone for good? She might as well get used to it, because soon he'd no longer be in this world. For all she knew, he was already dead, killed by a terrified guard or recaptured by warow.

No, he knows better.

Gríf knew that the warow were keeping an eye on them, and he knew about the guards at the front door. He had most likely left the house from the roof. But he also knew that he didn't stand a chance of making it into the stone circle, so he had left exclusively to get away from her.

Could she blame him, actually? She had met his worst enemy without telling him. She had plotted to kill him and utterly failed.

Afterward, she had come home and threatened Gríf's life because she had trusted a warow, the worst of them all, the one who had imprisoned Gríf.

But what right did he have to judge her? A devil who had taken the form of a wolf and used Slokna as his hunting grounds! What king of dark and bestial sorcery made something like that possible? She would never have believed it if she hadn't seen Gríf with her own eyes, occasionally so animalistic that she was willing to believe the wolf was still in him.

He had kept his mouth shut about the blood reading, too. The ability to sense, which he had single-handedly clawed into her. Gaula only knew what sort of filth had been put into her bloodstream, but it had given her a completely different life than she would have had otherwise. A heart that had always been in his power and, even so, he wanted praise because he had never used it on her?

What you can feel, you can also learn to control.

If he was telling the truth, then she was carrying a weapon against the vardari. A frightful ability to affect their hearts, which beat with his blood, and now he had cheated her out of the chance to learn. He had escaped and left her with a mysterious curse. He really was a devil.

So why did it hurt so Svartna much that he was gone? The pain sat like nails in her chest, jabbing in jerks when she least expected it.

She felt wolf breath on her heart and heard the sound of padding paws. From just a crack, Skarr pushed the door open wider with his snout and came out onto the roof. He scurried around acquainting himself before he sat down next to her. She had done her best not to get attached to him, but it was too late. Where would it end when a hunter fell for a wolf?

"Are they still at it?" she asked and burrowed her fingers into his fur.

Broddmar and the others were arguing down in the library, about everything she had told them. They were furious that Nafraím had sedated them and confused because she hadn't killed him when she had the chance. And none of them understood how she had managed to lose Gríf, allowed the world's most sought-after secret to slip between her fingers. She hadn't even managed to bring up her mother or Solde.

But they knew that she had painted herself into a corner. She had promised Nafraím that he would get Gríf and now she wouldn't be able to keep her promise even if she wanted to.

What am I going to do?

Skarr rubbed his muzzle against her arm, and she scratched him behind the ears. He was warm and indulgent.

"You have no idea what you're doing," she whispered. "You would have eaten me if you knew how many of yours I've killed."

The wolf stared at her with its yellow eyes free of prejudice. Kill or be killed, that was in the animal's nature. Skarr could live with the lives he'd taken. Could she? The memory of Nantes pushed its way into her head. That blond warow who had been eavesdropping at Haane's house, an antiques dealer . . . What kind of monster had she become? She knew nothing about him. Maybe he had never touched a hair on anyone's head, unlike Nafraím.

Nafraím deserved to die, for everything he had done. But as Broddmar had said, Nafraím was one of the first and there was every reason to believe he was the one keeping the others in check. The man she had intended to kill was possibly the best protection against the rest of the vardari. And now they had the same goal, but none of them had the means. Gríf was gone.

With that certainty came the pain, the nails in her chest. Was he gone forever, or would he come back once his anger had subsided? There were ten measly days left until the Yra Race. He knew the plan and knew there was no better way for him to get close to the stones. He would be there.

If he lives that long . . .

402

That thought poisoned her. Ate away at her arteries and veins. She needed to pull herself together and not let her emotions drain from her the willingness to act. She had a job to do and that was to keep herself and the others alive until the spring run. What would happen after that, only the gods knew.

Rugen was no threat since Nafraím had locked him up. But he could have caused his damage already, been to the other warow and told them that she had the devil. That was a vile, nagging risk of unknown proportions. She needed to disprove the rumors somehow and keep them at bay. Nafraím also needed to be neutralized, even if she couldn't kill him.

The task seemed impossible, and it was going to need to be solved whether Gríf came back or not. But how?

A noise broke through her uncertainty. A familiar, prolonged reverberation from out by Knokle: the Dead Man's Horn. In the middle of all of this. Juva pulled her hands over her face. She hadn't even had time to think about her job as a hunter, but this was bound to happen. The fact that she and Broddmar knew the wolf-sick had a chance of surviving didn't change anything after all. The hunt for them would continue, as always.

Skarr paced restlessly around her, aware of what the horn meant. Broddmar came out onto the roof. He stared at her, his eyes stunned at the impossible choice.

"What the fuck are we going to do, Juva?"

THE BIRDS

Juva tightened the straps on the bodice of her red hunting suit while Broddmar paced in circles in the foyer, talking to himself in half sentences.

"Jól preserve me, we can't just . . ." he muttered. "We do know that . . ."

Nothing she could say would help him. He needed to find a way to steel himself, simple as that. She hooked the folded crossbow to her back between the bloodskins and clicked her tongue for Skarr. The wolf came right away. He seemed to prefer her company presently.

He smells Gríf on me.

For a moment, she could swear that she could, too. A wild scent of leather and wood, which threatened to sap her of her strength.

Broddmar glanced anxiously toward the library, but the others couldn't hear them. They would stand their ground while the red hunters hunted the wolf-sick.

"Juva . . ."

"What?" She whirled around to face him, flinging up her arms. "What else are we going to do, Broddmar?! The horn sounded, and someone out there needs you! You can't just not do the job."

Broddmar looked far too old. His cheeks seemed more sunken, and in the close-cropped stubble on his head, she could see that his widow's peak had become more prominent. He chewed around, looking for words, but words had never been his strength. He sat down in peculiar harmony with the bones that formed the back of the bench.

"They could have a chance," he mumbled, a weight of guilt in his steel-blue eyes.

"Stand up, Broddmar!" Juva walked over to him and held out her hand. "What the fuck else are you going to do? Create warow out of all the wolf-sick and put them in cages until they either die or become like you? Their chances of living would be tiny, even if Grif willingly offered up his blood. And he's not here, so that's not an option anyway."

Because I let him go.

"This won't last forever, Broddmar," she sighed. "They don't need the wolf-sick to operate the stones anymore. Nafraím hasn't made any blood pearls since the Witness woke up. No dope means no wolf-sickness. It's just a matter of time before it's over."

She pulled him to his feet and studied him until his eyes hardened. He nodded grudgingly. Then she put the leather mask on over her nose and let him go out first. The guards had stopped being startled by Skarr. One of them bumped his fist against his chest as a sign of appreciation, which seemed in poor taste, a sort of thanks that they were going out to kill.

"Brenntorget is the closest guard booth," Broddmar said, nodding toward Nákla Henge. "We need to go there so we can . . ."

A runner dashed past them and Broddmar called after him. The boy came to a sudden stop, terrified when he realized who he was looking at.

"Where is this happening?" Broddmar asked.

The boy didn't need to ask what he meant. "Up in Herad," he replied, out of breath. "In the middle of Myntslaget." Then he ran on.

Ester!

Juva set out at a run up Skjepnasnaret and heard Broddmar following her. An eerie chill formed a clump in her chest, but she clung

405

to the knowledge that Myntslaget was a long street. Ester wasn't dead, of course not! Ester conquered life like no other.

They rounded Kingshill, and Juva steeled herself for the sight of the Ring Guard and the hearses, but Myntslaget lay deserted. Not a soul to see, even though it was afternoon. What was left of the storm blew desolately down the winding street, sweeping a handkerchief along.

Juva stopped outside Vinterhagen. Ester's guesthouse looked peaceful at first glance, sitting there. The rain had washed the sign and the gilded letters gleamed against the green background, surrounded by elaborate birds. Broddmar continued a little way up the street, stopped, and shrugged. No trouble or death to be seen.

Juva had the sense of being watched and turned around. A figure hurried away from the window inside the arms dealer's shop. She waved to Broddmar, crossed the street, and knocked at Agan Askran's place. The man who had sold her her crossbow peeked out a small window. It seemed to take him a moment to understand who they were, and then he opened the door a crack.

"About time," he mumbled. "What happened to the Ring Guard?"

"They're on their way. Where's it happening?" Juva asked.

Recognition flashed across his face, and he craned his neck to look at the crossbow on her back.

"Well that explains things." He smiled nervously. "In the guesthouse, but there's no one there anymore. Everyone stormed out in a panic; I have two people in the back room here. They say the old woman had a mouth full of blood and threw them out the door."

Juva's body felt numb.

Broddmar looked at her and said, "That doesn't necessarily mean that she's—"

"No."

They walked back over to the guesthouse. Broddmar opened the door and went in ahead of her, with nothing but a dagger in his hand. Juva raised her crossbow and followed him and Skarr up the stairs to the colorful great room. The place seemed dead. The only life was what was painted on the walls. They were surrounded by depictions of birds and fruit trees.

A table and a couple of chairs were tipped over and a painting by the door had fallen down, presumably because everyone had tried to get out at the same time. The crackling from the fireplace was all she could hear, and it seemed abnormal, as if something were missing.

The birds.

The twittering had been constant when she was last there. Now she couldn't hear a single little bird. The silence was sickening and a hint as to where Ester was. Skarr growled deep in his throat. Juva nudged Broddmar and gestured with her head to the double doors that stood open in the conservatory. She held out two fingers, the hunting signal for splitting up. Broddmar nodded, and they approached the doors from different sides.

Juva peeked in. The room was humid and lush with foreign plants that would never have survived even a day outside. Green vines and climbing plants from all corners of the world, gathered over the course of a long life. Daylight filtered down through gridded skylight onto an old well house in the middle, a circle of columns with a vaulted ceiling, like a sort of cage. The ladies usually sat there for breakfast or tea, but now the ornate chairs sat empty, aside from one.

Ester sat up against a column, her head lolling forward as if she were asleep. She was wearing slippers and an embroidered silk tunic. Her bone cane lay across her lap. She was surrounded by dead birds.

The birds lay strewn across the floor, their feathers bloodied. One of them was still alive, a house sparrow so delicate it would have disappeared in your hand. It flapped helplessly with a broken wing, unable to move, its beak half open.

Juva braced herself for what she knew was coming. Her heart shuddered, as if it were trying to shake off the sense of Ester and Skarr, without success. It was too painful to fight. But she couldn't let pity in, not now. This was a job, nothing else. She could feel her emotions later.

Skarr crept past her and snarled, his snout wrinkled to reveal red gums above his teeth. Ester recovered and looked up at them sluggishly. Blood filled the wrinkles around her mouth. She smiled with effort.

"Could you leash your animal?" Ester asked, short of breath.

Juva clenched her teeth. The sight of sharp fangs in Ester's mouth sapped Juva's defensive wall. Broddmar chased the wolf out, and then closed the doors so he wouldn't come back in.

"I meant the other animal," Ester said, pointing to Broddmar.

Juva took a couple of cautious steps toward the cage. A teacup shard crunched under her shoe. One of the blue cups, she saw, that had the butterflies on the inside. She stopped between two columns, without lowering her crossbow. Out of the corner of her eyes, she saw Broddmar sneak along a paved footpath in the forest of plants heading toward the back of the well house.

"Men," Ester snorted and set her cane on the floor. She rubbed the fist-shaped handle. "I was no older than you when I swore that my death would never take place at the hands of a man. I saw them for the animals they were. But who's the animal now, my girl? Who's the animal now . . ."

Juva felt the wolf-sick woman twitching inside her heart, tiny tugs that nibbled pieces off of it.

"Ester, what have you done?" Juva asked blankly.

Ester raised a ring-laden hand, a warning not to come any closer.

"I chased them all away before the thirst took me, but I'm old, Juva. It's got me now. And Jól preserve me, I intend to die before the animal comes out."

Juva blinked, her eyes hazy with tears. Her arm shook. Ester's bloody face seemed to waver in her crossbow sight.

"Aren't they magnificent?" Ester caressed the vines that climbed up the columns.

It looked like nature was enveloping her, demanding the old woman back.

Broddmar crept between the columns to stand behind Ester with his dagger ready. He watched Juva, and she realized that he was waiting for her blessing to proceed. How in heaven's name was she going to convey that to him? Ester hadn't killed anyone besides birds. To the contrary, she had saved lives because she knew what was coming.

The wolf-sickness didn't give a damn how well-deserved it was. Nothing could save Ester now—not even Grif's blood if it was true that few could bear the transition from warow to human. There was no doubt, only despair.

Juva nodded to Broddmar, but he didn't act. He just stood there with the dagger in his hand. His face contorted in a grimace of pain.

He's breaking down!

Ester suddenly raised her cane and jabbed it backward. It hit Broddmar in the crotch and he gasped. He dropped the dagger and fell to his knees.

"Not at . . . the hands of . . . a man!" Ester said, eyeing Juva through the same veil of madness as Rugen had. She dropped her cane on the floor and stood up as if she had never needed it. "They want to see you yearning for crumbs, and you're letting them. Teaching you to hunger. But you're stronger than them, Juva. Never go hungry. Promise me that. I have lived an unconstrained life and have no regrets."

Juva knew what she was being asked to do, but her finger sat frozen on the trigger and refused to budge.

Ester wiped blood and brown lip wax on her sleeve. "I told you, not that long ago, that I liked you because you're afraid of wolves. But it's not the fear that's worth liking. It's not the fear that *is* you, Juva. It's the will to face it. You are a wolf hunter, even though you fear them. You fear this, too, but you're going to do it anyway. For my sake."

Ester bared her teeth and came rushing at a tremendous and un-expected speed. Juva fired. The bolt tore out of the track and into Ester's chest. She continued forward for a second, as if she didn't understand that she'd been hit. Then she collapsed at Juva's feet and lay there motionless on her side. Her silk tunic bunched into glisten-ing wrinkles around the bolt, like a star.

Juva lowered the crossbow. Enough, enough already. Her body felt hard and cold, like a wall. The only thing that penetrated was the certainty that this had to end, never any more warow, never any more wolf-sick.

"She could . . . We could have . . . " Broddmar crawled up from his kneeling position, but then flopped onto Ester's chair and stayed there.

"No," Juva said.

She swept the broken glass aside with her foot and walked over to the bird that was floundering in its own blood. She squatted down, scooped the warm little body up in her hands, and wrung its neck. Then she picked up the dagger and handed it to Broddmar. He stared at it as if he had never seen it before, the look in his eyes, unguarded, completely unable to hide the burden he was carrying.

Never let them see a weak blood reader.

"We can't let people with wolf-sickness run around on the loose," she hissed, tossing the dagger on the table in front of him. "So what were we supposed to do, cage her? For how long, Broddmar? And what would she have to endure in terms of pain and losing her mind, while she waited for you to man up and make it stop?"

"He's changed everything, Juva." Broddmar's lips curled into a toothless grin as he stared down at his own hands.

She didn't need to ask who he meant. Her longing cut into her, merciless and raw.

"Yes, he has." She propped her hands against the table and leaned over the man falling apart in front of her. "Broddmar, to hunt wolves, you need to think like a wolf. You taught me that. Have you forgotten that yourself? No one can kill wolves without becoming one."

The words were meant for him, but they hit home in her. She straightened up and looked up at the ceiling. The light.

To hunt a wolf, you need to think like a wolf.

That realization forced both shock and grief, drawing a crystal-clear picture of what needed to happen. She would never win against the vardari or Nafraím by thinking like a hunter. She had to think like them. And she knew them. She knew what they were afraid of and what they longed for.

She knew what she had to do.

Skarr barked out in the great room. Shouts from the street indicated that the Ring Guard had finally arrived.

"Pull yourself together, Broddmar."

Juva pulled the pliers out of his belt and walked over to Ester. She forced open her wrinkled mouth and broke out the bestial canine teeth. Teeth were a currency in this cursed city. Broddmar usually delivered them to the Ring Guard along with the blood and was paid for his work. But not this time. No one would receive any money for this killing, never.

But Nafraím will pay for this. And I know how.

"Shall we ... You can't ..." Broddmar got up and came over to her.

"No. The blood isn't needed anymore. No one will bleed Ester."

Juva opened the doors and let Skarr in. She walked over to the window and nodded to the Ring Guard outside. They came storming up

411

the stairs and ran past her to where Broddmar was. He would have to handle the explanation. Juva needed to get out of there. Keep going, otherwise she would crack, like him.

She used to believe that she was cursed, that she made horrific things happen, a helpless child who burned drawings of the wolf to save herself and other people. But she had only been in the wrong place at the wrong time, met the devil and received her fear as a gift, the ability to sense.

Terrible things had always happened and would always happen. Her curse was to be the only one who could stop it, even if the price was as high as her life.

NAKED

Nafraím crossed Professor Dolg's Vei barely keeping himself from breaking into a run. He felt young as a foal on frisky legs. Blessed by a freedom from cares. He felt the card in his pocket, with the words that had set him in motion.

Juva Sannseyr is waiting in Svermeriet.

Before this morning was over, he would know where the devil was. The end was near. The closure he had fought and killed for. It was paradoxical that a man should need to fight with so much perseverance in order to die.

Nafraím greeted the man at the door and entered the hectic entertainment environment that was Florian's Parlors. The great room was almost full, mostly with guests from far away who had the place on their list of things to indulge in at some point in their life. The rest were regular guests from the city, who chatted over the teacups and had dressed to harmonize with the blue-green and gold interior.

A host hurried past him and in between the tables with his hands full of silverware. Nafraím followed him through the room toward Svermeriet, "the Swoonery," a far more intimate room just inside. The only thing separating it from the rest of the parlor was a magical wall of sea-green glass panels. He saw Juva's silhouette behind the glass.

The sight brought out the ache in his shoulder from her bolt, a sweet pain that made him smile. What was it about this young woman? Why had he risked so incredibly much to keep her alive? It was a true riddle. She lacked most of the qualities that he had learned to value. Good breeding, experience, patience . . . Sooner the opposite, she was far too young to have anything to offer, and there was every reason to believe she had not found her true self. She was nervous, distrustful, brusque, and hard to get close to.

But brave and bright, an excellent judge of character.

And she could sense him. She probably already knew he was there. He had faced hard times over the last several years, difficult days, when no achievement had felt worth the effort it was to live. But she was sitting in there, and she knew he existed. She confirmed his existence. And she hated him for that, enough to punish him for every single sin by shooting him with a bolt. Wonderful.

Nafraím ordered roe and tea for two from the hostess at the door. Then he smoothed his hair and walked into the private chamber.

Svermeriet had only one table, and Juva had seated herself with her back to the wall, of course. Her long, blond hair was charmingly unbrushed, and she wore a gray linen shirt. Simple and ordinary, but it highlighted her piercing, gray-blue eyes. She had pulled the sleeves down over her hands as if she were cold, and he saw that she had been crying.

He smiled cautiously, critically aware that he was the source of the problems in her life. He hung his coat on the peg and nodded at the hands she was hiding in her shirt sleeves.

"What is it this time? A dagger? Or are you planning to poison me?"

She smiled, even though her eyes said that she was no stranger to the thought.

"I'm not the murderer of the family."

Her words were brutal in all their simplicity, but they meant that she trusted him. Or she had received confirmation that his assumption about Solde was correct.

414

"Maybe not the only one, but clearly the best." He sat down across from her.

A look of disgust crossed her face. The battle she was waging against her own nature was captivating to witness. One day she would find her footing and accept the abyss she carried within her. That would be a sight for the gods. He caught himself hoping that he could partake in it.

A host came in with a tray, which he rested on the edge of the table as he unloaded silverware and bone bowls heaping with crackers and roe. He poured tea into the cups and disappeared with a tactless wink. Nafraím realized that he assumed they were lovers, an uncomfortable thought.

Juva put her hands around the cup, apparently for the heat, and looked at him.

"I have no idea where he is," she said.

Nafraím stared at her, studying her face for signs she was lying without finding any. She could lie about many things, Juva Sannseyr, but there was no doubt that the despair in her puffy eyes was genuine. He set down the teapot, weakened by disappointment and a smoldering rage.

"You gave him to someone else?" Nafraím feared the worst.

"No!" Her eyes opened wide. "No, I couldn't give him to anyone if I wanted to, not until I know where he is." She set down her cup and put her hands in her lap. "But I can find out. It's . . . complicated."

Uneasiness gnawed at him. He had expected a clear answer. He didn't have any patience left and he felt it in his jaws.

"Tell me what's going on," he said, "and let *me* judge how complicated it is."

"My mother tried to explain as she was dying," Juva said, staring down into her cup. "But she wasn't herself and I had no idea it was important. She said that Solde wouldn't be able to tolerate the inheritance, that it should go to me. Me, leader of the Seida Guild?! That was complete lunacy, and I didn't want the job."

Nafraím tasted a butter biscuit. The beads of fish roe popped as he chewed, blending with the sour cream. The girl was still telling the truth, there was no doubt about that, so he let her continue.

"But she said more that seemed even crazier. About the devil being real. The wolf, everything I had heard in the fairy tale, it was real, but I couldn't let anyone get him. I had to keep the hiding place secret, because they had done that for a thousand years. I thought she was raving."

"Where is he hidden?"

"That's just it," Juva said, her voice bitter. "I was supposed to find that out, from a man. I don't know who, but he was supposed to give me a letter with the details, in Jólshov, after mother's sepulture. But he never came. I think he saw you . . . So you have yourself to thank for that. If you'd left me alone, I'd know where he was now."

"So, you were supposed to find out where the devil is hidden, but the letter never came?" Nafraím leaned back in his chair.

"Oh no, I've received several letters. He's tried to find a meeting place and time, but he's afraid of the vardari. He doesn't feel safe, and he wants to have a lot of people around. The last thing I heard was that he's going to try during the Yra Race."

"The spring run?" Nafraím tried to hide his relief. "You're going to meet him in eight days?"

"No, not meet exactly." Juva shook her head. "This man doesn't want to meet anyone at all. He's just going to find me and give me the letter, nothing else. But it probably won't happen . . ."

Nafraím caught her eye and held eye contact. Was she toying with him?

"Do you still have the letters?"

"Do you think I'm an idiot?" She rolled her eyes. "Of course not, I've burned everything I've received."

"And you don't think it's going to happen, because . . . ?"

"Because he wants to meet where there's the most people, up at Nákla Henge, but he's afraid of the Ring Guard and security. He says they're keeping a closer eye than they used to."

"That's true, but security is a trivial problem. I can fix that. He should feel safe enough to give you the letter."

Juva pulled her hands over her face. Her eyes welled up.

"But I don't want it!" she said.

"What do you mean?"

"I mean what I say. I don't want the letter. I don't want to know. I never wanted any of this. I want my life back, my life the way it was before you got involved in it, before Mother died, before . . . before all of this."

Nafraím handed her a handkerchief and smiled.

"It will surprise you to hear that this, too, is a trivial problem," he said. "You see to receiving the letter, and I will be there to free you of the burden immediately. You'll never need to hear anything about the devil again, Juva Sannseyr."

"And no one will follow me or threaten me?"

"Never again, pretty girl. Here, take a butter biscuit. The roe is fresh and amazing."

"No, thank you." Her lips curled in distaste. "It looks like blood pearls."

"Same fish, actually, hvitharving. But blood free, I can assure you.

Nafraím helped himself to another biscuit with a growing appetite. All this time of doubt and threats, when all he had needed to do was promise her peace. Was it too good to be true? No, she had been through enough to want out of this. And even *if* she had wanted to trick him into some new trap, there were many better methods for doing so. He wouldn't be running any risk in the middle of the Yra Race.

417

"Then we're in agreement?" he asked.

"Just make sure that he doesn't see you first." Juva wiped away her tears and nodded. "Then he'll never give me anything, and I have no idea who he is, so I can't find him again."

"My dear, I just promised to give you your life back and free you from the devil. You should have a little more faith in me. You're making the only right choice, Juva." He took a large bite of buttered biscuit and managed not to smile.

"I know," she replied. "I'm eradicating wolf-sickness. And you people."

"You needn't look quite so pleased about it, now when we're having such a lovely time," he teased. "I brought something, incidentally."

He pulled the book out of his coat pocket and set it in front of her. A spark of curiosity ignited in her tired eyes, and that warmed him more than he had expected.

"It's a sort of diary," he said. "Things I've worked on, projects, if you will. Perhaps it will bring us to understand each other better."

She opened it to reveal page after page of his handwriting and a series of drawings. He pointed.

"These are the plans for the ice hall underneath Kingshill. For food storage. And that there was the first printing press." He smiled at the memory. "That wasn't my idea, I have to say. I worked with an exceptional woman, almost three hundred years ago now. And there's a formula for an anesthetic for a surgeon in Haeyna. I'm no doctor, but minor adjustments can make big differences. Very similar to the substance I used on the blood readers when . . ."

Nafraím swallowed his words, but it was too late. He realized that he had brought the book along in the hopes of seeing some change in the look in her eyes, of her viewing him differently, but he should have known better. She hadn't even seen twenty summers, and he . . . He had seen so many lives that he was inadvertently dwelling on the drug that had taken her sister from her. A bolt in the shoulder was far less than he deserved.

He had been naked, and she had seen him for who he really was.

"You must know that I'm so very sorry that . . ." he cleared his throat, "for all you've been through. I wanted you to see that perhaps it was . . ."

"Worth it?" She closed the book.

There was no indication that she would ever think that. The silence was stifling. The conversation seemed unusually difficult, and this wasn't a situation he had any experience with.

Nafraím sipped his tea. It was cold already. "If it's any comfort, I'll age and die with significant pain." He raised his cup again and clinked it against hers. "Cheers, Juva Sannseyr. To short lives and long consequences."

THE FOX

"You did what?!"

Broddmar's outburst made the baby wail in his arms, and Lok came to take over. Juva pulled Broddmar away from the others so they could talk in peace. She was no longer used to having people around.

The whole hunting team was there to celebrate Lok's newborn son having taken the water. She could see Embla, his wife, measuring Nolan in the dining room. Juva had hired her to sew outfits for the whole gang for the Yra Race. The house was teeming with voices, yet it had never felt so quiet. Her heart felt like it was dead now that Gríf was gone.

She was surrounded by strong, honorable men, whom she had learned to trust, but none of them was a part of her. Not like Gríf. The feel of him wasn't a sound, it was a presence, a pulse from within. Maybe that's how it felt to be pregnant? Juva peeked at the baby. She had no idea. She'd never been pregnant nor did she have any plans to become so. All she'd learned about how to raise a child was how *not* to do it. What in Drukna would she be able to offer a child?

She opened the lacquered cabinet and got out the whiskey, freshly bought for the watering.

"What I did, Broddmar," she said, "was buy us peace until the Yra Race. Nafraím won't bother us anymore."

She had lowered her voice in the hope of avoiding any conversation. This should be a day of joy, but the others drew closer, aware of what they were discussing. This pertained to all of them. They were involved now, whether she wanted that or not.

Broddmar looked around at them, seeking support. "You sat there in Florian's, the parlor *he* probably owns, and lied right to his face? Sure, you grew up with blood readers, but the man is a warow! He's as old as the foundation walls in Náklav. You can't fool him!"

Lok rocked his son in his arms and glanced toward the dining room, a sign that he had kept his word. Even his wife didn't know about Gríf or what had happened at Hidehall.

Juva poured a generous splash from the bottle into six glasses and downed hers right away. The gods knew she was going to need it.

"You can fool anyone," she said. "Especially men like him. The more they want something, the easier it is to convince them that it's coming. Besides, I used the easiest method to sell a lie."

"What's that?" Muggen asked.

"I told the truth. Mostly."

"You told the truth?" Broddmar sighed and sat down on the sofa. "You said someone was going to give you a letter in the middle of the Yra Race with information about where the devil is, a letter you promised to give Nafraím as soon as you got your hands on it. Where is there any truth in that? What letter? From whom?"

"The letter I'm going to write," Juva replied. "Which Hanuk is going to deliver to me."

"Me?" Hanuk chuckled shrilly. "I'm going to give you a letter about the devil?"

Juva shrugged. "You're the fastest runner of all of us," she said, pouring more whiskey into her glass. It made it easier to believe what she was saying. "We'll be dressed up, all of us, and surrounded by many thousands of other animals. No one will recognize you."

"No one is concerned about being recognized," Broddmar said, sounding discouraged. "What I want to know is what the heck you're planning to do after that! You're writing a fake letter full of nonsense about where the devil is, fine. We take part in the race, where Hanuk gives you the letter, and you give it to Nafraím. Also fine. But what happens when he opens it, Juva? What happens when he realizes that you've tricked him? This is the most poorly thought-out plan since the city's fifth bridge."

Juva stared into her glass, seeking reassurances that she did not find there. She had only told them half of it and they weren't even buying that much.

"It doesn't matter," she replied. "No matter what he does, it'll be too late. Gríf will have made it to the Witness and will be gone from this world. And Nafraím will be busy staying alive. Trust me."

The door knocker sounded on the front door and saved her from their objections.

"The city councilman is here," she said. "He's going to need the sofa, Broddmar."

Juva went out to the foyer and opened the door. Councilman Drogg Valsvik stood on the front steps, just as corpulent as she remembered him, but she didn't see any carriage. Had the man who had been trying to save heartbeats walked there on his own two feet?

Drogg held up a mask in front of his face, which transformed him into the world's fattest and most adorable fox, with a coat made of rust-colored yarn and pointy ears.

"Isn't it wonderful!" he exclaimed.

"You're going to run in the Yra Race?" Juva realized she was staring.

"Well, *run* is a generous word, Frú Sannseyr. I'll stick to the rear, with the walkers." He came in and warmed her with his gaze. It had a spark that she hadn't seen the last time.

"I owe you a thank you," he said as they made their way to the library. "You've blown some life into this old carcass. Our meeting got me thinking and it dawned on me that if I'm going to obey what a blood reader says, then I might as well choose a blood reader like you to listen to, right? One with some *joie de vivre* and benevolence, Frú Sannseyr."

Juva suppressed a giggle, unable to recognize herself in his description. It filled her with a challenging blend of shame and joy.

They went into the library and the guys all straightened up. Muggen smoothed the motheaten cape that was his hallmark without making it look any better, and Lok stood up with the baby in his arms.

"No, no, sit by all means!" Drogg waved for him to sit back down. "I'm only here to remind Frú Sannseyr about the speech."

The speech . . .

Juva inhaled through clenched teeth. She had pushed the whole speech so far back in her mind that it had disappeared under everything else.

"You are, of course, free to say whatever you'd like, but under the circumstances . . . " Drogg handed her a letter and their eyes med. "Well, I seem to recall that you prefer to be plainspoken, and we're suffering from an increase in wolf-sickness and dead blood readers now. You are also young, and newly in charge of the Seida Guild, so, naturally, we have some . . . shall we say, polite requests about what ought to be said. Read them, that's all the city council asks."

"Oh, to Gaula!" Muggen realized what was going on. "You're the Seida Guild! You're the old lady who has to give the speech at the Yra Race!"

"Yeah," Juva acknowledged. "Thanks . . . "

If I can stay alive until then.

"Is there anything more I can do for you, Frú Sannseyr?" Drogg asked, wiping away his sweat with his floral handkerchief.

Juva hesitated. She knew what she needed to ask for, but she also knew that the others were going to react.

"Yes, there is one thing," she said. "You can recall the guards. I don't need a security team anymore."

"I'll take care of that right away, Frú Sannseyr." Drogg smiled as if they shared a secret, and she realized that he thought they had both overcome their fears.

The guys stared at her.

"But . . . " Muggen said.

Hanuk poked him and he didn't say anything else. Broddmar turned his back to them and set down his glass, clearly unable to keep the emotions off his face.

The councilman said goodbye, waved to Hanuk, and left the room. The guys were deathly quiet as they listened to his footsteps in the foyer.

The front door had scarcely banged shut before Broddmar flung out his arms.

"You've got a death wish," Broddmar said. "Is that what's going on here? Or do you want us to move in and keep watch in shifts at night?"

He sat back down on the sofa. Juva steeled herself. This wasn't going to be easy to explain, but she needed them. She sat down next to him.

"No one can move in, Broddmar," she said. "We can't do anything unusual now. If we did that, it would draw their attention."

"What about the warow, Juva?" Lok said, looking up from the baby's face. "The ones who have been keeping an eye on you? Without guards, they'll be able to . . ." He didn't complete his sentence. Everyone knew very well what they might do.

Broddmar finished his glass and clucked his tongue on the roof of his mouth.

"You think Nafraím was the biggest danger?" Broddmar said, his knee whipping back and forth in a restless rhythm. "That nobody else will come here?"

"Quite the opposite," Juva said. She didn't dare look at him. "I'm sure they will come here."

"They're coming to kill you," Muggen said.

"No." Juva shook her head. "Not if they suspect I know where the devil is. They need him to survive. They can do a lot of things. They can threaten me or torture me. But they won't kill me until they know where he is."

"So, what's your plan?" Broddmar looked at her, his eyes tormented.

Juva gulped and said, "My plan is to let them capture me."

The silence was intense but brief. She looked up and saw that Nolan had also come in, clearly finished having his measurements taken.

"Why?" he asked.

Juva stood up. Their reactions were touching, but they made her doubt her decision. And she couldn't afford to do that.

"Because I have something to tell them, and I have no idea who they are. Even if I knew how to find them, they would never believe me if I sought them out. I'm going to let them come to me, and I'll tell them precisely the same thing I told Nafraím. That I have no idea where the devil is, but that Nafraím will know soon."

Juva could tell from the way they were looking at each other that they thought she was out of her mind. Muggen was the only one grinning.

"You're going to play them against each other!" he exclaimed. The others looked at him, equally confused. He raised his arms, as if the answer were obvious.

"It's logical!" he said. "If Nafraím thinks he's the only one who knows where the devil is, and the *other* warow think that only he knows where the devil is . . . Then she'll be safe, and they'll be preoccupied with each other. That's what she said instead, right, that when they see that Nafraím has the letter, he'll be busy saving his own ass."

The guys stared at him, as if he had just come down with wolf-sickness.

"What?" Muggen said with a shrug. "What is it?"

No one answered him.

"Wow. Sometimes I'm sure you guys think I'm an idiot." He took a glass of whiskey, which looked tiny in his hand.

The room dissolved into laughter and Juva's shoulders relaxed. She had them. They understood. But Broddmar wasn't laughing. He came over to her and whispered into her ear.

"And afterward, Juva? What will you do once both parties realize that you've tricked them?"

Juva didn't have an answer for him. She had no plan beyond the next eight days. After that was another life.

BAIT

Kleft was bathed in sunshine and made Ester's sepulture into something completely different from Mother's and Solde's. A worthy farewell for a woman who had lived long and unusually well. A fashionably dressed gathering of friends and business connections stood in a semicircle around the ramp. Juva recognized the young man from the guesthouse, the one who had been sitting in the corner embroidering. His bruise had faded. He was the only one who cried.

Juva was there as a friend, but also as the leader of the Seida Guild. She hadn't hesitated to accept the job of leading the sepulture. She was the one who had sent Ester to Drukna. It was fair and proper that she should do the sepulture as well since Ester didn't have any family.

She lifted the cloth from Ester's wrinkled face. Her mouth was half open and the sight of her missing canines brought about a sad feeling of helplessness. Would it ever end?

Juva hurried to give her the last waters from the horn before anyone came too close and noticed her missing teeth. Then she ignited the cloth. The yellow sparks from the seaweed oil spat into the sky. Broddmar and Nolan helped her tip the ramp and Ester plunged toward the ocean, just as sparkling in death as she had been in life.

Juva had asked Nafraím for Ester's death to be logged as natural, not as due to wolf-sickness, and to not feed her blood to the stones. He had kept his word.

It had been two days since Juva had seen Nafraím, two days since the guards had left the Sannseyr home, but there hadn't been any sign of warow. That made her more anxious than she dared let on to the guys. She was depending on their getting in touch. Otherwise, the plan would fail.

What if they don't come? None of them?

She could try to find them, but that would make it considerably harder to convince them about Nafraím and the letter.

The entourage broke up and strolled back down to the longship. It lay bobbing at the water's edge, with the fire-yellow keel that was supposed to keep Gaula at bay.

Juva spotted Ilja from the Seida Guild. The last time she had seen the over-decorated blood reader, she'd had the door slammed in her face and been called a murderer. Haane stood next to her with her head bowed and her hair in a straggly bun. She glanced up at Juva several times. She probably had something to say, but she never took that step. In the end, she was pulled along by Ilja, who whispered something to her, scowling in Juva's direction.

Those who had once been the Seida Guild still despised her, even though she was supposed to lead them. Or was it just fear? Was it too risky to be close to the person who had taken over for the dead?

Never let them see a weak blood reader.

Juva straightened her back. She had other things to fight besides the intrigues of people who didn't even dare to be part of the guild anymore.

Muggen and Broddmar came up alongside her.

"What's going to happen to Hidehall?" Muggen asked.

That was a good question without any clear answer. She hoped someone would take over running the place so no one lost their livelihood. Especially not Lok—things were tight enough for him with five kids. But he was independent and strong-willed, so the only way she had found to help was to overpay his wife for sewing their costumes.

"He has to turn up soon," Broddmar said, climbing aboard the boat and sitting down beside her. "We've only got six days, Juva."

She held back a bitter response. He didn't need to tell her that they didn't have much time or that Grif was gone. She knew that better than any of them, and every reminder tugged at her heart.

He would turn up again. It was the only way he could get home. And once he had finally left, she would be able to forget him. That was a lie she told herself repeatedly.

As soon as the ship docked in Corpse Bay, the mood among their entourage cheered up even more. A wake was being held at Jólshov and people were discussing the Yra Race. The long line slowly made its way up the hill and along the city wall toward Jólshov. They walked in through the gates and the feeling began immediately, little pinpricks in her heart with a pulse slower than her own.

Vardari.

Juva felt her palms grow clammy and her feet unsteady, weakened by a nauseating combination of fear and relief. They knew the city council wasn't guarding her anymore, and they were there. This was someone she had sensed before. Juva dug through her memories. This must be the woman she had seen at the tailor's shop, a distinguished lady in her forties in knee-high boots.

What should I do?

Juva suppressed her impulse to look around. It wasn't certain that this warow knew she could sense them, and that was an advantage she wanted to keep to herself.

She followed the others into Muune's Hall in Jólshov and sat down on one of the benches in a numb trance.

Muggen looked around the hall, which was known for resembling a vagina.

"Huh, that really looks a lot like a . . . Well, you know," he said.

The guys pretended like they had no idea what he meant and couldn't keep from laughing as he attempted to explain without using the actual word itself. Juva could barely follow what they were saying. She was wrapped in a fog of nerves. Broddmar asked her if everything was all right, and she forced herself to nod.

She had known that this would happen. She *needed* it to happen, but she had to dig deep to remember why. This was a fear she knew well, the merciless type that changed every plan, every choice, that devoured what you thought was important until there were only crumbs left.

She could still turn back. It wasn't too late. Tell the guys that she had felt warow outside and ask them to stay in the house overnight.

Until tomorrow. Or the day after.

No, this was her opportunity. If she didn't seize it, she would remain prey for every single warow in Náklav. Including Nafraím. She had to clear herself of suspicion regarding the devil and get them interested in one another, and it needed to happen before the Yra Race. It was now or never.

Juva got up with a strained smile. She said she didn't feel well and needed to go home. Broddmar and Muggen leapt up to accompany her, but she waved for them to sit back down.

"No, I'll go alone."

Muggen shrugged but understanding kindled in Broddmar's eyes. His face paled. Juva nodded to him and tried to say what needed to be said with her eyes, but there was too much.

"In a worst-case scenario, you guys need to get him home," she whispered. "And then we'll have won, in the long run."

In a worst-case scenario. If I don't come back.

She turned around and left the room. The prickling in her chest began again as soon as she stepped out the Jólshov gates. The sun was low in the sky now. She forced herself to follow the quiet alley along the city wall, up toward Bodsrabben, so they would risk showing themselves.

Far too soon, she heard rapid footsteps behind her. She gave a start, but it was an extremely human man, no fluttering. He asked the quickest way to Nákla Henge, and she gave him directions. She exhaled with relief as he turned around and disappeared around the corner.

Juva walked a few more steps and suddenly noticed how tired she was, dizzy even—difficult days, difficult weeks, far too many dead. Everything seemed to harden around her feet, and she stopped. Something was wrong. Something was seriously wrong.

She braced herself against the rough stone wall of a building, bathed in burning orange from the sun, and realized that the man had touched her hand when he thanked her. The wall caught her. Her strength vanished. She squinted at the sun and was extinguished in the fire.

NEEDLES

Where am I?

It was a lucid and intentional thought, the first she had managed to form. It brought with it an avalanche of others and a pounding headache. Juva had the suffocating feeling of being trapped.

She forced her eyes open. She was alone, but not locked up or imprisoned. Quite the opposite. The room was enormous, a banquet hall, filled with tens of thousands of little candles. Mellow flames as far as she could see.

No, it wasn't right. Juva squinted, blinked, and tried to focus again. The hall was smaller than she had thought but appointed with large wall mirrors in ornate frames. A row of candles in high candlesticks was reflected infinitely.

A banquet hall? No, there hadn't been any life there for centuries. The room showed signs of deterioration. Fading flakes of red paint curled around the cracks in the ceiling, and the mirrors were mottled with dark stains. It smelled like something nondescript and pungent. Vinegar?

Juva struggled upright. She was sitting in a wingback chair upholstered in red velvet. It seemed new, unlike the rest of the room. There was a plainer chair made of wrought iron next to her and a table with a silver fruit bowl. It was full of dried apples with brown spots.

In the middle of the room was a black tent with a hole in the canvas, a round window of dark glass. Was there someone inside? Was she being observed?

Juva smiled darkly. This was a stage, a play that would have been worthy of her mother.

A tingling began in her heart, an uncomfortable pulse that revealed she was no longer alone. She heard footsteps behind her, and a woman came into view, countless versions of her, reflected in the mirrors. She stopped at the black tent.

Juva had seen her before—at the tailor's shop, when she'd had the measurements taken for the red outfit. And apparently that hadn't been a coincidence. The woman had hardly looked at her then. Now she stared so shamelessly that it seemed menacing. The fact that her heartbeats felt like pinpricks made matters worse.

She had a distinguished face with long, pronounced cheekbones. The wrinkles at the base of her neck said nothing of how old she actually was, but Juva guessed she had been around fifty when she became a warow. She had a sharp look in her eye, but her heavy eyelids gave her an aura of superiority that could quickly become dangerous. Her fingers had dark stains on them. Ashes?

There was no indication that she planned to introduce herself. The silence grew steadily more onerous and finally reached a point where it seemed impossible to break.

This was a game, a blood reader trick Juva had learned before she had drunk her first beer. Silence could contain anything at all and gave a false impression of insight. It created fear and built expectation.

Juva hoped the woman had chosen this strategy because she didn't know what Juva knew. And vice versa.

"You have not been the easiest person to get in touch with," the woman finally said, as if that was sufficient explanation for why it had been necessary to abduct her.

Juva hunted for a good response, painfully aware that she only had one chance. She couldn't afford not to be believed, so she needed to spare the lies and guard her body, which often spoke before she did.

"Well, you folks definitely haven't been the easiest to avoid, either," she retorted, rubbing at the headache within her temples.

The lazy smile she received suggested that the woman found her answer entertaining. "You have nothing to fear from me," she said, looking away as she sat down in the wrought iron chair.

She's lying.

That certainty made the cold dread grow in her chest. The woman was dangerous, and it was going to be far too easy to act threatened.

She observed Juva, brazenly, as if she were planning to draw her. "I'm Eydala," she said. "And I hear you're fearless."

Juva couldn't help but laugh. The echo sounded shrill between the mirrored walls. Her? Fearless? That was so backward that it bordered on vicious. Eydala seemed satisfied with her speechless response.

"Where am I?" Juva asked.

"Don't you like it?" Eydala did not take her eyes off her. "It's sublime. I never tire of it. Every winter, another section crumbles away, making it even more beautiful. It was once a mirror workshop, owned by a family from Undst. A mysterious people, don't you think? They came here with their lone god and toothless threats of eternal torment for the greedy. Can you imagine how much conviction it would require coming here, to Náklav, and preaching moderation?"

She smiled and tossed her head. Juva realized that was how she laughed, noiselessly, only to herself.

Eydala leaned forward and took an apple, green and fuzzy with mold. Something moved where it had been sitting, crawled in between the other rotten apples. Juva nearly threw up. She stared at Eydala, who ate undisturbed.

A game. Relax. It's a game.

"But they had other thoughts, the Undstlanders, that we soaked up like mother's milk." Eydala glanced at the apple she had eaten from, without any hint of disgust. "The idea of the devil, for example, the tempter, the father of lies, a more polished and . . . palatable version of our own wolf, who gave the women the power to see him." She looked at Juva again. "A fairy tale older than sin and yet here we are, in the unlikely circumstance that *you*, a girl barely grown, a wolf hunter born blood reader, have him in your possession."

The words were out.

Juva jumped at a movement in the mirrors. Someone grabbed her from behind. She froze in panic. She struggled to get up from the chair, but was stuck, suffocating in the crook of a strong arm. Something tightened around her throat, cutting into her skin.

"It's a steel wire." Eydala raised her hand with its black stained fingers as if to hush her. "The more you struggle, the more you'll bleed. Nod if you understand."

Juva tried to nod, but the pain was unbearable. She stared at Eydala to avoid looking at her own reflection and the injury she had suffered. Her breath was stuck in her chest, frozen in the rhythm of the pinpricks from Eydala's warped heart.

She leaned toward Juva with that intense look again, as if she were seeing something pretty, something she wanted to etch into her memory.

"I don't intend to kill you, but you have something that belongs to us. It means nothing to you, but it is the alpha and the omega to me. Do yourself a favor and you can leave here safely. Tell me, Juva Sannseyr, where is the devil?"

The wire around her throat loosened slightly, enough that she was able to force out an answer.

"I don't know. I have no idea where he is!" The wire tightened again, and she screamed. "It's true!"

"You have a lover whose opinion differs. He says you have him in Hidehall."

"I lied!" Juva felt something run down her neck, and she couldn't hold back a tear. They transformed the room into foggy shadows. "I lied," she repeated and tried to swallow her way through the pain.

Eydala made a gesture with her hand and the wire loosened. Juva reached for her throat and gasped for breath. Her hand felt hot and wet, and she knew she had lost the upper hand. She was unable to evaluate her injury, unable to control her thoughts.

"Why lie about that?" Eydala asked.

"I lied . . . I lied to lure a man there, one of you." Juva remained seated, crouched over with her hand to her throat. "I wanted to kill him."

"You wanted to kill Nafraím? And here I thought you lacked ambition. So, what did you do?"

Eydala sat motionless like a painting with the rotten apple in her hand and a cool, interested look that would have made Nafraím seem tender-hearted. He had been right. There were far worse warow than him. That recognition writhed like a snake in her stomach.

"I shot him. With the crossbow." Juva wiped blood off her hand on the leg of her pants.

Eydala laughed, this time with a booming sound, revealing her fangs.

"Oh, sweet child! What I would have given to see that moment. I love moments, Juva. Small, frozen pearls of time. That's what drove him to me, you see."

Juva glanced reluctantly at the mirrors, but the man who had been holding her was gone. Her neck was sticky with blood and chased a new wave of fear through her body. Eydala continued, unshaken.

"Before him I was working on an instrument, an invention that would have made eternal life difficult. He has always liked games,

Nafraím. He loves calling himself a man of science, but what I was doing couldn't see the light of day. So, he gave me the choice: die, or cut off the project and become one of them."

"He created you," Juva stared at her.

Her words appeared to irritate Eydala, and she shifted in her chair to shake them off. "So you shot him," Eydala said. "Then what happened?"

Juva didn't dare move. Her neck felt like a burning knot, and she feared that the slightest motion would tear the wound. Her body was paralyzed with fear and rage, but she had chosen to be there. And this was the reason. This was the moment she had been waiting for.

"I said he would get the devil."

"The devil that you don't have?"

"When my mother died . . ." Juva closed her eyes for a moment, searching for strength. "She said he was real, the devil. That you people must never get him."

"And she told you where he is?" Eydala was on the edge of her chair.

Unable to shake it, Juva cautiously turned her head. The pain was hot and new.

You're a blood reader. Give her what she wants.

"No, but a man . . . a messenger is going to contact me and give me a letter. About where he is. But I don't want him. I don't give a damn about the devil, and I don't give a damn about you people! You're sick, all of you. I want my life back."

Eydala rolled her hand eagerly in a circle, as if to hurry her along.

"You're going to receive a letter about where the devil is?" she pressed. "Where and when?"

"It doesn't matter. I already promised Nafraím that he'll get the letter as soon as I've received it. Unread. Then he'll know where the devil is, not me."

"Where and when?" Eydala repeated tersely, leaving no room for objections.

"Up at Nákla Henge in the middle of the Yra Race. Nafraím will be there, and as soon as I receive the letter I was promised, I'll give it to him. I don't have any choice. I can't keep it."

"You're lying," Eydala leaned back again. "Why would you give the devil to the man you wanted to kill?"

Juva took a deep breath. "Because I've had it with mysteries and riddles," she said. "I've had it with death, with being victimized, threatened, and nearly strangled! And because Nafraím promised me he would kill him."

"He promised to do what?" Eydala stood up.

"He wants the devil because he wants to kill him." Juva glanced up at her and let her see the naked contempt. "He said he wants to wipe out the vardari, and I've got absolutely no problem with that."

Eydala took a couple of steps, stopped, and then a couple more, as if her whole body were contemplating this claim. After a painfully long spell, she came closer and leaned over Juva. She licked her blue-black thumb, which was clearly discolored in some way, a discoloration that was as everlasting as she was.

"Juva, I'll give you what you want," she said, wiping the blood from Juva's neck with her damp finger. "You'll get your life back. How does that sound?"

"Wonderful," Juva did her best not to bare her teeth.

It'll be over soon.

"After we've seen each other during the Yra Race, of course," Eydala smiled. "But if you breathe a word about this meeting to anyone, including Nafraím, then I'll be forced to . . . Well, you shouldn't believe that my need to find the devil is stronger than my need for revenge. That's good advice and you should listen to it."

Juva clenched her teeth and stared at the floor, where she saw black marks at each corner of the chair, as if to show that it needed to be exactly where it was and not a hair's breadth away.

Eydala's fingers touched Juva's jaw and unlaced her top to reveal her injured neck. Juva got a glimpse in the mirrors. A blue collar, saturated with blood. She closed her eyes.

Eydala put her hand on Juva's thigh and forced her knees apart.

"Sit still now. Don't breathe, don't blink, don't move. Look at the hole in the black tent and don't look away. Can you manage that, Juva Sannseyr?"

I can do more than you think. I tricked you, you damned bitch.

Eydala walked over to the black tent and disappeared through a curtain on the back side. The smell of vinegar grew stronger. Juva glanced quickly around, half prepared to run. The mood had changed, from life-threatening to creepy. She got goosebumps on her arms. And what in Gaula was that stench?

Juva stared at the hole and made an effort to keep her knees from shaking. What was going to happen and how much was it going to hurt? Her shirt was open down to her breasts and her neck pulsed with pain. She was sitting on display, without any audience other than her own countless reflections, and a completely ruined warow. A sick, old woman who got wet from seeing her humiliated. It was perverse.

But she had won. She had tricked a vardari, and as far as she was concerned, they could all send each other to Drukna, every last one of them.

Her body felt numb as Eydala eventually emerged from the tent. She took Juva's hand and pulled her to her feet. Juva was surprised that her legs were able to hold her up.

What just happened? Why had she just sat there?

"I would prefer that you don't know where we are," Eydala said. "I'm sure you understand. So, if you would allow me?" She held up a black scarf but didn't wait for an answer before tying it over Juva's eyes.

Juva was blind. All she could make out were points of light as she was led outside and into a carriage. It had started raining.

"Oh yes," Eydala said as she laced Juva's top back up at the neck. "The old woman's death was truly regrettable. Ester, wasn't it? It's sad how little a body tolerates at that age. Even blood pearls can be too much."

Juva stiffened in the carriage seat. What the fuck did she mean? She had murdered Ester? Given her blood pearls? Or was she just using that to hint at what she had the power to do?

The carriage door banged shut. Eydala's pins slowly withdrew from her heart, and Juva gasped for breath.

Don't cry. Never let them see a weak blood reader.

The carriage began to roll. The rhythm calmed her, safer with every bumpy stone. The rain drummed on the carriage roof. Her panic faded away, leaving behind something just as frightening. A certainty that what had happened would dawn on her soon, catch up to her, without her being able to run from it.

When the carriage finally stopped, she knew she was home. She loosened the scarf and climbed out of the carriage. Walked up the stairs without looking back and dug around in her pocket for the key. She let herself in and felt the house embrace her. She felt the same flutter she had known since she was seven, and which had been gone for almost five days.

Grif.

She heard voices and put her hand on the heavy wrought iron door so it wouldn't bang. Someone was arguing in the library. Broddmar and Muggen. Grif. It smelled like food, but all she could picture was that rotten apple.

Juva put a hand over her heart, and it felt like it might break. He was back. He was alive. The determination that had held her together was failing. She knew they were afraid for her and waiting for a sign of life, but she wasn't up to the thought of seeing anyone, at least not Gríf. It would break her.

She tiptoed up the stairs, through the attic and out onto the roof. She stumbled forward and grabbed the railing. Then her body gave in, pushing out deep sobs that ripped through her chest like vomit.

COME

The rage burned to the bone. A raw, untamable rage she had never felt anything like before. So why was she blubbering like a child? It was inconceivable.

Juva yanked at the railing and swallowed a scream. If she'd thought the gods could hear, she would have told them to rot even if the sky was crying with her. Lykteløkka, the blood reader street down below, tempted her like an abyss in front of the roof, but not even it could contain all the Svartna she bore.

Ester, whom she had slaughtered herself, like a wild animal. Mother, who had forced her on this path before she vomited herself to death. Nafraím with his silver tongue, the beginning of all misery, but whom she still couldn't manage to kill. Rugen, the rat king of betrayal, poor, pathetic fool. And Solde . . .

What in Gaula were you thinking, little sister?

The Seida Guild, which was crumbling under her laughable leadership. Blood and wolf-sickness. And now tonight she had stared straight into Drukna, gotten a glimpse below the surface of a dark, sudden drop-off that terrified her. Only now did she realize what she was dealing with, what Nafraím had created. She could feel every drop of rain on her tender neck. There were monsters out there.

But she had achieved what she wanted: peace until the Yra Race.

That thought made her smile, which made her throat burn. She would get Gríf home, send the damned devil away through

442

the Witness and out of this world for good. Slowly but surely, the vardari would rot and die out. Eydala, too, in far greater pain than this.

What came after didn't matter. As soon as he was gone, she wouldn't have anything more to lose. Fucking Gríf, the wolf that was tearing her apart, that she wanted to have sex with, that she wanted to kill. She wanted so much more of him than he was ever going to give.

Five stupid days of silence in her heart.

How am I going to handle a lifetime?

Her heart started beating out of step with itself as if it had heard her, and she realized that he was close. He had felt her when she came in, just as surely as she had felt him. Juva wiped her nose on her sleeve, grateful for the rain. Not in Gaula would he see her cry, even if she suspected it might be too late.

The wall was cold against her thighs. The rain seemed to collect in a compact form behind her. His heart was boisterous, indomitable, and she hated that he felt hers, too. Did he feel the same fury? The same aftermath from what she'd been through?

"Do you need an explanation?" His husky voice created a yearning in her stomach.

"No."

"Do you need blood?"

It took her a minute to understand what he meant. He could help. Patch her up without stitches, without scarring, the way she had seen him do with his own arm after Rugen went berserk. That he was asking also meant that Broddmar and the others had told him what she had done.

"No."

He stood behind her but put his hand on the railing next to hers. His claws, which had been so alien when she had first seen them, now felt so natural that her own fingers seemed meager, limited. He was a roving weapon, and what wouldn't she have given to be the same tonight?

"Show me," he said, against the back of her neck.

Juva turned around. He was so close that she had to press her back into the wall. He was wearing the black shirt she had bought him, heavy with rain along his shoulders. She swallowed the lump in her throat, raised her chin, and revealed her throat, so defiant that she felt annoyed.

He cocked his head slightly and eyed the wound. The railing creaked under his grip as if it were going to break.

"Don't you dare," she said, not recognizing her own voice. "Don't you dare come here feeling sorry for me."

"It would never occur to me. I save my pity for those who need it, the powerless."

He placed his fingers on her neck, stroked the injury. She jumped when his claws encountered resistance where the blood had clotted.

"I can heal it," he said. "Just a few drops, no pain."

Juva laughed bitterly. "So they can see that I have you? You might as well fly a flag on the roof up here."

His dark gaze hardened. "Provide relief, then? Take away the pain? Or do you need that to know you exist? Wolves need to know who you would have been without fear or suffering."

"Spare me!" Juva pushed aside his hand. "This wouldn't even have happened if it weren't for you."

"Do you think I'm not clear on that?" he replied.

The rain ran down from his black hair toward his quivering lips, which revealed his canines. Juva knew she should stop while she was ahead, but she couldn't. She wanted to see him just as angry as her. He had destroyed her, ruined her heart, and the only fair thing would be to ruin his as well. A heart for a heart.

"The gods only know what you're clear on and what you're not," she blurted out. "You haven't been here. You have no right to come back and guess who I am, preach about what *I* fear. I'm so tired of fear! I don't want to feel that anymore. The only thing I want to be afraid of is you, and you left!"

"I thought you didn't need any explanation?" He turned his back as if to go.

"I don't give a damn why you left. What I need an explanation for is why you came back." Her voice broke.

He turned abruptly to face her again and flung out his arms. "Because I thought you had set me free!" he snapped.

His heart swelled inside hers, strong and hunted. His shirt stuck to his chest. He closed his eyes for a second, exhaled and came closer.

"I thought you had set me free," he repeated softly. "But the longer I was gone, the less free I was. I came back because I'm still a prisoner."

His words absorbed her rage and she felt completely exhausted. She let her forehead fall against his chest, grabbed hold of his shirt to hold herself upright on her feet. His body stiffened as if he didn't dare breathe. His chin touched her temple. She raised her head and met that inky dark look that only he in the world had.

"Come," she whispered, and before the word was out, his lips found hers, wild, demanding from the first instant. She dug her fingers into his hair to keep him close. His fangs scraped her tongue and she heard herself gasp. She drank him in, drank in the rain, felt him harden against her thighs. Her body was suddenly wide awake. The blood rushed through her and coalesced into a throbbing knot between her thighs.

Grif . . .

He pulled free and backed away an arm's length. The door opened behind him and Broddmar came out. His gaze wandered between them, as if he were trying to read the mood. Then it locked on her. Juva put her hand to her throat, but he had clearly already seen the wound.

"I succeeded," she said, even though she didn't think it would make any difference.

"Good," Broddmar replied, his voice strained. "Nolan and Hanuk are taking the upstairs bedrooms. Muggen and I are moving in downstairs, so we can control the foyer."

"You don't need to . . ." She looked at him and realized it would be pointless to refuse his protection. What she was unsure of was who he wanted to protect her from.

MAGIC

Juva adjusted her position on the sofa and propped her sketch-book against her thighs, but the words for her speech didn't come any easier. The city council's suggestions were about as useful as a case of wolf-sickness, false assurances and toothless measures. She couldn't stand up in front of half the city and spew that nonsense, not that it mattered.

The library was quiet as the guys sat around the fireplace and ate. Juva had given up, it hurt too much to swallow, even if it was only soup. Gríf emptied his bowl and slurped up the rest with his claws while the others stared, apparently thinking they were being furtive. He was doing it on purpose, she was sure of that, to highlight his own alienness.

The guys had been staying there for a few days, but they were still uneasy around Gríf. Hanuk was the most unflappable, cheerful and unafraid to ask questions. Juva had eavesdropped as he received answers to things that she herself had been afraid to dig into.

Why should she ask? The more she knew about Gríf, the harder it would be to forget him, and tomorrow night he would be gone.

He still slept in the shaft, even though she couldn't understand how he could bear it. And every night, she struggled to keep from climbing down to him after the guys had gone to bed. Every time she closed her eyes, she felt the rain on her face and hard lips on her own.

Skarr curled up around Gríf's feet and he scratched him behind the ears. The wolf was going to be crazed with missing him when he was gone. Had he considered that at all?

Broddmar sat clucking with his tongue again, nervous about the next day, even though the plan was simple enough. They had reviewed it over and over again. The costumes, the race, the speech, the letter, and the element that was most foreign to them: the Witness, those tower-like walls that would take Gríf home.

Muggen came in and stopped in the middle of the room. He picked a fuzz ball off his shaggy costume, which looked about as good on him as a sack. His face stuck out in the middle of a round, brown board with ears attached to it.

"I was a bear last year, too," he grumbled. "Why do I always have to be a bear?"

Juva bit her lip to keep from laughing, and she could see the rest of the crew struggling to do the same as they leaned over their soup bowls.

Muggen sat down in the chair next to her and took the only untouched soup bowl. "There must be more than a thousand animals in the world. So why a bear?" He raised the spoon to eat, but the board around his face was in his way, causing him to spill.

The dimples grew in Hanuk's cheeks until he broke into a grating laugh.

"It's because you're huge, Muggen," Nolan said. "You could be a bear or a whale."

"But that doesn't matter," Muggen grumbled, yanking off his bear face. "I could have been a really big rabbit, for example."

"Next year, Muggen." Juva put her hand on his paw, the most artistic part of the whole costume. "Next year you can be a really big rabbit."

Muggen grinned with his underbite, and Juva felt a pang of sadness. For her, next year was not guaranteed, maybe not for the rest of them, either. The safest thing she could do for them all was to leave the city before the vardari figured out what had happened.

They heard a roar of laughter from the street, where the festivities were already well underway. It would continue all night.

Broddmar pushed his bowl away and said, "So, Juva, your job?"

"Up at the crack of dawn, put on the party clothes," Juva said for what had to be the tenth time that afternoon. "Then up to Nákla Henge before people gather there. I rattle off reassuring lies to the city council. After that, people move down toward the bridge. I position myself as close to the northern gate as possible, along with the crowd. Nafraím is guaranteed to be one of them."

"And that other woman?"

Eydala . . .

Juva nodded and fought her impulse to touch her throat. She had been close to taking hoggthorn the last few days but knew that was an old habit. It wouldn't help, not with the fear or the pain. Hoggthorn had only numbed her heart and now she knew why it beat as two.

"And you?" Broddmar asked, glancing at Hanuk.

"I bring the letter and meet Nolan at Nattlyslokket. We trade costumes in case anyone saw me leave here. Then I go down to the bridge for the race, which starts from Náklaport. I wait in the crowd until the competition runners have left and then run with the rest up to Nákla Henge. I look for you guys at the intersection before Kingshill and give the signal. I keep running and follow the flow around the stone circle, find Juva, and give her the letter. Then I vanish into the crowd."

"Muggen?"

"I go with the rest of you guys, and he . . . " Muggen pointed to Gríf. "We leave here together and head up toward Ringgata where the runners will be. When we see Hanuk in the rabbit costume and— Why does he get to be a rabbit? He's not that much—"

"Muggen!"

"Yes, yes! When Hanuk runs by, we blend into the crowd and go up to Nákla Henge. When we get there, Juva will have received the letter and will probably be busy with Nafraím, so we'll just be there in case there's trouble."

"Good." Broddmar nodded.

"And Gríf?" Juva asked, since Broddmar didn't.

"I go home," he said.

The guys looked at each other. He seemed to register that and was gracious enough to elaborate.

"I'll leave here with you and wait until I can see the end of the runners. Then I'll make my way up to Nákla Henge. I'll stay close to the stones at the turnaround so I can cut out of the crowd and run into the middle. Then home."

"How sure are we that the sculpture is a traveling stone?" Nolan asked, rubbing his knuckles.

"I'm wondering that, too." Lok chimed in. "I've never heard of that."

"And don't you have to do something specific?" Hanuk asked. "You guys were talking about magic."

Gríf stared at him with his inky black eyes and Juva could swear that he rolled them.

"Magic?" Gríf said, as if he had never spoken the word before. "This is not a fairy tale. I just need to embrace and awaken the Might in the stones. It can't be seen or heard. Relax, that's not anything you need to think about."

The guys exchanged looks again.

"Yes, it . . ." Muggen began, scratching his bald pate. "No, well, I guess it's not magic, at any rate."

"It sounds like magic," Hanuk said, "because that's not how we do it. But I guess it's just a new method. We use wolf blood, and that's not really any less mysterious when you think about it. The stones per se are pure magic!"

"They most certainly are not," Nolan snorted. "Ask the professors up at the college. The stone pillars are road markers that let us travel through the dream world."

"So why aren't there any dreams there? Just black as the night?" Lok folded his arms in front of his chest.

That question triggered a mild argument. Juva and Gríf exchanged a look. He smiled and shook his head. His heart warmed hers. It was as if they were having a secret conversation in a full room. And in the morning, he would be out of her life.

Juva stood up. "Well, you guys will have to agree about what the stones are on your own. I have a letter and a speech to write."

TO THE WOLVES

Juva spread on lip wax and watched her mouth blacken in the mirror. She looked like Mother. A young, but blond, Lagalune. There was a likeness she had never seen before, or she'd merely chosen not to notice in her quest for putting as much distance as possible between herself and the blood readers.

And now there she stood, looking like everything she had sworn she would never become: the head of the Seida Guild and a blood reader. But with a completely different view of blood reading than her mother had ever had—or the other blood readers, maybe none for several hundred years.

She had pulled the clothes from Mother's charcoal-black costume drama: a black lace blouse and ankle-length skirt, wolf teeth, bone runes, and Muune's moons dangling between her breasts. The only decoration that wasn't from her mother was the bluish-purple marks around her throat, a morbid finishing touch from the toughest months of her life.

But that had taught her the most important thing of all: who she was dealing with.

The notion that the vardari were dangerous meant something completely different now than it had a few months ago. She had seen that same insight in her mother's eyes when she died, at first incredulous and then bitter recognition as the word *dangerous* had become real. There was a vast abyss between knowing and understanding.

She could say the same about Gríf. Had Mother actually suspected what she had in the shaft? It was reasonable to believe that the superficial woman had never understood the significance of Gríf's blood, of the secret she, too, had inherited. But her words often whispered from Drukna.

Never let them get him.

Juva glanced at the letter that sat on the mirror shelf. A thick and yellowed envelope, sealed with black wax. Nafraím would open it right away and he would realize that she had tricked him.

It was foolhardy, she knew that. She should have done what the guys suggested, written a couple of pages of nonsense, drawn a made-up map and symbols. Then at least she would have bought herself a couple of days before he figured it out. But she was done being cautious, done hinting. There was only one thing to put in the letter and she wanted to see his face when he understood it. That was a victory she deserved to see.

Juva tied a dark silk scarf around her neck. Then she leaned closer to mother's ornate mirror and painted two white triangles on her black bottom lip. They looked like fangs when she closed her mouth. A moderate tribute to the wolf on this day of the wolf.

Gríf appeared behind her with a plague mask in his hand. He was dressed like a raven, with claw gloves and winglike rag rugs around his arms.

The mirror image of them both was a sight she wished she could have preserved for posterity, two gloomily dressed deviants, made for each other.

"Fangs?" he said, black ink swirling in his eyes, which were dwelling on her lips. "Not particularly . . . what do you call it? Effective?"

"More convincing than yours." She shrugged.

He laughed. A perfect sound that cut into her heart like a knife blade. She would never hear his laugh again, never see him again. He had lived for an eternity, but she had run out of time. She took a deep, troubled breath and clenched her fists in a vain attempt to gather her strength.

The door knocker banged in the foyer. The carriages had arrived. Broddmar stuck his head in with a silent question in his eyes. *Are you ready?*

Juva nodded and handed him the letter for Hanuk. Broddmar disappeared with it and the door knocker banged again.

She looked at Gríf, restless and despairing. What should she do, what should she say? He stood as dependable as a mountain, but his heart had falling beats, steadfast and cold, and she would have given everything she owned to hear him say something heartwarming. He ran his hand through his wild, shoulder-length hair and looked away.

She turned her back to him and left.

The guys were standing in the foyer, as if she were on her way to her own sepulture. The seriousness felt out of place given the costumes: Hanuk as a stag, Nolan as a hare, Broddmar as a wolf, and Muggen, wonderful Muggen, as a bear. Lok would show up later as a fox.

"You guys should be happy." Juva forced herself to smile. "This will be the easiest hunting we've ever done together and with the biggest catch."

She put on her backpack, fully packed with the harness, red outfit, and folded crossbow. As soon as her speech was over, she would change. If everything went to Drukna, she would need to be able to defend herself, not stumble around in a skirt and jewelry.

She walked out onto the front steps without looking back. The carriage puller was waiting outside. He helped her into the small carriage, closed the door, and walked around to the front to pull. The streets were already full of people in every conceivable type of outfit. Even the most restrained had paid for a tail or a pair of fur ears. Braided chains hung between the buildings, decorated with feathers, animal skulls, and elaborate eggs. For the birth. The spring equinox was the day of new beginnings. But nothing new could come without something else ending.

The puller shouted for people to get out of the way as he maneuvered the carriage up to Nákla Henge, where the enormous, verdigris gates were still closed. Juva showed her permit to the Ring Guardians, who let her in through the little door in the gate.

"Ah, Juva!"

There was no mistaking the fat fox. The city councilman stood just inside the door, along with a row of distinguished guests whom he seemed to take great pleasure in leaving. He pulled off his mask and regarded her with wide-eyed affection.

"Juva Sannseyr, you are the spitting image of your mother!" He put his hand on her hair, which she wore up in a braided bun. "Gorgeous, truly gorgeous. The Seida Guild has its star."

Juva felt suffocated. She wasn't there to be anyone's star. She was there to put an end to the warow and wolf-sickness and to lose the wolf who had been devouring her heart her whole life.

Drogg's cheeks were a hectic red, and he pointed up at the balcony that jutted out from the galleries. "We'll go up together. I'll officially welcome you and introduce you. You give your speech. You brought your notes, right? Remember to finish by declaring the Yra Race open. As soon as you're done and the cheers have subsided, people will start moving down toward the bridge. Holy Jól, we lucked out with the weather, didn't we? The most competitively minded of the runners will be at the bridge already. They don't take things lightly, that gang."

He talked faster than Juva could follow, but nothing he said was important.

"But the actual race does take a little time," he continued. "You don't need to think about that. You're free to do as you please, but there are a lot of people who would really like to meet you. We'll have a dinner at Náklaborg later with the Queen, as I'm sure you're aware, and that's where you ought to . . . Oh to Drukna, they're opening the doors now? Dear heavens!"

Drogg walked as fast as he could toward a group who were holding a rope across the front of the galleries to keep the audience back.

"The prize!" Drogg cried. "Who has the prize? Has anyone seen Sjur?"

Juva swallowed her nausea and walked up the stone stairs to the balcony. Her heart pounded in her chest without Gríf or any warow, merely out of fear. She had never given a speech in her life, and every word she had prepared the previous night was gone. From up on the balcony, she could see the entire stone circle in all its splendor. Sixteen black menhir, Náklav's heart. Each standing stone narrowed toward the top. They stood in pairs, smooth on the inside, so people might believe that, at one time, they had been united as one, and that the gods had cleft them.

The wolf blood that drove them flowed, hidden under the grating, but the Yra Race was sacred, so no visitors would come through today.

Aside from Gríf.

The Witness towered in the middle of the ring, under the column of daylight that came in through the opening in the domed wooden roof. Juva had never seen the greenish-blue sculpture from above before. It was three enormous walls that met in the middle, like a cloverleaf. According to Gríf, the walls were made of stone, only clad in copper, and decorated with the renowned clockworks, which were still moving. At the outside edge, each wall had an animal sitting on top: a raven, a wolf, and a stag.

Between two of the walls lay the invisible path to Gríf's world, a world only he could reach with the help of this Might he thought was a part of everything and everyone.

If I warn the Ring Guard now, he would have to stay here.

456

The gates began to complain as they opened and the crowd thronged into the square, a flock of wild creatures with animal ears, fangs, fur collars, and tails. Some had clearly spent their whole winter planning their costumes. Others had just pulled on a hood. She could see a couple of men wearing real antlers on their heads, as if it were a contest to see who could wear the heaviest set. Kids with noses and whiskers painted on in black challenged the guards by running back and forth between the stones.

A flutter in her heart revealed that Nafraím had arrived. She searched until she spotted him in the shadows underneath the gallery. But her palpitations were her own fault, not his.

What have I done?

So many people. So many faces staring up at her. How was she going to stand up there and pretend to be anything other than a girl? She wasn't her mother or Ogny. She was a hunter, dolled up in black lace and rattling bone jewelry.

The city councilman came up the stairs, wiping his sweat with a handkerchief. A few weeks ago, he would have insisted on being carried up the stairs. Every drop of sweat would have denoted a heartbeat lost. A shocking legacy from her mother, which Juva had succeeded in quashing.

He's wrong. I'm not the spitting image of my mother, and I never will be.

Drogg stepped out onto the balcony and boomed out a welcome. He spoke with genuine enthusiasm, and it struck her that he really was the right person in the right place, unlike her.

Panic began to sprout in her chest. Her hands grew clammy, and she knew she needed to get out of there. Juva withdrew back into the stairwell. She dropped her backpack and tore off her clothes. The blouse, the jewelry, everything. That wasn't her and it never would be. All she kept was the thin silk scarf around her neck. She pulled out the red outfit and fought her way into it with trembling hands, strapping the corset tightly so she would stay together. She hooked the crossbow onto her back and stuffed her other clothes into her backpack. She heard Drogg speaking louder, wrapping up.

"And with that I give you the new star of the Seida Guild, Juva Sannseyr." She could hear hesitant applause and Drogg's voice, nervous now. "J-Juva?"

She set down her backpack and stepped out onto the balcony. Drogg's chin dropped, forming her name silently with his lips. She hurried past him and looked out at the square. The crowd had grown frighteningly quiet, and she could vividly imagine what they were thinking. She was no blood reader. She was a bleeder. What was she doing being leader of the Seida Guild? Leader of a hunting team would have been more suitable. And she was a child, compared to old Ogny. Maybe they thought she'd been tricked into doing this, since no one else dared?

Her heart stung, once, twice.

Eydala!

The fear chilled her blood. The sensation of her caused Juva's throat to constrict, sent her back to a hall of mirrors. She clutched the railing. The words she was supposed to say refused to come. And that was exactly why she was standing here. Fear of the warow. Fear of wolf-sickness. She wasn't the only one there who was afraid.

Never let them see a weak blood reader.

Juva took a breath and said exactly what she was thinking.

"Fear," she yelled. "I know it. You know it. We know it, all of us, and fear is the reason I stand before you today."

Her voice echoed off the domed roof. The city councilman cleared his throat behind her, but she pretended not to hear him.

"I'm standing here because the leaders of the Seida Guild are dead, and the people who were meant to be their heirs are dead. I'm standing here because there isn't anyone else. Everyone else is scared, and with good reason."

458

The smiles faded in the sea of animal-like faces below her.

"I have buried seven women since midwinter, family and friends, lost to fangs, murdered by the warow and by the wolf-sickness they spread. They churn out blood pearls and poison us from the shadows. They sit in positions of power and have never had to answer for their sins."

The throat-clearing behind her grew increasingly frantic, and people were starting to gape. They exchanged looks, but she had nothing to lose anymore. She was about to lose everything she cared about anyway.

"The city councilman here would prefer that I not mention them. They want me to say that they have a handle on the wolf-sickness. They want me to say that each person we lose, each time the Dead Man's Horn sounds, is a tragedy, but that this will be a good year.

"Seven buried women is a tragedy. It's a war! The vardari wanted to break the Seida Guild and they almost succeeded. But only *almost*, because I'm still here. Not because I'm fearless, but because I've lived with fear my whole damned life, and I'm done kneeling down to it."

No one in the square was exchanging looks anymore. They stared up at her as if mesmerized.

"The Seida Guild has been meeting fear with false prophecies, accepting payment for made-up fictions that let you get a good night's sleep again. They say you will live a long time, be healthy, and marry the one you love. Simple, right? That's not blood reading. That's a betrayal of everything the Seida Guild was meant to be."

Juva knew not many people would understand what she was talking about, but she had to get through to the ones who were like her, the ones who could sense the warow. She had to get the word out.

"The first blood readers from the fairy tale, they took their charge seriously. They were there to sense evil and protect against the wolf-sick and the vardari. They were warriors." Juva hit her chest with her fist. "*We* were warriors, because I'm not alone. I know there are more of you out there who have more than one heart. The new Seida Guild is for you."

The fear she had felt was spreading now. It settled like a suffocating blanket over them all. She lifted them up, gave them just as little to lose as she had.

"Is it dangerous to resist?" she yelled. "Gaula, yes, it's dangerous, but it's also dangerous to live. You can die from that, or so I've heard."

That old joke lightened the mood among the crowd. A cautious laughter spread, wonderfully infectious. Her eyes roamed, looking for Eydala, but she couldn't see her.

"The Seida Guild has paid its debt to the warow, and we will never give in again. We must be true to our roots. And if anyone threatens a blood reader, then I will hunt them down and bleed them empty no matter who they are. I kill everything with fangs, wolf-sick or not."

"So, no, I'm not going to tell you that this will be a good year. It may be worse than ever. But you're Náklavites. You can take it. Because I can promise you that we will have fewer cases of wolf-sickness tomorrow. Fewer still in a month. And when you stand here next year, it will be another world, a world without the Dead Man's Horn, where no one—*no one*—is above the law. *That* is the new Seida Guild!"

The silence in the square was intense. She had hoped someone would dare to clap. She felt a kick to her calf and hurried to add:

"I hereby declare the Yra Race open!"

The crowd erupted into cheers. They could clap for the Yra Race. That wasn't dangerous. Unlike a girl declaring war against the vardari.

The councilman came up beside her, pressing his handkerchief to his forehead.

"You know," he said weakly, "the worst thing is that I warned them. I said you weren't going to make this easy. But even I wouldn't have believed—"

"I'm no idiot, councilman. I understand this might impact you, and I'm sorry about that."

He laughed nervously as he waved to the sea of people. "Well, I can assure you that the next city council meeting is not going to be a quiet one. But I'm safe. I warned them."

"About what?"

He put on his fox mask and looked at her.

"I told them the truth," he said. "I told them that Juva Sannseyr was the wrong woman to throw to the wolves."

TRACES OF BLOOD

People pushed their way out the west gate, some ready to race and others ready to party. Many had gotten off to an early start with the beer and were obviously planning to sing their way through the entire Yra Race. The square was a boiling sea of antlers, fangs, snouts, and tankards.

Juva picked up her backpack and followed the councilman down the stairs.

He lifted his fox mask and looked at her, as terrified as he was excited. "I can't believe I'm doing this," he said, "but running the Yra Race seems manageable compared to what you just accomplished, so Gaula take me, I'm in!"

He pulled the mask back down and walked over to a group of friends who stood waiting. Juva thought she smiled, but it was hard to say. Her face felt as if it were carved from stone.

She hurried on, knowing the best spots would fill up fast. She stood in one of the archways, as close to the running track as she could get, just beside the north gate. Slowly but surely, the round square emptied of people as the spectators were left standing in the galleries the whole way around. The spots on the second floor were the most expensive, so the best dressed were busy trying to be seen there, leaning forward and waving to people they knew.

Nafraím stood in the shadows, a couple of archways past her. He watched her with a silent approval that suggested her speech had pleased him. Juva looked away. There was no sign of other vardari, but the muted tingling in her heart told her that Eydala wasn't far away. Surely somewhere in the back on the floor above.

The hollow din of pleasant chatter spread beneath the domed roof as people waited for the runners. Hosts and hostesses wandered around selling overpriced wine and brown wolf cookies. They tasted like cinders, but traditions were traditions.

Several of the spectators had found space next to her, and they wanted to treat her to one. But she politely declined. Time seemed to stand still.

Juva studied the three sculptures on top of the Witness. They seemed wild, their designs unfinished, as if they had been made by a terrified artist in a hurry. The wolf's hackles were up and his teeth bared, a monster turned to stone that was going to take her own wolf away from her.

A horn blew above the western gate and a Ring Guardian called out something she couldn't hear. Excitement spread through the spectators.

They're coming now.

The gate was wide open, and soon thereafter, a group of five came rushing in, four men and a woman, all hot on the heels of the one in the lead.

The onlookers clapped and cheered as the five sprinted all the way around the stone circle, and out again through the other door in the gate. Another group of runners followed and did the same. The groups rushing in grew larger and larger and, eventually, the square was full with an unending stream of runners. Juva stood up against the column so she wouldn't get swept into the fray. The air filled with the smell of sweat, and she told herself that was why she was struggling to breathe.

As soon as the trophy contenders cleared out, everyone else arrived; then there was just as much dancing as running, but the onlookers cheered all the same. Juva stared into the crowd with her heart in her throat, tormented by Eydala's pinpricks and Nafraím's fidgety rhythm.

A man in a familiar hare mask approached quickly.

Hanuk!

He pulled into the outside of the turn and slipped Juva the letter as he ran past. He was one of thousands and no one had noticed him. Juva stared at the letter, which trembled in her hand. She looked up at the gallery.

Eydala stood in the archway, just above Nafraím, staring down at her with a grotesque hunger in her eyes. Juva took a breath and slipped into the edge of the runners, moving toward Nafraím. Her legs felt shaky, useless. People danced past her, dressed like wild animals. They were unruly, hollering, carrying on unaffected as if she weren't holding the end of the world in her hands.

She neared Nafraím. Up in the gallery she saw Eydala move so as not to lose sight of them. Juva stopped in front of Nafraím and handed him the letter. He took it and looked at her. She had no doubt that he could perceive her unconcealed agitation, but that didn't matter, not anymore.

Nafraím ran his hand lovingly over the envelope. Juva peeked up at Eydala, who smiled lazily and then disappeared into the shadows again. The pinpricks faded from Juva's heart as Eydala vanished. The eerie woman had seen what she needed to see. Nafraím had received the letter. He knew where the devil was.

For him everything was over, but he didn't know that yet himself.

Nafraím looked around and then opened the letter. He looked down into the envelope and pulled out the card. Mother's pale blood reader card made of whale cartilage, branded with the image of the devil. He stared at it, turned it over in his hand.

Juva could see the memory returning. He remembered that he had received this from her before. Realization dawned on his face, slowly, as if in a dream. His face wilted as he understood that he had been tricked, deceived.

Juva took a step back. Nafraím looked up at the gallery, his eyes darting around, realizing that he must have been observed by his own kind, but he wouldn't find them. Eydala had left.

He looked at Juva again. She realized that she had been expecting rage, an outburst, an attack, but his eyes contained nothing but unfathomable grief. His lips formed words that were almost drowned out by the noise.

"What have you done, Juva?"

Juva gulped. He had understood that he would never know where the devil was and that she had sold him out to his own kind, but the heady victory she had dreamt of did not materialize. Maybe because she had seen a deeper darkness than Nafraím. The man who murdered Solde, and the leaders of the Seida Guild, seemed downright humane following her encounter with Eydala, his warped creation.

He put the card back in the envelope, and stuck it in his pocket with his stiff, clumsy hand. He tugged at the lapels of his jacket as if to collect his thoughts.

"He's already gone, isn't he?" he asked, his voice hoarse. "Don't you understand, Juva? He's going to come back with the wolves. You've killed us all, every person in Náklav."

A flicker grazed her heart and then more. They grew into a new pulse, which pounded next to hers, familiar, loved and hated. Gríf.

No! It's too soon!

He was supposed to be among the last runners! He was supposed to give Nafraím plenty of time to react and get out.

Juva turned around. Gríf stood in the open square, inside the stone circle, the only fixed point in the middle of the maelstrom of people. Dressed like a raven in a plague mask. Suddenly she realized that she was staring, and that Nafraím was going to follow suit, but it was too late.

Nafraím gaped at the creature. His insight was written on his face, which had lost all its color. Gríf lifted off his mask and the two men stared at each other over the sea of people.

Juva threw her hand over her mouth and stifled a sob. This wasn't the plan. He was supposed to leave Náklav in silence. Nafraím wasn't supposed to know. No one was supposed to know!

Juva dropped her backpack and pushed her way between the runners. She was carried along by the crowds but fought her way forward until she stumbled in, between the stones. She thought she was going to fall, but something kept her on her feet, something that grew into her from the ground, an incomprehensible, violent force, which chased the blood to her heart and made time stand still.

The Might.

It was a certainty, strong as a mountain. *This* was what he had been talking about. This was the force that was meant to power the stones, power all life. She gasped for air, had a vision of a deserted square. Nákla-wall crumbled in a dream image, became a ruin. Juva stood motionless as eternity rushed by. Even so, she could still see the runners, as if they were ghosts. Why didn't they stop? Couldn't they feel that the world was coming undone? Was it just her?

Gríf stood before the Witness, just a step away from her, but he didn't seem to notice her. His black eyes burned at Nafraím from beneath his unruly bangs, a frightening promise after nearly seven hundred years of captivity. He held his head up and bared his teeth.

Her heart swelled, thundered as two, on the verge of rending. Something red moved on the ground. She turned and saw the blood come. It flowed up over the blood grating, around the entire circumference of the stone circle, and crept along the ground in toward Gríf. Grew like veins. The runners didn't seem to care. They danced on, planting their feet in the wolf blood, and covering the square in red footprints.

She stood with a broken heart in a sea of blood.

466

Nafraim's prediction. From the raven cabinet at home. Broken heart, blood, and ocean.

Juva heard a distant cry and saw the pale shadow of a Ring Guardian come running to chase them. Gríf seemed to wake up and suddenly reality was back. The guardsman raised his crossbow as he rushed into the square between the stones.

Gríf threw off his mask and grabbed Juva. His grasp ripped the buttons off her jacket. He held her as a shield in front of himself. His claws dug into her breasts, burning hot. Juva screamed. Gríf dragged her a short way before tossing her aside like a sack. She fell to her knees, clutching her chest. The bun on her head had come loose and her hair hung in tufts over her face.

She looked up at Gríf. His nose twitched as if he were about to eat her. She said his name, but no sound came out. He turned his back on her and walked toward the Witness as he pulled off his black outfit. He tossed it aside onto the ground, revealing his broad back.

Then he vanished between the stones.

Juva stared into the empty corner where the walls met, but he was gone.

Gone.

The storm in her body died, so abruptly that she broke down, collapsing on the ground. Her heart skipped several beats, and she thought it was going to stop. But then it continued, unsteadily at first, then in an even and painfully solitary rhythm.

Guards ran around the blood gratings, hunting for a leak they were never going to find. She was surrounded by thousands but had never ever felt so alone.

Broddmar came running and got her to her feet.

The guardsman with the crossbow stared at the Witness, unsure of what he had just seen. He looked at Broddmar.

"Did you see . . . ?" he began.

"Yes! He ran that way." Broddmar pointed to the west gate.

The guardsman blinked and shook himself out of his trance. He gave a quick laugh, obviously convinced that he had been mistaken about what he'd seen, and then ran toward the gates.

"Is everything all right?" Broddmar asked.

Juva nodded and hid the injuries on her chest. She looked for Nafraím but knew she wouldn't find him. Knew it, because she had only one heart in her body, and it had never been so small. A fragile, breaking shell with a solitary pulse, sore and sensitive, like breath.

MARKED FOR DEATH

Nafraím let himself in and was met by Ofre, who'd come to take his coat, but he kept it on. The estate master pointed to a letter that sat on a shelf by the door.

"It came while you were out, Master."

Nafraím glanced at the red envelope with Eydala's white seal and smiled bitterly. He let it sit. He could say with certainty that it contained nothing but a blank card. He had been marked for death.

She doesn't waste time.

He put his hand on his estate master's shoulder and led him into the foyer.

"Ofre, I'm afraid we've reached the end of the road."

"Master?"

"I've run out of time, and the last good deed I can do is release you. I know that this is sudden, but you need to leave me. And if you value your life, you won't dawdle. Pack your things, let the staff go, and leave here immediately. I've arranged for compensation, of course, enough that you'll never need to worry. You'll find the instructions at Náklabank. Will you listen to me, Ofre?"

Ofre hesitated. Nafraím could see that he wanted to ask questions, but he wasn't going to.

"Always, Master. Thank you, Master."

Nafraím took Ofre's hand in both his own.

"It is I who should be thanking you, Ofre. You have been an exceptional and invaluable help for many years. I'm going down to the study to arrange a package I need you to deliver for me."

Ofre looked down. A blush spread across his wrinkled cheeks. When had he gotten to be so old? Time passed too quickly, had always passed too quickly.

"Of course, Master. Shall I make tea?"

Nafraím forced himself to smile.

"We no longer have time for tea. Go now, and if you hear anyone come, don't let yourself be seen, not under any circumstances. Leave the house, through a window if you must. Do you understand?"

Ofre raised his chin, nodded, and left him, walking quickly. He stopped at the top step. "Master, what about the sick boy in the storeroom?"

"Don't give that a thought, Ofre. Go and pack now."

Nafraím climbed down the spiral staircase into the wine cellar. He lifted the dusty lid off the crate in the corner and took a two-hundred-year-old bottle of strong Martheng into the study with him. He didn't have a glass and lifted his hand to pull the bell cord but stopped himself. Ofre didn't work for him anymore.

Nafraím took off his coat and looked out the window. The ocean lay treacherously still. Black and still as a mirror, with rows of ships decorated for the Yra Race. He opened the wine bottle and took a swig, a sweet, burning mouthful of preserved fruit, leather, and tobacco.

He pulled Juva's letter out of his pocket. Stared at the pale bone card with the picture of the devil.

Seven hundred years ruined by a girl who had yet to see her twentieth summer. Death had caught up to him. Finally.

The girl had stripped him of his credibility and power, sent the devil home, and made the rest of the vardari believe that he was sitting on the secret of his whereabouts. Or at any rate, she'd told them that he intended to kill the devil and annihilate his own kind.

He had played with the highest stakes of all and lost.

Nafraím looked around the room, which showed the signs of an eternity of erudition, models, drawings, chemicals, and tissue samples. He had always believed he had done well, but today he had seen the truth in a black Vitnir-look. A near thousand-year-old hatred and a promise of revenge, the worst conceivable outcome.

His shoulder burned where Juva had shot him. That had seemed like a passing penance, he had thought, without suspecting that the punishment she had planned was exceedingly worse.

Had he wanted this? Had he somehow conjured up this downfall himself? This deception she had foisted on him?

Eydala would come, with the warow who were willing to follow her reign of terror. A world of torment lay ahead of him. And then if he were lucky, death would come.

Nafraím was not afraid of dying or pain. He would have suffered those anyway. He feared the rot that would relentlessly fill the void he left behind. He feared for Náklav's fate. And for Juva's.

He took another swig and walked over to the bookshelf. He carefully pulled out his most important diaries, the ones that needed to outlive him, and placed them into a sailor bag for Ofre. Then he wrote a short letter in haste and stuck it into the same bag.

A sound made him jump, glass breaking, commotion, voices.

Already?

Nafraím tossed the bag under the stairs and sat down on the windowsill with the bottle in his lap. He heard Eydala bark a command up in the front hall, followed by what he guessed was the sound of a door being ripped off its hinges.

He hardened his heart to the sounds of destruction and stared at the staircase, which someone was descending.

Rugen's sweaty face appeared between the bars. The young addict, sick from abstaining, grinned and yelled back up the stairs, "He's here!"

Then he stared at Nafraím, his eyes awash with schadenfreude.

That was absolutely the worst part of wolf-sickness. It did more than kill. It toyed with people. It found its host's worst traits and amplified them, without the individual realizing what was going on.

Nafraím took a mouthful of wine and stared out at the ocean for what he knew was the last time.

THE FIRE SNAKE

Juva ducked into the bathroom as soon as they entered Hidehall. She had to look at her wounds before the guys figured out something was wrong.

A hunting team wasn't stronger than its weakest member, and injuries were supposed to be shared right away, but this was something else. This wound penetrated deeper than any of them could comprehend, or fix.

He played me.

Gríf had used her, dragged her in front of him as a shield. Clawed her up and tossed her aside. Why couldn't he just have left and let her live believing that he cared, that something had grown between them? What kind of a monster was he, to so harshly expose what a fool she'd been?

Juva took off her red leather jacket while staring at the ceiling, blinking to stop herself from crying before she started.

Pull yourself together. You barely knew him.

She pumped water into the washbasin and unlaced her shirt. It was stuck to her with clotted blood. She moistened it and unstuck it from the wound, leaving her breast bare as she clenched her teeth against the stinging. The purpose of the red outfits had never been clearer.

She loosened the silk scarf that hid the bruises around her neck and dipped it in the water. Then she found the hand mirror on the shelf and held it up in front of her as she washed her chest clean.

The wound was smaller than she had feared. He had plunged two of his claws in deep, just above her breasts, and then dragged them up to the hollow at the base of her throat. He must have had some filth in them, too, because they had burned her skin, forming two thumb-length gashes, which grew thicker at the top. They mirrored each other so perfectly that it resembled a broken heart. Or a pair of fangs.

She stared at the mark. The mockery was so poetic that she could swear he had done it on purpose.

It still burned. Maybe it always would. Maybe she was doomed to burn the way she had burned so many wolves. To live the rest of her life with this pain.

Juva felt like she was going to throw up. She felt sick to her stomach, her body heavy with anger, with longing. She tried to suppress the truth, but it owned her now and would not let her escape.

She had believed she was loved.

How laughable could a person be? Gríf had been alive for almost a thousand years, and he would live for many thousands more. She was barely a ripple in one wave of his infinite ocean of time. She was just the person who had happened to find him and had the power to set him free.

Her heart felt leaky, like it was bleeding through the cracks. It wasn't pumping, it was trickling, and she caught herself hoping that it would stop beating. She was done.

She had accomplished what she had set out to do, and she could hear them talking about it in the common room. They had mixed feelings, that was clear. They had won, in the long run, and their joy was obvious. But they were also afraid of revenge. None of them had been sure that they could pull it off, but they had done the job anyway.

And no one else knew that the guys had been involved, so they were safe, even if Nafraím should manage to convince the other warow of what she'd done. She would do the wisest thing and leave Náklav. Put everything and everyone behind her. The Seida Guild would never gather around her after all.

The voices stole through the cracks in the old wooden door. Muggen and Lok were worried about Hidehall. It had belonged to Ester, and thanks to her charity, they all used it, and at a ridiculously cheap price. Now it would probably be sold, and the tavern would be expanded. There was more money in beer than in hunting.

"We have to ask," Lok said. "Kids are expensive. I need the job."

"Me, too," Muggen replied. "I guess you're in a better position, Broddmar, since you're a red hunter. That pays something."

Broddmar let out a little snort. "Ha, for how long?" Broddmar asked. "I'm wagering wolf-sickness is gone for the winter. They need fresh blood every year to keep themselves warow. That's what Gríf said."

Gríf...

His name was a punch in the chest. When in Drukna had she allowed herself to become so vulnerable? She knew he had used her, but it was as if her body hadn't understood that yet. It was reacting blindly to his being gone.

I can be gone, too.

That thought was appealing. Far from as frightening as she would have thought. Why should she continue when she had done everything she needed to do? At best, she was going to have to keep leading a Seida Guild that hated her. At worst, she would have to stand face-to-face with Eydala again and pay the piper for her deception. The guys might also suffer for it.

But if she didn't exist anymore . . . She could let the hunting team inherit the house, and none of them would ever need to worry anymore.

Juva laced the neckline of her shirt back up, hiding the mark Grif's claws had left. She took a deep breath and walked back out and sat down with the guys. They looked at her, all of them together, with the type of concern people feel when they think things have gone a little far. Muggen still had the brown cutting board around his face with the round ears.

Juva put on a stiff smile and raised the beer tankard, which was waiting for her. "Muggen," she said, "I know why you're a bear every single year."

"Oh yeah?"

"Because you like it."

The guys chuckled while Muggen stared thoughtfully at the ceiling, as if he wasn't sure himself. They were marvelous, these guys, and she had a damned duty now to help them. They had helped her.

She emptied her beer slowly, acting unaffected as she did so. Broddmar was the first to mention Gríf's behavior at the end, how he had shown up too soon and put the whole plan at risk. Juva shrugged and acted as if nothing had happened.

She sat for as long as she needed to before getting up to go. Broddmar and Muggen wanted to go with her, but she insisted on being alone. The vardari were busy with Nafraím. No one would do anything tonight.

Juva laced up her shoes, intentionally slowly so she could listen to the guys' voices a little more. Then she left Hidehall, following Taakedraget up toward Kingshill. The party was just getting started. People danced in the streets and stood around in groups outside the taverns, drinking. Spring equinox. A new beginning for everyone, and they didn't know yet how unique this beginning was. They had no inkling that six hunters had dealt a death blow to the warow, the city's most oppressive supernatural affliction.

Everything had changed, and in total secrecy—an invisible victory.

Juva took off down toward Lykteløkka. She walked for a bit and got the feeling that something was different without realizing why. Then it hit her.

The lamps . . .

The street was exactly the way she remembered it from her childhood. The lanterns were lit, hundreds of them. They burned beside the doors in red, orange, and yellow, an endless snake made of fire.

Juva nearly walked right into a lamppost, so blinded by the sight. The lanterns continued the whole way home, where she spotted someone on her front steps. A young girl sat there, waiting.

Kefla!

The twelve-year-old blood reader sat, leaning back, her elbows resting on the step above. She was eating a handful of wolf cookies she had probably stolen. She squinted up at Juva and grinned.

"I heard your speech," she said, with feigned indifference. "And I think you're either the toughest or the stupidest lady in the city."

"Couldn't I be both?" Juva asked, getting out her keys.

Kefla stood up. "So, uh . . . Don't let it go to your head or anything, but I think things are going to get worse for a while, and I think the safest place to be is with you."

Juva laughed, surprised at how much of a relief that was to hear. "Or the most dangerous," she said.

"How about both?" Kefla stuffed the last wolf cookie into her mouth and brushed the crumbs off her pants.

Juva unlocked the door and let the girl in. Kefla strolled into the foyer and stopped abruptly.

"Oh, Gaula, what a place!" She walked around in circles, picking everything up as she gaped.

Juva closed the front door and picked a letter up off the floor. It must have arrived after she had gone out that morning. She opened it and read it while Kefla darted around, cursing enthusiastically.

The letter was from Náklabank, an invitation to a meeting about the inheritance. There must be some mistake. She was finished with all the paperwork from the distribution of her mother's estate.

She turned it over and spotted Ester's name. It was in the middle of an unreal sentence about her having left everything she owned to *her*.

Juva dropped her keys but kept on reading.

. . . and must point out that this involves considerable business assets and funds, so a prompt meeting is called for . . .

"This is the nicest house I've ever seen!" Kefla said, scurrying over to her. "Can I pick a room? And I know about—this is top secret, you know what I mean?—but I know about another girl, who also gets multiple hearts from the warow. She has a home, you know, but her dad is a real son of a bitch. Can she move in here, too? It looks like you've got space."

Juva looked at her. The girl with the scab-like freckles was ecstatic, but that didn't hide the sincere hopefulness in her eyes. And she was right, the world was going to get worse and people like her would be caught in the middle of it.

"You know . . ." Juva said, rubbing her face. "We're going to have a lot of problems, but space isn't one of them."

Kefla flung her arms around Juva's waist. "You'd better not fucking think I'm crying or anything," Kefla mumbled against her chest.

"It wouldn't even occur to me." Juva smiled.

Kefla clung more tightly, as if Juva were her last hope. Juva stroked the girl's hair, far too aware that it was actually the other way around.

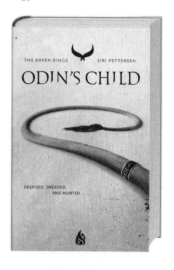